THE DEVIL OF IT IS . . .

Publius led Barry into the office. A woman wrapped in mobcap and regulation tent came forward, frowning suspiciously. Her eye lit on Publius. "You! I told you, we don't allow play-acting here! No point asking for a permit—"

"I know, Mrs. Hannah." Publius smiled. "I'm here to introduce Mr. Barry Tallendar."

"Pleased, I'm sure," she sniffed, then looked again. "Aren't you the fellow who played the Angel in *Gideon*?" Her eyes grew wide. "That's my favorite 3DT—and you were the perfect angel!"

"The last time someone told me that, I was ten years old." Barry held out a hand, smiling. "But I thank you."

"Oh, you even sound like an actor, with that funny talking!"

Alas the day, when proper speech must be labeled "funny." Barry kept his smile, somehow. "I wish to secure a permit to lecture."

Her eyes went wide. "Dearie me! Imagine—to hear the Angel speak!"

How fortunate that she had not seen Barry as the Tempter . . .

By Christopher Stasheff
Published by Ballantine Books:

A Wizard in Rhyme
HER MAJESTY'S WIZARD
THE OATHBOUND WIZARD
THE WITCH DOCTOR
THE SECULAR WIZARD*

Starship Troupers
A COMPANY OF STARS
WE OPEN ON VENUS
A SLIGHT DETOUR

**Forthcoming*

A SLIGHT DETOUR

Book Three of *Starship Troupers*

Christopher Stasheff

A Del Rey® Book
BALLANTINE BOOKS • NEW YORK

A Del Rey® Book
Published by Ballantine Books

Library of Congress Catalog Card Number: 94-94191

ISBN 0-345-37601-3

Manufactured in the United States of America

First Edition: August 1994

10 9 8 7 6 5 4 3 2 1

1

Ramou caught Larry by the shoulder and spun him around. Larry lurched back against the wall, clapping a hand to his shoulder. "Ow!" He stared up at Ramou in anger that turned to fear when he saw the look in his eye.

"Ramou, stop!" Suzanne cried.

"No, Ramou!" Lacey shouted. "Mr. Burbage, help me!"

I leaped to help even before she called. "Please, Ramou! Whatever his offense, it doesn't merit *this*!"

The lounge went into instant pandemonium as everyone tried to deter Ramou. We all knew how dangerous he might be when enraged. Well, no, not "knew," actually—but we feared the worst.

Ramou virtually shrugged off the hands that tried to contain him, though, and elbowed aside anyone who dared intervene as he barked at Larry. Larry shrank away, obviously terrified but still trying to look truculent.

"Strychnine!" Ramou stepped closer to him, crowding him, backing him into the corner. "That needle was tipped with strychnine!"

"Well, I didn't put it there!" Larry protested.

"Who else?" Ramou snarled. "You're the only one in this company who goes around picking locks! Opening every locker back there on New Venus—then Charlie turns up with a needle in his tights, and you're going to tell me you didn't put it there?"

"I didn't! I swear!"

"Yeah, every time somebody crosses you, you swear a blue streak. What's the matter, Larry? Did Charlie say something you didn't like, when he wasn't looking?"

Barry turned to Charles Publican. "Why didn't you tell us the needle was poisoned, Charles?"

"I didn't intend for anyone to learn of it," Charles said, pale-faced. He had good reason; Ramou was a martial arts master. It was very unlike him to lose his temper like this—and bullying certainly wasn't his style.

"I thought it was a practical joke," Marty protested.

"Yeah, a joke." Ramou was throttling the desire to throttle Larry; it was a visible effort for him to keep his hands on his hips. "Very funny, Larry. Very funny!"

"Ramou happened to come in while I was running a chemical analysis of the coating on the point," Charles explained. "He read the data off the monitor."

Larry bleated, "There are some people on this ship I wouldn't mind seeing dead, Ramou, beginning with you—but not Charlie!"

It was true. Everyone liked Charles Publican, and no one disliked him, though he was so reticent that it had taken all of us awhile to come to know him well enough to warm up to him.

"But, Ramou," I said, "didn't you tell me that the Man in Gray had been in the locker room just before we came in to change into costume? Or that you had met him coming up the stairs, at least."

That gave Ramou pause—and a spark of hope sprang into Larry's eye.

"We know nothing about the man, save that he must be an agent from someone on Terra," I went on, seized by inspiration. "For all we know, *he* might be capable of picking locks—and is far more likely to have access to strychnine than Larry would."

"There's no telling *what* Larry might get hold of!" Ramou snapped.

He was referring to Larry's attempts at smuggling. "Be honest, Ramou," I said. "You jumped to the conclusion that Larry poisoned the needle, and only because he could open Charlie's locker when none of the rest of us could. That's not even strong enough to be circumstantial evidence."

A shadow of doubt crept into Ramou's expression.

Marty stepped around to Larry's other side. "You don't really believe this joker has brains enough to plan something like *that*, do you, Ramou?"

Larry turned on Marty. "*You*, talking about brain power? You, the man to whom 'wit' is only half a word?"

Larry might have been in danger of a beating, but he still wasn't about to take a threat to his vanity without fighting back.

Marty grinned. "That's pretty good, coming from the man who thinks that only clothes can be 'smart.' "

Ramou stepped back a pace, frowning, puzzled.

Charles stepped in for the *coup de grace*. "Larry had no motive, Ramou. He wouldn't want my character parts."

That did it; Ramou's expression crumpled into shame and self-disgust. Charles was a utility actor, playing second comic parts and subordinate older roles; Larry was the company juvenile and aspired to grow up to be a leading man. He certainly had nothing to gain by Charles' death.

"Yeah, I suppose so," Ramou growled—but now, the anger in his face was directed at himself. "Sorry, Larry."

"I should think you would be, you pithecanthropus!" Larry stepped away from the wall, brushing imaginary wrinkles out of his clothing. "A cretin could have seen I had nothing to do with that needle."

Ramou's face darkened dangerously again, and Merlo stepped in. "Come off it, kid. Ramou said he was sorry."

"Oh, and I suppose you don't think I have any cause for indignation!"

"Yeah, you've got reason for a gripe," Merlo admitted, "but you've got a bigger reason to be thanking your lucky stars you're not in traction."

Larry muttered something about the technical staff always sticking together, then turned away. Lacey fell in beside him, murmuring reassurances.

Everyone relaxed visibly, but Barry remembered the original *cassus belli* and turned to Charles. "Do you really think this Man in Gray was trying to kill you?"

Charles shrugged. "It seems more probable that it was a case of mistaken identity, Mr. Tallendar."

"Either that, or the man is a psychotic who dislikes actors," Ogden wheezed. "A very wealthy psychotic."

Very wealthy, indeed. Space travel is extremely expensive. The only reason the Star Repertory Company could get off the ground was because Barry's brother happened to be one of the wealthiest tycoons on Terra. Intimidated by his older brother's success on the stage, he had eschewed the theater and gone into business. He could easily have bought and sold us all—and to some extent, he had. Had sold us his former mistress, that is—Marnie Lulala, our leading lady. He had bought us a ship and a tour, and she was the price we paid. One week in her presence, and anyone would understand why he had been willing to pay through the nose to have her escorted several light-years away from him. One could also understand why only light-years could be far enough.

On the other side of the lounge, the argument was still going on, but one of the principals had changed.

"Rash, if you're innocent, hyenas are morose!" Marty spun on his heel and went stalking off down the corridor.

"Coward!" Larry called. "Stick around for the last word!"

Marty turned back. "False advertising. I'd love to hear your last word, but I think you're planning to keep living awhile." He started away again.

"You don't get away that easily!" Larry ran after him, caught up, and said, "The only time you can think of a last word, is when you reach the end of a novel!"

"And I'm really looking forward to the end of this one, if it means I get to be free of you for a while."

"I'm not free, Kemp—"

Marty chimed in for the punch line. "But you're reasonable." Then solo, "Come on, Rash. That one was old when the iguanas told it to the first mammal."

And off they went down the hall, bickering.

I heaved a sigh of relief. "That lad Marty is a natural diplomat."

"I agree, Horace." Barry nodded. "He defused the situation very nicely. With only a few words, he managed to change it from an imminent beating into a verbal duel between himself and Larry. Amazing chap. Glad we chose him."

Then he turned a stern gaze on Ramou. "I hope you realize that you mustn't explode on so little evidence again, Mr. Lazarian."

The name itself was a rebuke; Barry had started calling

Ramou by his first name halfway through our abortive run on New Venus.

"Yeah, I know." Ramou looked so far down that he could have been playing Second Grave Digger. "I don't know what made me pop off like that, Mr. Tallendar. I won't do it again. Sensei would be ashamed of me."

It was, certainly, the only time I had ever seen Ramou truly lose his temper. He was a martial arts devotee, and his teacher had taught him at least as much about the philosophy underlying the art as about its methods of wreaking havoc. In fact, from the few comments Ramou had let drop, I gather that those principles were the core of his life, and had far more to do with not being violent than with doing it most effectively. In attacking Larry, Ramou had betrayed himself as much as his teacher.

"I understand that emotionally, you were reacting to a threat to a friend," Barry said, his tone much gentler. "It is one of the better aspects of a company of ours, that we begin to care about one another. But for that very reason, you must be certain of your facts before you accuse another company member of wrongdoing."

Ramou took it in good part, standing there with his hands on his hips, looking at the floor and nodding. "Yessir," he mumbled. "Yessir."

Well. There wasn't really much more Barry could say, when he took it so well and was so thoroughly accepting. For myself, I marveled at Charlie Publican's influence—for a quiet, retiring, near-nonentity, he had managed to win a great deal of liking from the other company members in a very short time. I wondered how he had managed it—he so rarely seemed to say anything at all. Of course, when he did, it was during a moment of crisis, which he nicely managed to alleviate.

"Well, that's done, then." Barry gusted out a sigh. "I *was* about to convene a company meeting—but under the circumstances, I think I will let it wait until after dinner."

I nodded. People are always much more reasonable with full stomachs. Not that Larry wouldn't harbor a grudge, of course. Ramou would not—but neither would he warm to Larry in any way. It might have had something to do with their both being interested in Lacey—or it might not, since

Ramou was also interested in Suzanne. More probably, it had to do with a fundamental philosophical disagreement: Ramou believed in treating everyone with courtesy, whereas Larry seemed to feel that politeness was only for those he acknowledged as his superiors, or who were in a position to benefit him—which company did not include Ramou.

Dinner was done, and the company assembled in the lounge with cheerful chitchat and laughter. One advantage of occupying a spaceship that began life as a luxury liner was that the food synthesizers all had gourmet dishes in their memories. *One* advantage, as I say—there were many others.

However, the liner had carried uniformed waiters, busboys, and maître d's; the tour ship was self-service in the dining room. Not the lounge, though—self-service meant free access to the beverage dispensers, and we did not want that. Not for Ogden—and, therefore, not for anybody. It wasn't just that Ogden would have been constantly drunk, no matter what his good resolutions—it was also that it would have killed him, sooner or later. Probably sooner, considering the heart attack he had suffered during the lift-off from Terra. So Ramou served, as he always did, in his capacity as general assistant—one more thing that no doubt encouraged Larry to believe Ramou to be an inferior. He overlooked the fact that they were both very young, and that in ten years' time, Ramou might very well be directing a play for which Larry was auditioning.

Yeah, I blew it, slamming Larry around like that and all but convicting him of attempted murder. I suppose it was because I'd been wanting to slap him around for a good long time, anyway—that, and the fact that he *had* opened all the lockers.

On the other hand, nobody seemed to be blaming me—except Larry, of course. He gave me an icy glare as he took his old-fashioned off the tray. I ignored it. Lacey was a bit reserved, but I knew that would only last until she needed a favor. Suzanne wasn't exactly warm and approving, but she did seem almost sympathetic, which made me wonder.

Appreciate, but still wonder. Maybe she figured Larry could try the patience of a saint, and lord knows I'm no saint.

Marty was the only one who actually mentioned the incident at all—sort of.

"So you used to be a short-order cook, huh, Ramou?"

"Short-order cook?" I frowned. "No—or at least, only for a month or two. Why?"

" 'Cause you got a great style for slapping a hamburger onto a flat surface."

Very funny; I gave him the dagger look it deserved—the one that's kind of pointless—and he understood there was no offense intended, 'cause he just grinned and took his drink.

"Could use a bit more vodka in this, Ramou," Ogden grumbled, heaving his vast bulk forward in the armchair just far enough to take the drink I was holding out. "Don't know why you won't let me have anything but screwdrivers, anyway."

I wouldn't let him have anything but screwdrivers for the same reason frat boys feed them to their dates—it's real hard to tell how much alcohol is in the orange juice. Truly is it said, "Beware of Greeks bearing gifts"—though I must admit we nonaffiliated types are apt to be a bit underhanded, too. Of course, I was working just the reverse of your average callow-youth ploy—putting in a lot *less* vodka than standard. "More vodka. Right, Mr. Wellesley." After all, I'd only put in a quarter of an ounce—what harm could three more drops do? After having to help Suzanne haul him to the infirmary, I was bound and determined to wean him away from the bottle.

The veterans were great—not a look of censure from a one of them. In fact, I could have sworn there was a gleam of approval in Marnie's eye, and Winston gave me a big smile as he took his glass, with a lot of emphasis on the "*Thank* you, Ramou." My immediate boss, Merlo, gave me the kind of look any master gives an apprentice who has done well, and silently toasted me. My spirits rose with his glass.

"Attention, please, everyone," Barry called out. He was sitting at a folding table in front of the 3DT tank, that being the focus of this end of the lounge—ever notice how the chairs are set up so everybody can get a look at their favorite stars? Captain McLeod was right beside him, so I had both my ultimate bosses at the same sitting. That's because my right hand is technical assistant for The Star Company, but my left hand is second officer—read: gofer—for the Starship *Cotton Blossom*. That's because a ship can't lift off without an official minimum crew of three—"official" because I don't really know spaceships from steamboats—lot in common, actually. But I'm learning, I'm learning.

"We had a surprising success on New Venus—" Barry began.

"Quite," Marnie interrupted. "I'm sure the petroleum company managers were vastly surprised."

"Surely they must have had some inkling that a revolution was brewing," Winston protested. As resident villain, he should have been scheming more than the revolutionaries, but he was more than happy to leave that to Barry and Horace.

"They should have been," Merlo said, "but who ever would have expected *Mac* . . . uh, the Scottish play, to trigger a revolt?"

"Looking back, it seems so obvious," Lacey said, with a knowing smile; she may have been the ingenue, but she was anything but ingenuous. "After all, the play deals with trying to build up a movement to kick out a tyrant."

"No wonder the management wanted to censor us." Suzanne leaned back with a sigh. My eyes swiveled over to her with an almost audible click; her sighs were very much worth watching. Soubrettes are usually well endowed, and Suzanne was keeping up their reputation. Keeping up my interest, too—I had to keep flirting with Lacey to counterbalance my interest in Suzanne. I was bound and determined not to be committed—which is to say, determined not to be bound. Not that I think Suzanne was honestly trying, mind you, but there were other girls who had. It was one of those hassles that had sent me to New York in the first place.

"You'd be worth censoring all by yourself, Suzanne darling," Lacey said sweetly. "Do you sigh that way often?"

Suzanne's eyes flashed dangerously, but she just smiled

and said, "Your eyes are so green this evening, Lacey darling."

"Yes, well, our surprise on New Venus notwithstanding, we actually made a profit there." Barry wrested them back to the issue by main force.

Beside him, Gantry McLeod nodded. "We came out with our fuel tanks full, and that's no mean feat, considering that water cost like gold on that planet. To actually come out ahead is amazing."

"Especially considering how badly they handicapped our attempts to advertise," Mr. Burbage put in.

"Quite so, Horace. Apropos of which, we sent Publius Promo on ahead by the fast mail ship, just before we lifted off from the Centauri space station—so hopefully, we will arrive at our next port of call to find our posters already on display."

That was bait if I ever heard any.

"Hopefully?" asked Winston, with his trademark sardonic lift of the eyebrow.

"Next port of call?" Ogden rumbled.

"What *is* our next port, Barry?" Marnie demanded, in her loftiest grande-dame manner.

"It's rather complicated," Barry began.

"Not a bit," Ogden returned. "Just tell us the name, there's a good chap."

Barry sighed and said, "Citadel."

Instant uproar. Everyone talked at once.

"Citadel? But they're Puritans!"

"From Elector Rudders to the Citadel deacons? Talk about frying pans and fires!"

"A planetful of religious fanatics? What shall we perform—*Saint Joan*?"

"Hardly—she was a Papist."

"Not the Shaw—they'll riot!"

"We could do the Shakespeare version from *Henry VI*—you know, the one-act where she really *is* a witch."

That quickly, they had gone from protest over the choice of planet to debate over the play. These actors are great people—well, mostly—but sometimes they don't make the world's greatest amount of sense.

"Please, people!" Barry raised both hands. "There are good reasons for it."

"Damned well had better be," Marnie warned, with fire in her eye. "Surely we're not going out of our way to visit such an abysmal setting!"

"Not at all . . ." Barry began, but Captain McLeod cleared his throat, and Barry turned to him, inclining his head. "Captain?"

"We're going out of our way by a little less than one light-year," McLeod said, standing. "Your director has told me that your next major stopover was intended to be Corona—the only habitable planet around 'Gemma,' otherwise known as Alpha Corona Borealis. Citadel is almost on a line between New Venus and Corona. Sure, we have to go a little out of our way—but it only adds another month to the trip time."

Everyone groaned.

"Add a week to that," Barry said, "a week on the ground. We're not planning a long stay, of course—but we should be able to realize a modest profit from the detour."

We all perked up at that. "How long would the trip to Corona be without the side trip?" Grudy asked, polishing her glasses. The old dear couldn't have lens surgery for some reason and, being a costumer, she did need close vision.

"About seventy-five days," Barry answered.

There was a rumble of alarm as everyone glanced at everyone else. Sure, each one of us got along with several of the others, and there were a few, such as Charlie and Winston and Horace, who pretty much got along with everybody—but the idea of being stuck with each other for such a long stretch bothered us all.

But something wasn't making sense. I frowned and asked, "If Corona is almost fourteen times farther away than New Venus was from Terra, how come it doesn't take us fourteen times as long to get there?"

Larry and a few others hissed at me to be quiet—almost as if asking the question would make the trip take that extra fourteen times as long. I ignored them and listened to McLeod.

"The actual transit time in H-space doesn't take very

long at all," he explained to me—and just incidentally, to everybody else at the same time. "Once you can go faster than the speed of light, you can build up a very fast speed indeed. The limiting factor isn't the ship or the fuel—we have a hydrogen scoop, and there's hydrogen in H-space, too. No, what limits how fast we can build up speed is our own bodies. We have to travel under constant acceleration, and if we let that go harder than one G, everybody would start hurting very quickly—not to mention a dozen other ailments that happen when your body has to try to work under heavier gravity than it was designed for."

Everybody glanced at Ogden, remembering his heart attack. The huge old actor shuddered.

"So most of the travel time is spent accelerating and decelerating," I inferred.

"Very good, Number Two!" Gantry's eyes gleamed. "That means that the farther we have to go, the higher the speed we can build up. The good part is that it's never going to take more than about one day per light-year, once we're going more than thirty light-years; a month is about the minimum travel time, and that's only if nobody minds being a little heavy all the way."

I nodded. "Minimum acceleration time?"

"And deceleration. The bad part is that thirty days *is* pretty much the minimum."

Everybody groaned.

Marty piped up: "But isn't Corona Borealis kind of in another part of the sky from the Centaur?"

I looked up at him, surprised—I hadn't pegged Marty for a man who would ever have looked up at the night sky.

"From Terra, yes." McLeod fairly gleamed with approval. "But not very much. Alpha Centauri and Terra are right next door to each other, in astronomical distances. I hate to say it, but when you can go so much faster than light as we can, four light-years isn't really all that much."

"So this slight detour would give us a break in the middle of the trip?" Winston asked.

"Not the middle," McLeod said. "More like one-third and two-thirds. Actual travel time to Citadel would be about three and a half weeks—twenty-five days."

"And twice that to Corona." Marnie shivered. "Why did

I ever involve myself with this calamitous undertaking? Not even room service!"

No one answered. We all knew why Marnie had joined us, and so did she—because Valdor Tallendar had given her an ultimatum: leave Terra with The Star Company and a fat settlement, or leave his house with as little as the courts would allow—and the judicial system may have recognized the rights of mistresses, but it hasn't been very generous about it.

Of course, I'm sure Valdor was much nicer about it than that. He's a top executive, after all—or was, until he bought the company—his first one, that is. No, he would have hinted, have laid it on thick about how she really needed to be back before her public, how badly they were missing her, how starved the poor folk of the outer regions were for theater, and so on. Marnie would have gotten the message; she's not stupid. Obtuse, maybe, but not stupid.

"Everything considered, I do think it's best to break the trip," Horace said. They pay attention when he talks, partly because he's an old hand who knows the ropes—sixty, at least—and partly because he's Barry's best and oldest buddy. Everyone knows that if Barry says it, he's talked it over with Horace first.

"Breaking the trip is fine," Winston said. "A stopover on Citadel is not. Are you *sure* this is well advised, Barry? They're Puritans, after all! The audience may be so small that we won't make back the cost of takeoff and landing!"

"It shouldn't be that expensive," McLeod assured him. "Citadel is more than half water—four big oceans, and half a dozen seas. H_2O won't cost all that much. What's the matter? Don't you folks think you can pull in even *that* much audience?"

Chorus of indignant exclamations, here—and the usual remarks about Gantry being a layman, and what did he know about theater? McLeod rode it out, smiling—they all knew the answer. He was an excellent example of your average audience member.

But not from a Puritan planet.

Finally, they settled down enough for somebody to think of the obvious question. "Have you ever been on Citadel, Captain?"

"Yes, Ms. Lark. Not much past the spaceport, usually—they have a few hotels nearby, just for travelers—but I did bring a package tour through once. They stopped there for the same reason we're going to—it was a convenient way to break the trip. Came to see Mount Tabor, of course."

"Of course" was right. Mount Tabor was famous—the most beautiful mountain in the Terran Sphere, if you don't count any of the spectaculars on Old Earth herself. Most painters reckoned it second only to Mount Fuji, and came just to set up their easels.

"But you wouldn't get much of a feel for the people that way, would you?" Lacey said doubtfully.

"Not much, no," McLeod agreed. "It was a package tour, as I said, and I think the Citadel deacons were worried that we might corrupt their youth or something. They escorted us out in hoverbuses, shadowed everybody the whole day as they wandered and hiked and painted and spun pictures, then herded us back to the spaceport."

"So what *do* we know about them?" Marnie demanded.

"We know they're starved for theater," Barry replied. "They should be willing to pay quite handsomely for the opportunity to witness a performance."

"Provided they wish to *go* to the theater," Ogden pointed out.

"*If* they have any money to spend," Marnie snapped.

"As to their desire to go to the theater, we note that when their ships land on Terra, the officers and crew go to a different play each night," Horace told them. "We have also looked into export records and discovered that they buy approximately fifty new 3DT epics every year."

"Well . . . those are favorable signs," Ogden admitted.

"Ramou?" Barry could see I was itching to get a word in.

"But they're just a bunch of farmers, aren't they?" I asked. "I mean, we studied them in our high school Tour of the Colonies unit—and from what they said there, nearly everybody farms, and the land's so rocky and poor that they just barely make enough to feed everybody."

"Not quite so," Horace told me. "They farm, yes—but they also raise a great number of sheep. Seems the beasts can graze nearly anywhere, and this particular breed has an amazingly soft variety of wool. So there's a very large weaving industry . . ."

"Why, yes!" Lacey sat up, eyes wide. "Now that I think of it, Citadel woolens cost through the nose when you're trying to buy clothes made of them. I haven't bought one of their sweaters since college!"

"Sweaters do seem to be about all they manufacture," Horace noted, "in plain colors, and the classic styles that never go out of date. As to other garments, no one off-planet seems to favor their idea of fashion."

"No, I don't know of anybody who really likes a basic sack for a dress," Suzanne said. "They seem to be designed to hide the fact that a woman might have a shape."

"If she did, I'm sure they would think it sinful," Marnie said darkly. "You don't mean to say they've become rich from exporting wool, do you, Horace?"

"That was the beginning," Horace said. "I did read what histories they had available in the New York library, though it was rather scanty. From the export of woolen cloth, they built an enormous shipping industry, second only to Terra's. Apparently their trading voyages last for a year or two, beginning by selling their cloth on one of the more advanced colony planets, where they buy manufactured goods and take them to one of the newer, less-industrialized colonies. They sell manufactured goods at a high profit and buy raw materials, then take those back to an industrialized world, back and forth several times, until they have finally amassed an amazing amount of money—whereupon they fill their ships with the sort of goods they don't raise or make at home, such as new looms—"

"And 3DT epics," Winston reminded him.

"Yes, and such stuff. So there's no doubt that a great deal of wealth is going into the planet. Surely they must be willing to pay a good deal for an evening's entertainment."

"It does seem probable," Ogden admitted. Marnie flashed him a skeptical look, but even she seemed more than half-convinced.

"I don't see that we can do less than break even," Barry said, "and I would expect a decent profit, such as we turned on New Venus."

"Let's hope it doesn't take another miracle, like a homemade revolutionary movement," Marnie sniffed, "but you do make it sound attractive."

"An audience is an audience," Winston agreed, "but one starved for entertainment is likely to be very appreciative."

Their eyes all gleamed at the prospect of applause. The only other time they ever looked that way was when somebody talked about making lots of money. Apparently, for actors, the two go together a lot.

"But what sorts of plays would we be able to *do*, Barry?" Ogden demanded. "I'd rather not end my days playing an archangel in *The Last Judgment*."

"I scarcely think it will be that," Barry said with a smile. "Their shipping industry is very active, as I've said, and their crews must spread the news of the outside world when they come home. I would expect them to be surprisingly cosmopolitan, at least as religious fanatics go. In fact, having to deal with so many merchants from pleasure-loving planets such as Falstaff and Meriera must have taken the edge off their fanaticism. I would expect them to be much more tolerant than rumor would have them—so we might attempt some drawing-room comedies, perhaps even a Molière."

"But not *Tartuffe*, eh?" Ogden said, smiling.

He got his laugh. Even I understood why—the play is a thorough slam on a religious hypocrite.

"But what if you're wrong in that guess, Barry?" Marnie asked.

"Then I suggest that we also rehearse the pleasant moral pieces of Hans Sachs," Barry answered. "If the Meistersinger of Nuremburg could entertain while enlightening a Medieval town, his plays should do well with a modern, but no less Medieval, mindset. We might also be thinking about *The Ten Commandments, Gideon, J.B., Samson. . . .*"

"But not Delilah," Marty piped up. "Little too racy for them, don't you think?"

He got his laugh, too, and Barry said, "I believe that will suffice for this evening. Drink and be merry, my friends, for tomorrow we rehearse."

2

"Ask 'em, Number Two."

"Number Two" is me. Merlo and I were currently on the bridge in our capacities as crew. At least one of us was qualified.

Of course, I was qualified, too—even a dropout electrical engineer can handle a communication system and sundry other odd jobs. "Spaceship *Cotton Blossom* requesting permission to land on Citadel. Come in, Citadel ground control."

"Citadel ground control here." It was a harsh, unsmiling voice—yes, you *can* hear a smile; it changes the shape of your mouth, which alters the overtones in your voice. Had a bit of a nasal twang, too. "What is the nature of your business, *Cotton Blossom*?"

"Entertainment," I replied. "We're a troupe of traveling actors, coming to perform on Citadel."

Ground control was quiet for a moment, and Merlo frowned. "Didn't Publius tell them we were coming?"

"That depends on whether or not your advance man was sober long enough," McLeod answered curtly. The curtness was understandable, coming from a periodic boozer. He never drank aboard a spaceship, but he made up for it when he went ashore.

"Cleared for landing, *Cotton Blossom*," the harsh voice said. "Blast Pit Twelve—southwest corner of the port."

"Blast Pit Twelve, southwest corner. Aye, aye, Citadel."

"We're lighting your beam, *Cotton Blossom*. Follow it in. Contact us just before landing."

"Will do, Citadel." I broke the connection and leaned back. "Doesn't sound too friendly."

"That's not part of his job," Merlo told me. "Twelve blast pits, huh? Not bad, for a colonial world!"

McLeod nodded. "It's a major shipping center, all right, Mr. Hertz. Don't forget, you're looking at one of the oldest colonies. They were shipping goods when your great-grandfather was wondering whether or not he should get married."

"Hadn't thought about it that way." Merlo leaned forward and keyed the pressure patch that locked the computer pilot onto the homing beacon. "Better make your final rounds, Ramou. We'll be starting descent in about fifteen minutes." He raised his voice. "Check ETA, voice readout."

"Sixteen minutes, seven seconds," answered the mellow voice of the ship's computer. McLeod kept it turned off most of the time, just communicated with it by keyboard and screen—said he could manage his ship better by feel than by voice, and besides, if there was one thing he couldn't stand, it was a mouthy ship. Me, I think he's just old-fashioned.

"On my way." I got up and went over to the drop shaft.

It wasn't too much of a tussle this time—except with Suzanne; she was in a playful mood, and I wasn't about to object. Everybody else has pretty much figured out by now that when I say it's time to web in, I mean it, and I'm not going to take no for an answer. Especially Larry, but he learns hard. I left Suzanne for last, to make sure I'd have an official interruption to save my face.

"Ensign Lazarian to the bridge," the speaker in her cabin crackled.

"Spoilsport!" She made a face at the speaker.

"Give me any more sport like that, and you'll sure spoil *me*." I tightened the webbing at her side.

She rolled enough to brush my fingers against her breast. "Complaining, Ramou?" Her eyes danced wickedly.

"Never," I assured her, and almost kissed her, but held off at the last second—I was still feeling guilty about Larry. When I glanced back from the doorway, she was watching me with big eyes, pouting.

I stopped on the way to double-check Ogden. "Just on my way back to the bridge, Mr. Wellesley." I deftly removed the glass from the table beside his acceleration couch, emptied it, refilled it with water, and put it back. "Everything still comfortable?"

"Just fine." Ogden sighed. "I'll admit that one has need of sanitary facilities frequently, Ramou, but not in the ten minutes since you last came in. Or were you more concerned about input than output?"

"Just reassuring myself in general, Mr. Wellesley. I don't intend to let you have another heart attack on me."

"I assure you, dear boy, I didn't intend to."

Then on up to the bridge. Merlo glanced at the clock. "Cutting it a bit fine there, boyo."

I looked as I slid into my couch; I had a minute and eight left till descent. "Hey, you said I had sixteen minutes."

"That wasn't supposed to include five for Suzanne."

"Some things can't be avoided," I sighed. "At least, not if you're going to be polite. Thanks for the call, Merlo."

"Always glad to be your social excuse," he answered, with irony.

"Clear us, Number Two!" McLeod snapped, and I hit the comm again. "*Cotton Blossom* to Citadel ground control. We're about to start our descent, Citadel."

"Clear for landing," Citadel responded—grudgingly, I thought. "Come on in, *Cotton Blossom*."

"No, do not!" It was a new voice, filled with a lot of crackle and hiss, but we could hear it—and it sounded familiar. Also frightened, but that was familiar, too. It was Publius Promo, our advance man. "Do not land, Captain! Repeat, do not! Tell Mr. Tallendar! This is a disastrous—"

A third voice broke in, iron-hard and angry. "Illegal transmission! Substandard equipment, degraded signal! Cease transmitting at once!"

"—mistake!" Publius finished. If he could hear the other voice, he made no sign.

"Relay to director's cabin," McLeod snapped, and I pressed a patch, calling, "Mr. Tallendar! Emergency! Publius!" Then I shut up, so he could hear the rest. Me, too.

"—disaster!" Publius was saying. "If you come in, you won't go out! They have it all planned, a fiendish system! Don't worry about me—I'm lost, and nothing can save me now! Save yourselves! Don't land on—"

A burst of static interrupted him, and the third voice snapped, "Cease unathorized transmission!"

Apparently, Publius did, because the static stopped, and Citadel ground control said, "Commence descent, *Cotton Blossom*, or make another orbit—you've almost lost your window."

"Directions, Mr. Tallendar?" McLeod said calmly.

"We don't abandon our own," Barry's voice answered. "If Publius is in trouble, it's because we've sent him there! We'll find a way to get him out—*then* we'll leave!"

McLeod nodded in approval. "Going down." He touched the patches that told the computer to start the descent.

The ship rotated on its axis—slowly, but faster than the fluid in my inner ear. Fortunately, I *like* roller coasters.

We'd been slowing down as we looped around the planet, the friction of the atmosphere dragging down our velocity fast. When the main thrust tubes were pointed at the planet, we started falling. Before we could start feeling the sinking in our stomachs, the computer lit the torch, and a pillar of flame cushioned us on our way down. Oh, we still felt as if we were descending—but not very fast. We were, of course, but it didn't feel like it. It's just the opposite of a lift-off—on the way up, you have to get going as fast as possible—escape velocity, and we'd already had occasion to get going faster than that, if we could have. For people who don't want us around, it's amazing how planetary governments try to prevent us from leaving. Of course, we suspect Elector Rudders might have something to do with that—he's afraid we might come home to Terra. We made him look bad enough, managing to escape when he was howling for our blood and trying to make sure we couldn't take it anywhere else; it would have made him look even worse, for us to come home for a triumphant season on Broadway.

The ship touched down with a jar that only rattled my dental work a little bit. Then the whole vessel seemed to relax and sigh and settle, and McLeod pronounced, "We're down." He hit the "all stations" on the intercom and announced, in his official captain's voice, "We have arrived on Citadel. Personnel may now unfasten their shock webbing. Everyone cleared for shore leave may queue up at the boarding ramp."

I always imagined I could hear a massed cheer when he said that. Just imagination, I know—he only had the intercom set on one way, and the skeleton of the ship couldn't carry *sound* that well.

On the other hand, I didn't know if they had anything to cheer about. Normally, everybody would be cleared for shore leave except one of the crew, and McLeod usually took that burden on himself—said that if he went ashore, he'd start drinking again, and he couldn't afford to do that until we got back to Terra. But Publius's call changed all that.

McLeod was on the horn with Barry. "What do we do about it, Mr. Director?"

"How did this call come in, Captain?" Barry's voice returned.

"Suddenly and with lousy reception," McLeod answered. "At a guess, he's cobbled together a homemade radio because they wouldn't let him use the real thing. Whatever kind of bind he's in, he's done something very brave in trying to warn us off."

"And even braver, in trying to sacrifice himself so that we, too, will not be trapped," Barry agreed.

They were both right, and I was surprised. From what I'd seen of Publius on New Venus, I had him pegged as the weak-kneed sort who'd collapse into a bowl of jelly at the first threat. Back there, he'd collapsed into a bottle. I guess he could summon up courage, if he had enough warning.

"It was a noble gesture, of course, but we cannot accept it," Barry said. "On the other hand, we must observe all due caution in our interactions with the inhabitants of Citadel. I think we had better begin with another short meeting. Summon the company to the lounge, will you, Captain?"

"Be glad to, Mr. Director, and I'll join you myself, as soon as I've made provisions for refueling. I think we may want to be ready for a quick getaway."

Hey, why not? Was there any other way to leave a planet?

* * *

The company gathered in the lounge with a lot of loud and angry muttering. They weren't happy about having to stay aboard ship a second longer than they had to. As Barry came in, Marnie pounced. "What is this asininity about, Barry? What could possibly keep us from going out?"

"A warning from Publius, Marnie," Barry said gravely.

The lounge went rock-still. Even Horace looked startled, and he had come in with Barry.

Then Marnie found her voice. "Warning? From the advance man? How silly! What does he wish to caution us about—low ticket sales?"

"He did not have time to say," Barry answered gravely. "We deduce that he was broadcasting with an illegal transmitter and had to turn it off before the authorities found him. As it is, he may be in for a jail sentence or worse, depending on local jurisprudence."

"A gallant man." Winston sounded impressed.

"Gallant indeed! What was he warning us about?" Ogden wanted to know.

"He told us not to land—that if we did, we wouldn't be able to take off again."

Controversy erupted.

"Ridiculous! This isn't the Middle Ages! If a visitor wishes to go, he's free to go!"

"They're a colony of Terra, not a sovereign government!"

"Whatever could be so disastrous as to keep us here?"

"Why did we ever land?" Larry squawked. "If he told us to stay away, we're out of our minds!"

Barry gave him a cold stare. "We do not desert our own."

"He's not *my* own!" Larry yelled. "I've scarcely met the old fool! If he's going to rot here, why should *I* keep him company? I've got my whole career ahead of me!"

"And it's going to be rather short, at the rate you're going," Horace snapped.

"Would you want us to fly on by, if *you* were the one who was stranded, Mr. Rash?" Barry asked.

Larry started to answer, but his voice caught in his throat.

"Whatever the difficulty, I highly doubt that it is insuperable," Barry went on, "though I can easily believe that one man alone might lack the resources to overcome it. If we are all together, we should be able to find a way out."

Everyone relaxed a little—or started to, but just then Captain McLeod came in and stepped up to mutter something to Barry.

"Let us *all* hear," Marnie cried. "We have the right!"

"But I don't." McLeod turned to give her a very cold stare. "As ship's captain, I only have the right to talk to you about shipboard rules, conduct, and safety practices, Ms. Lulala. Anything pertaining to your going ashore is for your director to say to you."

"Yes, quite," Barry said quickly, before Marnie could start arguing. "And you're quite right, too, Marnie—you should all learn it at once. I believe Captain McLeod has discovered the nature of the insurmountable obstacle that has kept Publius planet-bound. Captain, if you would be so good?"

"Well, since I have your leave." McLeod sighed. He turned to face the company. "I called the terminal to order refueling, and they told me I have to pay first."

"What's the difficulty?" Winston demanded. "Pay them!"

"I can't, Mr. Carlton. Seems they only accept their own local currency—for everything."

They were all talking at once again—exclamations of disbelief and outrage. Barry held up his hands, and when they quieted down, we could hear Larry saying, "What difference does that make? Just exchange some BTUs for seashells, or whatever they use for currency here."

"Can't," McLeod explained. "It's illegal."

This time the whole lounge went silent, appalled. Then Ogden found his voice. "But we can't be the only ones who have ever landed here!"

"Of course not," McLeod agreed, "but most of the others are cargo ships. They sell their goods for local currency, and they have enough to buy more fuel. Then at their next planet, they exchange Citadel talents for BTUs."

"Oh, so it's allowed off-planet, huh?" Marty sounded angry.

"Of course." McLeod shrugged. "Other planets aren't bound by Citadel's laws."

"Surely Citadel can't be so hypocritical as to exchange their currency for others; but not allow them the same courtesy!" Marnie declared.

McLeod only answered, "Why not?"

That stopped us all. Come to think of it, maybe it was a good question.

Barry sighed. "They might not even see it as hypocritical—just good business practice, keeping their own resources at home."

Horace nodded. "No doubt they think the rest of the Terran planets are foolish not to employ such a useful law."

"But it restricts trade!" Marty cried. "They're merchants! They *need* foreign currency!"

"And I'm sure they have plenty of it, in foreign banks," Barry returned. "Even in their own banks, no doubt. But not in circulation on their own world."

McLeod nodded. "I never thought about it before, because I didn't have anything to do with the arrangements—but the tour groups I brought through doled out spending money to all the tourists, before they left the ship. They must have taken care of their currency exchange on another planet and brought the local stuff here."

"Coals to Newcastle," Ogden grumbled. "My heavens! Who'd ever have thought there would be a good reason?"

"I understand the Eskimos have been buying refrigeration units for several centuries now," McLeod said dryly.

"So what do we do?" Suzanne asked.

"We perform," Barry said, "as quickly as possible."

"But what about our shore leave?" Lacey cried.

Barry shrugged. "You can wander about and look at the sights all you like, Ms. Lark—but don't try to buy anything. Oh, and if they have cabs, don't take one. We won't be able to pay the fare."

There was a dark silence. Barry looked around, frowning, wondering why.

Then Winston voiced what we were all worrying about. "Are we sure we will be *allowed* to perform, Barry?"

"Why—I can't think why not." But Barry paled; apparently, he was finally willing to consider the matter seriously. "However! That is a problem for another day. For now, let's go ashore. Enjoy the dirt, friends."

* * *

I'd be a liar if I told you the news didn't dampen our enthusiasm about seeing a planet again—but our spirits picked up as the hatch opened. We streamed out of the airlock and down the boarding ramp. Suzanne tossed her head back, letting her hair blow loose in the wind. "Fresh air! Oh, doesn't it feel wonderful, Ramou!"

"Sure does." I grinned. After weeks of canned air, it would have smelled wonderful if I had been downwind of a fish factory.

"Perhaps a little *too* fresh." Larry wrapped an oversized duffle coat more tightly about him. I glanced at him, deciding he was overdoing it—he just wanted an excuse to bring along that huge coat, with the deep pockets. I suspected he had a dozen more pouches on the inside, and wondered what he had brought along to sell to the natives *this* time. On New Venus, it had been cigarettes, plus matches—that on a world where the oceans were made of petroleum, and possession of matches is a capital crime!

"Get used to it, younker," McLeod called down from the hatch. "Temperature never gets much above twenty-five."

He meant centigrade, of course. About sixty degrees, on the Fahrenheit scale they still used back in Detroit.

Larry shuddered. "Absolutely beastly!"

"You could stay home," I suggested.

"No, no!" he said quickly. "Cabin fever! Anything's better than staying inside that tin can a moment longer." He eyed the surrounding terrain and added, "Though maybe not for long."

I had to agree, though not out loud. Looking around from the top stair of the boarding ramp, I had to admit that I had never seen a place that looked so bleak and hostile. It was flat almost all the way to the horizon, though there was a suggestion of low hills right at the edge. The sky was leaden, and the wind whistled around the docked ships and cut like a knife.

There were only five or six ships, too, most of them cargo shuttles, squatting over the charred bowls of blast pits. There were twenty of those black rings—I counted them later—and they really added to the sweetness and gaiety of the scene, especially with so few ships on them. "Slow day," I muttered.

"What's that, Ramou?" Suzanne asked.

"I said, 'okay.' " Why depress her, too? She wasn't obliged to share my moods. She wasn't even my girl. Not my choice, but she'd made it clear, though gently, that she didn't intend to get tied down to any one man for a long time yet. Of course, the tone of her voice, and her movements and gestures, were always hinting that she'd like to, so I kept my hopes up. On the other hand, I wasn't about to put all *my* eggs in one basket, either, so I kept up a healthy flirtation with Lacey. Wouldn't want Suzanne to get complacent, after all.

" 'Okay' is entirely a matter of opinion." Marty blew on his hands and rubbed them. "But Larry's right, for once—it's better than being shut up aboard. 'Course, I don't know if there's much point in exploring . . ."

"I know what you mean," Lacey agreed. "No money, no shopping."

"Probably no stores, anyway—or nothing we'd recognize by that name," Suzanne said. "And we can't see the sights much, without a cab."

"Who said there were cabs?" I rejoined. "But hey, who needs money? We'll walk. After all those weeks of dropshafts and companionways, I could do with a hike."

Suzanne's eyes lit. "Yeah!"

"You don't suppose the sun ever shines here, do you?" Marty asked.

"Has to, or the farmers wouldn't be able to grow anything," I said. "Probably shows up on alternate Wednesdays." But I did wonder what they could grow, with such low temperatures. Cabbage? Lichens? How about a nice algae soup? I eyed Marty's choice of wardrobe, and decided he'd been prudent.

He was wearing a baggy sweater and a huge scarf wound around his neck. On second thought, maybe Larry *did* need a coat, though one his own size might have done better. Me, I was wearing my good old synthetic jacket that looked just like leather—nothing else could have taken that many scars and still come up fighting. The girls were taking advantage of the excuse to wear sweaters, too, though big and baggy they definitely weren't. Suzanne was winning, but Lacey was definitely giving her a run for her money. "And to think I almost wore a skirt!" Lacey said.

"Trousers do have advantages, don't they?" Suzanne watched the steam from her breath drift away, dissipating, and smiled with the delight of a child. "Do you think we ought to wait for the vets?"

We were labeling the more mature actors as "veterans," since that's the way they seemed to think of themselves. There was a pretty sharp age gap—the four of us under thirty, Barry and Horace and Grudy and Winston and Marnie over forty—never mind what Marnie claimed—with Charlie and Merlo somewhere in between.

"Let 'em catch up," Marty suggested. "We can wander around the tarmac and breathe the air for a little."

So we did, gazing in delight at a real sky, feeling ground under our feet that wouldn't go away if the gravity generator failed. But it got old pretty fast—very old, and very cold.

"Well, that's fresh air." Lacey shivered. "Nice to visit, but I wouldn't want to breathe here—if I could help it."

Suzanne nodded. "Sweater weather is wonderful, but I forgot my mittens."

Marty nodded, too. "Into the terminal, right?"

"Right!" both girls said.

"At least it's a different view than we see inside of the ship," Larry groused.

So we headed for the door marked CUSTOMS. But as we came up, an official came out. At least, I assume he was an official, because there was a badge on his gray shirt, right next to the suspender. He wore a flat, black, brimless hat that fitted low on his scalp—harder to blow off, I guess—and black trousers that lapped over boots. I shuddered; he didn't look all that different from a prison inmate.

"Hi!" Marty said brightly. "We've come to visit your lovely planet!"

"You cannot," the apparition said, out of a jaw like a nutcracker's. It was surrounded by a fringe of beard—he needed it, in this weather.

"We can't?" Suzanne gave him her most winsome smile

and biggest blue eyes. "Why not?" She managed a very discreet wriggle.

He drew away from her as if she had the plague. "Because you're not properly clad!"

"Properly clad?" Fortunately, Suzanne's eyes were already wide.

"How do you mean?" Lacey stepped up, not at all winsome. "We're covered from head to toe!"

"You might as well wear nothing at all, in those second skins you have on your tops! And your limbs! You're showing your limbs!"

Suzanne looked down, as if to make sure her pants hadn't blown away when she wasn't looking. They hadn't; they were still right below her sweater. "There's not an inch of skin showing!"

"Nay, but one can see that you have limbs! Disgraceful, 'tis provocative! Have you no shame?"

"Not what you mean by it, no." Lacey's voice flattened, and my stomach sank. I'd seen her in this mood before. "If you think inhibitions that make a woman subservient to a male-dominated culture are 'shame . . .' "

"Then we'll try to deal with your cultural norms," Marty interrupted smoothly. "Just what sort of clothing did you have in mind, Officer . . ." His gaze flicked down to the nameplate above the badge. ". . . Officer Abimilech?"

"Not men's!" The man wrinkled his nose, pointing toward Lacey's trouser legs, and for a second, there was a gleam of desire in his eye. Only for a second; he squelched it quickly.

Lacey noticed and let her lip curl—for a second. "You mean we *have* to wear skirts?"

"Not skirts—dresses, decent dresses!"

Lacey started a hot retort, but Suzanne restrained her with a hand on her arm. "What sort of dresses?"

"Why, dresses that cover you, all of you!" Abimilech declaimed. "Cover you from your chin to your toe!"

"Cut loosely, of course."

"Oh, aye! Loosely, fully! With sleeves to your wrists, and a high collar that covers all your neck!" He snorted in disgust. "I'll wager you don't even have such things."

"You lose." Lacey turned away, back toward the ship. "Come on, Suzanne. Let's go see Grudy."

"Just a minute, darling—I see a chance to get some local currency." Suzanne stopped her, looking back at the customs man. "You really want to wager?"

"Nay, of course not!" The man's head snapped up as if he'd been slapped. "Gambling's the devil's game! 'Twas only a manner of speaking!"

"Odd manner, if you don't believe in gambling," I said, frowning.

"Why, don't you see, young man, that if you gamble, the only thing you can be sure of, is that you'll lose your soul! So we say, 'I wager' when we speak of certain sin!"

Suzanne turned away with a shudder. "Talk about a jaundiced way of looking at life! You were right, Lacey—let's go."

They turned away, pacing off toward the ship fast—but a last comment wafted behind them: "Talk about sexist!"

Abimilech's eyes grew round, and his face grew red with horror. "*What* word was that you said?"

" 'About sixes,' " Marty said quickly. "That's their dress size."

Abimilech looked skeptical, but he had even less of an idea about women's sizes than we did, so all he said was, "Do they truly have dresses?"

"Yeah, but not the kind you just described," I said.

He gave me a vindictive smile of triumph. "So they'll not be back!"

"Oh, I wouldn't say that." I bridled, but held myself in—I was on his territory. "They're very good at improvising in a hurry." For some reason, I had a hunch I shouldn't tell him we'd brought our own costumer along, or that all she had to do to produce a dress was key in the style on a machine.

Mostly, though, my mind had locked on Suzanne's idea about raising local currency. If these people had to import everything but wool and food that could be grown with a short season, there was a good chance they might be interested in some of the gourmet items we could produce with the food synthesizers. "Are we allowed to bring in edibles?"

"Nay, of course not! No planet in the Terran Sphere will let you import comestibles without a license, and a dozen tests to make sure they've no virulent germs!"

"The old story." I sighed. " 'Leave it to the paid professionals.' How about knicknacks and gewgaws?"

"I should say not!" Abimilech exclaimed self-righteously. "Waste good brass on idle toys? Nay! Destroy the moral fiber of our young folk, would you?"

I stared; that was putting it a bit strongly. "So what *can* we sell?"

"Nothing! What little we need from off-world, we'll have our merchants buy, and our customs agents certify under a deacon's inspection! We'll have none of your Devil's toys and temptations brought to our hale planet!"

"What are you afraid of?" Larry asked, in his nastiest tone.

I stiffened and saw Marty's jaw clench.

Abimilech's eyes narrowed. "Afraid of mortal peril for our souls, but even more, for those of our young folk! 'Lead us not unto temptation,' as the Lord's Prayer says! Oh, we'll not hesitate to admit being afraid of the Devil, be sure—but be even surer that we'll boast that we fear the Lord!"

Larry drew breath, and I grabbed his arm and turned him away before he could start blasting. I needed a quick change of subject. "Larry," I said as I strolled him back toward the ship, "You heard what the man just said. Whether the unofficial import business is right or wrong, it's illegal."

"Civil disobedience, Ramou! An unjust law should not be obeyed!"

"Very Thoreau, aren't you?" I shrugged. "Hey, it's your conscience—and if you were the only one who was going to have to pay the price, I'd be the last one to try to impose my morality on you. Unfortunately, though, your ideas of morality could wind me into the stockade, here—along with Lacey and Suzanne, and nice old folks like Horace and Grudy. So, everything considered, I'd have to say that, just as a matter of good social interaction, you ought to obey the local laws."

He fixed me with a glare that couldn't quite hold focus. "My principles are none of your affair, Ramou!"

"I just explained to you why they are."

"We are free to choose our own moral codes!"

"Yeah, but if they clash with society's, we have to be ready to pay the price." I tightened my grip on his arm. "*Alone*, Larry. Now, you wouldn't have been planning to set up a traveling retail business here, would you?" I gave him a friendly pat on the ribs.

They clacked.

"Interesting haberdashery." I slipped a hand inside his duffle coat. He yelled and slapped at it, but I was too fast for him. My hand came back out with a rack of 3DT cubes. "What's on 'em, Larry?" I glanced at the titles. "*A Night on the Town—High Stakes—Watch 'Em Run*—let me guess. Drinking, gambling, and horse racing. Right?"

"None of your business!" Larry snatched the cubes back.

"Very much my business—and the rest of the company's, too." I tapped his other side; it rustled. He clapped a hand over it, but I was faster again, turning away from his frantic grabs as I leafed through it. "Wow! Is *she* ever built! So is he, for that matter—wish I had pecs like that." I turned the page. "Getting right down to the issues, aren't they?" I turned one more page, stared, then guessed. "I press the little red square in the lower right-hand corner here, and she moves, right?"

"Not very much." Larry had jammed his fists into his coat pockets.

I glanced down at them. "What do you have in there? Hashish? Instant-gin powder? A miniature nuclear bomb? I know it doesn't take much plutonium to make a big bang . . ."

"Ramou!" Larry paled. "You don't think *I* would market tools of destruction, do you?"

"Why not? You've got enough in there to guarantee all of us get destroyed. What did you do? Find out the itinerary from Barry, and lay in trade goods for every planet?"

"Of course not! You know he and Horace hadn't worked out the tour yet! We did have to leave in a bit of a hurry, after all."

"So you brought whatever you thought would sell well, in general—which means everything that might, on most planets, be considered illegal, immoral, or both." I shook my head. "Didn't you stop to think that the rest of us might wind up in jail with you?"

"None of us will wind up in jail, Ramou! I *am* discreet, you know!"

"Discreet." I tapped a coat pocket; it sloshed. "That's your idea of 'discreet?' Well, I'll tell you, Larry—you carry on the way you're doing, and we'll *all* be discrete—discrete particles, inside an execution chamber that disassociates our molecules into their constituent atoms! I know I'll have to return to dust some day, but I'm in no rush to hurry the job."

"They'll never know . . ."

"Just like the customs agent on New Venus didn't find your cigarettes, huh?"

"They were sophisticated, high-tech! These savages—"

"—Aren't savage," I interrupted. "They may dress old-fashioned, but I'll bet you they have state-of-the-art snooper equipment all around that doorway we have to walk through. In fact, we're probably going to have to walk through a regular tunnel of them. So do me a favor, will you, Larry?" I clapped him around the shoulders and turned him toward the ship, walking fast. "Clean out your coat, will you? Leave all your pocketfuls behind—and come out wearing a tighter jacket. Just for my peace of mind. Okay?"

"The last thing on Earth I'm worried about is your peace of mind!" he snarled, but he kept walking. Didn't have much choice, of course.

"But we're not on Earth," I reminded him. "Why make a fortune, when you'll only be the richest man in prison? Put 'em away, Larry—put 'em all away. You'll thank me, someday."

He didn't, of course—ever. Admitted I was right, six years later when he was in his cups—but he never thanked me. Par for the course—and for Larry.

3

The vets came trooping across the tarmac, or whatever the spaceport's apron was made of. Marnie was at her most vivacious, chatting with Charlie and Winston, laughing, eyes glowing. I felt a lurch somewhere inside, and for a second, I could imagine what she must have looked like when she was twenty.

I could see it in Ramou's eyes—the sudden awareness of Marnie as a woman. I honestly believe he had never seen her in that light before, nor realized just how beautiful she had once been—that, in spite of the fact that he must have seen her in at least one 3DT epic during his formative years. She still was beautiful, of course, but no longer in the way that appeals to callow youths with an overabundance of hormones. I found her far more to my taste than Suzanne or Lacey, for example—until she opened her mouth. She had all the winsome charm of a barracuda, and it neatly canceled all the attractions of her face and figure.

I could see Ramou making the same comparison, with similar results; the admiration in his gaze calmed to wariness and courtesy once more, as he fell in beside me.

"Weary of the great outdoors so soon?" I asked. "Or did Larry need an escort back to the ship?"

"Not just an escort—a frisker," he said.

"Oh." I raised my eyebrows. "More contraband?"

"In spades," Ramou confirmed. "Why does that guy feel that he always has to play the angles, Horace?"

"An inborn trait, no doubt—though it may have been aggravated by his professors; I understand many of the college acting coaches are teaching their students that they should take any advantage they find—particularly, that they must toady to those in power and ingratiate themselves in any way possible, if they want to be cast. The attitude carries over to other aspects of life." I said it absently, however, for I was scanning the little group at the gate—and noticing that it was down to one: Marty. "I take it the young ladies had to return to the ship, too?"

"Only temporarily." Ramou glanced at Marnie. "Uh, you might want to batten down the hatches, Horace."

"Prepare myself for a tirade? Why, what happened to the girls?"

"The customs agent wouldn't let them through the door. They were dressed wrong."

"Oh, my." I glanced at Marnie. "So that is why Grudy was not ready to join us. Tell me the worst, Ramou—how extensive did they wish the ladies' costumes to be?"

"Well, he was willing to let them show their faces and hands."

"How kind of him, not to insist on veils and gloves! He wanted total coverage, then?"

"Just like your insurance agent advises—top to toe, and your basic umbrella."

"They want the dresses as loose as they think actresses' morals to be?" I shuddered. "I don't relish breaking the news to Marnie."

"Better that it come from one of us, easier if it comes from a junior." And before I could stop him, Ramou had stepped around me and over to Marnie. I made a frantic grab, but he was beyond my reach and in front of her, walking backward and saying, "Uh, Ms. Lulala?"

"Yes, Ramou! Isn't it lovely to . . ." Marnie ran out of gas on the first kind word she had ever said to him. "You have something unpleasant to tell me, haven't you?"

"Yes, Ms. Lulala." Ramou swallowed. "It has to do with why Suzanne and Lacey went back to the ship."

"Did they? We must have come down to the hatch just after they'd . . ." Marnie came to a halt; she must have been realizing that the girls could not have been returning to their quarters, or they would have met in the lift. We older folk hadn't been *that* far behind them, after all. "They didn't go back to their cabins—so they must have gone below."

"Yes, Ms. Lulala."

"Where to, Ramou?" Her voice took on its first touch of iron.

"Just a guess, you understand . . ."

"Ramou," Winston said quietly, "this is not the time to hedge. Tell us in straightforward terms."

"They went to see Grudy," Ramou said. "Customs won't let them loose on Citadel unless they're dressed like Whistler's mother."

Marnie was very quiet, but her eyes narrowed and her whole body stiffened.

I stepped up behind Ramou, to give what little support I could.

It started low, but built rapidly. "Why, those narrow-minded, hidebound, Puritanical, hypocritical, sanctimonious pharisees!" She was in full voice, now. "How *dare* a bunch of arrogant, bigoted *males* try to dictate so basic an element of a woman's *life*!"

"Dunno, ma'am," Ramou muttered. He was looking a trifle tattered, but he was holding up well against the blast.

"Why, they're positively medieval! Don't they know that such tents are a sign of female subjugation? By what right do they think they can imprison us, subjugate us to their whims?"

"Religion," Ramou muttered.

"Blasphemy, you mean! Any religion that could condone feminine oppression is contradicting the fundamental tenets that every major religion professes! No, not 'condones'—justifies! Excuses! Rationalizes! It's nothing but masculine insecurity in sanctimonious robes!"

"Yes, *ma'am*," Ramou said with approval and admiration. I felt similarly—I hadn't known Marnie was capable of such eloquence.

"There is no need for me to submit to such bigotry! I can pass the time quite pleasantly aboard the ship!" She turned on her heel and started back toward the ramp.

"Quite so." Charles fell in beside her. "If you want fresh air and open space, all you have to do is step outside and walk around the blast pits. Not much more to see outside the fence, anyway."

"Nothing!" Marnie snapped.

"And you don't really *need* to perform."

Marnie's stride faltered.

"They will probably make an execrable audience, anyway," Charles went on.

"Don't try to cozen me, Charles Publican!" Marnie warned.

"I wouldn't think of it. Just ask yourself, Ms. Lulala, if you would *really* want to perform in front of an audience of Puritans, in *any* costume. Why, they will probably give only grunts of disapproval where you would expect laughs—having grown up without comedy, they probably think that even laughter is sinful."

Marnie stopped in her tracks.

"Do spare us a kind thought as you relax in a soft chair with a martini and a cigarette, though," Charles pleaded. "We will be confronting the heathen on their own territory, for I doubt that we'll find a temple of Dionysus on this forsaken rock."

"If you had the slightest bit of sense," Marnie snapped, "You'd come back with me and stay inside, too!"

"Indeed I should," Charles agreed. "In fact, if it weren't for the small problem of acquiring more fuel, I definitely *would*—and I suspect that everyone else would, too, after one look at Citadel. I congratulate you on your good sense, Ms. Lulala."

"*Thank* you, Charles." Marnie picked up the pace again and hurried toward the ship.

Charles turned back, strolling toward us.

"Neatly done, I must say," I told him as he came up to us. "Emotional blackmail, threats of deprivation, and exploitation of guilt feelings, all in a few sentences. I didn't know you could be so underhanded, Charles."

"You're right, of course, Horace. I'm quite ashamed of myself." He looked anything but.

"Also very skillful," Ramou put in. "Had a lot of practice on undergraduates, Prof?"

Charles smiled slowly. "Why, Ramou, how uncharitable of you!"

"Especially if I'm right," our dropout said brightly.

"It was a bravura performance." Winston was eyeing him rather warily.

"Indeed," Barry agreed. "Remind me to employ you against the recalcitrant whenever we encounter them, Charles."

Charles looked up at him in feigned surprise. "But I thought you had planned to, Barry. You did say we were going to perform here."

Ramou looked up past him. "That was fast work!"

We all turned to look. Sure enough, there came Lacey and Suzanne, pacing side by side, holding purses at their waists, the very picture of Young Mother Hubbard off to the supermarket for doggy bones, complete with voluminous ankle-length dresses, poke bonnets, and completely unpainted faces.

"She's trying to hold it down," Ramou muttered, "but the way Suzanne walks, no costume in the world can hide."

He was quite right; Suzanne had only to breathe in order to attract the male eye. Lacey was much less voluptuous, but walked with a swing to her stride and a glint in her eye that made her the target of every male eye whether she was angry or not.

"The young Puritan lads will be following her like iron filings after moving magnets," Winston said.

"Like electrons to the anode," Ramou agreed.

"Partly from sheer shock," Barry said. "I doubt they've ever seen any women like these."

"If they did, they gave each one a scarlet *A*," Winston said.

But Charles turned to Barry in curiosity. "You said 'partly.' What was the other part?"

"The reputation of their profession," Barry said dryly.

He was quite right, of course. Actresses have had reputations for loose conduct since the seventeenth century, though it stopped being deserved in the nineteenth—and in the twentieth, it was no more true of actresses than of any other group of women. It was even more true of men, of course, but the double standard prevailed.

Lacey and Suzanne came up, faces flaming. "This is ridiculous!" Suzanne snapped.

"Degrading!" Lacey flared.

"Just pretend you're onstage, in a costume," Barry said

in soothing tones. "That will be true, to some extent—and true for all of us, not just for you ladies."

"She comes," Winston said quietly.

We turned to look. Sure enough, there came Marnie across the tarmac, skirts whipping about her ankles, face pale with anger. Behind her, Grudy was just coming out the hatch, escorted by Merlo.

"I hope you are proud of yourself, Charles," I said sourly.

"Did I do that?" Charles murmured. "Oh, my!"

"Well, you certainly do meet the letter of the law," Barry said as Marnie came up, "or rather, the niche. But frankly, my dear, you couldn't look dowdy if you tried."

"Then this certainly is the acid test," Marnie said, still fuming. "No cosmetics, not an inch of skin showing—not a curve!"

"At least, as long as you stay out of the wind," Winston said, eyeing her critically. "I'm sorry, my dear, but I'm afraid they will still count you as a provocative moral hazard."

"You say the sweetest things," Marnie said in a tone drier than any martini—but she looked somewhat mollified.

"I am so glad you have decided to take pity on the poor natives and lend them your presence." Charles took her hand in both of his. "Not to mention lending us your support."

"*Me*, lend *you* support? Well, I'm glad you see it that way . . ."

"I do indeed. But to what do we owe this fortunate change of heart, dear lady?"

"As if you didn't know! Well, if you must have it said, I did feel that I might be shirking my duties . . ."

That, I decided, must certainly have been a first.

"So I went down to the costume shop to discuss the issue with Grudy. She was just finishing buttoning Lacey and Suzanne into their tents—"

"Buttoning?"

"Oh, yes!" Marnie lifted her eyebrows, nodding. "They're devotedly primitive here, you know. Absolutely no seamzip allowed, no flat fastenings of any sort, short of hooks and eyes—and they must all fasten up the back! As if buttons on the front of a dress could be provocative!"

I could think of a few oversize zippers I had seen, that had definitely had that effect—making a man ache to reach out and pull to discover what treasures lay beneath. Still, I had to agree with Marnie—buttons are so cumbersome that their location would not be much of an inducement.

"Well! I had barely poked my head in past the jamb, you see, and Grudy nodded to a sack hanging in the corner and said, 'There's yours, dear.' I mean, what could I say?"

"You couldn't disappoint the valiant woman, of course," Charles agreed. "I am so relieved, Ms. Lulala! If we must confront the barbarians, surely it is best to do so all together."

"I agree, but I fear it is a trifle impractical," Barry said. "I really believe Horace and I must seek out Publius without delay and discover what is to be done—if anything."

"All the more important that the rest of us be together," Charles said firmly.

"Quite so," Winston agreed. "May I suggest, young friends, that this time we *not* separate by age? I realize we more mature specimens may be a bit of a drag on your high hilarity . . ."

"Not at all, Mr. Carlton," Suzanne said quickly.

Lacey chimed in, though I suspect from different motives. "We'll be very glad, sir. In numbers there is strength."

Citadel may have been Gothic in its attitudes, but not in its technology—although nowhere in the spaceport terminal did we discover anything remotely luxurious. There were no refreshment dispensers, no billboard screens—no advertisements of any sort, for that matter—and no 3DT screens. In any Terran spaceport, there would have been several metered screens wherever there were waiting chairs, and a large free one in the bar.

Of course, the Citadel spaceport had no bar. For that matter, the chairs in the waiting area were unpadded and looked singular uninviting—very functional, Bauhaus at its bowziest. The colors were cheery, though—muted pastels in a variety of shades. Apparently the Puritans weren't totally grim.

Customs took awhile, of course, even though we had no luggage with us. The inspectors glared at us suspiciously as we came out of the detector tunnel, as if to say they knew we were hiding contraband somewhere, even though they could not prove it and had no grounds for a strip search. They were probably right—but the contraband we were carrying was in our minds. It is impossible to exclude new ideas completely, of course, but the colony of Citadel certainly made a conscientious effort in that direction.

They did, however, have a communications booth.

Barry stepped into it, raised a hand to punch in the standard "information" code while he fumbled in his pocket for his credit card—and froze.

"What is the problem?" I asked.

"There is no card slot," he said. "It requires coins."

I stood frozen for a moment myself. Then I said, "Local currency, of course."

"Of course," Barry confirmed.

I took a deep breath. "Perhaps information is free, even to us off-worlders."

Barry's face lit. "An excellent thought." He checked the number from the base display on the screen, then entered the code. "Capital, Horace! I have the directory!"

"Excellent," I sighed.

"Now let us see if they have him listed." Barry pressed the SCROLL patch. "He can't have been here more than a week or two . . ."

I frowned, concerned. "And with the need for local currency, he may not have been able to afford a comm set . . . How *has* he acquired cash, I wonder."

I shuddered to think of the most probable answer—that he had not. But no, that was ridiculous—advance men were always careful to procure a minimum amount of local currency before they departed for the next stop on the tour. Additionally, Publius had sent a distress signal to us, which meant he obviously had managed to procure the necessary components for a minimal transmitter. That, in turn, implied that he had obtained local currency with which to purchase those components—or was a more accomplished thief than I had ever thought him.

"There is a listing." Barry was immensely relieved.

"And an address?"

"Fortunately, yes." He copied down the listing, then pressed END on the keypad and tucked the address away as he came out of the booth. "Now our only difficulty is discovering a means of transportation to that address."

A difficulty, indeed.

At the terminal exit, we came out through a genuine door—steel and glass on hinges, the first time I had ever seen one on a public building. Apparently force curtains were a luxury on a colony planet.

There were no taxis.

Indeed, there was very little of anything. The walkway just outside the door was paved, in some quaint native varient of plasticrete—shaped like a huge teardrop, the narrow end terminating at a single, gleaming rail.

There was no road.

"How the deuce are we to go into the city?" I asked.

"Presumably, aboard whatever conveyance rides that track." Barry looked rather gloomy. "Quite democratic—no matter how wealthy or important you become, you must take the same public conveyance as everyone else."

"Unless, of course, you have a flier of some sort," I hazarded.

Barry nodded. "A good thought, Horace. I believe the *Cotton Blossom*'s lifeboats might be useable within atmosphere. Perhaps we should return to the ship and discuss their use with Gantry."

In private, of course, Barry and Captain McLeod were on a first-name basis; they seemed to respect each other, even to the point of friendship. In public, however, they were still quite formal.

A silver gleam appeared way off to our left.

"Perhaps we should attempt to cope with the native system first," I suggested, "since it does not appear that we will have to wait terribly long."

"Well, thank heaven for that!" Barry sighed. "I feared the car would not come at all, at least on a regular schedule. There does not appear to be terribly much traffic at this spaceport."

"Not passengers, perhaps," I said. "But if they really do

have extensive shipping, the crews must need to go into the city and come back fairly frequently."

"Meaning several times a day? Well, we are fortunate in coincidence. However, how shall we pay for the ride?"

As it eventuated, we had no need. The long silver car drew up beside us; the door opened, and steps swung down; a dozen bearded men in short blue coats, long blue trousers, and black boots climbed down, joking and chatting, and filed past us with only an incurious glance. That surprised me, until I remembered that these were merchant spacemen; off-planet people were nothing new, to them. I found myself hoping that the attitude was prevalent among their compatriots.

"You have one minute to board," a synthesized voice announced.

I looked up at Barry in surprise; he looked at me with the same emotion evident. Then, in unison, we shrugged and climbed aboard.

"There is no fare box," Barry said, looking about.

"Transportation is free, to the public of Citadel," the computerized voice informed him.

I throttled a lingering trace of honesty, but Barry could not. "We are visitors to the planet."

"Transportation is free to the public," the computer insisted stubbornly. "Fifteen seconds to board."

We exchanged a glance and shrugged again.

"Five seconds to board," the car announced.

A lone spacehand stepped in, clad exactly as the recent arrivals had been. He flicked a glance of appraisal at us, then sat down, took a small black book out of a coat pocket, and began to read.

I found myself grateful for his rudeness. "We had best seek seats," I told Barry.

"Yes, we really should," he agreed.

We found facing seats in the middle of the car. Unfortunately, that put us directly across from the spaceman, but they were the only facing seats in the car. He had taken the others so that he could put his feet up.

"Departing," the car informed us, and slid smoothly away from the terminal. It swung about in a wide loop and headed back in the direction from which it had come.

We both looked out the window—or rather, the transparent side of the car; three feet off the floor, the metal ended, and the steelglass began.

"This must become rather hot when the sun is shining," Barry offered.

The spaceman looked up, then quickly back to his book.

"Perhaps it is rare enough that it is scarcely a problem," I offered, "or perhaps the roof darkens automatically under solar radiation."

"More likely the last." Barry gazed out the window. "The fields seem to be fertile. There must be *some* sunlight."

It certainly did not seem so at that moment. The land stretched away to the horizon, broken only by the occasional house and barn. Then something came in view that seemed extremely incongruous. I leaned forward, barely restraining myself from pointing. "Can that man really be plowing with a team of horses?"

"As I live and breathe, he is," Barry marveled.

And he was. Oh, he was riding, not walking, and the plow was carving five furrows rather than one—but he was nonetheless laboring in antique fashion. We were silent, struck by the incongruity of staring at such a sight through the transparent wall of a modern monorail car. I almost felt as if I had stepped through a time machine, back into nineteenth century Terra.

Barry broke the silence. "They must have tractors available! Why do they not use them?"

"Perhaps it is only this individual farmer," I suggested. "Perhaps he cannot afford modern equipment."

Barry frowned. "That would scarcely seem to be in the best interest of the society as a whole."

"Perhaps they have adhered to an early form of economy, as of farming," I conjectured. "Primitive forms of capitalism assumed that the interests of the state would be best served by individuals competing for profit."

"True, but in the modern day? Certainly every society has seen that it must supply each individual with the means of productivity, in order to make the society as a whole prosper!"

"You're both daft," said a voice.

We both jumped; we had completely forgotten our silent companion. I turned to him, recovering my composure. "Am I really? What could be the reason, then?"

"Why," said he, "the need for hard work. You must tire the body, you see, if it's not to get into mischief."

I couldn't quite believe I'd heard that. I just sat, gazing at him. Then I said, "I see. The motive, then, is religious?"

"Religious?" he cried. "Nay, 'tis common sense! A man's a hotbed of energies, don't you see, and if you don't drain them off in productive pursuits, they'll explode in destructive ways—destructive to himself, aye, but to the rest of us, too!"

Yet he had maintained that it wasn't religious.

"A fascinating concept." Barry nodded thoughtfully. "But surely a man cannot be as productive with a team of horses as he would be with a modern tractor and a twelve-share plow."

"Productive enough," our informant snapped. "What do we need with more, anyway? We've surplus enough so that grain would rot in the bin if we had more."

"You could export it," I suggested.

"We've the government farms for that," he retorted, "and they produce all we can export, as 'tis. Nay, let him farm who can, and he who will not, let him pay the price of his sloth!"

I chilled inside, realizing that he was talking about starvation—but Barry only tilted his head to the side, eyes alight with interest. "What of him who *can* not?"

"Cannot labor?" the spacehand frowned. "You speak of the feebleminded, then, or the injured or deformed. Well, they shall live, though simply. The deacons allot food and tools and clothing to all, aye, and fuel, too, in the cold months. None starve, if they cannot work."

"What of those who *will* not work?" I asked.

"Then they shall be clapped into prison, as they deserve, and forced to find labor on the government farms, since they will not seek it by themselves!"

I shuddered for Publius.

"So the deacons supply all the necessities, and everyone has to work." Barry seemed genuinely interested. "But if someone wants more than the minimum—say, money for pictures of his children—he must do extra work for it."

"Aye." The man looked at him strangely. "Is it not thus everywhere?"

"Well, there are societies that are not so open about it. I take it that beginning a business is one way in which a man may perform extra labor?"

"Aye, and one that brings greater brass for the hour's effort, if he can save enough coin to begin."

"Accumulation of capital," Barry translated.

For myself, I wondered if the local currency really was made of brass. "I take it, then, that business is encouraged?"

"Aye."

"Because it occupies a person's time and energy, and provides occupation for other people?"

"Well, that, of course," the man conceded.

" 'Of course'?" Barry leaned forward. "There are other reasons, then?"

"Aye. It brings profit."

Barry stared. So did I.

Then Barry shook himself. "Is that alone sufficient reason for the deacons to endorse the activity?"

"Of course! Does the Bible not set that as reason for doing or not doing? Does not Ecclesiastes say, 'What shall it profit a man that he labor long under the sun'?"

" 'What shall it profit a man if he gain the whole world, but lose his immortal soul'?" I murmured.

He turned to me, eye quickening with interest. "Ah, then, you've read your Bible!"

"I have read it," I acknowledged, "but I am certainly no scholar."

The spaceman nodded. "A becoming modesty, sir, becoming!"

As modesty, the statement was indeed becoming, and would probably never arrive. "Is anything that brings profit right, then?"

"Aye, if 'tis true profit." He raised an admonishing forefinger. "Mind you, gambling is not—for though there is a chance of profit, there is far more chance of losing your capital."

"As there is with entertainments," Barry suggested.

"What—music?" The man shrugged impatiently. "There's no great cost, only the price of an instrument."

"But it encourages people to dance," I pointed out.

He nodded. " 'Tis good excercise, that profits the body."

I gathered he was not speaking about slow dancing. I had the good sense not to ask.

"Have you been to Terra?" Barry asked.

The man wrinkled his nose. "The fleshpots of corruption? Aye."

"They have entertainments there, such as 3DT spectacles . . ."

"Oh, we have them here!" The man sat back, comfortable in his sophistication. "Easter would not be Easter without the Oberammergau Passion Play."

"Surely not." Barry paled a trifle. "Of course, to be at Oberammergau in person, to watch as they performed it . . ."

The spacehand's eyes kindled. "Aye, that would be excellent!"

So they did not object to live theater per se, then—as long as its subject was spiritual.

Barry leaned back. "The live theatrical displays in New York, now—"

"Sinks of sin!" the man said promptly. "And if we'd any doubts of it, Elector Rudders has reminded us all, three months past! We heard and saw him on 3DT, denouncing the immorality of it!"

"Indeed." Barry was quite pale now, and I was not feeling any too enthusiastic myself. "However, I understand that the theatrical producers do make a handsome profit . . ."

"They could not, if none went to cast away their hard-earned brass on such a waste of time!" The man smiled, at ease, glancing out the window. "Aye, 'tis good to be back on Citadel, where such nonsense would not be tolerated."

"Is it indeed?" Barry whispered.

4

They made us take the customs tunnel slow, ostensibly to make good and sure we didn't have any contraband. I wondered if their sensors really could pick up drugs and alcohol. Even if they could, they *had* to be able to work faster than *that.*

Lacey came out with her skirts flouncing and her face burning.

"What's the matter?" I asked.

"Those hormonal hypocrites!" she hissed. "They just made us go slowly so that they could get a good look at Suzanne and me with X-ray vision!"

Personally, I didn't think the customs officers were going to get turned on by skeletons, no matter how feminine—but you never can tell. Besides, I remembered how flesh shows up as a ghostly image on X-ray plates, and decided to play it safe. "You don't suppose they could really get excited by looking at a foggy image on a low-resolution viewscreen, do you?"

"When they've been completely deprived of the sight of the female form divine for all their lives?" she returned. "You bet a ghostly image could turn them on! Besides, what makes you think it's all that ghostly? For all you know, they could have 3DT screens in full living color, with high resolution that shows every detail! They could have had sensor after sensor showing us first as we look to the eye, then without our outer gowns—just our slips—and so on! An electronic striptease! They might even have recorded it to drool over at home!"

What could I say? She might have been right. Though personally, I think she was showing an excellent imagination. First time she'd showed any sign of it, too.

Of course, it could have just been conceit.

But Suzanne came out blushing and shuddering, with her arms clasped about her.

"What's the matter?" I was instantly hovering, ready to comfort.

"Must be my imagination," she muttered.

"What must?"

"I kept thinking those men were watching me on their viewscreens and drooling as they looked through my clothing. Isn't that silly of me? It's impossible, isn't it?"

I decided Lacey might have had a point, but all I said was, "The kind of surveillance they're giving us would be enough to make anyone feel a little paranoid." The girls had me wondering, though, if they were the only ones who had been scanned so thoroughly.

Larry came out red-faced and snarling. "Don't think I'm going to thank you, Ramou!"

"Wouldn't think of it," I said slowly. "Why—just because that bank of sensors would have detected every cigarette, every bit of paper, every holo cube you had on you? Of course I wouldn't expect thanks."

"Fortunate, because you're not going to have any! Though I suppose I might say you've made up for your boorishness at the beginning of the trip."

I clamped my jaw shut, repressing the urge to be boorish again—to the point of giving him a valid insurance claim for a new set of teeth. With any luck, he probably didn't even have Partial Medical. "Think nothing of it, Larry me lad. Not being dragged off to jail with you is thanks enough for me."

Suzanne looked from one to the other of us. "Am I missing something here?"

"Yes," Lacey said, "and from what I can see, we should be glad of it. Let the boys play their silly games, Suzanne. We don't have to join in."

They might not have had much choice, if Larry had walked through customs with the load he'd been carrying. I wouldn't have put it past the Citadelites to clap us all into irons on the general principle that if one of us was willing to break the law, the rest of us just hadn't had the chance yet. Guilt by association, and from their point of view, we were probably a guilty association. If one of us reflected on all, I certainly didn't want Larry's face reflecting into mine.

Marty came out whistling, though.

Suzanne stared. "That didn't bother you?"

"Hey, I'll take all the attention I can get! I just love it when somebody's sure I've done something, but they can't tell what."

"But you haven't," Larry objected.

"Makes it even more fun. Know why they hide inside a booth with the viewscreens?"

"The better to watch us, my dear," Lacey said sourly.

"No, because they knew Marnie was coming, and they didn't want to be there when she exploded."

But she didn't explode; she came stalking out of the tunnel, face flaming. "The very idea—treating us as if we were common criminals! I've endured many customs passages in this profession, but this has definitely been the rudest of all! To think that they won't even greet you with a live human being until the end of the gamut! Even then, all he will say is, 'Please proceed through the gate'! No matter what I said, that was all—'Please proceed through the gate'! He even had the audacity to appear amused!"

I had to give the man credit. Anybody who could weather one of Marnie's tantrums with a smile had a very strong stomach—or a very sadistic bent; he might have been enjoying watching her get angrier and angrier. I've known some of those.

"It *was* rather embarrassing," Suzanne said. "Creepy, in fact."

Marnie shuddered. "I know what you mean. Absolutely no reason to feel violated, of course—just a figment of my imagination, I'm sure. That makes it worse, in a way."

Lacey frowned. "Interesting that all three of us had the same feeling."

"Let's see how Grudy feels," Suzanne said.

But it was Winston who came through next, strolling and looking quite dapper. "At least they were kind enough to shoot my better profile. Of course, they also shot my worse one—but, *que sera, sera.*"

"Easy enough for you to say," Marnie said acidly. "All those years on 3DT—you're used to the cameras."

"And I assure you, I played to them every inch of the way. Do you know, though, I actually felt that their surveillance was—shall I say, 'intrusive'?"

"You, too?" Lacey stared.

Marty frowned. "I feel left out."

"Don't worry, Martyn—it won't be the last hostile audience you play to," Winston assured him.

Ogden waddled out, wheezing. "I dare say! If that didn't set me up for cybernetic implants, nothing will!"

I wondered if he would have had a heart attack, if he'd had medical aids implanted. "Just as well you didn't, Mr. Wellesley—that barrage of rays and waves would have knocked them haywire."

"Always have been an advocate of nature's way," he said.

I could have debated that. Okay, Nature does turn fruit juice into wine—but she doesn't distill it.

Charles came out with an affable smile, but there was a tension to his body that I didn't usually see. He nodded pleasantly to all of us, but didn't say anything.

Winston broke the silence. "Novel experience, isn't it, Charles?"

"Yes, and one I'm not anxious to repeat," he said. "Did you all note a feeling of anxiety increasing as you went through the tunnel?"

We all looked startled. I thought he'd described it just right—by the time I'd finished the gamut of sensors, I was feeling as guilty as if I'd been trying to smuggle in a cannon.

"Kind of like going on in front of an audience that's loaded with rotten tomatoes?" Marty asked.

That broke through; Charlie smiled. "Now you know how you'll fare in front of such a group."

"Yeah, I'll get cocky. They're gonna dare me to make 'em laugh? I'm gonna dare them not to!"

I looked at Marty in surprise. I'd known he had courage of some sort; now I knew what kind.

"You suspect something, Charles," Winston said softly.

Charlie nodded. "They were using subsonics on us—a frequency that induces anxiety."

We stared at one another, flabbergasted.

Then Winston found his voice. "To what purpose?"

"So that anyone with a guilty conscience will confess," Charlie said, "which, in this case, means anyone attempting to smuggle in contraband. He will come out in a state of nervous collapse which, given the religious teachings he has grown up with, can only be ameliorated by confession."

Then Marnie's face darkened. "Of all the low, conniving, underhanded tricks! Can these people possibly claim to be ethical? I'm going to tell them exactly what I think of a religion that allows them to deliberately torment their fellow creatures." She turned away toward the customs agent at the end of the tunnel.

"Marnie!" Winston cried in alarm, but Charlie just put up a cautioning hand. "Gently, Ms. Lulala. It's quite possible that it could just be a side effect of their detection equipment."

Marnie hesitated, then scowled at him. "You don't believe that for a second, Charles Publican!"

"No, I don't, actually," Charlie said. "But I can't think of a reason for their trying to make us all anxious."

Grudy came out of the tunnel, pale and clutching her handbag with both hands. "My heavens! What an unpleasant experience!"

"You, too, eh?" Ogden grunted.

"Oh, yes! Suddenly, I'm very anxious about dying! I'm old enough that it could happen soon, you know—and for some reason, I find myself thinking of the afterlife with dread!"

We all stared at one another, appalled.

"Did I say something?" Grudy asked.

"Possibly the truth," Charlie said grimly. "We were just wondering why the Citadelites would use their customs booth to give us all a dose of subsonics that would induce anxiety. I think you have just confirmed my guess, my dear."

"To put the fear of God in us, as the old idiom has it," Ogden growled.

"Or the fear of hellfire," Winston modified. His face darkened. "How positively immoral!"

"All's fair in war and proselytizing," Charlie said grimly. "Perhaps it does reinforce the average Citadelite's religious faith—but in our case, it was far more interesting as an index of our personalities. Grudy, my dear, I never knew you were religious underneath it all."

"I still think 'underneath it all' is what they were really after," Lacey snapped.

Merlo came out scowling. "Boy, they really want to grill you inside and out here, don't they?"

"Anything bothering you, Merlo?" Winston said casually.

Merlo shrugged impatiently. "Nothing major. Oddest thing, though—halfway down that tunnel, I started worrying about having to cobble together a set for the *Last Judgment*, then for the whole blasted *Mystery Cycle,* and make it all portable. . . . What's the joke?"

Marty and Larry had erupted into shouts of laughter, and the girls had dissolved into giggles. The rest of us were smiling, some more broadly than others, and Marnie was laughing with a vindictive note.

Winston clapped Merlo on the shoulder. "My friend, it is delightful to know a true man of the theater."

"Uh, thanks, Winston. Honored." But Merlo was looking around him suspiciously. "Somebody want to let me in on the funny?"

"Of course, of course—but let us do it as we pass out of this terminal, shall we?" Ogden chuckled.

We turned and moved toward the exit, Charles saying, "For the meantime, Merlo, let it warm your heart to know that you are no doubt the first one to discomfit our friendly and welcoming customs agents."

We all glanced back, and sure enough, the customs agent at the end of the tunnel was glaring after us, puzzled and angry. We managed to keep the burst of laughter down to a chortle as we shoved through the door, then let it out with a shout once we were outdoors.

"I'll get a cab," I offered, and went to look while Winston let Merlo in on the joke. I heard the laughter behind me, and grinned. Star Company, one—Citadel, zero.

Then I looked around me and realized Citadel was one point higher up than I'd thought. There weren't any cabs.

I came back just as the laughter was dying down into chuckles. It expired as they took one look at my face.

"Don't tell me there is no cab!" Marnie gasped.

"Okay," I said. "I won't."

"You mean we'll have to *walk*?" Lacey cried.

But Charlie looked around and pointed. "Perhaps not. There is *some* mode of transportation, at least."

We all looked, then breathed a communal sigh of relief. "A monorail," Marnie sighed.

"Yes." Ogden frowned. "Now all we need is a train."

It came eventually, though by the time it did, we were reduced to swapping stories about disasters on stage. That meant all I could do was listen, since I hadn't had any experience before this. It was enough to give me earthquakes in the belly—if the customs tunnel had been bad, this was worse!

Still, though, the car did hiss in and sigh as it settled down on the rail. Then the doors opened, and a resonant voice said, "This car will depart in five minutes."

"Just time enough for me to climb in," Ogden said, and moved toward the door.

Just as he reached it, two Citadelites appeared in the doorway, staring at us in surprise, then in suspicion—or at least, *he* did. *She* was wide-eyed in wonder at actually seeing somebody out of uniform.

Then *he* saw Lacey and Suzanne, and the suspicion disappeared as his eyes bulged.

I felt my own eyes bulging as I looked at his female companion, and my whole body seemed to vibrate. She was a real and rare beauty, easily the most beautiful girl I had ever seen, tied for first place with Suzanne and Lacey. Long, abundant curls rolled to the shoulders of her dark blue broadcloth dress; her eyes were large, her eyebrows fine, graceful lines, her nose small and perfectly formed, making a man ache to kiss it—and to go on below, to those luscious, full, red, red lips, seeming more red because she wasn't using any lipstick or rouge. She looked back at me, and the deep pools of eyes widened; I felt the connection, and I knew she did, too, like a charge running through us. I felt ashamed and guilty at the same time that I felt charged and hyped—she might have been his wife, or his fiancée.

I didn't let it worry me too much, though—not from the way he was looking at Lacey and Suzanne.

Lacey saw the advantages immediately. "Why, *hello*," she trilled. "What a pleasant surprise!"

"Ye-yes, miss," the young man managed. "Yes, 'tis."

"Let me get out of your way." Lacey stepped aside, and the rest of us took our cue and backed off, though Suzanne flashed Lacey a look of annoyance—no doubt for having thought of it first, because by the time she turned back to the young couple, she was all syrupy smiles. "Are you outbound on a spaceship?"

"Well, not yet," the young man hedged, and the girl said, "We are looking for work, do ye see. Would you be spacefolk?"

"Oh, travelers from another planet, at least," Lacey said. "Looking for work, you say?"

"Aye. I labor on the government farm now, and my sister—" He nodded at the young woman. "—has not yet found a husband, so she must seek employment, too, or come labor on the farms in the kitchens, or such."

"Kitchens?" Marnie bristled. "What sort of work are you looking for here, child?"

Me, I didn't care whether she was applying for the position of scullery maid or queen. She was his sister, nothing more—that was what mattered. I felt the slow grin spreading with the warmth that coursed through me, knowing she was fair game.

The young woman stared at her. "Cleaning, likely, ma'am—the kitchens are small here, for there are only the ground crews and controllers, and mayhap one crew a day." Her eyes were huge; I wondered why, until I realized she had probably never seen anyone like Marnie before.

"Only cleaning or cooking?" Marnie said dangerously—as dangerously as the rumble that comes before the volcano erupts—but Winston flashed her a warning look, and Ogden turned to her with a finger across his lips, and she subsided, simmering. Remembered she was a guest in a foreign land, probably—or maybe had a sudden feeling of vulnerability.

"It is what a woman does best," the girl said, "and I would not be capable of lifting and hammering, as the men must." She extended a hand. "I am Prudence. Who be you?"

"Prudence!" her brother snapped, no doubt thinking she was not living up to her name.

"Oh, be not so oafish, Elias!" she scolded, like sisters everywhere. She turned back to us. "My brother is Elias, if ye would know."

"Pleased to meet you." Winston raised a hand in greeting. "I am Winston Carlton, and these are my friends, Lacey Lark and Suzanne Souci . . . ."

"How delightful!" Lacey gushed, pressing Prudence's hand, then dropping it quickly to take Elias's callused paw. He started as if she had touched him with a live wire, then smiled, dazed.

Suzanne smiled, too, warmly, as she shook hands with Prudence, then with more than warmth as she took Elias's other hand—Lacey seemed to be reluctant to let go. Elias's head swiveled to Suzanne, and his smile gained an *l*—from dazed to dazzled.

Me, I felt a surge of jealousy, so hot it scared me. Larry wasn't looking any too happy, either, and Marty was looking very unsure.

Winston wasn't letting us rest. "Ramou Lazarian." He gestured toward me. "Larry Rash."

We stepped forward to shake hands—and I was astounded to discover just how big Prudence's eyes were. My heavens, that girl was beautiful! Without makeup, even, and her hair unstyled, just falling loose. I was amazed that her cheeks were so rosy, and I knew darn well that the color was natural. The strands of hair peeking out from under her bonnet were the color of corn—of course.

I had to say something. "Charmed." It came out as a bit of a croak, and Suzanne shot me a quick frown, concerned.

Prudence dimpled prettily and made a sort of half curtsy. "And I am pleased to meet you, Mr. . . . Lazarian?"

"Very good!" I said, surprised and approving. "Not many get it right on the first try!"

"Not many would wish to," Larry snapped, elbowing me aside. "A pleasure to meet you, Miss Prudence. You are a spot of life and loveliness in a singularly dreary landscape." He brought her hand halfway to his lips, then hesitated, as if unsure whether or not the gesture would be misunderstood.

Lacey joined Suzanne in her glower. So did Elias.

I had to admit Larry did it well—in fact, I hadn't known he could be charming when he wanted.

But Prudence did it well, too—she blushed, lowered her gaze, and gave him the same sort of half curtsy she had given me. It hit me like a sledgehammer—she knew exactly what effect she was having on Larry, and why!

Therefore, it followed, she knew what effect she was having on me, too. Our sweet and innocent little country miss wasn't quite so naive as she seemed to be.

Winston cleared his throat. Larry glanced back at him in annoyance, but stepped aside as Winston said, "Our leading lady, Ms. Marnie Lulala . . ."

Marnie stepped up, with a smile that was so artificial I practically heard it creak, and pressed the girl's fingers so briefly that you would have thought she had leprosy.

Or tried to, anyway. Prudence's hand clamped tight as a vise as her eyes went round. "Leading lady! Are you an actress from the 3DT, then?"

"An actress, yes." Marnie wrested her fingers free by main force. "And though I must admit to having appeared on 3DT when I couldn't avoid it, I would much rather be known as a theatrical professional."

"Theater! Oh! You mean . . . putting on a play, right here, yourselves?"

"With an audience of live people, instead of 3DT cameras." Winston intervened smoothly. "Yes, that is exactly what we mean, Miss Prudence. We have come to perform for you and your fellow citizens." But there was a shadow of anxiety across his face. "You mean you have not heard we were coming?"

Prudence turned her wide eyes from side to side. "No, sir. Not a word."

We all exchanged a look of alarm. No posters, no announcements of any kind—and we all knew what that meant. Publius had run into trouble trying to promote the show.

But Winston was too thorough a professional to let concern show in front of an audience. He went on down the row. "Mr. Charles Publican . . . Mr. Merlo Hertz, our set designer . . . Ms. Grudy Drury, our costume designer . . . Mr. Ogden Wellesley . . ."

"Mr. Wellesley!" Prudence gasped, giving him the huge eyes. "Oh! Are *you* the man who was Isaac in *Jacob and Esau*?"

"Why, yes." Ogden's smile widened into something more than public politeness. "Though there was considerably less of me at the time; that was quite some years ago."

"Years ago! But we only saw it last Harvest Home!"

Time for another round of startled glances, and a thrill of foreboding. If they were still going after antique religious productions, what chance did we have with a contemporary secular comedy?

Maybe none. Maybe everything. Could go either way, but not much in between.

"Theater must be wonderful!" Prudence clasped her arms tightly and hugged herself, shivering. "To make the word of the Lord come alive so!"

"Well, it isn't always the Bible stories that we present," Ogden said, with a bit of a guilty glance at Winston.

I stared. What kind of magic did this kid have, to be able to make *Ogden* feel guilty?

Lacey was looking rather jaundiced herself, but Suzanne decided to do something about it. She sidled up to Elias, purring, "And do you enjoy watching Bible stories on 3DT, too?"

"Oh, yes!" But his eyes were all for her, and he couldn't help a quick glance down below her chin. "For little ones, the words of the Bible are so hard, but to see the stories come to life, with real people to watch, is amazing! And you are one of these . . . actresses, is it?"

"Well, I try." Suzanne lowered her gaze modestly.

Lacey started to say something, then bit it back.

"Try? Then you've not been about it long?" There was a sudden new intensity in his voice and his gaze; it shriveled me inside. Did he scent a soul that could be saved?

"Only a few years." Suzanne carefully didn't say how many. "But I've fallen in love with it, you see—there's no feeling of . . . fulfillment . . . like giving an audience the hopes and dreams they need."

Elias nodded, the intensity transforming, his eyes burning

as he watched her. I wondered if Suzanne was intending double entendres, or if I was just hearing them. Elias was—or at least, seemed to be hearing more than she was saying.

Prudence realized that, too. She stepped over and took his arm. "Come, Elias! We have held these people long enough!"

"I fear 'tis true." Elias turned away with her, but cast a regretful glance back at Suzanne.

"A pleasure to have met you." Winston shook the young man's hand firmly, which forced him to take his eyes off Suzanne. He turned, startled, then blushed as he shook Winston's hand. "We shall look forward to your performance with eagerness, sir."

"Oh, yes!" Prudence trilled. "We have *never* seen a living show before!"

As I said—could be great, could be rotten.

"This car will depart in one minute," the monorail informed us.

"Has it been four minutes already?" Lacey caroled. "My, such a pleasant time! Wonderful to meet you, Elias—and you, too, Prudence."

"And you, Miss Lark," Prudence said, with a warm smile that seemed so genuine it made me think she had the talent to be an actress, herself. She turned about to take us all in, eyes wide again. "And all of you! Oh, I am so thrilled!"

"Then we shall count on you to be in the audience," Winston said, with his warmest smile before he turned away to the car.

Suzanne stepped toward the monorail, profile to Elias as she sighed, "It would be so nice if we had someone with us who knew the planet and could tell us what we're seeing!"

"It would," Lacey said, all sweetness and light, "but they don't seem to run to professional guides here."

"Or at least, only for tourist groups," Suzanne agreed, with another sigh.

Elias jarred to a halt, staring back at them. Prudence looked up, nettled—and Larry stepped up to catch her hand again. "Farewell, fair one! It would be so pleasant to enjoy your company a few moments longer—but fate and the monorail do not permit!" He half raised her hand again, caught himself, and dropped it with an apologetic smile, then turned away to the car.

Marty rolled his eyes up.

"Hey, give a fellow professional credit for a good performance," I whispered.

"I would, if I'd seen one," Marty hissed back.

"This car will depart in thirty seconds," the monorail warned.

"Aboard, my friends!" Winston cried, making shooing motions. "We do not want to have to wait for the next one, especially since we do not know when it will come!"

"In twenty minutes," Elias called out.

Suzanne looked back to blink gratitude at him with long lashes. "Oh, thank you, Elias! It's so troublesome, trying to learn the local ways!"

Prudence came to a decision. "Come, brother! There will be time enough to speak of work later—there are many hours to the day!"

"But we have taken leave for the purpose." Elias gazed longingly after the monorail.

"And we shall fulfill that purpose—later!" Prudence gathered up her skirts and hurried toward the car. "We cannot leave visitors with no knowledge of the town! After all, is it not our duty?"

If it was, they were the only ones on the whole planet to who had thought of it.

"It truly is." Elias hurried after her, his smile spreading. "We are required to tell all who ask about our Church, are we not?"

I resolved not to ask.

I stood aside for them, saying as she passed, "It's really good of you, Miss Prudence."

She flashed me a smile that would keep me for a week. "I rejoice to help where I may."

"No, really! It's asking too much of you!" Suzanne cooed as Elias stepped aboard.

"I could not see ladies go without guidance," he said with a very warm smile.

I stepped on behind him, a split second before the door

closed. I had to hand it to Suzanne and Lacey—they knew how to work fast.

And, I had to admit, so did Larry.

Lacey stared past Elias at the vista unrolling outside the window. "Is it so flat everywhere here?"

"Oh, nay." Elias smiled, excitement in his eyes. "There are hills by the rivers and, way inland, there are mountains."

"So it's just around the spaceport that the land is like a table?" Suzanne asked, all wide-eyed and ingenuous.

"It is—for they needed flat land where the ships would come in, you see. They are atmosphere craft, after all, and many of the smaller ones still glide in, so they need a great deal of flat running space."

"I suppose they would," Suzanne marveled. "Now, why didn't I ever think of that?"

Lacey's eyes flashed, and I could see her jaw tighten—only because I was sitting across from Prudence, and Lacey was right there over her shoulder in the next seat. Larry was sitting next to Prudence, so he had the benefit of profile, and Marty was sitting next to me, looking decidedly frustrated—but it was like a well-designed theater, there really was no bad seat.

"It seems so strange that you have no theaters," Lacey said. "If seeing Bible stories come alive is thrilling, children in school would find it even more inspiring to perform the roles of saints and heroes."

Elias's eyes went wide with surprise. "Why, what an amazing thought! Surely it must be even as you say!"

"Has anyone ever told you why they don't have theaters?" Suzanne asked.

Elias shook his head. "No one has even thought of it, for all I know."

"But your spaceship crews see live theater when they stop on Terra," Winston said from across the aisle.

"Aye, so I hear." Elias looked up at him, long enough to be polite. "My eldest brother is a space trader—first officer, as of last year—and he tells us that one must choose very carefully in going to the theater there, for there are many, many immoral plays in the cities of Old Earth."

"That is true, sad to say," Winston confirmed.

I was sure big brother was careful about the plays he chose, all right. I just wondered which ones he was selecting. After all, he had to witness wickedness firsthand if he was going to tell how horrible it was, didn't he?

"Would you believe it," Elias said, "some of those actresses in New York and London and Paris wear almost nothing at all when they go out there in front of all those people?"

"That much?" Marty muttered, but Marnie glared him to silence, and he shriveled up inside his jacket. Overdid it, of course.

"There are actresses who are indiscreet," Lacey said sadly.

"Aye, and he was warned against them, when first he went aboard a merchant ship! Warned that actresses might corrupt him! Surely the folk who said that had not seen two such lovely ladies as yourselves, so demure and modest!"

Merlo had a sudden coughing fit.

"There are members of our profession who are somewhat less than virtuous," Lacey said sadly, but Suzanne gave Elias a mischievous wink.

"Beware, kind sir! I might corrupt you while you aren't looking!"

Elias joined in the laugh that followed, albeit his was a bit nervous.

Prudence heard and glared back over her shoulder.

Larry moved in to distract, fast. "We're not really the monsters they say we are, Miss Prudence."

She turned to him, her own smile warming in response to his. "I would scarcely think you were, Mr. Lash, though surely . . . what is the matter, Mr. Kemp?"

"Hiccups," Marty answered, and took another deep breath.

Larry flashed him a glare, but he wasn't looking.

"Well, if they tell stories like that about us, no *wonder* they don't want children learning about theater," I said, trying to sound hearty.

"True, Mr. Lazarian." Prudence gave me that dazzling smile again. "But I am no child."

It was hard to tell with that voluminous dress, but I was inclined to agree.

"Then I'll tell you what," I said. "We'll tell you about theater, and you tell us about Citadel. Fair enough?"

Her smile was vibrant—at least, it made me vibrate. "Fair indeed! Ask what you will!"

"Anything?" Marty said, with an overearnest grin and an eager gleam in his eye.

Prudence lost her smile and drew back, startled. Elias turned around, frowning, suspicious.

"Don't pay any attention to him," I advised. "He's just hamming it up."

"Hamming?" Prudence asked with a pretty frown—she must have been somewhat reassured.

"Overacting, dea . . . ah, Prudence," Marnie explained from across the aisle, working hard at being sweet. "Speaking his lines with too much emotion and not enough conviction. Martyn does it for comedic effect, though. He is our comic."

" 'Comic'?"

Marnie took a deep breath and a firm hold on her patience. Marty stepped in fast, grinning. "A funny man, Miss Prudence—or funny woman, of course, but the term is usually applied to guys."

"Possibly because more men than women enjoy making fools of themselves." Lacey gave Marty a look of scorn. "Often misplaced."

"Hey, I've gotta try for every laugh I can get," Marty protested.

"I know." Larry sneered. "You get so few of them."

"Only when *you're* in the house." Marty played to Prudence again. "Besides, female comics get better treatment—they call them 'comediennes.' "

Prudence watched this exchange wide-eyed, but with a growing smile. Marty noticed and winked at her. "I wasn't serious, Miss Prudence. That would take a major effort for me."

Finally, Prudence laughed, and Elias relaxed, but was still wary.

"Let me rephrase that," Marty said. He clapped a hand over his forehead and wiped it slowly down over his face, emerging with a very serious expression. "Can we really ask you *anything* about Citadel?"

Prudence erupted into peals of laughter, and Elias chuckled a little.

Marty nodded at him. "Coming from *you*, that's a compliment."

The smile disappeared, and Elias looked lost.

"He means that you are usually so serious, that a chuckle from you is as good as a belly laugh from someone else," Suzanne explained.

"Oh! Thank you, Ms. Souci!" He turned back to her, eyes glowing. "What is a 'belly laugh'?"

"Why . . ." Suzanne faltered, surprised that he didn't know the term, and Winston stepped in smoothly, albeit from the next seat over.

"It refers to laughing so hard that your stomach hurts, young man."

Elias stared. "Why would my stomach hurt from laughing?"

"Because that is the true source of your breathing," Winston explained. "You think of breath as coming from the lungs, no doubt, and of course it does—but the muscles that fill and empty those lungs are the diaphragm and *transversus abdominis*—your belly muscles."

"Nay!" Elias frowned. "Surely it is with our chests that we breathe!"

"Far less than you would think," Ogden put in. "They only top off the bottle, so to speak. Have you never been struck in the stomach, young man?"

"Why—of course," Elias said. "What boy has not?"

"Quite true. And when you have suffered such a blow, you no doubt have noticed that you cannot breathe for a minute or so. That is because your abdominal muscles have been momentarily paralyzed."

"If you doubt us, ask your doctor," Charlie said. "You'll find he confirms the truth of what we've said."

Elias's eyes took on a new light. Up till then, I think he was prepared to believe that everything we'd said was a lie. This time, though, he'd caught us in a truth.

"Well, then!" I slapped my knee, turning back to Prudence—I hadn't really taken my eyes off her for more than a few seconds. "That makes two things we've told you about theater—what a comic is, and how an actor breathes."

"Why, so you have!" she said in surprise. "Well, then, ask about Citadel. It is our duty to answer, to explain the faith to all who wish to learn. What do you wish to know?"

"Well, this isn't directly about your religion," I said, "though I'm sure it has its roots there. Why doesn't your government allow any kind of money but your own? I mean, they won't even let us exchange our Terran coins for Citadel cash. Why?"

"I . . . I do not know," she faltered. "Women are not schooled in money, or its ways. Perhaps Elias can tell you."

Marnie's eyes flashed at this further sign of female subjugation, and Lacey didn't look any too happy, either—but Suzanne cooed, "Oh, do tell us, Elias!"

"Why, I shall be pleased to." The look he gave Suzanne said he'd be willing to explain anything, if she were the one who asked. You'd think a guy who grew up with a sister like that would be used to feminine beauty, and hardened to it—but you know how it is, brothers never think of their sisters as beautiful, except maybe in the most objective, analytical way. "I shall be glad to explain," he told her, "so far as I know it. If we do not have off-planet money here on Citadel, you see, we cannot buy off-planet goods, when travelers offer them to us. We are thus strengthened against the temptation to corruption which they represent."

Larry stared, realizing that even if he had been able to smuggle in some vice, he couldn't have sold it.

"Corruption?" Ogden frowned. "But who would try to bring such things to Citadel?"

Now it was my turn for a coughing fit.

Larry looked up, startled, then turned away quickly, looking guilty.

Personally, I thought Ogden was a fine one to talk. Give him a chance, and he would have brought in a barrel of whiskey. Though I'll give him this, he wouldn't have tried to sell drinks—he'd have given them away.

Elias turned to him, earnest and sincere. "They would not think they were bringing in things of vice, sir, for they are so used to them on their home planets that they no longer recognize devices of Satan when they see them."

"Just what did you have in mind as 'devices of Satan'?" Marnie asked, with a hard smile and a glossy stare.

"Oh . . . for women, face paint and luxurious fabrics, and suchlike." He squirmed, uneasy under Marnie's scrutiny without knowing why. "For men, vain attire, tobacco, strong drink . . ."

"Strong drink?" Ogden stared. "You ban whiskey and gin?"

"I know not those words, but I know that strong drink is Devil's blood, sir, or even the demons themselves! Nay, assuredly the folk of Citadel would not have such!"

"Maybe beer?" Merlo ventured.

"Surely wine is acceptable!" Marnie protested.

Elias actually gained an air of authority as he scowled, shaking his head. "Beer makes a man take leave of his senses, and wine is worse! Nay, only grape juice is permitted, and that at service!"

Winston nodded thoughtfully. "I see what you meant, about our not thinking of such things as decadent or corrupt. Yes, we might indeed have brought along a bottle of Chartreuse, unthinking."

Elias nodded, obviously enjoying being right. "This is why our customs men must search so diligently. They cannot depend on an air of guilt, when the perpetrators think they do nothing wrong. And, of course, this is why the currency law must be so strict. If we do not allow folk to change our own money into theirs, there can be no temptation to buy or sell—for if only other governments and corporations can exchange Citadel cash for your worldly money, then smugglers cannot profit, even if we were to buy their goods with our own cash—for once they arrived at their homes again, the smugglers would not be able to turn our cash into their own coins."

Just for the record, Prudence had followed this exchange without any trouble at all. She had obviously already picked up the basics of currency exchange, even if she wasn't supposed to. Presumably her male relatives had discussed the issue in front of her, figuring women either couldn't understand such complexities, or weren't interested.

She leaned forward now, eager for information—and probably also eager to change the subject. "But enough of money, and suchlike boring matter! What else can you say about theater?"

"Mostly that we're in deep trouble," Lacey said, "considering what Citadel's people think makes for moral corruption."

5

The monorail stopped at a plasticrete plaza in the middle of the town. As we stepped down, we saw a large sign proclaiming that the town was HADLEYBURG—nothing more, and nothing less; certainly no words of welcome.

Barry bowed to our loquacious friend. "Thank you for your kind instruction."

"I am ever glad to speak of the Church and the Lord," he assured us. "May you prosper." And with that much of a greeting, he turned away.

Barry straightened, watching him go with a frown. I stepped up to him and said, "Fascinating."

Barry nodded. "Indeed."

"But before we discuss the implications of his disclosures," I said, "perhaps we ought to discover a means of transportation to Publius' address."

"This train will depart in five seconds," the monorail announced.

"Transportation?" Barry looked up in surprise. "Surely our feet will suffice, Horace." He stepped away from the sign and waved his arm. "There is not so much of Hadleyburg, after all."

The monorail sighed into motion, then swept away with a smooth susurrus of displaced air. I found myself looking out over low buildings, most of them built of wood and fieldstone, generally fieldstone. I could see down the broad central street to the edge of town quite clearly. "Yes," I said. "We could visit every address in town before dark, could we not?"

"No, but we could have, if we had started with dawn's first light." Barry consulted his note. "Twelve-twelve

Twelfth Street—that should not be difficult to discover. Let us seek."

We walked away opposite to the direction our informant had taken. Barry glanced back. "He is out of sight. What do you think of that encounter, Horace?"

"Rather unpromising," I said. "It would seem that if we wish to have an audience, we must do a medieval mystery play."

"And though we have several mysteries we might excel in, they have more in common with Agatha Christie than with Christian teachings," Barry agreed. "Still, perhaps we can entice the public if our offerings appeal to their underlying values. What would you say those are, Horace, if our erstwhile fellow passenger is indicative of his people?"

"The work ethic, certainly—that work is good and right in itself, and idleness is wrong." I stopped and looked around; we had come to a corner, but I could see no street sign.

Barry looked around us, too, with a frown. "Presumably the natives know each street by sight, and they have very few visitors."

"Then why name the streets at all?" I asked. "Well, let us keep walking until we discover some indication." I set off down the street that intersected the plaza—and tripped, barely catching myself in time to avoid a bad fall.

"Steady, old fellow." Barry reached out to catch my arm.

"Thank you, Barry. What the deuce did I trip over?" I turned back, looking down, and saw a six-inch-high cube of stone. "What is *that* doing there?"

"Waiting to trip the unwary pedestrian." Barry looked more closely. "No, wait! It has writing . . ."

I was too busy limping away pain to read. "What does it say?"

"On this face, 'Transit Plaza.' " Barry stepped around the stone ninety degrees. "And on this, 'Ninth Avenue.' "

I halted. "Street signs!"

"Where you would least expect to see them," Barry agreed. "Perhaps they interfered with the view."

I pursed my lips, gazing at the words. "Ninth Avenue. Wasn't Publius' address Twelfth Street?"

"It was indeed." Barry looked up, stroking his chin.

"Perhaps we should go further in this direction, and find Twelfth Avenue."

"Or perhaps," I said, "we should walk along Ninth Avenue, and it will lead us to Twelfth Street."

Barry smiled. "Amusing, is it not?"

"It shows a singular lack of imagination," I agreed. "Or is it the secret desire of every little town to be New York in some mysterious way? Well, let us wander."

We stepped off down Ninth Avenue, and the contrast with the street of that name in Manhattan was enough to make me shudder. It was lined with glorified log cabins—glorified in both size, and in being made primarily of fieldstone; the land must have been rocky indeed, when the original colonists landed. None were more than three stories tall, and most only one.

However, it was twice as wide as Broadway—heaven only knows why. And it was clean.

Scrupulously clean; I wondered if that was due to the enforced efforts of those who chose not to work. Again, I thought of Publius and shivered.

The thought reminded me of the ethic we had been discussing. "So you think that this colony is primarily a product of the work ethic?"

"No," said Barry, "for that ethic is itself only the product of a more fundamental principle: the prudential ethic."

"Ah, yes." I nodded, remembering my college literature classes. " 'That which is right, is also profitable.' And of course, in practice, it very easily becomes inverted."

" 'That which is profitable, is also right.' " Barry smiled thinly. "Of course, that variation was never openly admitted."

"Be fair, Barry—the early bourgeoisie probably did not even realize they were operating on such assumptions."

Barry nodded. "Though by the time devout sea captains were smuggling opium from India into China, they surely should have known their own beliefs well enough to acknowledge them."

I shook my head. "They were men of action, Barry, and of business. They were not introspective; they never stopped to ask themselves why they were doing what they were doing. They only knew that there was profit in it, so they did it, and never asked whether or not it was right. Religion, after all, was only for ministers, in church, and on Sundays."

"Unless it had to do with sex," Barry said, "though there are rumors as to who really owned the brothels in Cheapside."

"Oh, *dealing* in sex was well enough, as long as one did not spend one's own money on it," I pointed out. "If others wished to do so, why, then it was profitable—for the landlord."

"A very personal interpretation of basic principles, was it not?" Barry smiled thinly. "One concerned oneself with one's own style of living, and if others wished to be foolish, well, that was all to one's own benefit. The morally proper were entitled to profit from the morally deficient."

"Very self-centered," I agreed, "which is no doubt what allowed those sea captains to set up a triangle trade without asking themselves who would be hurt, or whether it was right or wrong."

"To maximize profit, never travel in an empty ship." Barry nodded. "So if you are transporting manufactured goods from England to India, sell them in India, then spend the gold to buy something that will fill your hold cheaply, but that can be sold at a high profit . . ."

"Such as opium," I finished. "Then take it to China, sell it at a high profit, and invest the money in Chinese goods that will sell for another high profit in England. Triple profit from one voyage—fabrics to opium to tea."

"Or West Indies molasses to New England rum, to African slaves." Barry nodded, his mouth tight. "Never mind that your profit comes from the lifelong misery of kidnapped, beaten human beings and their widows and orphans—or that, in order to create a market for your rum, you are bringing thousands to alcoholism."

I nodded. "Or that, in order to create a market, you must lure hundreds of thousands of Chinese into addiction—it is their own moral weakness that allows them to be exploited."

" 'You can't cheat an honest man,' " Barry said grimly, "and that makes it all right to cheat everyone else. So . . ."

" 'Never smarten up a sucker or wisen up a chump,' " I

quoted, with a sardonic grimace. "And they claim *we* are immoral."

"Be fair," Barry said. "They would never dream of interfering with our right to perform on Terra—or Corona, or Falstaff."

"But on their own world, we are only an opportunity to spend money without profit." I nodded. "Well, Barry, we will just have to find some way to make our performances profitable for their souls."

"That, in itself, is easy," Barry said. "I have never produced or directed a play that was not fundamentally moral—even if it did show immoral actions as an example of the violation of an ethic, and the havoc that ensues—nor have I ever performed in such a play."

"The context has always been profoundly moral." I nodded. "Here, however, I think our hosts will not be at all concerned about the ethical context—they will only be concerned with the surface morality."

"Which eliminates *Didn't He Ramble*; the setting of the converted bordello would obscure the speculation about the fundamental predatory nature of our species," I said, "not to mention most of the English classics, and virtually all of Shakespeare."

"*Ow!*" Barry stumbled.

I stopped abruptly. "Why, we have come to a corner, haven't we?"

Barry limped back, glaring balefully at the cube over which he had tripped. "Twelfth Street! Twelfth Street and Ninth Avenue! Scarcely the environment that I associate with that address, but an intersection nevertheless. Now we have only to find Number 1212."

"Which way?"

"When we know nothing, either will do. Let us follow our political inclinations, and turn to the left."

So we did, and went off down Twelfth Street, wondering whether we were going north, south, east, or west. No doubt the sun would eventually shine and tell us.

"Here?" I stared up at the picture emblazoned over the doorway. "This is Publius' abode?"

"I doubt it." Barry looked about him. "It scarcely seems

to be the sort of establishment that would offer accommodations."

The picture was of food and drink—rather Spartan fare: bread, milk, and a bowl of porridge.

"This is, however, the location at which he can be contacted." Barry pointed to the small cube jutting up from the pavement on the corner. On one face, it read "Twelfth Avenue," and on the other, "Twelfth Street."

"Twelve-twelve," I summarized. "At the corner of Twelfth Avenue and Twelfth Street. Quaint. At least I shall know how to find, eleven-ten-, or eighty-six."

"Presumably, there are other designations for buildings between corners," Barry said, "but they need not concern us now. Let us enter, Horace."

We went in.

It was a rather barren room: fieldstone walls, plasticrete floor, and wooden tables with straight chairs about them. There was a pass-through window at the back. A man in an apron looked up and came toward us. When he saw we wore overcoats and no beards, he began to look suspicious, but he forced himself to sound polite as he asked, "Will you dine, strangers?"

We exchanged a glance, remembering our dearth of local currency. "Actually, no," Barry said. "We have come seeking a colleague of ours—a Mr. Publius Promo."

"Oh, the show fellow, is it?" the man said, letting his contempt show. "The charity case." He turned back toward the pass-through and called, "Promo! Folk to see you!" Then, with a glance back at us, he growled, "Bide," and went back toward what I presumed was the kitchen.

Barry and I exchanged looks of alarm. "Charity case?" he whispered.

A stocky man came out of the back room, drying reddened hands on a stained apron. He saw us, and his face lit with delight. "Mr. Tallendar! Horace! Thank heavens!"

Well, at least he was sober.

Publius besought his employer for a few minutes to chat with us, and the restaurateur reluctantly gave him permission to do so.

"Seat yourselves, seat yourselves!" Publius urged, and turned away toward the kitchen again.

Barry and I exchanged puzzled looks, then shrugged and went to a table in a corner, as far from the kitchen as possible.

Publius brought cups and a steaming pot. "A little tea, at least, they won't begrudge me! Welcome, welcome! I am *so* glad to see you, so relieved—but so distraught, too. Did my message not reach you?" He poured tea.

"It did," Barry assured him, "but we could not leave a member of our company stranded."

Publius froze in midpour, then set the pot down with a shaking hand and collapsed into a chair. Suddenly, he went completely limp and bowed his face into his hands. "It is so good of you, so good," he said, his voice thick with suppressed sobs—or perhaps not so completely suppressed; when he looked up, there were tears in his eyes. "For your sakes, I wish you had not come—but for my sake, I am glad that you did, so glad!"

"We could not leave one of our own in dire straits," Barry said firmly. I believe it must have been excellent acting on his part; for my own, I felt tremendously shaken at discovering Publius in the role of dishwasher! Not that he had never done it, of course—we all took menial jobs during the early years, when we were auditioning as often as we could and hoping for the next casting, to relieve us of the drudgery.

"But how is it we find you as a menial in this establishment?" Barry asked. "Come now, have a good strong drink of your own tea, and tell us!"

Publius did as he was bidden, and the taste of the tea did seem to restore him a bit—but a muscle in his left cheek began to twitch. "It's this confounded currency dilemma, Mr. Tallendar. They won't let you have but a few hundred, and the cost of room and board is exorbitant! I was almost flat within a fortnight. By that time, of course, I had come to realize how complete a trap this would be, so I spent the last few shillings on an electronics kit, hoping to be able to warn you off."

"You succeeded, and it is our own decision to ignore

your warning," Barry assured him. "But how did you manage?"

"Ah, well, as to that, the landlord of this dining hall is my landlord indeed. He feeds me and allows me to sleep on a pallet in the back room, in return for which, I wash dishes and peel vegetables, and any other chores he may find."

To see him reduced to such labor in middle age angered me. "Surely he pays you some sort of wage!"

Publius shook his head, jowls shaking, doleful as a bloodhound. "The prices are unbelievable, Mr. Burbage."

"I am 'Horace,' " I reminded him, "and this gentleman is 'Barry,' not 'Mr. Tallendar'."

In retrospect, I am not sure I would have encouraged such familiarity, if I had not felt so sorry for the poor chap, and so angry at his persecutors—but Barry must have been feeling something of the same, for he nodded his head. "We are fellow professionals, after all. Still, I wonder that you must work for food and board—a local told us that the government provided all necessities."

"To citizens." Publius held up a forefinger. "Only to citizens. If I became a permanent resident of Citadel, and a convert to their variety of Christianity, the necessities would be provided—but only the bare necessities. Of course, I would then have to go into business, for which I lack the capital, or take whatever form of work they assigned me on the cash-crop farms."

"Is there no alternative?" I asked.

Publius shrugged. "Service in the Lord's Army is mandatory—they have never fought a war, but the soldiers function as a police force. Fortunately, I was too old to enlist, or I might have had no choice, citizen or not. A young man may choose the navy instead, of course—it functions as a merchant marine. Needless to say, I am too old for that form of duty, too—at least, too old to begin it involuntarily."

That puzzled me. "I thought the merchants were private."

"They are, to ensure that the government itself takes no risk—but the trading companies must hire ships and crews from the navy. The terms are an outright fee plus a percentage of the profits."

Barry raised his eyebrows. "Very profitable—for the government!"

"Oh, and for the merchants, too, Barry!" Publius hastened to assure him. "After all, they must have some incentive to undertake the risk of investing in a voyage."

"Plus," I said, "the government must have someone to tax."

"And they do, they do!" Publius nodded so vigorously that his jowls shook again. "The government takes out its share before it transfers the money to the company—only they don't call it 'tax' here, you see. They call it 'tithing.' "

"But don't tithes go to the Church?" I asked.

Publius turned a blank stare upon me. "What is the difference?"

I hadn't known he had a knack for sarcasm. At least, I *hoped* it was sarcasm.

But Barry was still grappling with an earlier statement. "The government passes the profits from the voyage to the company?"

"Quite so. Money coming in from shipping goes to the government first, so that it can change off-world currency into local; they don't allow a single farthing of any other coinage to enter circulation on Citadel. The company is paid in local currency; then it pays the captain and crew."

"So in addition to everything else, the government receives the benefit of the exchange rate!" Barry nodded, the cynical gleam in his eye again. "For a spiritual organization, the Church does rather well for itself."

"Only in its mundane aspect, as the government," Publius clarified.

His earnest tone struck a chord of foreboding in me; I hoped he was not beginning to feel that there was some sense in this totalitarian system. Well, if he was, no doubt the company of fellow professionals would soon clear that from his soul.

"I trust you were not thinking of signing on for a voyage," Barry said.

"Once you had been warned away, I might have tried to do so," Publius admitted. "I understand that the captains and shore patrols keep a very vigilant watch over their sailors in foreign ports, but I might have managed to jump ship anyway."

"Surely they would have seen that you were too old for such rigors!"

"Yes, and sent me to harder labor on the government farms." Publius shuddered. "I did not mind hard physical labor in my youth, Mr., ah, Barry . . . but in middle age, it could prove decidedly unhealthy."

"Especially since they seem to prefer not to use machines unless it is absolutely necessary." Barry nodded. "No, for you to convert would be to submit to tyranny."

"Not to mention total hypocrisy." Publius nodded. "Under those circumstances, the proprietor of this establishment *is* being charitable to allow me to work for my room and board." He shrugged, spreading his hands with a rueful smile. "I have been stranded before—but never, I think, quite so thoroughly as this."

As we all might be, I realized, unless we could generate some local currency. A chill seized me at the thought of ending my days on so desolate a rock as this.

Publius leaned close, and whispered, "To make it worse, I haven't been able to find a single drop of alcohol—the whole planet's dry, every single citizen a teetotaler!"

"Which they can accomplish easily," Barry said grimly, "by merely prohibiting the importation of alcoholic beverages. Surely there must be some local, illicit distilling?"

"If there is, it is very well hidden," Publius said. "I am told that the penalties for it are quite severe."

It was sensible, in its way; after all, the planet had no moon. I shuddered at the thought of having to perform with Ogden, this far away from a bottle. It would be very good for him, no doubt, but extremely unpleasant for the rest of us. In fact, I dreaded the thought of being away from the ship with him at all—and it was a positive nightmare, imagining what would happen if these Puritans' police caught him with a bottle! I began to understand why Barry was so determined to build a theater in the cavernous cargo hold.

"Certainly a hideous state of affairs," Barry agreed, "but I can see from your expression that you fear you have worse to tell. Have you not been able to arrange for a hall?"

"No, Mr. Tallendar." Publius swallowed thickly, summoned all his nerve, and blurted, "On this benighted planet, theater is prohibited!"

"Illegal?" I stared in horror.

"Absolutely," Publius said, and he looked ready to weep again. "Theater in any form; even 3DT exhibitions are limited to those chosen by the deacons!"

" 'Chosen'?" I echoed. "Not 'approved'?"

"Not," Publius confirmed.

"They have gone beyond mere censorship, then." Barry sat back, frowning. "Do you mean that, in order to present a play, we must find some way to make the deacons choose our production?"

"No, Barry. The deacons' secretary made that quite clear to me—live theater will not be permitted in any form."

I turned an uncomprehending stare upon Barry. "Why would that be? Why would they present selected 3DT productions, but not allow live theatrical presentations of the same material?"

"Perhaps it has to do with the physical proximity of the actors, and especially actresses," Barry conjectured. "There are precedents in the early days of theater, when the government seemed to think the actresses were merely prostitutes advertising their wares."

"And to prove themselves right, they seduced the actresses, then banned them." I nodded. "Or perhaps it might be the uncertainty factor—you can never be sure that an actor will speak exactly what the playwright has written for him."

"If Shakespeare could not be sure of it, why should the deacons?" Barry nodded. "That, too, makes sense."

"Still, our informant's notion seems entirely adequate, for this culture," I said, "simply that a play is an opportunity to waste money."

"On the surface, at least," Barry said. "But I would incline more to the notion of an underlying emotional prejudice; any reasons given are only excuses."

"No matter the rationale, gentlemen," Publius said quietly, "we are faced with the fact: The law forbids theater in any form."

"What *is* allowed?" I asked.

"Concerts are acceptable," Publius said, "if the music is uplifting."

Barry nodded. "Classical, then, with a preponderance of Church music. I would assume that sermons are also permissible."

"Yes, for those who are certified as ministers of the Citadel Church."

"Certainly," Barry said dryly. "Not a complete guarantee that the Church will approve the sermon, but almost one. And if the Church approves it, I assume the government does, too."

"Of course." Finally, Publius smiled. "On Citadel, the Church and the government are one and the same."

"Of course!" I stared. "A theocracy! I should have realized it sooner!"

Barry nodded. "Government by God—or God's appointed ministers, at least. Do they allow *any* entertainments?"

"Sporting events are legal—but only soccer, gymnastics, and boxing."

I frowned. "They object to football?"

"Yes—there is too much gratuitous violence."

"The same would apply to hockey, no doubt," Barry said, and Publius nodded.

I could understand that. "Baseball?"

Publius shook his head. "The deacons suspect it of having sexual implications."

I threw up my hands in exasperation. "If baseball is counted salacious, then we certainly cannot present anything!"

"And if we cannot perform, we cannot earn local currency." The twitch was back, and Publius's eyes started to fill again. "And if we cannot earn local currency, we cannot buy fuel for the ship to lift off—and we are stranded here!"

"Not necessarily," Barry said grimly. "There are still several alternatives."

"What?" Publius pounced on it.

"Surely we cannot get out and push!" I said.

"No," Barry said, "but even one who is not a minister might present a lecture. Can he not, Publius?"

"I have heard no law against it," the advance man said slowly, "though I assume the person in question would have to show the proper credentials."

"I am officially a master of arts," Barry said, "and my diploma is one of the few items I treasure sufficiently to have brought with me."

Possibly, I thought, because it took up little space and had little mass—but I did not say so. In fact, it was more likely a matter of the diploma being in with his valuable papers, and of his not taking time to sort in the rush to pack. "But on what topic shall you lecture?"

"On heads," Barry answered.

"Of course!" I should have realized it. When our professional forebears ran afoul of city elders who had outlawed theater, they supported themselves by presenting lectures on heads. If they could do it, so could we.

But Publius looked dubious. "Surely the deacons will see that for what it is—a blatant attempt to amuse! And if they do, then what can we do, M . . . Barry? We will be quite thoroughly marooned!"

"We will find a way, my friend. It is not the first time actors have been stranded, nor will it be the last. They have always found a way to return to civilization."

"Or settled down where they were." Publius shuddered. "I never thought I would end my days as a farmer, Barry!"

"Nor shall you," Barry said, with grim determination. "The stars await us, Publius. We shall not be mired here. Come, thank your employer for his kindness, resign, and let us return to the ship—we have, at least, that much of culture and refinement here."

Publius rose, with every sign of relief. "I shall do so immediately! Oh, thank you, Barry, thank you!"

As he bustled away, I leaned close to Barry and murmured, "It is quite unnerving to see him reduced to such a state."

"Especially since the same fate might befall us?" Barry shook his head, smiling slightly. "Has it occurred to you that the government may have let us land in order to gain another dozen laborers?"

"The thought had crossed my mind," I admitted, "though I thought it more likely that they sought to trap a few more souls to force into their version of salvation."

Barry nodded grimly. "I think that we had better perform quickly, Horace. We must see to gaining permits and booking a hall."

6

Prudence stared, and Elias began to look very self-righteous indeed. "How is this, Miss Lark? Surely you do not intend to corrupt our citizens with your playacting!"

"Why . . . no, of course not," Lacey stammered.

I felt sorry for the guy—his goddess was developing feet of flesh and bone, and the transformation might work its way up.

Once again, Winston interposed smoothly. "Certainly not, Mr. Elias! But as you have just noted, what you deem decadent, may seem normal to us—possibly even innocent and wholesome. The comedies and dramas we have rehearsed may prove quite unacceptable by Citadel's standards. How are we to know what may offend, and what may not?"

"Ah! The very point, the very point!" Elias relaxed, his goddess back on her pedestal again. He smiled, hands folded in his lap. "You have but to bring the words of your plays to the deacons, and they will be happy to tell you which passages are sinful, and which are not."

"I just bet they will," Marty muttered.

I gave him an elbow in the ribs and said, "We can't be all that far off by your standards, Elias. The theater does have some principles of its own."

Lacey had to smother an exclamation, and Marty stared at me in amazement. Ogden had to cough, and Marnie did a double take.

Prudence glanced at them out of the corner of her eyes, but Elias just turned around to smile at me. "There, I could not think you were completely devoid of morality! What are these principles, Mr. Lazarian?"

"Just 'Ramou,' please," I said. "I don't like the sound of

my last name. The main principles were laid down by Aristotle, thousands of years ago, Mr. Elias—and since some of his ideas were incorporated in early Christianity, they shouldn't be too alien."

Marnie looked startled, and Ogden nodded surprised approval. Suzanne stared at me in amazement over the back of the seat, and Larry eyed me suspiciously—they both knew I had been an engineering major, not a literary scholar, and that I hadn't even finished my third year.

What they didn't know was that Horace had been answering every question I'd asked, and he had gone off on broad tangents; and Merlo had a tendency to do the same, while we were working on sets and lights. I had listened with every ounce of concentration—the theater bug had really bitten me hard. I just wished Horace were here for my term exam.

"True." Elias frowned. "Though those early Christians were Papists, and the true faith not yet thought of. What principles are these?"

"Well, Aristotle laid down a lot of rules for how to write plays," I said, "but the ones that govern right or wrong in content are decorum and catharsis."

" 'Decorum' has a righteous sound," Elias said, nodding. "What is 'catharsis'?"

Prudence began to show signs of impatience; this wasn't the part of theater that she wanted to hear about. But Elias ignored her, fastening on what I was saying; surely questions of morality were far more important than anything else.

" 'Catharsis' meant purging the audience of all the emotions that led to evil behavior," I said, "by watching somebody else suffer because of having committed the same deeds the audience members are tempted toward."

Elias scowled. "Purging such desires and impulses is good—but this has a sound of showing immoral deeds right there, in front of the folk themselves."

Ogden nodded. "That usually occurs, yes."

"Will not that tempt the audience to do those very deeds?"

Prudence looked up, interested again.

"Aristotle says no," I explained. I didn't tell him that I

thought Aristotle had been very naive—but then, he was used to an audience that saw plays maybe one week out of the whole year, not one that was bombarded by 3DT every day. "People are apt to think twice, when they see the crime punished—or, even more, see that the crime brings its own punishment."

"The wages of sin," Elias mused.

"And nobody likes to see them paid," I agreed. "One critic said it's a matter of seeing immoral actions within a profoundly moral context."

Marnie was looking skeptical—she knew very well that only in the best plays is the context profoundly moral. In the lighter stuff, the immoral acts may be shown clearly enough, but they're not always punished—or not very harshly. And, of course, the modern theater allows a lot of plays with sinners who don't get punished, and plays that glory in their depravity. Can't say too much against them, either, 'cause some of them are really fine drama. At least, so says Horace.

I tried to get away from the issue. " 'Decorum' you know about—it's a matter of not putting anything in front of the audience that isn't absolutely necessary to make the point . . . I mean, the moral. For example, you might show the villain's dead body, but you wouldn't show him being killed."

"Wherefore not?" Elias frowned. "We must take arms against Evil, Mr. . . . Ramou. We must show the agents of good defeating those of wickedness."

I perked up; this guy was talking my language. "Oh, there's a lot of stage combat, of course! Later generations of actors realized that Aristotle wasn't right about everything."

Prudence shuddered. "Must you always show people smiting one another?"

"Only if it's well done," I assured her.

"But do you show nothing of why folk prosper, or why they fail?" Elias demanded.

"Well, we do show true love being rewarded for persevering under adversity," Suzanne replied.

Prudence turned around to look at her, interested—but

Elias said, "Nay, nay! We speak of material gain, sister—of virtue rewarded, and vice punished!"

"There are a lot of plays along that line," I said slowly. I couldn't offhand think of any, though, so I said, "But what kind of actions do Citadel people think should be rewarded?"

"Thrift," Elias said immediately, "and hard work. Prudent living, and careful management of money, to yield profit."

Suzanne stared, then recovered and batted her eyelashes at him with a smile. "Are those your only virtues—just business?"

"Oh, nay!" Elias said. "They arise from the deeper virtues—constancy and modesty, for a woman—and chastity."

Marnie held her face rigid and fought for sweetness in her tone. "Is chastity only for women, then?"

"Nay, surely not!" Elias cried, afronted. "Men are obligated to chastity, too, Miss Lulala! From chastity arises thrift, and from thrift, prosperity!"

Lacey frowned prettily. "Thrift arises from chastity? I don't understand."

Elias turned to her, then blushed and turned away. "I am glad to learn that."

That actually left a gap for Prudence to get a word in. "Constancy arises from faith, Miss Lark, as does courage—though for myself, I think hope is a part of courage, too." She turned those huge blue eyes on me. "Who would have the strength to persist and strive through day after day of this mortal life, if we did not have the hope of something better to come?"

It must have been the acoustics—there couldn't really have been an echo to her words, a hidden meaning. Surely the Puritan maid was too innocent for that.

"So faith and hope are key virtues because they give rise to the others," I said. "But how about charity?"

"It is incumbent upon us all," Elias said complacently, "to aid our less fortunate brethren. But they, too, must strive, do you see?"

"Is that all charity means to you?" Suzanne asked, batting those eyelashes again. "Just giving money to the poor?"

"Surely it is more!" Prudence protested. Again, she turned to me. "It is the love of those who are close to one another, too, and share the joy that arises from their love." And those huge blue eyes were promising joy indeed. I reminded myself that she was only thinking of the pleasures of the spirit.

Lacey glanced at her, frowning, but Elias took charge again. "Vice is punished, and virtue is rewarded. This it is which kept our colony alive during the bitter, early years of colonization—but hard though the times were, our ancestors still rejoiced, for they were free to worship as they would, without the interference of the agents of Satan who continually paraded temptations before them—temptations to idleness, and expensive pleasures; to gambling and drinking away their money, to squandering it on loose women and wild living. And it is these virtues that keep us prosperous today, that make our fields yield rich harvests and our captains high profits. They may all be summed up in one word, the cardinal virtue for which my sister is named: prudence. For prudence is the fruit of all the other virtues, and in its own turn, their key."

Suzanne and Lacey just sat, staring at him, not quite believing their ears.

Beside me, Marty muttered, "Tell me again how these people are gonna spend money to see a play."

"Sheer novelty," I hissed back. "Besides, they've all got to come see it so they can tell each other what's so horrible about it."

"I thought they were Puritans, not critics."

Deceleration made us sway suddenly, and the computer-voice announced, "We will be arriving in Hadleyburg in thirty seconds."

"Well!" Suzanne pulled her bright face back on. "Thank you for such an enlightening discussion! Now, though, I think we'll ask you to give us a tour of the town!"

"I shall be delighted," Elias said gravely.

But he was a little late—when the doors slid open, we found a reception committee ready and waiting.

They were all wearing the same kind of dark blue jackets

and blue canvas trousers. When they saw us, they sent up a roar that didn't quite have words in it, and wasn't *quite* angry. . . .

"Step aside, young woman!" the biggest one called at Prudence. "We want to talk to them playacting folks!"

"What about?" Elias asked, amazed.

"Not your worry, young'un! Just step aside, now."

Some of them were holding sticks. I could smell trouble and felt the old eager smile tugging at the corners of my lips. I guess I let it show, 'cause Merlo started looking nervous—he knew from experience that when I begin to look that way, there's a fight coming. Mind you, he doesn't mind a good fight, but he thinks I go after them a little too quickly. "I'm one of the playacting folk!" He elbowed me aside and stepped to the front. "What do you want?"

"This car will depart in five minutes," the computer informed us.

"Merlo, you forget yourself!"

Merlo looked up in complete surprise, off balance—and Marnie took advantage of it to step past him and out the door. "If you do not know how to receive your public, be sure that I do! If there is tribute to be received, I shall have it!" She turned to the mob with a gracious smile. "Good afternoon, everyone! I'm Marnie Lulala!"

She stopped them for a second, it's a fact. Even at forty, Marnie was a beautiful woman—and these were hard-bitten frontiersmen for whom a lady of her beauty and poise was as rare as a flowering tree on the high plains. They stared, and I saw a few jaws loosen, a few sticks lower, a few fists unclench.

Then the leader's face darkened as if he were remembering his duty, and his fists knotted again. "We know what you are, you shameless woman! Come to corrupt our young folk and bedazzle our young men!"

Marnie stared, taken aback for a moment, and Merlo nudged her. "Yes," she murmured to him, "your crowd." She stepped to the back.

Merlo stepped to the front again. "I love you, too, sweetheart. What do you want?"

"We want you gone!" the man called, and all his mates shouted agreement behind him. "Josh, there, rode in with two of your folk and found out you're fixing to put on an ungodly playacting show! We're here to tell you Hadley-burg doesn't want your kind!"

"Aren't they jumping the gun a little?" Marty asked somewhere behind me.

"Yes," Winston answered. "They're supposed to wait until we've performed a few days and run up a hotel bill, before they run us out of town."

"An immoral, obscene playacting show!" the man shouted. "Scarlet women, parading right out there where anybody can see their ankles! We won't have it, I tell you!"

But I could see a couple of the men in the back eyeing Suzanne and Lacey, and thinking twice.

"Not at all!" Lacey cried. "Scarlet is my worst color!"

"*What* immoral plays?" Merlo demanded.

"What do you want, a name of one? What does it matter? They're *all* immoral! Or most of them, anyway. Nay, we have come to tell you to go back where you came from."

"Why, we would be glad to," Winston said slowly, "if your spaceport would accept our Terran money for your Citadel fuel—but they will not."

"Then you must find honest work and earn your bread by moral means! And we are here to see that you do!"

I was grinning openly now, and that made Merlo really nervous. He called out, "We'll be very moral, our plays will be downright illuminating! But that's the only kind of work we can do, to earn our fuel!"

"Then get you back to your ship until the government finds work for you!" The ringleader shook a fist under Merlo's nose. "Or we shall *make* you go back!"

Marnie boiled over. "So that's what this is all about, is it? Trying to reduce us to slaves! What else did you have in mind for us? Or are you going to try to claim there is no crime here?"

There was a collective gasp of shock; these guys had no trouble understanding what she was hinting at. They'd been raised to think dirty, so that they would be able to see sin coming a long way off and avoid it. Well, they could see it coming, anyway—the jury was still out on the avoidance charge.

"How dare you hint at such things!" The ringleader stared, aghast. "Surely you can be no lady, if you know of them!"

Prudence glanced from one to another, wide-eyed. "Know of what?"

"Later, dearie," Lacey said, "and not without a permit from your parents."

Prudence flushed. "I am a woman grown!"

"Be still, sister!" Elias commanded, backing up. "And come away!"

"Good idea!" Suzanne turned after him. "Let's all go!"

They were heading for the monorail door, but a couple of the gang leaped to head them off. "Nay! You shall not flee!"

"But you wanted us to go," Suzanne protested, and the men hesitated, confused—that happens, when you haven't figured out your real motives—and while they were hesitating, the monorail door slid shut. They looked up, startled, just in time to see the car glide down the track.

"Take these two lambs to safety!" The ringleader waved them away, and two rear guards started herding Elias and Prudence out of the line of fire.

"Nay!" Elias protested. "We have spoken with these people—they are good folk!"

"They have pulled the wool over your eyes, boy," the ringleader told him, "beguiling you with false smiles and fair words."

Elias reddened, and I guessed the ringleader's calling him "boy" had been a big mistake.

"They are not evil!" Prudence cried. "They—"

"Be still, woman!" the ringleader roared. "It is not your place to speak in matters of weight!"

That was a bigger mistake; all three actresses turned on him at once. "How dare you tyrannize the child that way!" "Just who do you think you are, trying to tell women to be insignificant!" "Why, that's absolutely Paleolithic! You blatant sexist!"

"*What* . . . did . . . you . . . say?" the leader gasped.

Marnie stared, lost. "What? I give up."

"That . . . that word!" the leader managed, in a strangled tone.

"What . . . 'Paleolithic'?"

"Not that! The other!"

"Really anxious to hear me say it again, aren't you?" Marnie said in her most scathing tone. "What was it? 'Blatant'? 'Sex—' "

"Again! She said it again!" another man bleated.

"Have you no shame, woman!" the ringleader snapped.

Marnie stared, unable to believe her ears.

"It's not the '-ist' that's bothering them," Winston confided. "It's the—"

"Don't you dare say the word!"

"My heavens!" Winston stared. "Not even a mention of it, eh?"

"But of course," Marnie said, eyes narrowing. "If you can't say the root, you can't say the compound word—and if you don't have the word, you can't express the concept. Very neat—women can't even talk about being exploited!"

The ringleader scowled. "I do not like the tone of your words, missus. Surely you must not perform where our young folk can see you!"

"Not to mention your womenfolk," Marnie said, with sarcasm.

"Them least of all! We'll not have them learning to be painted hussies and scarlet women! Be gone back to your ship, all of you!"

"We can't," Winston said reasonably. "You blocked us from the monorail."

But one of the crowd was noticing the look on my face, and frowned. "What troubles you, young man?"

"Just exasperation," I said.

"At what?"

"You and your cronies. I mean, if all you're going to do is talk, why should I stay around?"

"Ramou!" Marnie snapped, and Merlo groaned.

Elias made one last try. "Their ways are not ours, but they are not evil!"

"Lad, lad!" the leader said sadly. "You have let lascivious glances and lewd talk corrupt you already!"

"Are you the constable?" I asked. "Or maybe the chief of police?"

"Nay." The sailor scowled. "We are honest citizens, who

do not wish your kind among us!" But he glanced aside at Suzanne with a covetous gleam in his eye, that gave the lie to his words.

It also gave me a push toward mayhem. "If you're not official," I said, "you have no right to stop us. Stand aside, please."

"Ramou," Lacey said nervously, "I don't think you—"

"Ramou," another bruiser sneered. "What sort of name is that? A girl's name, sure!"

He wasn't the first one who had ever pulled that line on me, but he was the only one who hadn't wound up in traction for it—yet. "It's a name with a great tradition behind it," I said, "and I'll be delighted to bring that tradition for your moral improvement. Now, please get out of the way—we're law-abiding citizens, and the law doesn't prohibit us from walking down your street."

"Maybe the law doesn't," the ringleader snarled, "but we do! Get them, men!"

And he swung that huge hairy fist at me.

I leaned aside and rolled back, just enough to take the punch on my shoulder. "Ow!" I yelled, very loudly and theatrically. "I've been hit!"

"Hold on, Ramou . . ." Merlo began, but the mob cut him off. With a concerted howl, they struck.

"Girls in the middle!" I shouted, and jumped in front of Suzanne. A fist slammed at my head; I blocked it downward, and it slammed into my chest instead. It hurt, and that got my adrenaline flowing. I grabbed the guy's jacket and yanked as I kicked his feet out from under him, then used him to block the club that his buddy was swinging from my left. On my right, I heard Merlo grunt with pain, then the solid meaty sound as his fist connected. Larry bleated in fear, which was good—if he was scared enough, he might actually accomplish something.

The club-swinger tried again, and I stepped toward him just enough so the guy on the right missed me with his left hook—and far enough back so the club went past me. I stepped in before the swing finished and rocked him with a blow to the head. He slumped and went down, but there wasn't time to watch—Marnie called, "Ramou! Behind you!" and I had to whirl and crouch in time to duck the fist that whistled over my head. I came up to give him a jab in the short ribs—and something made a loud crack that filled the world, a world of sudden pain, and I was seeing double. I fell and rolled away, hearing somebody roar with triumph, a roar that turned into a yelp of pain. My vision cleared in time to see a big bruiser hopping on one foot, holding his shin, and Suzanne taking aim at the remaining shin with a needle-toed shoe. Behind her, Winston was blocking one punch and returning another. Suzanne kicked; the fellow fell, and Grudy caught him around the neck, hugging his head in a hammerlock for Lacey to beat on.

I rolled to my feet, coming up inside the guard of a fiery-eyed man who was reaching for Suzanne. He blinked in astonishment before I caught him in the solar plexus, and he fell away gagging. I saw Marty yank a guy's beard, and he stumbled forward into Larry's fist, but he swung blind and connected, knocking Larry loose. Then the ringleader loomed up in front of me, yelling with a mouth full of cavities and swinging a fist the size of a ham hock. I caught it, turning as I grabbed his jacket, crouching, then surging up to throw him over my shoulder—and into two more who were diving for Charlie and Winston.

Merlo reeled back in front of me, blocking punches by a very religious Neanderthal—then suddenly ducked and swung in, hard, catching the guy in the belly. The fanatic bent over, gargling, and Merlo slammed a fist into his jaw.

The ringleader scrambled to his feet, snarling, and lunged at me. He must have been groggy; I stepped aside and slammed another punch into his head. He went down like a steer in the slaughterhouse, clearing the way for me to see Winston sweeping one guy's feet out from under him and the last lummox scrambling upright just in time for Charlie to deck him with an uppercut.

And, that quickly, it was all over. I looked around me, panting. Marty was down, with Suzanne just now dropping to sit beside him, and Larry was kneeling with his head in his hands, but Lacey and Marnie were already hovering over him. The rest of us had some bad bruises, Suzanne included, but we were intact.

On the sidelines, Elias and Prudence stared. "How did you do that?" she gasped.

Admiration from a beautiful woman always makes you feel good—but this might not have been admiration. "Experience," I panted, then turned an approving gaze on Winston. "A little martial arts training when you were a kid, huh?"

Winston grinned. "Just a little." He dabbed at a streak of blood over his eye with his handkerchief.

"Quickly!" Grudy gasped. "Let's get away while they're unconscious!"

But I shook my head. "Can't do, Ms. Drury. Got to make sure nobody's hurt bad, first."

"But they will seek revenge! They will call out the law!"

"Have to take the chance," I said.

"Got to wait for the monorail, anyway," Merlo pointed out.

"Oh . . . yes, we do." Grudy looked apprehensively at the rail.

I went over to the ringleader and knelt down to check his pulse. A shadow fell across me, and I looked up, surprised and braced.

It was Marty, standing there with his left hand over his bruised face and one of the goons' clubs in his right, lifted and ready to plant. He looked scared as a tuna in shark country, but he was standing by manfully.

"What's that for?" I asked.

"Just in case he suddenly gets a lot better," Marty croaked.

I couldn't help the grin. "Your support warms my heart, Mr. Kemp."

"I'll warm his head," he returned. "Just check him out quick, okay, Ramou?"

"Will do." I checked; the guy's pulse was strong and regular. I probed beneath the dark spots that were working on becoming bruises, but I didn't feel anything broken. On the third probe, though, he stirred, with a groan of pain.

"He's all right." I stood up and went over to the next one. Over to my right, I saw Suzanne kneeling to check one very lucky casualty, with Merlo hovering over her. Like Marty, he was holding one of the dropped clubs. Charlie was checking up on another goon, with Winston backing him up. Larry and Lacey, of course, were standing back watching.

When I had checked my fourth one, I stood up to see Suzanne standing, too. "That's five," she said. "They're going to have bad headaches, but they won't need a hospital. They all ought to have themselves checked for concussion, of course, but I know none of them will."

"Sure—they're big and tough and strong." I grinned, stepping over to her. "Do you always fight as well as you nurse?"

She looked surprised, then stepped up close to me herself, her eyelids growing heavy, lips relaxing into lazy smile. "No, I usually nurse as well as I fight."

As wit, it wasn't much, but the way she said it, and the look in those bedroom eyes, sent a charge of desire running through me that was more sudden and intense than anything I'd ever known—almost as frightening as the first time I'd felt desire at all, back in elementary school, staring at a precocious classmate.

"I'd love to find out from personal experience," I breathed, moving a little closer.

She swayed to within an inch of me. "All right, then—I'll come nurse you."

We stood centimeters apart, the air between us almost crackling, and I knew she was feeling it, too.

"I hate to break this up," Marty said, "but your first customer's coming around."

I stepped away, pivoting, desire transforming instantly into battle lust. The ringleader was sitting up. He looked up at me, scowling.

I went over and reached down a hand. "Feel like getting up?"

"Aye—and thank you," he grunted. He took my hand and pulled. I was braced in case he might try to pull me down, but he didn't, only pulled himself up. "You hit hard, young fellow, but you hit clean."

"That's the name of the game. I don't think much of people who use clubs, though."

He turned to glare at me. I met his gaze with a level one of my own, and he looked down, ashamed. "No," he mumbled. "We should not have done that."

He hadn't, of course—but he hadn't tried to stop anybody else from using them, either.

A couple of his buddies levered themselves off the ground a little, moaning. "Call the watch," one growled.

"Nay!" the ringleader barked. "These folk have fought bravely and fairly. It is not a style that we know, true, but it is clean for all that."

"Karate is just dirty fighting," one surly one grumbled.

"It is not, for I have known excellent men who fought in that style. Aye, it is not my way to mix boxing and wrestling—but all is fair, in a brawl!" He turned to me. "You have proved your courage, strangers, and we'll not seek to harry you further."

"Not so long as you honor the commandments and the law," one of the guys on the ground growled.

The ringleader glanced down at him impatiently. "Of course, as long as they honor the law—and the faith." He turned back to me. "But you would not think to *not* honor them, would you?"

"Not if you can punch like that," I ad-libbed. After all, I hadn't read the law he was talking about.

He looked surprised, then barked laughter and clapped me on the shoulder. "Aye, you're a brave and worthy one! If the rest of your folk are like you, you'll bring no harm to Citadel."

"Then why have we suffered cracked heads this day?" his buddy demanded as he heaved himself to his feet.

"Why, to make sure of them!" He turned back to me. "And you of us. Am I not right, stranger?"

"Oh, you've won my respect, all right." I stuck out a hand. "Ramou Lazarian."

"Zachariah McPharlin." He shook my hand. His was broad and hard, but his clasp was no rougher than my own. "Will you see Hadleyburg, then?"

A whisper behind me grew into a hiss. I looked up and saw the monorail car sliding in to a stop. "Not just now," I said. "I think we'd better get back to the ship and freshen up first."

He looked me over from head to toe, then glanced at the rest of the company. "Aye. You are the worse for wear. My apologies."

"No hard feelings." I didn't tell him I could only speak for myself. "Right now, though, I've got kind of a headache. Need any help getting any of your buddies back to shelter?"

"Nay." He grinned, looking out over the fallen. "They've seen worse than this."

Only the truth—most of them were back on their feet, and I felt a sudden urge to be back at the ship before they could have second thoughts. "Well, we'll see you in the audience, then," I said, and held out my hand again.

"That you will." He shook it, grinning. "Be welcome in Hadleyburg."

"Thanks." I grinned back, then dropped his hand and turned away, spreading my arms wide to shoo people. "Let's load up, folks! Back to the ship for R and R."

"Rest and recreation?" Merlo looked at me as if I were crazy.

"No—repairs and refitting. All aboard!"

Nobody really argued, but as I came close, Marnie demanded, "What was all *that* about, Ramou?"

"Just establishing our bona fides as trustworthy people who aren't agents of temptation," I said.

She halted, staring. "How can a brawl prove that?"

"Dunno if I can really say—but it works. You may notice that these folks are down on sex, but they have a lot of respect for violence."

She still stared. "You mean that because we could outfight them, we are morally acceptable?"

"No—because we put up a good fight, and fought clean. None of us chickened out; even the girls stood up for themselves. That was all that was necessary. We didn't really *have* to win."

Marnie turned away, shaking her head. "I shall never understand men! Honestly! Such little boys!"

"No," I said softly, after her retreating back. "Boys are little men." Then I followed.

Prudence stepped up. "Surely you will not go back to the spaceport just because of a few ruffians!"

I stopped and turned to her. "You might say that. Not because we're afraid, of course, but because we don't want to be seen in public looking like we've just been through a food processor."

Her eyes began to widen, and I felt early tremors, but Elias stepped up beside her.

"But you have come all this way! Do you not wish to see Hadleyburg?"

I turned and looked out over the plaza. There were low buildings on the far side, most made of fieldstone with some wood. Three broad streets debouched onto the plasticrete, and I could see straight down each one until the buildings stopped. Here and there, a roof shouldered above its fellows, but most of them were only two stories high. A few shop signs creaked in the wind, and I didn't think any of them were going to light up at night. Of course, it didn't help that the day was overcast—I found out it usually was, in the afternoons—so the net impression of the place was all brown and gray, dingy, dim, and grim. Also sober, severe, and humorless.

"I've seen it." I turned back to the monorail, then remembered my manners and smiled at Elias and Prudence. One look at her was enough to set that surge of desire clamoring through me again. She could tell, and I can't tell you how I know she responded, except to say that her eyes widened a little, and her posture became more relaxed. For a Puritan, she looked downright sultry.

Elias stiffened.

"Thanks for all your information." I shook hands with him.

"But we were going to conduct you on a tour of the city!" he protested.

"I think we'd better make that another day," I said. "Somehow, I've lost interest just now—and I think most of my friends have, too."

"But you must let us show you about!" Prudence stepped forward and caught my hand in both of hers. It galvanized me; her touch was electric, and those huge blue eyes were staring up into mine, churning up everything my ductless glands could spurt—and some of my ducted ones, too. "I would not have you think that all folk of Citadel are so unmannerly! Some among us can be very hospitable indeed!"

Elias frowned at her, not liking the tenor of the conversation, but not really seeing anything he could object to.

"You and your brother have been more than courteous," I assured her. "Downright friendly, in fact—and I'm sure we'll give Hadleyburg another try. Not today, though—we're a little worn out. First day trying to get our land legs back, and all."

Prudence came to a sudden decision. "Well, if you must go, you must." She gathered up her skirts and bustled toward the car. "Come, brother! Did we not set this day to go to the spaceport and inquire after work?"

"But surely not now!" he protested.

"Why not?" she answered, and stepped up onto the train.

There really wasn't a very good answer to that. Looking perplexed and exasperated, he followed.

I was careful to let him get in between us; I was still disconcerted by my body's reaction to Prudence. No, can that "my body" stuff—it's a lie. *All* of me had reacted to her, and right after I had felt that huge surge of desire for Suzanne, too. I followed, disgusted with myself. What was I, a drooling dog, to forget everything and run panting after every female in heat that happened by?

Yes. Exactly. The animal in us never dies. Which made me unworthy of any good woman's attention.

Suzanne was looking at me strangely. I gave her a guilty glance, transformed it into a feeble smile, and turned away to climb aboard the car before I could feel that surge of desire again, or communicate it to her.

7

Since we were coming in last, Prudence and Elias sat down with me—of course. I glanced around, but everybody else was ensconced talking to everybody else, though Suzanne did cast an anxious glance my way.

Anxious? What about? We had already won the fight.

"I hope you do not have this sort of welcome every time you arrive on a new planet," Prudence said, leaning forward a little, hands clasped in her lap.

"Hard to say," I answered. "This is only our second stop—but I wouldn't say our reception on New Venus was exactly warm and ecstatic."

"New Venus! Oh! Such a wonderful name, such an air of beauty!"

"Sister," Elias warned, "beware thoughts of vanity."

She ignored him as he deserved. "A world so close to Terra! What is it like?"

I smiled. "Sorry to disappoint you, but it's just one big company town. The only business there is pumping and shipping oil and its derivatives. Everything's pretty dingy, and nobody has much to look forward to."

"Do they not?" she said, in a very subdued voice. Her gaze strayed to the window, and I realized, with a sinking stomach, that I had just described Citadel. Well, not the company town part—but the dinginess and boredom, at least.

Elias stirred uncomfortably. "Surely then, your playacting enlightened their lives."

I don't know why that term "playacting" bothered me, or why I felt mulish about the "enlightenment" part—couldn't people just have fun?

Of course not. Not on Citadel.

"It certainly seemed to liven the place up," I agreed—which has to be the most understated description of a revolution that I have ever uttered. "Of course, they wouldn't let us perform just *any* play—they had a specific one they wanted."

Elias perked up at that. "You will perform whatever play your audience wishes, then?"

"Oh, yes, pretty much. Of course, there are some plays we *wouldn't* do."

"As is proper!" he exclaimed. I agreed, though I didn't think we had the same kind of play in mind.

But Prudence was getting impatient; she had other topics on her mind. "What is it like, on Terra?"

Thin ice, here—especially with her brother watching, and her bright eyes so eager. Caution warred with my natural instinct to impress a pretty girl.

Elias saved me. "Hold, sister! I wish to learn of this play they performed!"

She flashed him a mutinous glare, but she subsided. Marnie noticed and turned to frown. Elias blithely ignored her.

I figured I'd better answer. "The Scottish play, the one Shakespeare wrote."

"Macbeth?" Elias asked.

Heads turned to stare in alarm all through the car. I felt a cold chill down my back, myself. It was ridiculous—we weren't in a theater, so saying the name of the Scottish play couldn't bring us bad luck—but I wouldn't have said that word, myself. I was amazed to realize how quickly I had become superstitious.

"That's the one," I agreed. "Of course, we had no objection to performing it . . ." Black looks from several of the company members, but I plowed on. ". . . since it *is* a classic, and an excellent play."

"What part did you play in it?" Prudence asked eagerly, leaning forward, those huge eyes gazing at me in admiration.

Why was I feeling wary? Her questions were anything but personal.

Because she was beautiful, that's why—and seemed to be showing an undue amount of interest in me. Enjoyable, of course—any man likes to have a beautiful woman show interest in him—but any amount of interest seems undue, when you're as homely as I am. I mean, if it weren't for my chin, I'd look like a Neanderthal. Of course, it might help if I combed my hair back, and let more forehead show, but I didn't really think so. No, if a woman's interested in me, she's either impressed by all the wrong traits, or she wants something.

Of course, there's Suzanne—but she's interested in everybody. Being in the same class with seventy-year-old Ogden Wellesley is flattering professionally, but not personally.

"I was just a spear-carrier," I said.

Blank looks of incomprehension from both of them.

"That's slang for a person who doesn't have any lines," I explained. Of course, I *had* spoken—two lines, but I wasn't about to admit it. "He just walks around wearing armor and carrying a spear. One of the soldiers in the battle scenes."

"Oh." Prudence looked disappointed. "You are not an actor, then?"

"No, I'm the technical assistant. That's supposed to mean that I help the technical director—Merlo, over there; he's also our set and light designer."

She blinked, then frowned, puzzled.

"You don't just turn on some lights and put up some walls," I explained. "You have to plan them out ahead of time. Here, I'm sure Merlo could explain it better than I could. . . ."

"Oh, nay!" She put out a hand to stop me as I started to get up. The hand brushed my forearm, setting up shock waves that worked their way inward fast. I sank back.

But Elias had seen the physical contact; his face darkened. "Sister . . ."

"An accident, Elias," she said quickly, then turned back to me. "How is it, then, that you were on the . . . stage, do they call it?"

"They do," I said, "though in this case, it was a gymnasium floor." Glad of the chance to change the topic, I said, "Do you have a theater here?"

"Oh, nay!" Elias said, affronted, and Prudence hurried to explain.

"There have never been actors here before you. There is a meetinghouse, but that is for worship."

Elias nodded. "The armory is your most probable place."

Well, back to the gym.

Then it hit me—why did they have an armory? Who were they going to fight? They were the only ones on the planet!

I was about to ask, but Prudence was talking again. "There are halls for attending lectures—several of them, so that those who have heard one speaker today, may hear another tomorrow."

"Lecture halls?" Charlie said, interested. "On what topics do your speakers lecture?"

"Anything that will improve the soul," Elias told him gladly. "Philosophy, theology, metaphysics . . ."

It sounded like a really jolly evening.

Prudence took advantage of the diversion of Elias's attention to get in another question. "Is it true that, on Terra, there is a continuous riot of pleasure seeking?"

"Always one great big party?" I smiled. "No, Miss Prudence, I'm afraid that's a myth. Oh, there are parties every night somewhere, sure, and there are people who are rich enough to spend every night in a club that serves alcoholic drinks and has a dance floor, maybe even a band and some singers—but most of us have to make do with 3DT, or hanging around on somebody's porch, waiting for pretty girls to watch."

"Then it is true," she breathed.

Elias turned around, suspicious and watchful. "What is true?"

"That the people on Terra spend their days working for a living, the same as you folks do," I said, with a meaningful glance at Prudence. "And what do you do during the day, Miss?"

"Oh, keeping house, mending, making clothing." She dismissed the topic with an impatient shrug. "It is all very boring."

"Sister!" Elias remonstrated.

"But what do *you* do during the day?" she asked me.

So I was supposed to do all the talking, then. I suppose, from her point of view, anything we folks from off planet were doing was by definition more interesting than the things she knew.

"We rehearse," I said. "One play in the morning, another in the afternoon, then perform a third in the evening, when we're on a planet. Twelve-hour days about half the time. Of course, that's what the actors do. Merlo and I only rehearse when they draft us for bit . . . uh, for small parts."

"What do you do while the others rehearse, then?" Her eyes were wide and admiring.

I decided, *What the hell, might as well enjoy it*, and let myself preen a little bit. "Merlo designs the set for the next show, and we build it."

"Build it!" Elias perked up. "Then you actually do work with your hands?"

"Oh, yes," I said. "Of course, we've got equipment that makes it possible for two men to do the whole job, but we two men do have to do a lot of hauling, not to mention hammering and sawing."

"I would be very interested in seeing such equipment," Elias said.

Prudence glanced at him, annoyed.

"I'd love to show you," I said slowly, "but I don't know if you're allowed to visit a ship in port."

Prudence stilled, her eyes becoming very intent.

"Can you not bring out your tools?" Elias asked.

I shook my head. "Too big, most of them—and very solidly bolted down. Everything has to be, aboard a spaceship."

"Aye, I can see that would be so," he said with regret.

"Surely there must be some way for you to visit," Prudence urged.

Elias nodded. "There must. I shall have to speak with the deacon."

Suddenly, I was afraid of what I had started here. I wasn't all that sure that I wanted these two getting in the way aboard the *Cotton Blossom*—and I knew Barry wouldn't. Bad precedent, and all that.

"Perhaps the deacon would be willing," Prudence said,

"if you told him that such equipment could enhance your own industry."

"I assume you speak of an inner drive," Charlie asked, "not a factory?"

Elias turned to him. "She does indeed, sir. I pride myself on just such a sense of industry—but only as it is evidenced by my working, of course, and so far as is seemly."

Charlie shook his head. " 'Pride' is an ambiguous term when you are discussing spiritual values, young man. Perhaps what you are referring to as 'seemly pride' would be more accurately termed 'self-respect,' and unseemly pride could be termed 'arrogance.' "

"A good thought," Elias said, surprised to hear an actor talking about moral matters. " 'Self-respect' I could accept, sir, but I am not sure that 'arrogance' is quite what I mean by 'unseemly pride.' "

" 'Impudence,' perhaps?"

"Perhaps," Elias said slowly, "though I hesitate to use any word but 'pride'—for it is pride, we are told, that is one of the seven deadly sins."

"Yes, but surely that speaks of the sort of pride that sets itself up as being above the laws of God or man." Charlie beckoned. "Do come over here, young man, if we are going to talk at any length. I'll have an infernal crick in my neck, if I crane about to talk to you behind my seat much longer."

"Well . . ." Elias was tempted, but he glanced at Prudence, as though reluctant to leave her unguarded.

"Oh, go along with you, silly!" Prudence waved him away, the gesture covering her elation—but not terribly well. "What could befall me, here among so many folk, and with you close by?"

"Aye—'tis so." Elias stood up and stepped over to sit across from Charlie, bright with anticipation.

"Of course," Charlie said, "the seven deadly sins are a medieval concept. Are you sure they are still valid, in the modern world?"

You can't blame him. He thought he was doing me a favor.

Prudence turned to me with a gleam in her eye, all eagerness. "So you build while the actors rehearse, then perform with them in the evening! Is there no time for anything else in your life?"

"Such as socializing?" I smiled. "We always get together to chat for an hour or two after the evening rehearsal or performance. It takes awhile to calm down after you've been keyed up for an audience, after all."

"Those must be delightful evenings—so many fascinating people!"

"You'd be surprised." I smiled. "It only takes a few weeks before you've all heard each other's jokes. But it is warm and cozy, for the most part. We have our arguments, though."

"Oh, but such conflict could not trouble you!" Her eyes glowed. "I saw how skillfully you fought today, how valiantly!"

Hey, I'd already made up my mind to enjoy her admiration—especially since I was rock-sure that I wasn't going to enjoy anything else about her. But the sheer presence of a beautiful woman is pleasure enough, and it's much greater when she's looking up at you through long lashes, with glowing eyes. I grinned. "I like the occasional fight, yes—as long as it's not serious."

She stared. "Those spacehands were not *serious*?"

"Oh, they thought they were," I assured her, "and if we had chickened out, or fought dirty, they would have been—would have run us out of town any way they could, with high-powered weapons, if they had to. But when we stood our ground and defended ourselves, that proved we were good people, basically—self-respecting, and no guilty consciences, if you understand me."

She shook her head, blinking in pretty confusion through those long, long lashes—incredible, without cosmetics! "I do not. How could fighting prove that you felt no guilt? Guilt for what?"

I shrugged. "For trying to lead them astray, I guess. You'd know better than I would—but I think they suspected that we were dishonest people who were trying to make money by corrupting them."

"But you . . . I mean, of course you are not!"

So she'd been secretly suspecting that, too, eh? But if that were the case, shouldn't she have been trying to avoid me, not cozy up to me? I put the mysteries of the female mind behind me and said, "Of course we wouldn't dream of any such thing. We're all solidly moral, in our own ways—well, most of us, at least. It's just that our moral codes aren't all the same as our audience's."

She looked faintly disappointed—as I say, the female mind—but she pressed. "Different in which ways?" And, before I could answer, "You all believe in free love, do you not?"

Well! I'd read about that term in my history books, from the dim dark days five centuries behind us. Odd that it survived somewhere. "Some do, some don't." I wasn't too sure who didn't. "Depends on the person. It's not a prerequisite for the acting profession."

That faint look of disappointment again. "Do you?"

"Maybe in theory—but not in practice. Besides, 'free love' means just that—free, without constraint or coercion. Both partners have to be consenting, or it's not free—and the only way to be sure both are consenting, is for both to be eager." She was blushing furiously by this time, so I shrugged and wrapped it up. "What it really comes down to is, you and your fellow citizens are safe from us on that count, Miss Prudence."

"Or, at least, from yourself." She smiled, but surely I was imagining the trace of scorn on her lip. She was too innocent to know what I was really talking about, anyway.

"Well! And what is the topic of *this* little discussion?"

I looked up. It was Larry, more jovial than I'd seen him in a long time. He invited himself to a seat, favoring Prudence with his warmest smile. "What are you hashing out?"

Prudence frowned, puzzled again, but I said, "Love—and morality. Nothing you'd know anything about, Larry." After all, I figured Prudence deserved fair warning.

Wrong guess; her eyes lit with interest as she turned to Larry.

He was busy giving me a look of disgust. "I'm an existentialist, Lazarian—a firm believer."

"Only in the parts you find convenient," I retorted.

"Of course." He smiled. "That's the great appeal of existentalism."

"Only if you debase it," I said.

Prudence was glancing from one of us to the other with blank incomprehension. "What is this 'existenshil . . .' what did you call it?"

"Existentialism," Larry said.

"A do-it-yourself morality kit," I explained, "at least the way Larry practices it."

Upholstery sighed, and Lacey sat down across from Larry. "I heard someone mention love. May I sit in?"

"Of course," Prudence said, with her broadest smile.

It was a relief having someone else around for her to focus on.

"Don't believe a word they say, dearie," Lacey confided. "Men are all the same."

"But these gentlemen seem so much more . . . *tolerant* than our menfolk!"

"Only another lure for the innocent," Lacey assured her. "Do you know the story of Chicken Little, my dear?"

Prudence stared. "Of course!"

"Well, he's Foxy Loxy." Lacey nodded toward Larry. "Stay out of his cave."

Prudence stared in surprise, then dimpled merrily.

Larry's eyes sparked, but he smiled and said, "Of course. That's *your* territory, isn't it, Lacey?"

"If I wanted a caveman, Larry, I'd look in the museum—but that's *your* territory, isn't it?" She turned back to Prudence. "Just how far astray was Ramou trying to lead you, my dear?"

"I think he was trying not to lead me astray at all," she returned, "and having heavy going."

And the two of them were off into a discussion of the foibles of mankind, which they both seemed to agree far outnumbered the foibles of womankind. Larry sat there and smoldered, casting occasional venomous glances at Lacey, which she blithely ignored, and stabbing stares at me, for having got there first, and wasted the opportunity. He seemed to feel it should have been his.

Of course, there hadn't been any opportunity, really. I had Prudence pegged now—she wanted the excitement of pursuit, but was granite sure she wasn't going to get caught.

Not that I was about to try, anyway—the last thing I needed was a charge of corrupting the morals of a maiden, on a Puritan planet. Let Larry get himself fried—or married, as the case might be.

No, scratch that. I glanced at him with concern, noting the sunny smiles he was giving Prudence, just in case she happened to turn his way. If he got in trouble, we all got in trouble. I decided to make Larry my pet project for the next couple of weeks, and to try to raise his moral standards, whether he was willing or not.

Personally, I thought "not" might be more fun.

The girls were still chatting as we came into the terminal and strolled up to the customs tunnel.

"Thank you so much for guiding us!" Lacey turned and caught Prudence's hand. "You've been so much help, really! We know so much more about your world, now!"

"Oh . . . why . . . we were glad to be of assistance," Prudence said, a little taken aback.

"Aye, it was our pleasure." But Elias was looking surprised and disappointed, too. "Call on us again, if you have need of us!"

"Oh, we will!" Suzanne turned to beam at him. "But how will we find you?"

His face cleared considerably. "We live at Number Eleven, Fourteenth Street, in the house that was our parents'. Anyone can guide you to us."

"Then don't be surprised if we come calling."

"Don't be surprised, indeed." Charlie clasped Elias's hand firmly. "Thank you for a most enlightening chat, young man. I find your theology quite interesting."

"Thank *you*, Mr. Publican!" Elias shook his hand. "Your conversation was stimulating. I will be eager to renew the discussion; I am always glad to explain our faith."

While they were fighting the rearguard action, the other members of the company had prudently been lining up at the customs tunnel. "Is it *really* necessary to be searched again?" Marnie demanded loudly. "We're only going to our ship! We'll be back tomorrow, or certainly the next day!"

"Absolutely necessary," the guard said, wooden-faced. "We must be sure you are taking no illegal goods to your ship, you see. Passport, please."

Marnie gave him her most theatrical sigh as she fished in her belt purse.

"Passports?" Prudence stared, dismayed. "Must you have a passport for nothing more than to go to your own ship?"

"Seems so," I commiserated. "Your security guards are mighty strict." Inside, of course, I was jumping for joy with relief.

Prudence turned on Elias. "How can we be given passports?"

"Why . . . I do not know," Elias confessed. "But I shall learn it!"

"Sorry." I seized her hand and gave it a shake. "Got to run. Can't keep the rest waiting, you know."

"Yes—good-bye." Larry took her hand, almost caressing it. "I hope you will come and see us again, when we have rented a hall."

Prudence's smile bloomed, and she blushed prettily, lowering her gaze. Elias noticed—finally—and gave Larry a look of stern indignation. Too bad Larry had just turned away to customs.

Charlie was the last to leave the siblings. "We shall surely send someone by to let you know when we've hired a hall," he promised. "Good-bye for now, young folk."

"Good-bye," they both said, and Charlie turned, walking away from them and toward me—and customs. Then I turned around to step into the tunnel, and endure the gamut.

When I came out, all four women were hugging themselves and shuddering. "They may be innocent," Lacey was saying as I came up, "but it certainly *feels* as if they're doing something!"

"We shall never know," Winston said, trying to sound sympathetic.

"Prurience aside, the rays they use can't be very good for us!" Grudy said.

"They probably don't do you any harm," Merlo said, "as long as you only get blasted with them once every few months."

Marnie looked up, appalled. "But we are considering being dosed with them twice a day! For at least a *week*!"

Winston nodded grimly. "We may have to speak to Barry

about taking up temporary accommodations in Hadley-burg."

Suzanne shuddered. "I hate to think what their idea of a standard of living is!"

"Hard beds and straight chairs." I put an arm around her, hugging. "And a meal ticket to a soup line. We'll find a better way, Suzanne."

She flashed me a brief smile of gratitude, but her eyes were haunted. "You're a real comfort, Ramou. I just hope you're right."

"At any rate, we're done with them for now." Winston looked up as Charles came out of the tunnel. "All together now? Good. Let us return to our proper places, my friends."

We trooped back aboard the ship, feeling singularly weary and worn. Nobody made any move to go to the cabins—by common consent, we all headed for the lounge with its big, soft easy chairs, its deep carpet, and its sense of warmth. And its drink machines.

I started punching in orders. "It wasn't really all *that* cold out there, folks."

"But you didn't even ask before you coded for hot buttered rum," Marnie pointed out. "I'll have Irish coffee."

"Mexican coffee for me, please."

"Hot Long Island iced tea."

I brought Ogden his, more tea than alcohol—lots more. As soon as I stepped away, Suzanne started punching. She brought a tray around for the other veterans, leaving Larry and Marty to punch up their own—I had already taken care of Marnie and Grudy.

We sat down, took a sip of something hot, and expelled one unanimous sigh of relief.

"Well," Marty said, "at least we have some idea what we're up against, now—thanks to Prudence and her brother."

"Not 'Elias and his sister'?" Lacey said pointedly.

"*You* focus on Elias, if you want to."

Lacey shuddered. "No, thank you. Oh, I'm sure he's very nice and all that—but he *is* a bit of a cold fish."

"Not to mention his being a sexist," Marnie said. "I feel sorry for his sister."

"Oh, she seemed well enough able to take care of herself," Lacey said, and beamed at me. "She certainly seemed taken with *you*, Ramou."

"Wasn't she ever!" I said. "How come you all left her to me?"

"I was sure you could cope," Lacey said. "After all, she *is* just a sweet young thing. How was I to know she'd make a play for you?"

I stared. "She didn't! I mean, it may have looked like that, but she was really just asking about what it's like in theater!"

"Making you feel like the big, all-knowing, sophisticated hunk, no doubt." Lacey did seem to know the techniques. "And—'love and morality,' was it?"

"She was saying that all theater people must be loose and lewd," I protested. "I was trying to say we weren't!"

"Nice trick, if you can do it," Marty said. "Me, I almost lost it when Elias said how he'd been told actresses would try to corrupt him. It was all I could do to keep from saying, 'What about actors?' "

Winston exhaled with a long whistle. "Oh, I am so very glad you did not say that!"

"Perhaps we should rename the ship," Charlie suggested. "Instead of the *Cotton Blossom*, it should be the *Sodom and Gomorrah.*"

I frowned. "Why is it the *Cotton Blossom*, anyway?"

"That was the name of the showboat in Edna Ferber's novel," Merlo told me, "the book that was adapted into the pioneering musical drama."

Charlie nodded. "Before that, it was the name of several of the more famous showboats—the real ones, that used to play the Mississippi river towns."

"Several?" I stared.

Charlie nodded. "I presume that the first one was very successful, so the name became a sign of good fortune."

"A charm, you mean." I pursed my lips. "Y'know, Barry wants us to outfit the whole hold as a regular theater . . ."

"I wish he had." Marnie shuddered. "Every time I think of going through that customs tunnel, I get gooseflesh all over again. It would be so much nicer if we could just stay here and let the audience come to us!"

"You weren't saying that a few hours ago," Winston reminded her.

"I hadn't met the gentle citizens of Citadel then, or seen how depressing the landscape is! I swear, this ship never seemed so cozy before."

"Quickest cure for cabin fever I ever saw," Merlo opined. "Suppose we could bottle some of Citadel and sell it on the open market?"

" 'Broad-spectrum panacea'!" Marty proclaimed. " 'Cures all sorts of impatience, frustration, and general discontent'!"

Ogden nodded. "Anyone who thinks he has it bad, need only try a dose of this."

"Oh, surely we're being unfair!" Grudy protested.

Nobody answered.

"Well . . . perhaps not," she conceded. "That poor child Prudence *did* seem to be champing at the bit."

"At the chains, you mean!" Marnie shuddered. "We forget how fully we women have been freed from the prison of men's subjugation of us!"

"Three hours ago, I would have resented that statement," Merlo said. "Not now."

"He didn't seem to boss her around *that* much," Larry objected. Lacey cast a startled glance at him.

"No, but when he did, it never seemed to occur to him that she might resent it," Marnie said bitterly.

"She didn't obey, though! When he scolded her or rebuked her, she ignored him!"

"Purely their own personal relationship," Marnie assured him. "They both knew he could enforce his dictates by law, if he wished."

I was about to challenge that—not that I disagreed, mind you, but I hadn't seen any real evidence—until Winston nodded. "It was in their attitudes, in their tones. She knew she was getting away with murder, and could do so only because her brother cherished her too much to punish minor infractions. At a guess, I would say she is the elder."

"Even so," Suzanne said, "he was interrupting her every other sentence, and all she could do was glare and bear it."

Ogden nodded. "One of those cultures in which women are only *meant* for bearing."

"And pleasure," Lacey said darkly.

"No, I wouldn't even say that," Ogden said, "at least, not within the bonds of marriage."

"Hey, you're not being fair," I objected. "We're just assuming they've got brothels hidden away somewhere."

"Oh, I'm sure they're illegal," Winston said. "But human nature is human nature, and not even the Puritans were able to change that. Haven't you ever read *The Scarlet Letter*?"

"I'm more concerned with what we *have* witnessed," Marnie said. "You made a nice try at letting her talk, Ramou, but he always took it away from her, even when you asked her directly!"

I looked up at Charlie with sudden realization. "It wasn't *me* you were trying to bail out by sidetracking Elias—it was Prudence!"

"I thought I would be helping both of you, actually," Charlie answered, and Suzanne gave him a frown.

"She had a lot of spirit, for a member of the downtrodden," Marty pointed out.

"Yes, she did, really." For once, Larry agreed with him. "Tremendous vivacity! I was amazed she could seem so enthusiastic about life, forced to wear that ugly sack!"

I nodded. "Personality plus. You'd almost think she doesn't know she's been ground down."

"But she will, she will," Marnie warned them. "As the years go by, this oppression will erode her spirit more and more. Her eyes will lose their sparkle, her hair will lose its luster; her shoulders will droop, her mouth will sag. She will rarely smile, and never, ever laugh."

Larry stared. "Surely not!"

"That would be a crime," Marty said, staring, appalled.

I shuddered at the thought, then looked up at Marnie, frowning. "This is moral?"

"Not a bit." She smiled sweetly. "Perhaps we should do something about it."

8

I'm not sure I wanted to hear what she had in mind, so maybe it was just as well that Barry and Horace got back just then.

They came in looking as if they had just been through the mill, and I don't mean the one in Paris. Maybe the one that tossed Don Quixote around—but Publius came trotting right behind them, looking almost cheery. Certainly vastly relieved. We all stared. Then we cheered.

Publius looked around, dazed and amazed, then smiled and waved. A second later, he realized where credit was due, and turned to bow toward Barry and Horace.

"Hail the conquering heroes!" Winston called.

Ogden echoed, "Here, here!"

"Saved from bondage!" Publius cried. He plopped down into an empty easy chair and sighed. "It is so good to be home again! Soft chairs! Carpet! Heat!"

We all stared.

Barry and Horace lowered themselves carefully into recliners and went limp, sighing, leaning back; the recliners adjusted to cradle them. I leaped for the drink machine and punched up hot buttered rum for both of them.

"Thank you, lad." Barry looked up at me with a weary smile—and I was appalled. He actually looked old. Sixty isn't all that ancient these days—in fact, it's barely middle-aged—but Barry looked at least a hundred.

"Do we have to go out again?" Horace murmured. "Can we not simply stay in here?"

"We know what you mean," Winston assured him.

But Ogden huffed himself up and said, "You'll get over it, Horace. Everyone who lives in New York feels that way once in a while."

"Yes, but when it passes, they have New York just outside the window." Horace's nose twitched at the aroma of the rum. He opened his eyes, saw, and a beatific smile spread over his face. He took it, looking up at me. "Ramou! So good of you, my boy!"

"It seems to have been a harrowing day," Winston said carefully.

"It has," Barry said, leaning his head back and closing his eyes. "Perhaps we should make a pact not to tell one another about our travails."

"An excellent notion," Ogden rumbled, "but one that is bound to invite disaster. Really, Barry, we must insist."

"Maybe we ought to ask Publius," Merlo said. "He's looking in better shape than either of them."

"Only relief in being back in civilized surroundings, and among friends," Publius assured him. "The Citadelites do heat their houses as much as they absolutely have to, but not a jot more."

"Or their hearts," Marnie said sourly. "But tell us the worst, Publius. Didn't you make arrangements this time? Or did you fail again?"

"Marnie!" Barry chided, lifting his head to frown at her, but she kept her gaze fixed on Publius.

He shifted his chubby bulk uncomfortably. "Yes, I suppose that is the long and short of it. But I did succeed in sending you a warning!"

"I suppose that is something," Marnie said, "though not much. What is your excuse this time?"

"The best, Ms. Lulala—they wouldn't allow me."

"Allow you?" Winston frowned. "Allow you to do what?"

"Anything," Publius said. "Wouldn't allow me to put up posters, wouldn't allow me to rent a performance space—wouldn't allow anything."

A shiver of foreboding rattled down all our backs. I had to know, though. "Why, Publius?" I asked. "Did you get the wrong person angry on the way through customs, or something?"

"Not at all." Publius braced himself visibly. "You are *not* going to like this."

"You may be certain of that!" Marnie said. "Get it over with!"

Satisfied that we were all properly warned, Publius nodded and said, "They don't allow theater on this planet. Not any kind of theater. None at all. The closest they come is the public exhibition of a few carefully selected 3DT epics—the ones that will be morally uplifting and, essentially, religious teaching tools."

The announcement was greeted with a stunned silence.

Then Marnie turned on Barry in rage. "You! You incompetent, shortsighted, naive juvenile!"

"I admit it." Barry moaned, head back, eyes closed. "I admit it all. It was my idea, my proposal, myself who pushed it through. I have brought us all into disaster."

"Not at all!" Horace lifted his head, frowning. "I discussed the idea thoroughly with you, old chap, and concurred every inch of the way! The responsibility is as much mine as yours!"

"Oh, don't think that way, Mr. Tallendar!" Suzanne hurried over to his side, almost in tears. "It was only a mistake, that's all. You couldn't have known!"

"Of course he could, if he'd done his research!" Marnie snapped.

"No, he couldn't!" Suzanne turned to her, shielding Barry. "These Citadelites are careful not to let the rest of the Terran Sphere know anything more about them than they absolutely have to! Even the people who have visited here don't know they're so insanely strict and . . . and . . ."

"Ascetic," Winston murmured.

"Ascetic! Even Captain McLeod had been here before, and *he* didn't know! How could Barry and Horace have found out?"

"If they couldn't find the information," Marnie grated, "they should not have considered the visit!"

"But they *did* have information," I told her, "as much as anyone has about this place."

Marnie glared at me furiously, but before she could say anything, Winston said, "Aren't we rather missing the point?"

"The point!" Marnie spun to him. "The point is that we cannot perform, and if we cannot perform, we cannot earn local money, and if we cannot earn local money, we cannot buy fuel! The point, Winston, is that we are stranded on this dried-up harsh little backwater! Stranded in a cultural desert!"

"Quite so," Winston said. "Therefore, the point we must consider is: 'How are we going to get out?' "

"Good question," Ogden rumbled. "We can't just sneak out the back way while the desk clerk isn't watching, you know. How *do* you escape from a planet?"

"Without fuel?" Larry spat, his eyes blazing.

"You don't," Marty said with a hangdog expression.

"We could just stay on the ship, couldn't we?" Grudy asked hopefully. "We may not have enough fuel for lift off, but we can power the food synthesizers and the drink dispensers."

"For the rest of my *life*?" Lacey cried, verging on hysteria. Her eyes streamed, and Suzanne took an involuntary step toward her. Then she took two more, knelt, and held out her arms. Lacey went rigid, wavering for a moment, then reached out herself and collapsed into Suzanne's arms, sobs racking her chest.

Barry and Horace both bowed their heads, looking very old indeed.

"Won't work, anyway," Ogden opined. "Sooner or later, they'll want us to pay more port fees—in local currency."

Winston and Merlo looked up at him in surprise; Ogden wasn't usually so practical.

"That's true," Merlo said slowly. He was the first officer, so he knew. "The usual port fees, they'll accept in Terran currency—but after two weeks, or whatever the standard turnaround time is here, they'll start charging overtime."

"But surely they will accept off-world money!"

"I haven't asked," Merlo said, "but I'll bet Ogden has guessed right."

"And how do we get local currency if we can't perform!" Marnie demanded.

"We lecture," Barry said, with closed eyes, head back.

Everyone was quiet, startled, except for Lacey's sobs, which were calming now.

"That's right!" I cried. "Elias said they go to lectures for recreation! Anything that's spiritually improving!"

"Elias?" Barry lifted his head, actually reviving a little.

"Spiritually improving?" Marnie stared at me as if I were crazy. *"Us?"*

"We can be very spiritual, if we have to be," Winston assured her, "and quite intellectually uplifting, I'm sure."

"What about, though?" Ogden rumbled. 'What lecture can we present?"

"A lecture on heads," Barry said. "It brought our professional forebears through the worst the Puritans could throw at them, and it will save us, too."

We all stared, except Charlie; he just nodded judiciously.

"What," said Marty, "is the lecture on heads?"

"He should have said, 'lectures,' actually," Horace explained. "We think there were more than one."

"You 'think'?" Marnie said. "You don't *know*?"

And Marty asked, "Do you have the script?"

"Alas, no, to both questions," Horace returned. "There is only the reference to it, among the founding fathers of the American branch of the profession. Occasionally, they would arrive in a New England town to find that plays had been prohibited since their last visit. At such times, they would eke out a living by delivering lectures on heads."

"If it worked for them, it can work for us," Barry said. "In any milieu in which the only entertainments allowed are lectures, readings, and concerts, we should do brisk business."

"If we have anything to do at all," Marnie said scathingly. "Do you have any idea what these 'lectures on heads' were?"

"I'm afraid not," Charlie said, quite unexpectedly. "Unfortunately, none have survived from the early days when they were the fallback of the early companies attempting to tour the New World."

Marnie spun about to face him. "What do *you* know about this?"

Charlie gave a modest shrug. "Just something I picked up in my reading."

"You certainly seem to do a lot of reading!"

Charlie gave her his most charming smile. "When your face and form are as undistinguished as mine, you have to indulge in the quieter amusements." He turned to Horace. "Have you any basis for your script?"

"None," he admitted. "We will have to reconstruct it as much by imagination as by anything else. It seems obvious, from the title, that the subject of the lecture would be heads—but phrenology had not been invented when the early American actors delivered their speeches, so I think we may neglect the scientific approach to describing the human cranium."

"Maybe they were talking about heads that were no longer on bodies?" Marty suggested.

"A worthy idea." Horace ignored the exaggerated gagging in the background. "If such were the case, the head of John the Baptist would come first to mind."

Winston nodded judiciously. "Appropriate, for our current prospective audience."

"And not at all repellent, to you," Marnie gibed. "Any 3DT villain has handled dozens of amputated heads!"

Winston took it without batting an eye. "Yes, but only prop heads, to be sure."

"Still, I think the general principle is clear," Charlie said. "We are talking about the heads of famous people. Should we restrict ourselves to those who have had their heads cut off?"

"An excellent thought." Horace was fast reviving under the stimulus of conversation. "Certainly that could be the topic of one lecture—a sort of cautionary tale."

"You mean, 'Don't do this, or your head will be up here, too'?" Marty asked.

"Quite so—and a brilliant notion, Martyn!"

"Huh?" Marty looked all around him. "Who, me?"

"Indeed!" Barry leaned forward, energy beginning to flow again. "We illustrate the lecture—have the heads lined up on a table, for all to see!"

"Prop heads?" Marnie asked, with some trepidation.

"No—living heads! Several actors sitting beneath a counter, with holes cut in it for their heads to poke through!"

"Hey, great idea!" Marty sat up, grinning. "And the heads talk back?"

Horace started to answer, but Barry said, "Not at first,

Martyn. That might bring it too close to becoming a play. Let us attempt it with the heads merely grimacing, and see if the censors will let it pass. If they do, we might try the occasional line of dialogue."

"Comic, of course," Marty said.

"We will include the odd bit of comic relief, I am sure. However, the preponderance of the speech must be serious, at least at first."

Marnie frowned, beginning to catch their enthusiasm in spite of herself. "Can you really hold an audience with unrelieved seriousness?"

"I believe we can make it sufficiently dramatic, yes."

There was an actual ripple of laughter at that—anyone who had played in a thriller knew that they could keep an audience on the edges of their seats, if they did it right.

"John the Baptist as a murder mystery?" Marty hazarded.

"Did Herod really do it?" Lacey caught the mood.

"It could be that he has just been receiving bad press all these centuries," Larry offered.

"No, I think we had better stay with the established villains, at least at first," Barry said.

I was beginning to make a catalog of all his "at least at firsts." When he decided to pull out all the stops, this speech could become very interesting.

"All very good, for a beginning," Charlie said, "but won't there be some restrictions on who may deliver a lecture, and who may not?"

"I am officially qualified," Barry said. "I do hold a master's degree."

"Yes, but you are not a minister."

"Oh, so *you* will deliver the lecture!" Marnie said, bridling.

"I am afraid so," Barry answered, "at least . . ."

"At first!" everybody chorused.

Barry looked around in surprise, then gave us a rather sheepish smile. "Yes, I have rather been doing that a lot, haven't I? I am beginning to be eager to design a lecture without the precautions."

"Not . . ." Horace began.

"At first!" we all finished for him.

"But will they accept your credentials?" Charlie asked.

"That remains to be seen," Barry said grimly.

Charlie pursed his lips. "I should think you would need something resembling a text to show them."

"Yes, I should think so," Barry agreed. "I shall have to see what I can draft tonight."

"I could rough something out for you."

Barry bowed his head, taking a deep breath. "I . . . am very grateful for your willingness, Charles. . . ."

"But you think it might be a bit too academic?" Charlie smiled, amused. "No, I wasn't thinking of the actual wording, Barry—more of an outline."

"That could be useful," Barry said slowly.

"Hey, I could whop something out, too," Marty cried. "Different topic—and probably for 'not at first.' But it might come in handy, some time."

"Strike while the iron is hot," Barry agreed. "Write what the muse brings." He turned to the rest of us. "If any of you others feel like drafting some notes, or even a few paragraphs, I will appreciate all donations."

"Who do you think you are, the United Charities?" Marnie scoffed. "Still, I might have an idea or two, myself . . ."

Barry didn't look terribly reassured, but he said, "Thank you, Marnie. I would be interested in the woman's viewpoint."

"The deacons won't," she said grimly, "but I shall write it anyway."

"So, then! Armed with a rough draft, I shall beard the deacons in their den!" Barry turned to Publius. "How do we begin? Walk in, or ask for an appointment?"

"We can begin with the municipal offices," Publius said. "I haven't inquired about lecturing, but I assume there must be a standard procedure for it, since it seems to be done regularly. I shall go in to town tomorrow and make the appropriate inquiries."

"Since I am the one who intends to lecture, I had better go with you," Barry said. "Certainly it will be more efficient, if my signature is needed on a document or two."

"Speaking of efficiency," Merlo said, "maybe Ramou and I ought to spec out the lecture hall, and make sure it doesn't have any unpleasant surprises, like no P.A. system."

Everybody shuddered, remembering trying to perform the Scottish play in a vast gymnasium with no audio equipment except what nature provided.

"Yes, a good idea." Barry nodded. "Publius, do you know where they would go?"

"Yes, I do—the main lecture hall was one location I did note, since it seemed as close as we would come to a theater." Publius turned to Merlo. "It is at the corner of Fifteenth Street and Fifteenth Avenue, right in the center of town."

"Center of town?" Merlo asked, puzzled. "Fifteenth and Fifteenth is the center?"

"How creative," Larry sneered.

Publius nodded at him. "As you note, creativity is somewhat low on their list of virtues. The town is a grid—'streets' run east and west, while 'avenues' run north and south."

"They might not approve of New York," Horace mused, "but one of the original pioneers probably came from there."

"Who would know better why to disapprove of it?" Barry said, with irony.

"But," Merlo said, "if Fifteenth and Fifteenth is the center of town, that means there're only thirty streets and thirty avenues."

"Thirty-five, actually," Publius said. "The town has grown a bit since it was first laid out two hundred years ago."

"Only five more streets in two centuries?" Merlo shuddered. "Not exactly a metropolis, is it?"

"No. The majority of the people do farm, after all—it's only the merchants and space crews who live in Hadleyburg. And the deacons and other central-government workers, of course."

"Of course," Ogden said. "I'll wager Hadley was the pioneer from New York."

"Hadley? Oh, you mean the man after whom the town was named." Publius nodded. "I would agree with that guess—but I don't really know."

"But," I said, "if this small town is the biggest city on the planet, where else can we perform?"

"Nowhere," Barry said grimly, "so we had better impress the deacons with our offerings. Let us go to dinner, friends, then adjourn to drafting ideas and scripts. We must lose no time, no time at all."

There was a stack of hard copy waiting beside Barry's place at the breakfast table the next morning. He sat and lifted the top page, ignoring his meal. After ten seconds, his eyebrows rose. After thirty, he looked up at Charlie. "This is good, Charles, very good indeed! I did not know you were so gifted a writer!"

"I'm not," Charlie confessed. "I roughed out a sequence of ideas, as I promised, then turned them over to Marty, for his treatment of them, and another copy each to Winston and Marnie. Then, before breakfast, I took the liberty of combining them, taking what I considered best from each draft."

"When do I manage to deliver my own ideas in my own words?" Marnie demanded.

"Peace, my friend." Barry held up a palm without taking his eyes from the hard copy. "Let us see if we can perform this first script without incident, before we discuss providing others . . . Yes, eminently satisfactory!" He tucked the copy into his portfolio. "In fact, excellent. And these others?"

"The ideas you asked for," Marty said. "Nothing to do with the script you just read. That's my outline for a lecture on folly, on the bottom there. I think Ogden's is on top."

"Order of seniority," Ogden rumbled. "May I have more, ah, 'orange juice,' Ramou?"

"Sure, Mr. Wellesley." I set the glass down and took away the empty. He didn't seem to be noticing that he was almost down to straight O.J. by now.

"I shall look forward to reading them with the greatest of pleasure," Barry promised, "but just at present, I think I had better eat and run. The municipal offices open in a half an hour, Publius?"

"Forty-five minutes," Publius said. "We should just make it."

"We'll ride in with you." Merlo tucked in his last bite

and stood. "I'll just pick up a cup to go, and meet you at the air lock."

" 'Fraid you'll have to clean up by yourselves this morning, folks," I said. "Duty calls—or at least, Merlo."

We cycled through the air lock, hiked over to the terminal, and ran the Customs gamut again. Horace shook himself as he came out. "I really wonder if whatever sort of rays they are using in there are truly beneficial for us, Barry."

"I cannot believe they are," Barry answered. "If we were staying here more than a week, I would see to securing hotel facilities—if we had local currency."

"Well, hello!" a sunny voice cried.

I didn't freeze, but I slowed down to a crawl. Then I lifted my head, turning slowly, forcing a grin.

There she was, hurrying toward us, all rosy and blushing, eyelashes fluttering—and I felt my heart give a sudden lurch. Oh, but she was beautiful! I couldn't help wondering what the form underneath the billowing dress looked like—a wondering that was fast becoming a longing, one that was making me ache in all the wrong places. Suddenly, my smile wasn't forced at all. In fact, it was growing.

Merlo was smiling, too—he wasn't anymore immune than I was. But Barry, Horace, and Publius were looking up in surprise—gratified surprise, but surprise nonetheless.

She gave them a bright "Good morning!" on her way past to me, then said, "Good morning, Ramou!" head tilting to the side, smile sweet, eyelashes fluttering.

"Good morning, Prudence," I returned. "Have any luck with your job hunt?" I really wanted to ask, "What the hell are *you* doing here?" but it sounded nicer this way. Besides, I didn't really care what she *was* doing here—I was just glad of it.

"Oh, very well! They thought I was so promising that they asked me to come back today to talk to the superintendent!"

"Great!" I couldn't help meaning it. "When's your appointment?"

"I've just finished. He thought I was very promising, too."

Whatever the promise was, I was sure it wouldn't be kept. "But no job, huh?"

"They'll let me know tomorrow. Are you going into town now?"

"Yeah, we're on our way." I turned to Barry and Horace, stalling. "Prudence, these are my bosses."

Her eyes lit up.

"Barry Tallendar," I said, "our managing director—his associate, Horace Burbage—our advance man, Publius Promo . . ."

She gave each of them a shy smile and her hand. "What is an 'advance man'?" she asked Publius.

He puffed himself up. "I go in advance of the company, miss, to rent a theater or some other kind of performance space, and arrange for publicity."

She trilled a laugh. "You must have found it very difficult, here on Citadel! How could you rent a hall, with none of our money?"

Publius' smile curdled. "That, as it happened, was the least of my problems. As you guessed, though, I made absolutely no headway. I am more than glad to turn the problem over to Mr. Tallendar."

Prudence turned to Barry, blithely unconcerned that she might have offended Publius. "Will you manage to provide us a sight of real live actors, sir?"

"Of the actors, yes," Barry said, taking her hand with a slight bow. "Of the play, perhaps not. But my friend, Mr. Burbage and I hope to persuade your authorities to let us lecture, at least."

"Oh, I shall *so* look forward to your speech!" She turned to Horace. "Will you be lecturing, too, Mr. Burbage?"

"I fear not, Ms.—" Horace said, smiling warmly as he took her hand.

She frowned prettily, head tilting to the side again. "Why did you call me 'miz'? I'm not married!"

Interesting that she'd taken the first chance to mention that . . .

Horace looked up in surprise. "Have I offended by local custom? Believe me, my dear, I did not so intend!"

She trilled another laugh. "What a pretty speech!"

"It is my stock-in-trade," Horace assured her solemnly.

"In our world, Miss Prudence, all women are addressed as 'Ms.'—capital M, small s, period. It is an abbreviation for both 'Miss' and 'Mrs.' "

"Why, how wonderful!" she cried. "Then you never need worry about whether a woman's married or not, to know how to address her! But doesn't it make it possible for you to—" She blushed, lowering her eyes. "—make advances toward a married woman?"

"A gentleman would never ever make such advances unless he was sure they were desired," Horace assured her, letting her ignore the possibility that a married woman might want to be advanced upon.

Merlo cleared his throat, ostentatiously glancing at his watch-ring.

"Oh, yes! Forgive us, Miss, but we must hurry to catch the monorail!" Barry bowed and turned away.

"Oh, if you are going into town, may I ride with you?" Prudence cried. "It is not quite proper for an unmarried woman to go about unescorted."

Barry paused, then turned back with a broad smile. "We should be delighted. Let us make all due speed, though—machines do not wait on our convenience."

"So we must wait on theirs," Horace said, offering his arm.

She took it with obvious pleasure. "What a gentleman you are!"

"The benefits of urban culture," Horace assured her. "In fact, we refer to such gestures, and the attitude underlying them, as 'urbanity.' "

Out through the doorway they went, Prudence asking question after question, Horace answering gravely.

Merlo edged over to me. "Tough luck, kid. Looks like the veterans get all the attention today."

"Do you see me crying? I guess she just prefers suaveness to muscles."

Merlo shrugged. "Women like rank, and they outrank you. They also look richer."

I nodded. "Let the old guys enjoy a little adulation for a while." I caught Horace's eye and gave him a look of thanks. He winked and turned back to Prudence, answering another question. I told Merlo, "Just fine with me."

It wasn't, though. We sat down on the monorail with her next to Barry and across from Horace, heaping flattery on them by the bushel, asking questions and listening in wide-eyed wonder. I was amazed that they were falling for it. Okay, I had, yesterday, but I had an excuse—I was young and hyped on hormones.

Still was. I found myself resenting Horace and Barry for getting all her attention, and felt this unsettling impulse to gain some status, be number one, so the pretty girl would come after *me*.

Stupid, I know—but okay, I was jealous.

So was the spacehand who sat in the corner, glaring at us—or maybe he was just suspicious. I nudged Merlo, nodded toward our fellow traveler, and muttered, "I think she has a chaperone after all."

Merlo glanced at him out of the corner of his eye and nodded. "So do we."

9

Prudence broke off from them at the monorail stop, though. "Thank you very much for all you have told me, gentlemen! What a wonderful, magical world you inhabit!"

"You wouldn't say that if you had to endure twelve-hour rehearsals," Horace assured her, "or cudgel lines into your memory at the last moment. But it has been a pleasure talking to you, Miss Prudence."

"And you, sir! May I guide you anywhere?"

"No, I've already been where they're going," Publius said, "the municipal offices."

"Oh!" Prudence said, eyes wide.

"We must see about permits, and other such boring impedimenta," Barry lamented. "I trust we shall see you in our opening-night audience, Miss Prudence."

I had a notion they were going to be seeing her a lot sooner than that.

They bowed over her hand and turned away to start hiking, and Prudence turned to Merlo and me, all rosy-cheeked eagerness. "How delightful they are! And where are you off to, Ramou?"

"The lecture hall," I told her. "Fifteenth at Fifteenth."

"Oh, good! That's on my way home! You don't mind, do you?"

Of course we didn't mind—except when she was talking to the other guy. She did a marvelous job of splitting her attention between the two of us, though—no small feat, considering I was quite content to keep quiet and watch. But she kept asking me every other question, and whenever those huge eyes were on me, and that smile inviting, I found I just couldn't keep the answers down to one sentence. It occurred to me that the girl was wasted out here—

she should have been a police interrogator. With her asking the questions, the Spanish Inquisition wouldn't have needed any torturers.

Of course, that probably would have taken the fun out of it, for them . . .

Finally, we reached the corner of Fifteenth and Fifteenth—which looked just the same as everyplace else we had passed on the way: broad streets, exact right-angle corners, low stone-and-wood buildings, gray and brown, discreet signs only, and those painted or carved next to the door. But the stumbling-stone did say "15" on each side, so we were in the middle of town, all right.

We halted, and Prudence said, "Oh! Are we here already?"

"Sure are." Merlo put out a hand. "Nice talking to you, Miss."

"Oh, I'll come along! I may be able to help."

"I don't think . . ." I began, but Merlo's elbow in my ribs dissuaded me.

"We'd love it," he said. "Maybe you can tell us how to find somebody to talk to."

"Oh, certainly! The office is right inside, but up one flight of stairs!" She hurried away in front of us, through the door.

"Never turn down help from a local," Merlo told me as we went in, "especially a young and pretty one, when you're dealing with people who don't trust you."

"Why wouldn't they trust us?" I said, my voice low.

"We're from out of town," he answered, then stepped through the door.

Prudence was already halfway up the spiral stairs as we came in; we had to hurry to catch up with her. I caught a glimpse of flashing ankles, and was amazed at the thrill it gave me—when everything else is covered up, even ankles become alluring!

We caught up with her at the top of the stairs, and she stepped over to a cloudy-glass door. "In here."

The door was labeled HALL MANAGEMENT. We let her lead the way in.

An old battle-ax in a mobcap and brown sack dress looked up, frowning over the tops of her glasses at us. I wondered about the glasses, then realized that a frontier planet wasn't apt to have the facilities for lens surgery, even though it was standard back on Terra. "What are you doing here, Prudence?"

"I was on my way home, Mrs. Hopstead, and these gentlemen were good enough to escort me." She held out a hand toward us. "They are from off-planet, and are interested in our lectures."

Mrs. Hopstead gave us both the leery eye. "Escorted you, eh? In public, I hope?"

"On the streets, and the monorail—and there were three of their fellow passengers in the car with us, and a spacehand."

I was amazed that she took the inquisition so matter-of-factly.

"You'd be those actor people, wouldn't you?" Mrs. Hopstead demanded.

"When we have to be—but most of the time, we're the people who build the sets and set up the lights." Merlo held out a hand. "Merlo Hertz here, and my assistant, Ramou Lazarian."

She ignored the hand. "We don't allow playacting here!"

"So we've found out." Merlo drew the hand back slowly. "But we have a master of arts with us, and he's inquiring with the municipal offices to see if they want him to lecture. We came ahead to see if you've got the facilities to make it possible."

"Possible!" Mrs. Hopstead exclaimed in indignation. "I should say it's possible! We have excellent facilities, young man—excellent!"

"I hope so," Merlo said. "Could we see them, just to make sure?"

Mrs. Hopstead glared at us. "I don't have the authority!"

"Oh, may they talk to Mr. Langan, then, ma'am?" Prudence asked eagerly. "I'm sure he won't mind!"

"You're sure of more than I am, then," she grumbled, "but you're a good child, Prudence, even if you are a bit too dreamy. I'll ask him for you." She pressed a patch on her desk and asked, "Mr. Langan, we've two strangers here from off-planet. Could you talk to them a minute?"

"If I have to," a crackling voice answered from thin air. "Be right out."

A door at the back of the room opened, and a tall, thin man in the regulation blues stepped out. He wore a scraggly beard and a glare. He altered the glare into a beam when he saw our guide, though. "Why, Prudence, child! What are you doing here?" Then the smile vanished, and he stared, horrified. "You're not with these two strangers, are you?"

"Yes, Mr. Langan," she said. "I met them on the monorail, and thought I should be hospitable—for the Book tells us to be kind to strangers."

"Well, there's some truth to that." He stumped over to us and snapped, "Who are you?"

"Mr. Langan, this is Mr. Merlo Hertz, and his assistant, Mr. Ramou Lazarian," Prudence said. "They're the builders for the playactors who landed yesterday."

"Builders, eh? Well, maybe there's some hope for you," he said, but from his jaundiced look, he didn't really believe it. "I hope you don't think you're going to put on a play in my hall!"

"Not since we found out they're banned," Merlo told him. "But we were thinking about a lecture."

"Oh, were you, now! And what would you be lecturing about?"

"Not us—our managing director. I'm not sure about the topic, but I think it's going to have something to do with the follies of mankind and the disasters they can bring."

He tossed it off as if it were a shopping list, but old Langan's glare softened. "Could be worthy." He sniffed. "Want my hall, does he?"

"Yeah. Could we take a look at it?"

"Why?" Langan demanded.

"To make sure it's what our director needs."

"What he needs! Be sure it's what he needs! It's the finest lecture hall on the planet, as good as you'll find in any college back on Terra! You don't need to see it to know that!" And he turned to go, but Prudence stayed him with a hand on his elbow. "Please, Mr. Langan. It would be so hospitable of us just to let them have one little look, when they've come all this way."

He hesitated, glancing from her to us and back again. Behind him, Mrs. Hopstead's suspicion sharpened.

"Well, it can't do any harm." He relented, stepping back toward us. "But just a few minutes, mind! I'm a busy man, with more than enough to do!"

"A few minutes will be fine," Merlo promised.

"Well, then, come along," Mr. Langan grumbled, and stepped past us toward the door.

Merlo exchanged a look of triumph with me, then went after him. I followed, telling our interference-runner, "Thanks a lot, Miss Prudence. You've just saved us a lot of trouble."

"I am very glad to help." She gave me a melting gaze. "But please, can you not call me just 'Prudence'? You have already let me call you Ramou."

"Sure, if it's acceptable by local standards. There isn't some local convention against calling unmarried women by their first names alone?"

"Oh, no!" She laughed, making my heart skip. "It is simply that we do not call strangers by Christian names alone, until we know them well enough so that they are no longer strangers."

"Nice to know I'm not a stranger." I grinned. Still, it did seem to me that only a few hours' acquaintance scarcely qualified us as old friends.

"Not a stranger, and, I hope, a friend, and one who will become very close indeed." She gave me a merry glance that was nonetheless all eyes, and the eyes with a very warm invitation to them. I could feel my hormone factory gearing up for overproduction.

Then she turned away, and my whole body dropped down a thousand RPMs—until she appropriated my arm, and my biological tachometer registered revving up again. I smiled, hoping I wasn't showing how I was feeling—but she smiled back, and I felt that magical moment of contact that tells you when both of you are attracted to each other. Our eyes filled each other's gaze for a few seconds that seemed to last hours, and it's a good thing she broke it in time to see the stairs, or we would have gone tumbling down headfirst. As it was, I held my gaze a few seconds longer as my feet followed the steps of their own accord while I drank in the sight of her profile, the cascade of her hair, the sweetness of eyes and lashes, little nose and full lips . . .

Then I thought of Suzanne, the woman who had most recently had that effect on me, and felt a surge of guilt. I turned to watch my great clumsy feet, reflecting that guilt was irrational—Suzanne hadn't given me even the hint of a commitment, only some heart-stopping looks that made me feel as if she wanted more of me, much more and much more intimate—and the occasional kiss had been everything her eyes had promised; they had been very occasional, and entirely too few. She was an actress, after all, and might be conveying more than she meant—or showing what she very genuinely felt, but only at the moment. As to the deep, soulful glances, I'm beginning to think every woman learns how to do that on cue; they must be born with it, or pick it up in grade school.

So I took the hormone charge in stride, and Prudence's glances with a grain of salt. We'd see if she looked at the other guys that way. After all, Larry was very handsome. Very.

At the bottom of the stairs, Mr. Langan turned and headed further into the building, where a set of double doors blocked our way, real wood gleaming with wax and polish. I stared, taken by the sight of the grain. It was a golden wood, fine-grained, with swirls and whorls like those in fingerprints, but nestled inside each other and against each other. "Beautiful wood!" I said. "Where do you find it?"

"Eh?" Langan looked up, startled. Then his grouchiness lightened a little, and he said, "We grow it inland, a few hundred miles from here."

"Where does it get that wonderful swirling grain?" Merlo asked.

"From branches that jut out every few centimeters. They pull together as the tree grows—and they're mountain trees, so they're gnarled and twisted."

I frowned. "How can you cut them up for lumber, then?"

"Oh, we've developed saw tables that will do it, following the contours of the wood by computerized sensors. Then we nest the boards against each other to make a wide slab." Langan shrugged. "Awkward it may be, but it's what we have to do if we want wood—it's one of only a few kinds that grow here."

"Worth every second of the time!" Merlo averred.

"Yeah! Lovely, really lovely!" I breathed.

Langan looked up at us, gratified, and nodded. "Then you'll appreciate our hall." He turned back to the door.

Out of the corner of my eye, I caught the expression on Prudence's face. She was looking irked, for some reason. Couldn't be very important. I watched Langan instead.

He pressed his thumb against a plate, and the lock clicked open. I was struck again by the odd contrast between the antique and the ultramodern on this planet. "It's almost as if you won't use anything modern unless you have to, but if you do have to, you use the absolute latest and best."

"Why, that is it exactly!" Prudence said, surprised and pleased, and Langan nodded. "You're beginning to have some understanding, young fellow." He opened the door and went on in.

As we followed, Merlo brushed against me and muttered, "Just don't understand too much, okay? They might decide to keep you."

That sent a chill through me, and as I followed him with Prudence still on my arm, I resolved not to be quite so obliging and sincere.

We came into the hall, and my first impression was of starkness, bleakness, rigid straight lines and geometrically perfect shapes and angles. Then I looked again, and began to see a warmth and beauty I wouldn't have expected.

Okay, so you could have called it stark and antiseptic, if you wanted—or you could have said it was clean, light, and airy, almost Japanese in its simplicity and the harmony of its proportions. Of course, it helped that the sun had finally come out, and its light was streaming in the huge, tall windows that made up most of the northern wall, while clear light came in the matching row of glass from the south. The hall was rectangular, with a raised platform at one end—I would have said it was a stage, except that it was too shallow, and had a built-in lectern. The seats stood in rigid rows, but staggered so you might have a chance to see over the shoulders of the people in front of you. They were unpadded, of course—but at least they were real seats, and had armrests; I had been half expecting benches. They were made of plastic, and the walls were plaster, painted stark white—but the stage and lectern, and the window frames, were all of that wonderful golden swirly-grained wood. In its own severe way, it was beautiful.

"Very nice," Merlo breathed, looking around him.

I nodded, feeling my spirit lift as I looked about. "Nice indeed."

There was a little pause, while Mr. Langan tried to hide a smile of pride, and Prudence watched us with a little frown puckering her flawless forehead.

Then Merlo came back down to earth. He stepped up on the platform, looked out over the seats, and frowned. "Light."

"Beautiful, isn't it?" I said.

"Yeah," he said, "but it plays he . . . uh, havoc, with lighting effects."

"Oh." I looked around, suddenly remembering that whether or not we called it a lecture, it was still going to be theater. "That's right." I looked up at the windows, but I didn't see any blinds. "I guess Barry speaks at night."

"He'd have to, anyway—but we'll have to wait until after dark." Merlo turned to Langan. "What time is sunset, around here?"

Langan frowned. "Right after dinner, this time of year. No time to work in the fields after."

Late fall, at a guess. I thought it would have helped if he could have told us an hour, then remembered that he *had* told us what was important: by the time people were done eating and ready to come to the theater—excuse me, lecture hall—it would be nearly dark.

"Anybody ever want to use projections in their lectures?" Merlo asked.

"No, can't say as they have," Langan answered. "If the words ain't good enough for 'em, why would they be giving a lecture?"

"To make their ideas more clear, and more effective." Merlo was in professional mode at the moment, no time to make fun of the hicks in the sticks. He stepped down from the stage. "So you don't have window blinds."

"Blinds? No." Langan snorted. "You'll have to wait till dark to start, all right."

"That's what I thought. What kind of lights do you have?"

Langan just pointed to the globes hanging overhead. No crystal chandeliers here, never mind how effective they are for spreading light—this hall just had a dozen white globes hanging over the seats, and one to either side of the lectern.

"We like to put extra light on the speaker, and half light on the audience, so that the speaker stands out more," Merlo explained. "Can your house lights . . . uh, the globes over the audience . . . can you dim 'em, or just turn 'em on and off?"

"Turn 'em on and off, o' course," Langan said scornfully. "What's 'dimming,' anyway?"

Their homes must have been very functional.

"Turning lights on or off gradually," Merlo explained. "Could we bring in some lights of our own?"

"I haven't even said you could have the hall yet!"

"No, and we haven't asked, because we want to find out whether or not we can do all the things we need." Merlo was really being very diplomatic. I guess he respected Langan, just because his hall was so good.

"You mean you don't want my hall if you can't use your lights in it?" Langan wasn't sure whether or not he liked the sound of that.

"Didn't say that, Mr. Langan. Frankly, it's a lovely hall, and I think Mr. Tallendar—he's our managing director—I think he'll want to speak in here, as soon as he gets a look at it. I think he'll like it so much he'll change his presentation to fit the hall."

Safe guess—we *had* to perform, and Barry was going to have to take what he could get.

"We just want to know what he can and can't do," Merlo finished.

"Well . . ." Langan looked around him, mollified by the flattery. "I suppose you could bring in a few of your fancy lights . . ."

"How much power do you have available?" Merlo asked.

"Huh?" Langan looked up, startled. "Power? Same as everybody! Fifty amps at two hundred fifty volts."

Merlo nodded, gazing upward, mentally placing lighting instruments. "Limiting, but we can manage. Alternating current?"

" 'Course! What do you think, I got my own generator? For *that* kind of current?"

"I didn't know," Merlo told him, "but I've worked places that did."

Langan snorted. "Musta been *way* out in the boondocks!"

I smothered a laugh that came out as a snort, winning a frown from Prudence, and even Merlo had to look down for a moment. When he looked back up, though, his face was clear. "Way out indeed, Mr. Langan. We'd have to bring in three poles to hang the lights from."

"Poles! Where you gonna hang *them* from?"

"We don't—they stand upright. We call them 'booms,' short for 'boomerangs.' "

"Boomerangs! Like them sticks that always come back when y' throw 'em? What do you call them *that* for?"

"I don't know, but I think it's because they used to stand right behind the returns—those were tall uprights at either side of the stage, blocking sight lines so the audience couldn't see the people backstage," Merlo explained. "We'll pad everything heavily, make sure they don't come within two feet of touching any of your walls, don't stand directly on your floor." Merlo glanced down, admiring. "Hardwood. Lovely."

"Yes, 'tis," Langan said, mollified again.

"Not that swirly golden stuff, though—what did you call it?"

"Mountain oak," Langan said, "and you're right—the floor's different. It's white teak."

It really was almost white, with a very fine tracery of straight grain.

"No relation to the Terran woods?" Merlo asked.

" 'Course not! Local, every one! We just call 'em that!"

"Didn't bring any Terran wood seeds with you?"

"Oh, we have 'em, right enough, and they've changed to fit the climate and the soil chemistry. More expensive, though—and to tell the truth, I like the local woods better. Not for furniture, of course, but for structure."

"I can see why." Merlo finally tore his gaze away from the vegetation and looked up at Langan. "Well, we'll tell Mr. Tallendar about this, Mr. Langan, and he'll probably send Mr. Promo around to talk to you about booking the hall."

"Promo! That little fat guy who's been nosing around town the last month?"

"That's him, though he's not all that fat anymore."

"Why couldn't he do all this before you came?"

"Seems to be a problem in permits," Merlo said, "us being from off-planet, and all." Which was true, as far as it went. "And they won't give permits without talking to Mr. Tallendar."

"I thought this Promo guy was talking about putting on great big fancy plays!"

"He was," Merlo acknowledged. "Mr. Tallendar decided lectures would be more appropriate to the audience here."

Langan frowned. "What's he going to lecture about?"

"Vice and virtue," Merlo said—and that was true, as far as it went, too. True of most Western drama, in fact. Come to think of it, most drama, period.

As we came out of the building, I said, "Nicely done, Merlo. Very nicely done, indeed."

Merlo shrugged off the compliment. "Not exactly the first site survey I've done, apprentice."

"And not the first time you've had to butter . . . uh, establish rapport with a local?"

"Not that, either," Merlo agreed, "not that it took much doing."

Maybe he was just aware of a local eavesdropping—meaning Prudence. "You had him pegged for an amateur carpenter?"

Merlo nodded. "Right off."

"How?"

Finally, Merlo grinned. "It takes one to know one, Ramou. Come to that, how come that mountain oak lit your smile, too?"

"Hey, I wouldn't know which side of a knife to use!"

"No, just how to take it away from a thug. Remind me to teach you some basics, Ramou." He turned away, hands in his pockets, grumbling to himself. "That's the trouble with the craft, these days. No respect for the materials. No rapport with the resources. No love of the work for its own sake."

He bulled on ahead of us, and Prudence turned to me with wide eyes. "He sounds like one of us!"

Why did those words give me a chill?

Prudence needed walking home, and I certainly wasn't loathe.

She opened the door to the house and called, "Elias?"

There was no answer.

She turned to me with a smile of apology. "Elias is not at home, so I cannot invite you in."

Funny how cultures change things. For a Terran girl, that would have been the signal that I *could* come in.

"Well, thanks for your help," I said, hands in my jacket pockets.

"It was my pleasure," she returned, taking a step closer, beaming up at me. She hovered there, waiting.

It could have been an invitation to be kissed, and every fiber of my being wanted to taste those ripe, lucious lips. I felt my head lowering, almost as if something were drawing it down, an inch away from hers, and I forced my mouth to talk so it couldn't do anything else. "Maybe I'll see you again soon."

"Perhaps you shall," she whispered, lashes fluttering as they fought to hold up the great weight of her eyelids. "Perhaps we might even find a few minutes alone, with none to watch."

That didn't quite sound like the demure and innocent Puritan maid she seemed to be. I couldn't help wondering if this was how girls found husbands on Citadel—and that vagrant thought was enough to keep me from lowering my lips that final inch. "I'll look forward to it," I whispered. "Take care of yourself."

"I will," she whispered, "for you."

The intimacy, the promise of those words, the sweetness of her breath, set my head buzzing. I stepped back a little before it was too late and pressed her hand, feeling my smile turning foolish. "Say hello to Elias for me."

Her face twisted with annoyance; then she laughed. "I shall, if I see him—but I shall say hello for Mr. Hertz, too."

So she didn't want Elias to think we'd been alone—which made me wonder about her hints for the future, even as they made regret stab through me, self-anger at an opportunity wasted. But I forced a grin and dropped her hand, stepping back further.

"See you next time," I said, and waved to Prudence as I turned away. I looked back just before I turned the corner, and she was still there, watching us go. My heart sang as I stepped out of sight. Maybe I wasn't anything to Suzanne but a friend and a chance for a fun game of flirtation, but to Prudence, I was something considerably more.

Maybe.

Or maybe not. Was she genuinely swept away with emotion? Was she really that strongly attracted to me?

It would have been nice to think so, but somehow, I found room to doubt it.

That's my problem, you see—that I'm so very susceptible to the ladies. Even if I know they're scheming, I'm still so fascinated that I forget everything except that heavenly form, those soft red lips, those mascaraed eyes . . .

So how come I'm still single? Because of my mother, whom I loved with every fiber of my being until she married that pompous ass, and my father, may his life be filled with bitches. If it worked out so badly for them that he walked out before I was even born, what are the odds it could work out right for *me*? I know I'm a rat, you see—an ill-tempered, violent rat, held in check only by the philosophy of martial arts that Sensei somehow planted in me and nurtured until it flowered. Odds are that if I every really got intimate with a woman, I'd wind up losing my temper with her someday, and I'd hate myself forever after. More to the point, if a louse like me got married, how long could it last? So every time I'm on the brink of anything remotely resembling a commitment to a woman—and that's pretty often—something within me pulls back, gets wary, says *no*! At the slightest sign of anything serious, my heart chills, and I find a way to say "Good-bye."

Except for the first time, of course—the first time, the flood of emotions carried me away so hard that I ignored the warning bells. I was in love, totally and a hundred percent, all the way into bed for a long, long night.

It lasted a week.

It lasted a week, and she got bored with me, and told me very nicely to stop coming around. It hurt, and hurt bad—but what else could I expect, with a face that would make a very handsome chimpanzee, but not much of a human male? Ever since then, I've listened to that little voice inside me that says, "Hold back!"

So I listened to it this time, too. I knew I might regret it, but I wouldn't be sorry.

Then I turned the corner, and I *was* sorry.

There were four of them, and they were all tall, scowling, and thick with muscle.

I stopped, every nerve thrilling with adrenaline.

They just stood there glaring at me, their hands balled into fists. They were young—their beards weren't very thick. Their heads probably were, but not their beards.

I gave them my friendly, loose smile, the one that makes me look like a chump who can be beaten up without any risk, and waited.

Emboldened by it, the one in front said, "We do not want strangers about our womenfolk!"

"I was just giving her an escort home," I said, "and from the look of you, she needed it."

"We would not turn on one of our own!" one of the boys in back protested.

"No, unless you thought she was encouraging a stranger," I said, "and you could jump to that conclusion as soon as you wanted a fight."

The kid turned red in the face and lunged forward, bringing up his fists—but the one in front stopped him with a hand across his chest, never taking his eyes from me. "Nay, Jeremiah. Do not let him taunt you. Let us seek to make him see reason first."

"Oh, I'm very reasonable," I assured him.

"And when you were standing so close to Prudence, just now?" Jeremiah bawled. "Did you seek to 'reason' with her? Or to *corrupt* her? Let me smite him, Nahum!"

"Nay, Jeremiah," the leader said, still holding him back. "Stranger, will you undertake to stay away from our women?"

"Sure," I said, "if they stay away from me."

"You must send them away!" another ranker shouted. "We will not have them near you!"

I shook my head. "No. That would be very rude."

"Rude!" the fourth kid bawled. "We shall be rude to you, and worse, if you go near them! If they come, send them away!"

"They'll get mad at me, boys—unless you want me to tell them, 'Sorry, can't talk now. Your young men told me not to.' "

"He mocks us," the third one snarled, and started for me.

"Nay, Hezekiah!" Nahum put out his other arm. "Stranger, give us your promise, or I shall loose them!"

"Who gave you the authority?" I countered. "You don't look like police."

"The Lord has given us authority! We must act in defense of our sisters, as He wishes!"

"It seems more likely to me that He'd want them to be able to do as they thought right," I pointed out. "After all, He gave *them* free will, too."

"He debases holy doctrine by using it to excuse vice!" Jeremiah cried.

"He does indeed." Nahum's face went hard as he dropped his arm. "Teach him the fear of the Lord, brothers."

10

I was glad Merlo wasn't there. He would have found a way to stop me.

They came for me with fists windmilling, about as scientific as an avalanche. I ducked under Nahum's first punch; his second caught me a glancing blow on the head—painful, and justifying what I wanted to do, but not enough to slow me down. I came up inside his guard with a quick combination of punches. He stumbled back, looking surprised, and I took off running.

I made about fifty meters with shocked silence behind me. Then they shouted and came pelting after.

I ran about half my ordinary speed, and they galloped flat out. I glanced behind and saw that Hezekiah was way out in front of the other two—good. I waited a few seconds longer, until I could hear his feet pounding close behind me, then stopped and pivoted, ducking and swinging a roundhouse right.

I caught him right in the belly, with all his own momentum. It damn near shoved my arm back into my shoulder socket, but he folded over my fist and went down, way down. He sank to his knees, hands pressed to his middle, making strangling, gargling noises.

"Hey, are you hurt?" I meant it; it was scary. I dropped down beside him and started massaging his lower back, though I didn't think it would do much good. Nothing really to worry about—but there was always the chance that I had damaged something inside him. He wasn't going to be able to breathe for a few minutes, though, and that's very, very scary indeed. He'd need some moral support at least.

His friends came pounding up and hovered, at a loss, not

knowing what to do. They could see I wasn't hurting him, was even trying to help. I looked up at them, nodding. "That's right—nothing we can do, except wait till it passes. It will, though—and he'll have a sore stomach for a couple of days."

They looked a little reassured, but very puzzled—I wasn't following their script.

I was following my own just fine, though. Oh, I wouldn't have tried this in New York, or Detroit, where I came from, or even the rougher neighborhoods of some of the smaller cities—but these boys were nice kids, really, and they were basically moral, though I wouldn't have agreed with their mores. So with them, it worked.

Nahum came galumphing up behind them, a bit on the woozy side. He saw what I was doing and frowned. Here was the dangerous part—it was his pride against his innate decency. He might decide I was evil just to save his own face.

Fortunately, just then, Hezekiah gave a rattling gasp, and I knew his diaphragm had unkinked. "There you go!" I slapped his back—gently. "Just takes a little while. You'll be breathing fine in a minute or two."

He proved I was right by drawing another breath.

"He'll be okay now." I stood up. "Hurting, but okay." I stepped into the middle of the street, bringing up my fists—clenched Korean style. "Who's next?"

There was a startling lack of interest, Jeremiah and Number Four glancing covertly at each other. Before they could toss a coin, though, Nahum stepped out and said, " 'Tis me. You have only scored me once, after all."

"And you scored me." I nodded. "Ready when you are."

That easily, I had turned a gang into four single combats—because they were basically decent. And from my helping Hezekiah, little though it may have been, they knew I was, too.

Nahum's fist came fast and hard, a low left I was expecting, the high right I was expecting to follow it, but the next left came in high, when I had expected low. It caught me off guard; I blocked it, but not too well, and his fist clipped me on the jaw. Pain shot through the side of my head, and I skipped back, to give it a little time to clear, and Nahum followed in fast. For a few seconds, it was all I could do to block his punches, and some of them got through—pain seared my ribs, shot through my belly. I ached to jump and kick, but I knew they'd count it cheating—I had to stick to boxing. That was all they'd understand, since I had cut it down to single combat.

Then my head cleared, and I blocked the next punch, then feinted. Nahum moved to cover the feint and got my fist in his face. He dropped his guard, startled, and I hit hard and fast with a punch to the chest and another to the gut. He folded halfway, grunting, and swung in an uppercut.

I almost got out of the way in time.

Since it was "almost," I got a very good look at his fist, just before it crashed into my face. I saw it coming enough to roll back with it, but my face screamed with pain, and my head rang. I leaped aside, then gave ground in quick jumps while he came at me in a lumbering rush—so when I crouched down, hunched over, and spun with my back to him, he slammed right into me. It threw him off just enough so that I could whirl and follow back in with three punches to the midsection and one to the jaw. He straightened up, wavered for a second, then fell back.

Jeremiah and Number Four leaped in to catch him in the nick of time.

While they had their hands full, I whipped out my handkerchief and pressed it over my face. It came away red, so I knew I had a bloody nose. I pressed the handkerchief back and breathed through my mouth, waiting for the blood to clot. "Better . . . mop him off."

Because I wasn't the only one with a bloody nose, you see. Up until that last punch to the jaw, we were just about even on points.

Nahum struggled upright, but he leaned heavily on Jeremiah. Hezekiah came up and handed him a handkerchief. He mopped a little, then pressed it into place as I had and turned to look at me. We traded stares, looking like a couple of bandits, and there was silence for a minute. Jeremiah and Number Four glanced at me as if they were thinking they ought to take their turns, but weren't quite sure.

I grinned at them under the handkerchief.

Finally, Nahum heaved himself up off Jeremiah's shoulder, swayed a little, then took a step toward me, holding out his hand. "You fought well and cleanly, stranger."

"So did you." I shook his hand. "The name's Ramou."

"Ramou?" I could see the frown under the bandanna. "What kind of name is that?"

"French," I said; then, before he could suggest anything else, "Sure you're okay?"

"Oh, yes," he said. "Welcome to Citadel, Ramou."

"It's fascinating being here." I turned to the others. "Good meeting you, guys."

"And good to meet you," Jeremiah said, though he didn't look sure about it.

"Just stay away from our girls, all right?" Hezekiah asked.

"I won't make the first move," I told him, "and I'll try to tell them a gentle bye-bye if I can. But I won't be rude, and I won't give them the cold shoulder."

"You haven't told Prudence 'bye-bye,' " Nahum pointed out.

"She's hard to resist," I told him. "Give a guy a break, will you? Could *you* tell her to get lost?"

That drew a small laugh, and Nahum admitted, "Nay. But give her no more encouragement than you can help, eh, Ramou?"

"I'll try," I told him.

He cocked his head to the side, frowning. "Think of it this way: if you burn for her so badly that you must be with her always and forever, then you must become one of us, for she'll not leave Citadel."

"*Now* I can see your point."

I disagreed with his reasoning, though. I wasn't at all sure Prudence wanted to stay on Citadel. In fact, now that I thought about it, I was pretty sure that she didn't.

"Horace," Barry said, "do tell me that you are not actually developing a fondness for this place."

"Oh, no, certainly not!" I protested. "It is just that I have begun to see, shall we say, a few redeeming virtues here."

After all, very few people would have wanted to be Shakers, but a great number of people wanted to own the furniture they built. It was something of that sort, with Citadel.

It was only my second day on the planet, but it must have been one day too long, for I was beginning to find a curious charm, even beauty, to the way they constructed their buildings. Of course, natural materials always have their own beauty, and a house that is built of small boulders mortared together, with timber frames holding the courses in place, has a charm all its own. The wood was a lovely hue, too, a deep brown, with a darker veining of rippling grain. They were very thrifty, so the front windows on the first floor were made of bottoms of bottles, melted together with additional glass to fill in the empty spaces; they admitted light, but not a great deal of vision. The street was almost Elizabethan in appearance, which made it seem very attractive.

Of course, it helped that the sky had brightened, and a glowing spot in the clouds promised that the sun might actually break through—no doubt that enhanced the appearance of the town; but I had a notion it was the morning's chat with Prudence that had really done that. There is nothing like the presence of a sweet and beautiful maiden to improve a man's outlook on life.

Publius stopped by the panels of a door that glowed with the golden highlights of wood, framed in more of the same material. "In here, gentlemen."

Over the door was affixed a brass plate that read MUNICIPAL OFFICES. Direct and to the point, these Citadelites, no question about it.

Publius held the door, and we went in. Then Barry held the inner door for Publius and myself. As I stepped through, I looked for another door to open—I might as well take my turn.

It was interesting that the good folk of Citadel had kept the quaint old custom of vestibules, to prevent loss of heat—a sort of warmth-lock, we would think of it today. Pioneers do not have energy to spare for such frivolities as force-curtains. The spaceport terminal, of course, was relatively recent, built after the merchants had begun to redirect the current of money to flow into Citadel, but even it had only the traditional doors.

We went in, and Publius led the way to an office labeled PERMITS. We went inside and discovered a chest-high counter, with several desks behind it. A woman wrapped in mobcap and regulation tent came up toward us, frowning suspiciously. Then her eye lit on Publius. "You! I told you, we do not allow playacting here! There's no point in your asking for a permit, because there aren't any!"

"I know, I know, Mrs. Hannah." Publius gave her his most ingratiating smile, hands up to placate. "We are not here to inquire about a play. May I introduce my principal, Mr. Barry Tallendar, and his assistant, Mr. Horace Burbage."

"Pleased, I'm sure." She sniffed, then looked again. "Horace Burbage, did you say?"

"That is myself." I stepped closer to the counter.

"Are you the fellow who played the Angel in *Gideon*?"

"No, that was my friend, Mr. Tallendar." I nodded at Barry. "He was good enough to obtain a part for me as Gideon's father."

"*You* were the Angel?" She turned to Barry, eyes wide. "I thought 'twas the other way around!"

"I'm afraid I don't have the figure to appear tall and distinguished," I confessed.

"But you were so good! As the father, I mean." She hadn't turned away from Barry. "And you were the perfect Angel!"

"The last time someone told me that, I was ten years old." Barry held out a hand, smiling. "But I thank you, ma'am."

"Oh! You even sound like an actor, with that funny talking!"

Alas the day, when proper grammar and useage must be labeled "funny"!

"And an actor I am, have been all my mature years," Barry assured her, "though some of us mature earlier than others. I am honored to discover that one of my performances has come to Citadel."

"Oh, it came many a year ago, sir! My, but you must be a God-fearing man, to play an angel like that so well!"

Barry kept the smile, somehow. "I am essentially religious, though my ideas on the subject are rather difficult to categorize."

She frowned. "Does that mean you don't belong to any church?"

"That is the sum of it, yes," Barry admitted. My heart sank, and we stood and waited for the ax of petty authority to fall.

"Well, let us tell you about *our* church, sir!" the woman said earnestly, leaning over the counter. "If you have a hunger in your heart, our church may fill it."

"I would be fascinated," Barry murmured, half in shock, "but I fear time does not permit . . ."

"No, no, not on city time! But if you seek, sir, I shall be glad to guide you, yes, after the day's work is done!"

"I appreciate the offer," Barry assured her, "and I hope I shall have the time to benefit by your kindness—but at the moment, I must consult you in your professional capacity."

"Oh! Surely, sir! And what was it you were wanting?"

"I wish to secure a permit to lecture."

"*You* are going to lecture?" Her eyes went wide. "Dearie me, how wonderful it will be to hear the Angel speak!"

"Not the Angel, I'm afraid," Barry said, smiling. "Only the actor."

"Well, yes, of course!" But inside, so deeply that she probably was not aware of it, she still equated the actor with the role. She had first seen Barry playing the Angel—therefore, he would always be the Angel to her. It was just fortunate for us that she had not seem him as the tempter in *J.B.* Of course, that had been a much younger Barry.

The woman took out a form, then stilled, frowning down at it. " 'Qualifications to speak'—I can't just put down 'actor,' that doesn't qualify you for anything spiritual."

Well, she was entitled to her own opinion.

"I am a master of arts," Barry advised her.

"Master of arts?" She looked up, startled. "You mean you paint pictures, too?"

"Oh, no! Well, that is, actually, yes, I do, but only for my own amusement, and only when there is time. I certainly do not do it professionally, nor is it the area in which I took my degree."

"Oh." The woman looked disappointed. "What art *are* you a master of, then, sir?"

"Well, the theater, of course," Barry said, "but more specifically, Dramatic Literature."

You could hear the capitals as he said it, and the woman was impressed without knowing why. "And is that what you're going to lecture on, sir?"

"In a manner of speaking," Barry said slowly. "My topic will be 'The Vices and the Virtues.' "

She was startled again, almost as if she had seen a donkey open its mouth and cackle. "Really, sir? Is that Dramatic Lit . . . whatever?"

"It is," Barry assured her. "As the Middle Ages were ending, the good people of the towns and villages developed a form of theater we call the morality play, in which the characters were personifications of the vices and the virtues."

"Each vice and virtue appeared as a human being," I explained, "sometimes with a name that indicated what his nature was. Everything he did, everything he said, showed that vice in action."

"Only menfolk?" She seemed a little doubtful. "No women vices?"

"Oh, there were some," Barry admitted.

I wondered why the woman suddenly seemed so wary.

"Well, it's too big for me!" She slapped the paper down in front of Barry and said cheerfully, "You'll have to take it up with the deacons, sir."

"The deacons themselves?" Barry feigned surprise, though he'd been expecting it all along.

"Oh, yes, sir! They'll want to deal with this themselves, you being from off-planet, and an actor! I mean, if you were a minister, or a master of philosophy or such, there wouldn't be the hint of a problem, I'd just have you fill out the form and give you the permit—but I've never had any other kind of a speaker apply before, and to be honest, I just wouldn't know what to do!"

"Well, if you say so," Barry said. "In that case, I would like to make an appointment to speak to the deacons."

"I'll make a note of it." The old dear scribbled on a

notepad, an actual paper notepad. "You can talk to them this afternoon, sir, at one o'clock."

"So soon? Why, what a pleasant surprise!"

"Oh, yes, sir. They meet every day at one, to discuss everything and keep things running smooth. There's other things they have to talk about today, but I know they'll want to see you right away."

That, I decided, was not necessarily a good thing.

Barry checked the watch on his finger. "Almost twelve o'clock now—you do use the Terran time scale?"

"Yes, sir. There's twenty-six hours and some for this planet's rotation, but we add the extra in at night, so folks just get a little extra sleep. If you'll set your watch back an hour now, and again at noon, you'll find it works out even."

I didn't quite follow the logic of that, and could see that Barry didn't either, for he gave her a pleasant befuddled smile and said, "Does that make it ten o'clock now?"

"No, sir, it's nine. You didn't know about the difference yesterday, you see, so it crept up on you."

Barry looked dazed, but took a stylus and dutifully reset his watch. "Nine o'clock, then. Let me see, if we went back to the ship, we would have an hour or two there before we came back—but there is that excruciating trip through customs, and I confess the walk is less than delightful . . ."

"If you'd like to wait here, sir, there's a canteen in the basement." Our hostess scribbled on a form and handed it to Barry. "There! That's your appointment form. You just show that at the canteen, and they'll give you something to drink now, and dinner at noon."

"Why, thank you!" Barry said, pleasantly surprised. "I'm afraid we cannot pay, though, since we have no Citadel currency as yet."

"That's all right, sir—it's free, as long as you have business with the deacons."

I wondered if it would have been free if she had not taken a liking to Barry.

"What a delightful system," Barry said. "We shall certainly avail ourselves of your hospitality—but before we do, I think I would like to see a little more of downtown Hadleyburg."

Publius stared at him as if he were insane.

The lady nodded. "Just as you please, sir. There's some very nice old buildings only a block or two away, built right after the First Landing—and the landing site itself is marked, with the Meetinghouse of Safe Landing right beside it. It's very popular with the merchant captains and their crews."

"As I should think it would be," Barry averred. "By the way, where will we meet the deacons?"

"Up the stairs, sir—the double doors, right at the top. That's the deacons' chamber, and there's plenty of room for any who care to hear what's going on. If the door's locked, that just means they're in private session, and you'll have to wait a bit. It won't mean they're not meeting, though."

"Thank you for the advice." Barry reached out a hand. "And for all your courtesies."

"Oh, it was nothing, sir!" She took his hand, dimpling, and actually dropped him a little curtsy. "After all, it's not every day we have an angel walk through these doors!"

I couldn't help wondering if mere Barry Tallendar would have impressed her at all, in any way. But the Angel, of course, was another matter.

We said cheery good-byes and thank-yous, and regrouped outside the office as the door closed behind us. Before either Publius or I could begin to comment on the amazing scene we had just witnessed, Barry said, "Yes, I think a brief stroll might be helpful—give us a feeling for our potential audience, so to speak. Publius, can you guide us to these sites the good woman mentioned?"

"Well . . . I think so, Barry." Publius led the way back out of the building.

The door closed behind us, and Barry forged ahead without waiting, down the steps and to the corner. Then, finally, he halted with a huge gusty sigh. "Well! Thank heaven for that role in *Gideon*!"

"Yes, indeed," I agreed. "And we had only thought of it as a great *artistic* opportunity."

"I would never have guessed it would have saved us on a foreign planet," Barry admitted. "Perhaps I should have done more religious drama."

"Well," I said, "we both carried spears in *David* when we were rank beginners, if you'll remember."

"And didn't you list King Hiram in your credits, Barry?" Publius asked. "In that 3DT travesty of *Solomon*?"

"Well, yes, but I scarcely think the King of Tyre would inspire much respect here," Barry said, "or the tempter in *J.B.*, though it is rather hard to make the point of the play without him. Still, all in all, I am rather glad that I have not discriminated against religion in my choice of roles."

Publius showed us the sights, such as they were, although I would have been hard put to tell you the difference between any two Citadelite buildings. They were all half-timbered and made of fieldstone, though some did have stucco, and the arrangement of gables was slightly different, occasionally—but by and large, the founding fathers had hit on a design that worked, and their descendants had felt it was better not to meddle with proven success. In some ways, the attitude struck me as pervading the entire colony.

The monument to the founding fathers was equally revealing—only a plain slab of rock with the inscription,

On this spot,
The spaceship *Gabriel*
First landed on this world-Citadel,
Bearing colonists to labor for
The glory of the Lord.

It was plain and severe, only a dressed stone slab that called to mind a tombstone. It evoked visions of hard-bitten men in worn clothes, and flint-faced women in long skirts, climbing down a boarding ramp and setting right out to begin digging boulders from the ground to make their houses. If they were not hard when they disembarked, they soon were, for the labor must have been strenuous for that first generation—and for the second—wearing all the "silliness" out of them, leaving room only for stern duty and grim purpose. I could not help but think that lives so lived were not the worship God desired.

As we were going back to the Municipal Offices, the sun came out again—and I could scarcely believe the difference it made. Grim and dingy stone was transformed into a glittering coruscade—apparently there were many grains of mica in the local rock—and the timbers of the buildings glowed with a richness and warmth one would not have suspected. Instead of a stern and forbidding aspect, the town now wore, if not a semblance of happiness, at least a feeling of security.

I hoped it was not misleading.

It was brisk, mind you. We seemed to have come in during autumn. "Is the harvest in?" I asked Publius.

"Most of it," he said. "Enough so that everyone can take an evening off to attend a lecture."

"Are there many sunny days here?"

Publius shook his head. "I can only speak for a few weeks, mind you, and this *is* autumn—but I have seen sunshine on only three days out of seven, here."

Everything considered, we were rather glad to step back into the warmth and glowing woods of the Municipal Offices building.

We went down the stairs to the canteen, as they called it, though it looked to me to be a full-scale cafeteria. We each took coffee—there was nothing else available, breakfast being over and lunch not yet served. On the other hand, there was no one waiting to take money, either—apparently, refreshments were gratis to all those working here, or having business to transact. The coffee was not the beverage I was familiar with by that name—I doubt the genuine article could have grown in so cold a climate—but it did have a rich and nutty flavor that was quite acceptable.

We passed the time by going through the script in some detail—Publius had told Barry that there were seven deacons, so Barry had brought ten copies. We went through it with an eye toward revisions, and altered wording here and there, but otherwise left it intact—Charles and his collaborators had really done a very good job. It occurred to me that Martyn might do well as a speech writer, if he ever tired of acting. Certainly his prose would make the average politician seem much more interesting.

After the once-over, we put the scripts away and chatted idly, having lunch—the appointment note did indeed protect us from the need to pay—and vying to see who had the most interesting story to remember. Publius had done service as a comic actor in his youth, before he despaired of becoming a star and took to the advantages of a regular paycheck, so he was as well versed as we in good dialogue and rich anecdotes. We finally had to tell him to tone down his recitation—we were attracting entirely too much attention by the quantity of our laughter. Not that there was none from other tables, of course—but it was decorous and disciplined. I felt the insane urge to stand up and tell a tale that would send them all into gales of laughter, not only puncturing their Puritan pomposity but even annihilating it. However, I had to keep reminding myself that they had a right to their way of life and their own system of beliefs, no matter how wrong they might seem to me.

I wondered, though, whether all of them really subscribed to those beliefs. It seemed incredible that no one had ever been born on Citadel who had too merry a temperament to fit in, too skeptical a mind to blindly accept everything the deacons taught, too sensuous a disposition to accept the ascetism of stone and timber. What did they do with their misfits, here?

From what I saw about me, I could only think that they bludgeoned them into conformity, probably at a very young age—but what happened to those few who were stubborn enough to hold out, who never would be reconciled? Was there a secret colony of art and senuous living, deep in the interior? Did they export hedonists to the distant planets? Or did they clap them into prison—for surely, on a world governed by deacons, a direct violation of a commandment would be a crime, and an indirect violation, a misdemeanor.

But I was letting my imagination run away with me, and probably doing the good citizens of Citadel a grave injustice in the process. We finished our meal, drained our coffee cups, and mounted the stairs to confront the deacons.

11

There is this that all government chambers have in common—the need to impress the visitor with the power and importance of those who govern, and of their right to do so—the need for pomp and majesty, if you will. Admittedly, this is difficult to achieve in an extreme Calvinist culture, with its prohibition on ornamentation and luxury, but the deacons managed it.

The deacons' council chamber was the only room we had seen that eschewed polished hardwood floors and completely avoided paneling in that wonderful, soft, golden wood. Their importance was established by the carpet that covered the entire floor—gray, and with a pile thick enough to cover your toes. The walls were bare plaster, but with a horizontal rail painted maroon—the only element of color in the room, presumably for the assistance of the old and infirm. I saw the need for it as soon as I looked at the deacons.

They sat on a dais two feet high, and the ubiquitous carpet climbed its sides and ran under their feet. It would have been an excellent place to panel with that golden wood that would have fetched a king's ransom on Terra—but here, it was ordinary, and the deep-piled carpet was the luxury, no doubt because it had been imported—never mind that, on Old Earth, it would have cost far less than real wood. In terms of impressing the locals, it was well calculated; for impressing visitors from Terra, it was a miserable failure. However, it did impress us with the grimness and seriousness of the deacons—and of the culture which they represented. It was Hadleyburg in miniature, and without the sun.

Atop the gray carpet, there were several dozen rows of

chairs, and they were actually upholstered, in charcoal gray. That alone told one that those who met in this chamber were important—and that any business transacted would take a long time. Why else would the seats be padded?

The deacons could have used some upholstering, too. They were lean and spare, men with gnarled hands that had known much toil. Their beards were gray, but their clothes were work clothes like every other man's—though these were not faded and worn; again, proof of their importance. Blue, I saw, was not the only color permitted—merely the most popular. Some wore brown, some wore gray. Only one wore black, and he was very old, and in a wheelchair; I assumed he was in mourning.

Three others were in wheelchairs, four wore hearing aids, six wore glasses—apparently aural surgery, like lens surgery, was pointless luxury here. Personally, I would have chosen as they had, rather than trust the local doctors. I suspected that anesthetic was counted a vanity, too, except in the most extreme cases. I wondered about their teeth.

They all looked up as we came in, and their communal stare was unwavering, unblinking. Also unnerving, but I had faced hostile audiences before.

A man in his middle years came toward us, carrying a note board of some sort. He was clad as the deacons were, in what one might call mock working clothes. "Gentlemen?" he said, frowning. "You are the actors."

It occurred to me that he should have reversed the question mark and the period.

"We are," Barry said, "and I have submitted an application for a permit to lecture. I believe I have an appointment with the deacons; my name is Barry Tallendar."

If the secretary recognized the name, he gave no sign, only glanced at the note board. "Yes, your appointment is registered—at least you are punctual, anyway. I am the executive secretary to the deacons."

"Of course," Barry murmured. The secretary frowned, puzzled, but I caught Barry's meaning—since the post held power and influence, this was one secretary who would not be a woman.

I also noticed that the executive secretary did not feel obliged to mention his name.

"In view of the unusual nature of your case, the deacons have decided to speak with you first." He gestured with his note board. "This way."

We followed, myself thinking, with some exasperation, that the man didn't even know how to deliver a straight line.

He lined us up between the front row of seats and the dais, but pointedly did not invite us to sit. I didn't mind, under the circumstances, since it put our eyes only a little lower than those of the deacons, giving us that much less of a psychological disadvantage to overcome. The deacons must have been intensely curious about us, to have forgone the pleasure of emphasizing their importance by keeping us waiting for an hour or two. Or, perhaps, they classed us as a major danger to the state, to be dealt with as soon as possible.

"Barry Tallendar, eh?" The oldest deacon rattled a hard copy and glanced at it ostentatiously. "You are a master of arts?"

"I am." Barry held out a small rectangular case. "Here is an authenticated copy of my diploma."

The nearest deacon took it with a poor grace, gave it a cursory glance, and passed it on to his neighbor, eyes returning to Barry. The chairman, or chief deacon, or whatever he was, waited until the paper came around to him before continuing. Then he glanced at it, handed it on, and asked, "A master of arts in theater, eh? What sort of a college gives a degree in theater?"

"Most of the colleges and universities on Terra, sir," Barry answered, poker-faced. "It has become a major field of study, encompassing four thousand years of history and theory, and a huge catalog of dramatic literature—which, is of course, my own area of expertise."

The chairman let the "of course" slide by him and asked, "Do you really feel it is a valid field of study?"

"Why, of course!" Barry said, surprised, but the chairman was holding up his hand, not done. "By that I mean, should your degree in any way be classed with a master of arts in philosophy?"

"Not with it, but within it," Barry said. "All branches of Western knowledge had their beginnings in the philosophy of the ancient Greeks, and every one of them contributes information which bears on the ultimate questions of philosophy. That is why scholars in so many disciplines receive the degree of doctor of philosophy."

A long, lanky deacon frowned. "Do you honestly compare playacting to philosophy?"

"No, I compare the plays themselves—only not 'compare' so much as 'embody.' Many plays center around philosophical issues, such as Samuel Beckett's speculations on the need to purge ourselves of materialism, or Weiss's presentation of nineteenth century Germany philosophy in his play *Hölderlin.* To a lesser extent, one can argue that no play can be truly trivial, that every play can and does teach something, whether the playwright is aware of it or not."

"I hope you do not consider presenting plays whose writer paid no attention to what he was teaching!" the lanky deacon exclaimed.

"Quite right," Barry said, "I don't."

A stocky, grizzled deacon scowled. "Do you mean to say that plays can teach religion?"

"I do," Barry said. "That is how theater originated in ancient Greece, and again in medieval Europe—by presenting religious myths and stories, by making them come alive on the stage. Peasants who would doze through the sermon in church paid attention to the same ideas embodied in plays presented in front of the church doors."

"I can see that you believe what you say," the chairman said, scowling, "or are very clever in seeming to believe it. But tell me this: What in this study of dramatic literature would concern sober, God-fearing, and industrious folk, such as all of us, here on Citadel?"

"Many things, sir, but particularly the ways in which the playwrights and actors of the late Middle Ages presented the issues of conscience in their morality plays. There, every vice and every virtue was embodied as a living character, and the common folk were able to see them fight out their struggle for men's souls. They witnessed the efforts of the tempters and the struggles of the angels, wrestling for the souls of ordinary people. In at least one most notable play, that person was actually named 'Everyman.' "

"You make this sound like *Pilgrim's Progress*," the youngest deacon said. He was frowning, of course—they all were.

Barry nodded. "Bunyan's story is quite apt. It was drawn from the same sources as the morality plays and employed the same techniques in presenting its moral fable."

The deacons were beginning to look rather dazed. But the chairman made another valiant try. "Do you mean your lecture will be a sort of *Pilgrim's Progress*? Why not just read them the book?"

"I can do that, of course, if you think it would be appropriate," Barry said, "but if you'll pardon my saying so, it is a bit elaborate, and far too large an undertaking for a first presentation. I had planned instead to offer some cogitations on the subject instead." He opened his briefcase. "Here is the text of the speech I had been considering. Would you like to see it?"

Neatly done, Barry old soul, I thought, suppressing a smile. He had invited them to censor his script—making it obvious that there was nothing harmful in it. Or should I say, nothing that Barry considered to be harmful.

"We would like to, yes." The chairman seemed surprised, and almost hid it. Barry handed the stack of documents to the nearest deacon, who took one and handed them around.

The chairman riffled through his copy. "It seems long enough, Mr. Tallendar."

We had made progress, I noted—Barry was being addressed by name.

"It is planned to last one hour," Barry explained. "Anything less, and your good citizens would not be willing to part with money to hear it."

"Money?" The youngest deacon looked up in surprise.

"Oh, yes, Solomon," an older deacon said wearily. "He did not come all this way for the sole purpose of improving our souls, you know."

"I hope that my presentation will have that effect," Barry murmured, "though I must admit that I do expect to be compensated for my pains."

"Herod . . . Salome . . . John the Baptist . . . there is certainly much to laud in this," the chairman said, paging through the script. He turned a page and stopped, staring.

"Julius Caesar? What has he to do with the story of Salome?"

"There is an affinity of vice," Barry explained. "Herod's undoing was his lust for Salome, which became more important than the word of God, given by the Baptist. Caesar's undoing was his lust for worldly power, which blinded him to the will of the gods he worshipped."

"False gods, sir!"

"False gods," Barry admitted, "but since he died before the birth of Christ, he did not have the Gospels to guide him. However, he could have hearkened to the precepts of his own heathen faith."

"A telling point," another deacon admitted.

Deacon Number Six nodded, turning a page, lips pursed. "There is virtue indeed, in this discussion. It would prove uplifting, edifying." He looked up at Barry. "Though there is perhaps a bit too much of levity in it."

"The occasional witticism serves to refresh the audience, and sharpen their instincts," Barry explained. "It is not the only device for achieving these effects; I have used others."

"I hope you do not describe the vices you speak of in great detail," deacon Number Four cautioned. I craned my neck and saw he was on page twelve—the description of Salome's dance. "We would not wish you to kindle the very desires that you claim to abhor!"

"I certainly hope that I will not," Barry said, with some asperity. "If you will turn to the description of Salome's dance, you will see that I make it quite clear that her movements were lewd and obscene, but do not describe them. In fact, you might say that I only define them."

The deacon nodded, eyes on the page. "So I see." Surely he did not really sound regretful; it must have been my imagination.

Deacon Number Five looked up at the chairman. "I cannot see any real danger in this, Joshua. Indeed, if it were a minister who stood before us with this same text, I would not doubt him for a moment."

"Nor I," agreed deacon Number Seven, "though I have only seen one or two preachers who could make the word so vivid as this." He looked up at Barry. "Will your speaking be equal to the vivacity of this text, sir?"

Indignation flashed across Barry's features and was gone. "I certainly trust that it will, sir!"

"Well, I'll tell you what, Mr. Tallendar." The chairman closed his copy of the speech and laid it flat on the table before him. "For this first lecture, why don't we pay you out of the public purse, and you offer your speech free to all who wish to see it, eh? And if we don't like it, of course, we won't pay."

"An interesting thought," Barry said slowly, "and a very productive one, for me—a free lecture should make my audience interested in future ones, even though they must pay. But there would have to be, shall we say, a minimum amount that I would consider adequate compensation for my efforts."

"Adequate? What would you consider 'adequate'?"

"Oh, let us say . . ." I could almost hear him mentally estimating the cost of a full tank of water and dividing it by a week's worth of lectures. ". . . two per person, and your hall presumably holds several hundred . . ."

"Five hundred at a time," one of the other deacons informed him, "A thousand dolors, then? That seems a bit high!"

"How much bread will a dollar buy?" Barry asked, bracing himself for a longer stay.

"Dolors, man, not dollars! Money is sorrow, and we must ever bear that in mind when we hear its name! And one dolor will buy ten loaves of bread."

I did a quick mental conversion into kwahers. I could see that Barry was doing the same; he winced. "No, I'm afraid a thousand dolors for a presentation would be the least that I could ask with any self-respect. To charge less would be to undervalue my own efforts and thoughts."

"You have a high opinion of your own worth, Mr. Tallendar!"

"Mine, and the efforts of several of my colleagues, sir. They will assist me in making the presentation more vivid."

"More vivid?" The chairman immediately sensed danger. "In what way more vivid?"

"By the use of lighting, to enhance the impact of my words, to concentrate the audience's attention and direct it—and by the exhibition of the faces of the personages I discuss."

"And how will you achieve that?"

"By my colleagues impersonating the people in question. Only their heads will be visible, the rest of their bodies hidden by a high table, so that their heads will appear to rest on its surface."

"An ingenious device." The chairman frowned, trying to find a reason to object to this strategem, but seeing no legitimate grounds. One of his subordinates saved him. "And will they talk, these heads?"

"No, sir. I shall be the only one to utter words."

"Then why not merely use drawings of these heads? We have screens and cameras; you could project them, so that the audience could see them more clearly!"

"An interesting notion," Barry said slowly, "and one much worth experimentation. We are not prepared for it at the moment, however."

"They shall have to work with the older technology, Joram," another deacon said, "and surely there is virtue in simplicity."

Joram closed his mouth with a snap, looking annoyed, but not really able to argue against one of their cardinal virtues.

"Are we agreed, then?" The chairman looked around, caught all their gazes, and nodded. "We are." He turned to Barry. "You may present this speech as we have read it here, Mr. Tallendar, and we shall pay you a thousand dolors, so that the public may attend it free."

"Thank you, gentlemen." Barry inclined his head. "I am very pleased, and trust that you will be, too. But there are still two items to consider."

The chairman frowned; he'd been planning to dismiss us. "What are those?"

"First, that we cannot rent a hall without local currency."

"There's no problem in that," the chairman assured him. "The halls are all common property, though there is a manager appointed to each one." He turned. "Joram, you are deacon of education; will you see to it that these folk have the use of the main lecture hall?"

Joram nodded. "I will be pleased."

"We shall deduct its cost from your thousand," the chairman told Barry, turning back to him.

"Ah—yes. Of course. And the other issue is related—what shall we do if more than five hundred people wish to attend the lecture?"

"I do not truly expect it," the chairman said, frowning. "Never have we had more than one hall can hold, never! Still, if it were to happen, you would have to send some away disappointed, and tell them to come another night."

"Yes—but would they not feel cheated, to have to pay on that other night, when others have seen it already, for free?"

"The point is well taken," Joram admitted.

"It is," the chairman agreed reluctantly. "Very well, sir—if you present your lecture more than once, we will pay you two dolors for each person who attends."

"How kind of you! There remains only the question of how we are to notify the public of this event, and of your generosity."

"Oh, yes." The chairman switched his gaze to Publius, frowning. "That fellow there wished to despoil our walls with garish pictures, did he not? And was distressed to learn that we had no broadcast stations and would not allow him to include his own glaring display at our 3DT evenings."

"My apologies," Publius said meekly, "but there is so little known about your world in the rest of the Terran Sphere."

"A condition that we heartily approve! Nay, there must be none of this 'advertising' of yours, none of this seeking to persuade people to waste their hard-earned cash on frivolities. You may set forth nothing but a dignified announcement, printed words only, and it must be posted only where there are boards set up for the purpose."

Publius nodded. "I know where they are, now."

I frowned, knowing how little good printed words would do on a public bulletin board—few people look at them daily, even if they should happen to pass near. "We have had inquiries already, as to our intentions in coming here. Surely you would not object to our answering such questions by word of mouth?"

"Aye, if they are asked." The chairman was wary again.

"Indeed, we would require that you state your business clearly, and with no prevarication."

"There shall certainly be no hedging," I assured him.

Barry glanced at me askance, as if wondering what I had in mind—but Publius knew, and could barely suppress a grin.

"That much, you may do," the chairman confirmed. "Have you any other points of interest for us to ponder?"

"No, I think not," Barry said. "That will do quite nicely, thank you, gentlemen. You have been courteous indeed, and we very much appreciate your consideration."

I could not help but think that he sounded like a form letter.

"We are always pleased to offer hospitality to the stranger in our midst," the chairman assured him. "I shall look forward to your speech, Mr. Tallendar. When will you present it?"

"As soon as the hall is free," Barry said.

"Why, the hall is free tomorrow evening!"' Joram said, a gleam in his eye. "May we look forward to your speech at that early hour, Mr. Tallendar?"

For just a split second, Barry looked dismayed, and I'm afraid I held a similar expression for a bit longer. But Barry recovered smoothly and gave them a slight bow. "Tomorrow night it shall be, then! I shall look forward to having you in my audience, gentlemen."

"And we shall look forward to being there," the chairman promised. "Good day, Mr. Tallendar."

We turned and went out. The chamber doors had scarcely closed behind us when we both turned on Barry. "Are you insane? How can we possibly be ready so soon, with a piece we have not even read through, much less rehearsed?"

"I am the only one who needs to memorize," Barry said grimly. "Surely the rest of you can learn where to grimace in thirty hours."

"But how will you memorize a whole hour in one night?" Publius wailed.

"By iron discipline and hard work," Barry said. "Please, gentlemen—no more until we are out of the building."

I glanced around and saw three people watching us curiously. I smiled at them and turned away to follow Barry down the stairs and outside.

"Now, Horace!" Barry said as we descended the steps. "What stratagem did you have in mind when you requested permission to answer questions? A word-of-mouth campaign?"

"Precisely," I answered, and Publius explained.

"We send everybody out into the city in groups of two and three, to tell the Citadelites about our show . . . I mean, your lecture."

"But we only have permission to answer the questions they ask!"

"Come now, Barry," I chided. "If I cannot entice a person to ask the question that I wish to answer by this time, I deserve never to have heard of a talk show!"

Publius nodded. "I know where the printer is, and . . ." He broke off, staring. "We forgot to ask them to pick up the tab for the posters!"

"No need, old chap," Barry reminded him. "We have our own high-speed copier aboard ship. All you need do is prepare the prototype. Come, gentlemen—back to the *Cotton Blossom*. There is much to do."

There certainly was.

When we came back aboard the ship, we homed on the lounge like horses to a stable. We found Merlo and Winston pretending to chat with each other, but actually watching with varying degrees of amusement and concern as Suzanne applied various potions and unguents to Ramou's bruises. He had his shirt off, and we may be forgiven for thinking that the zeal with which she applied the balm to his chest and shoulders may not have been entirely due to her instinct for nursing. "All over a local girl!" she was saying. "And don't try to tell me that it wasn't her fault!"

"It wasn't," Ramou said.

"I told you not to tell me that!"

"The local boys decided to enforce their territorial rights to her, without her even knowing about it."

"Oh, don't you believe it for a second, Ramou! If they saw the two of you, I'll just bet that she saw the three of them! She'll get you into trouble, and she'll treasure every minute of it!"

"So will I."

Suzanne slapped his shoulders hard enough to raise a startled cry, then kneaded them as an excuse. "Stay away from her, Ramou! Honestly! Can't you control your raging hormones just a *little*?"

"No, but you can." Ramou caught her hand. "Save me from her, Suzanne."

She stared at him for a moment, then pulled her hand free and turned away. "Come on, Ramou. You know I can't let myself get tied down yet."

"Yeah," Ramou said ruefully, "I know."

Oho! thinks I. What have we here—*two* cases of fear of commitment?

"So go on, Suze." Ramou sighed. "Leave me naked in the cold, harsh world. Cast me unprotected to the wolves—or at least, the vixens. Just don't be surprised if I decide to go hunting."

"Don't try to lay the guilt on me for your own philandering!" Suzanne turned on him. "Really, Ramou! Any woman who took a chance on you would deserve whatever she got."

"Yes," Ramou said, looking straight into her eyes and suddenly very serious. "She would."

Suzanne just stared at him for a minute, then turned away, blushing.

I decided it was time for a politic interruption. "My heavens, Ramou! Are you hurt?"

"When he can talk like *that*?" Suzanne cast him a glance of exasperation. "The only thing he's suffering from is testosterone overload!"

Barry said, with real concern, "You haven't been antagonizing the locals, have you, Ramou?"

"No, sir." Ramou grinned. "*They* antagonized *me*. But we worked it out."

"By great tact and diplomacy, I see. Merlo, I must protest! He should never be allowed out alone!"

"He wasn't," Merlo said. "I left a young lady with him."

Ramou nodded. "No trouble until after I'd seen her

home. But don't worry, Mr. Tallendar—there are no hard feelings on either side."

"I rejoice to hear *that*—I suppose," Barry said dubiously. "Are your bruises all we have to show for our day's effort?"

"We actually did get something done, aside from establishing rapport with the locals," Merlo said.

"Oh," Suzanne said, "is *that* what they're calling it these days?"

"She doesn't understand fighting," Ramou explained to me.

"As long as fighting was all she had in mind, Ramou. How was the hall?"

"Great." Ramou beamed as he pulled his shirt back on. "Classic in its simplicity and its proportions, well lighted, airy . . ."

"Well lighted!" Barry said, startled. "What on earth are we to do about lighting effects?"

"Wait till after dark," Merlo told him. "That's what we'll have to do anyway, according to the hall's superintendent. He says the audience isn't free in the daytime."

"But don't worry, boss, I checked their eyeteeth," Ramou said.

"You *are* in a good mood today, aren't you? Well, you'll be glad to know that we actually will be able to rent that hall."

"Excellent!" Winston rose and went to the call patch, beaming. "I think the whole company will wish to hear this. By your leave, Barry?"

"Yes, why not?" Barry sighed. "There's not a moment to lose." He collapsed into a recliner and leaned back; it molded itself to maximum-recovery position.

Ramou stepped over to the beverage dispenser. "Would you like your resuscitation hot or cold?"

"Hot," Barry answered, "but with some kick to it. That concoction you fed us yesterday will do nicely, Ramou."

"Just hot buttered rum." he said. "Horace? Publius?"

"Why, yes, thank you, Ramou," I said, letting myself go limp in the embrace of a recliner.

"Already have it, Ramou." Publius lifted his glass in salute. "But thank you anyway."

Marnie came in the door. "What is the call to arms?"

"Good afternoon, my dear." Barry lifted his head with a tired smile.

Marnie made a jerky movement toward him, jerky because she stopped it almost before it started. She came slowly to sit near him. "Are these Citadelites so wicked, then?"

"Oh, no, they're quite upstanding! That is the problem, I suppose—that, and their deep-seated conviction that we must be out to corrupt them."

"Only insofar as we cannot avoid," Winston said.

Barry looked up with surprised approval. "Very good, Winston. Yes, I suppose to some extent, mere contact with another culture is apt to corrupt them, by Citadel's standards. Still, let's keep it to the minimum."

"Keep what to the minimum?" Larry demanded as he came in.

"Corruption," Ramou answered.

"Must we?"

"I'd rather avoid it entirely, but that doesn't seem to be possible," Barry sighed. "Good afternoon, Lacey . . . Grudy . . . Marty . . . Gantry."

"Sounded interesting, with a general call," McLeod said, taking an armchair. "Think I want to be in on this."

"Yes, I think you do. Are we all met? Ah. Ogden."

"Something with alcohol, Ramou—enough so that I can taste it," the old ham grunted as he sat down.

"Hot buttered rum." Ramou set it in his hand, then stepped back to give me a reassuring look from behind Ogden. I relaxed, reasonably confident that the cup contained heat and butter, and a solution of something flavored with rum extract.

"Well, my friends, the long and the short of it is that we have permission," Barry said. "We shall perform—or at least, I shall, while a few of you assist me in dumb show."

"Getting a head of ourselves," Marty quipped.

"Of course, you have to read a script tailored to suit their prejudices," Lacey said acidly. "This goes beyond censorship!"

"True, young lady, but playwrights have always had to write to please the audience available, with the minimum offense given," Barry sighed, "except for those brave few artists who have let the chips fall where they may, and have managed to avoid starvation only because of the infatuation of academic critics."

"The sooner we perform, the sooner we can leave this miserable dirt-ball," Marnie said. "When do we go on, Barry?"

"Tomorrow night."

"Tomorrow night!"

"Impossible! We can't be ready!"

"I haven't even drawn up a light plot . . ."

"Peace, my friends." Winston held up his hands. "First, let us hear the whole of it. *Then* we can panic."

12

The squawking modulated down to grumbling, then stopped.

Winston nodded, satisfied, and turned with a politely interested expression. "Barry?"

"Thank you, Winston," Barry said, with a gratified nod. "You will understand, my friends, that we are in no position to cavil at any caveat of our capt . . . ah, hosts."

"You mean, if you don't say what they want you to in that speech, they won't let you speak again." Lacey's face was thunderous.

"Precisely. And I must speak, or we will not have local currency with which to buy fuel—and if we cannot buy fuel, we are stranded on this planet for the rest of our lives."

Ogden frowned. "Surely your brother Valdor can send local currency in some fashion."

"Perhaps—if we can notify him. But the deacons have all the channels of communication in their hands."

The remark struck dead silence. Everyone glanced at everyone else, beginning to realize what total power we were confronting.

"But why should they wish to keep us here?" Marnie cried. "I should think they'd be glad to be rid of us!"

"I do not believe the deacons are concerned about our capacity to disrupt their society, Marnie," I said. "They can enforce their dictates very simply—if we are obstreperous, they will not give us food."

"But why should they *want* to keep us?" Marnie cried again. "Surely not to gain another handful of workers!"

"There is that," I said, "but I believe their motivation is more subtle."

Charles nodded. "They intend to reform us, by their standards. They want to save our souls."

The silence fell again, everyone staring, appalled.

"It is fully within the capacity of the zealot's mindset," Charles assured us all.

"Well, I don't know about the rest of you, but I have no intention of being reformed!" Marnie leaped up, eyes flashing. "Not by their standards—and by my own, I have no need of it!"

Barry nodded. "I see no sin in cosmetics and attractive clothing. In all other respects, I see no real wickedness in our behavior."

"Sexual behavior?" Ogden rumbled.

"What two people do together behind closed doors is their business alone, Mr. Wellesley!" Lacey turned to him, red-faced. "Theirs and no one else's!"

"I couldn't agree more," Ogden assured her. "Why is it that every generation of young people feels that it is they, and they alone, who have fought the sexual revolution? However, I suspect our reluctant hosts do not agree with your stand at all."

"But isn't it just a matter of being honest about it?" Suzanne said. "Do you *really* think your average Citadelite is any more virtuous in private than any of us?"

"We have no hard evidence to the contrary," Barry pointed out.

"True," Charles said, "but if the behavior of people in earlier Puritanical cultures is anything to go by, Citadel should have its share of illicit sexual activity. They are human beings, too, after all, and some of the stronger physical drives will not be denied. They, too, must be tempted, and a fair proportion of them are bound to succumb."

Lacey shuddered. "What a horrible way to think about sex! It may leave the sheer physical pleasure, but it takes away all the joy of it."

"And the joy that two people may take in one another. Yes." Barry nodded. "The relationship is polluted by unnecessary guilt—and makes a surprising number of people decide that they must be wicked by nature, so there is no point in their trying to be good."

Winston stirred restlessly. "We could go on all day about

the failings of a Puritanical culture, my friends, but that would not change the fact that we are well and truly caught. We must perform, or we shall not escape—and we must keep our performance within the bounds of their taste, or they will shut us down."

Lacey shivered, hugging herself. "I hate this! I never thought I would give in to censorship!"

"Every artist does, who needs an audience," Barry said, "except for the very lucky few whose work happens to be what their societies require. We, however, are not among those who conform without realizing it, and we must therefore perform as our audience demands, or cease to perform at all. For this little while, at least, we must speak the words the censor puts in our mouths. What we will say after we have escaped, we shall discuss when we come to it." He turned, noting a sudden gleam in Martyn's eye. "I never knew you were a playwright, Marty."

"Neither did I," Marty said, "but after this, I just might give it a try."

"I shall look forward to reading your work with interest," Barry promised, inclining his head.

Lacey and Larry sat up straight, looking startled.

"For the moment, however, we must perform as the deacons intend—and the sooner we begin, the sooner we can leave. That is why I made no objection when they bade us perform tomorrow night."

"An excellent point," Ogden rumbled. "By all means, let us begin as quickly as we may!"

"Well, when you put it *that* way . . ." Lacey said.

"Anything to get out of here as soon as possible!" Marnie said with disgust.

"Well said, stout hearts!" Barry said, smiling at them with pride. "However, we have more to do than merely to rehearse. There is a problem with publicity."

"Surely that's Publius's affair!" Grudy protested.

"It is. Publius?" Barry turned to the advance man.

Publius forced a wan smile. "The only advertising the deacons will permit are discreet notices on public bulletin boards—no pictures, no inflammatory language."

"*This* is an advertisement?" Marty asked.

"Technically, yes, though I would term it merely an announcement. They will, however, allow us to answer questions when we are asked."

Marty grinned. "Oh. You mean we should walk around and make sure we're asked."

"Exactly." Publius beamed. "Now, I might suggest a few techniques for eliciting questions from passersby. . . ."

"We can develop our own, thank you," Marnie informed him—and indeed, everyone was grinning as they anticipated their word-of-mouth campaign.

"Well," Publius said, miffed, "if you do have questions, I will be delighted to advise."

"Where do we get the tickets?" Lacey asked.

Publius looked startled, then confused, and turned to Barry.

"I don't remember the deacons mentioning ticket sales," I said.

"They did not," Barry confirmed, "and I believe they would decide that distributing tickets to passersby is considerably more than answering questions. No, you just spread the word, my friends. The audience may secure their tickets at the door."

Larry scowled. "Will they, though? If they leave us without a ticket in their hands, won't they just forget about it?"

"Oh, I don't think so." Winston grinned. "If you lived in a place where the only thing to do at night was to go to a square dance or a concert, or listen to a lecture by one of your neighbors whom you had heard a dozen times or more, would *you* forget a performance by a professional entertainer whom you had never seen before, except in a 3DT epic?"

Everyone shuddered, visions of home movies plodding through their heads. " 'Tis a consummation devoutly to be wished," Ogden rumbled.

"After all . . ." Winston smiled. ". . . the deacons may call it a lecture, but we know what it *really* is."

Barry nodded. "A one-man show, by any other name, is still a one-man show."

"*One* man?" Marnie stiffened in indignation. "I thought there were several others of us involved, too!"

"Indeed there are, my dear; you will pardon the clumsiness of the phrase. However, we will not need all of you for this first attempt—and since there is so little time, we shall divide the responsibilities according to the cast list. Those not appearing as heads in this first presentation, will be detailed to walk about the town and elicit questions to answer."

"Can we use shills?" Marty asked.

The question took Barry by surprise. "Shills? You mean locals who have agreed beforehand to ask you questions on cue?"

"Delightful!" Publius grinned.

"Well, yes, it would be a good technique," Barry said slowly, "but I would caution you against having one of your fellow actors dress in local garb and false beard for the occasion, Martyn. There is something of the small-town mentality here. These people have seen each other every day of their lives and will be quick to identify someone who is not truly one of them."

"Right, boss." Marty saluted. "But I was thinking of some genuine locals."

"Hey, yeah!" Ramou grinned with delight.

"Ramou, you stay away from her!" Suzanne scolded.

"What—that snake charmer Prudence?" Lacey stared. "Yes, Ramou, stay away! She's poison in a sugarplum!"

"Interestingly descriptive," Barry noted, "but the caution might be apropos. However, Ramou, as soon as you are done assisting Merlo in moving whatever articles you intend to use for the performance, I would appreciate your escorting some of our publicity-tellers."

"A good thought." Winston rubbed a bruise. "The locals might become excessively zealous again."

"You bet I'll escort 'em!" Ramou said. "Sell the show, too."

"Yes, there is no reason why you cannot be a teller yourself," Barry agreed.

"But there's only one of me," Ramou objected. "Can we make sure everybody goes in threes, and in mixed couples?"

"Why, yes, if you think it necessary," Barry said slowly. "Do you really forsee trouble, Ramou?"

"Not really, but it never hurts to be sure. I don't know

what the local boys really think of off-planet girls, but I'd rather not find out the hard way."

"Or what they think of our boys, either, eh?" Ogden chuckled.

Ramou shrugged. "That, too. Nobody's come right out and told me that if I'm an actor, I must be gay—but it doesn't hurt to be careful. A society like this might have some reactionary attitudes."

Winston shuddered. "Yes, I think all due precautions are in order." Then he stared, electrified. "My heavens! You don't suppose that tussle yesterday morning was designed to discover whether we were or weren't, do you?"

"Could have been one of its purposes," Merlo allowed, "but there were several motivations pushing those boys, and I don't think they were aware of more than one."

"Danger of corruption by city slickers." I nodded, with a sardonic smile.

Barry shook his head sadly. "Be charitable and friendly, but with all due caution as you go out among the heathen. Now, as to who will *not* go out among the heathen . . ."

Everyone sat up straighter. Lines or no lines, an audience is an audience, and a part is a part.

"Perhaps I should describe the 'lecture' first . . ." Barry began.

"Not really necessary," Winston told him. "We have made a good beginning already. We took the liberty of reading through the script in your absence."

"Very good, Winston! And all of you! My thanks—it was fortunate that you decided to be ready for all eventualities."

"No, Winston decided it." Marnie glared at the arch-villain. "I didn't know you could be so inexorable."

"Any 3DT villain learns the persistence of menace, my dear. I think you'll find that we all have some idea of how and when to react, Barry, no matter how we are cast."

"Gratifying to know," Barry assured him. "Now as to the casting . . ."

Everyone leaned forward.

"Suzanne will undertake the part of Salome—"

"Suzanne!" Lacey cried. "Why not *me*?" Then, before

anybody could tell her the obvious answer, "All they're going to see is her head!"

"Luck of the draw, my dear, nothing more," Barry said airily, "and before you ask, I am really not interested in auditioning either of you in the belly dance. Marnie will portray Herodias, Salome's mother . . . Ogden will portray Herod . . .

"I have escaped the villain?" Winston cried. "Delightful! Congratulations, Ogden."

"Why, thank you, Winston," our three-hundred-pounder said affably. "After all, by this point in his life, Herod *was* somewhat advanced in years."

"Never fear, Winston, you will not be spared," Barry assured him. "Horace will portray John the Baptist . . ."

"Please do not tell me my part will be cut," I protested.

"Don't worry, old chap—*none* of you has much to say. Think of it as having the finest costume onstage."

"A silver collar," I grumped. "A very *wide* silver collar."

"Precisely. Other than that, Grudy, you will only need headresses . . ."

"I have the designs ready for your approval, Barry," she assured him.

"Wonderfully fast work! Really, my friends, your promptness shames me."

"You *have* been rather busy, old chap," Winston said dryly.

"Well, I like to think I have not completely wasted my morning. Now for the second part of the program! Winston, you will portray Julius Caesar . . ."

"*Et tu*, Barry!" Winston said.

"Yes, I have had luncheon, thank you. Lacey, you will portray Calpurnia . . ."

"Calpurnia?" Lacey cried, startled. "But she doesn't *do* anything!"

"In this version, my dear, none of you will do anything," Barry assured her. "Charles, you will be Brutus—and that, my friends, will suffice for the nonce."

"You mean the lecture will please the clergy?" Marty asked.

"No, Marty," Barry sighed. "The good people of Citadel are Calvinists. They may have ministers, but they certainly do not have nonce." He waited for the groan to pass, then said, "We will begin rehearsal after dinner—right through the play once, then run it for continuity. Tomorrow morning we will work Part One intensively, while the actors from Part Two stroll about town, ostensibly seeing the sights. At noon, they will return to work Part Two, and the morning's actors will become the afternoon's announcers."

"Except for those of us who have no part at all," Larry said darkly, "which just happens to be limited to Marty and myself!"

"Younger limbs can walk longer distances," Barry explained airily, "and according to the traditional division, men have more stamina than women."

"Sexism and nonsense!" Marnie scoffed.

"True," Barry agreed, "but we do have more men than women in this company . . ."

"A situation which should be rectified!"

"Rather difficult, when the pool of available actors is thirty light-years away. You may remember that we did originally have two other actresses in the company, but they withdrew at the last minute—prudently, no doubt, but unfortunately, considering that you ladies must therefore undertake more work."

"Oh, I don't mind!" Lacey said. "Especially since it gets me out of being the town crier for the morning."

"Quite so." Barry glanced at his watch. "It is four o'clock, which leaves us approximately two hours for rest and recuperation before we meet for dinner. Enjoy it, my friends—you have a very demanding twenty-four hours coming up."

He rose, and everyone took that as the sign for adjournment, turning to one another and talking with far more enthusiasm than the situation warranted. I rose, too, and went over to Barry to say softly, "I do hope you will take advantage of the lull to take some rest, old fellow."

Barry smiled wanly. "I fear I must begin learning my lines, Horace."

Winston came up just in time to hear that. "Yes, quite a challenge," he said. "However shall you memorize so much so quickly?"

"I may be able to help." Charles joined the conference.

"You remember the prompting units that Ramou and I were developing on New Venus?"

"Why, yes! You don't mean to say they are perfected?"

"Not quite, but we do have a one-person modification—a small portable computer with a hidden earphone, that will feed you your lines at the touch of an inductance patch."

"Ingenious! But I surely shall not be needing prompting for every sentence."

"Nor will you have it," Charles assured him. "The computer will keep track of which sentences you have delivered, so that the touch on the patch will feed you the next line you *haven't* spoken." He held up a small black box with two thin wires emerging from it. A brass figure adorned the end of one. "This is the patch, disguised as a lapel pin. You have only to grasp your lapel, in the traditional orator's gesture, and you will hear your next words."

"Delightful! I thank you from the bottom of my brain box, Charles! However, I shall still need to memorize as well as I can, in the time remaining."

"True," I said, beaming, "but now you can take time for a nap."

We usually rehearsed in the hold, but it was huge and cavernous. Since the set for this presentation consisted of six chairs and a high counter, like the one in your favorite tavern but with six head-sized holes in it, Merlo and I set it up in the lounge.

As for the scenery—in stock? What's "stock"? For us, it's a computerized catalog with pictures and descriptions of all the standard set pieces and scenic units. We select the one we want, feed its code into the computer, turn on the forming unit, and voilà! Out comes the prop, in whatever color we specify. Only the one color, of course—we have to paint the trim by hand. But, hey, there has to be some room for artistry.

"We'll drape it tomorrow," Merlo told Barry. "Tonight, I want to be able to see what's going on underneath the table, so I can make sure everybody's chair is the right height for them, and nobody's uncomfortable. It's going to be a long sit, after all."

"It will indeed," Barry agreed.

It was going to take quite some adjusting, too. All the heads had to be at the same height, of course, since they were all supposed to be sitting on the countertop—but the heights of the actors varied considerably, from Ogden who, although he wasn't as tall as he once had been, was still six feet four inches tall—to Lacey, the shortest, who was only five feet five inches. The chairs had to make up the difference in height, which meant that each had to be fitted exactly to the actor. Merlo and I had taken measurements that afternoon and cobbled up rough chairs accordingly, but that didn't mean they'd really work out right. I mean, there wasn't more than an inch or two leeway for anyone.

Barry summoned his actors. "Attention, people! This is the set—and all the set we will have for this venture."

A ripple of laughter passed through the assembled troops.

"Merlo informs me that it will be draped tomorrow, but tonight, he wants to be able to see what needs adjusting. Now, Marnie, you sit here, nearest the right-hand end and the speaker, since you will be first named—then Horace, then Ogden . . . and finally, Suzanne. Then, for Act Two—pardon me, *Julius Caesar*—Winston, then Lacey, and finally Charles. Everyone know your place? Very well, places, please!"

Everyone got up and went over to find their chairs, grumbling. Ogden sat down—rather carefully, until the chair was done groaning—and started to slide into the counter, then halted, staring. "I say, Barry, this won't do!"

The counter was halfway across his chest.

"You must have one of the young ladies' chairs," Barry said. "Merlo, whose is whose, here?"

"Names are carved into the top of the backrest," Merlo grunted. He came up to the playing area. "See? Says 'Lacey,' plain as day!"

"A rather cloudy day," Ogden said ominously. "You have painted over them with the same color as the rest of the frame!"

"Of course. I didn't want the names to glare—it would have ruined the look of the piece."

"I'm afraid aesthetics must yield to utility in this instance, Merlo." Barry sighed. "Would you label the chairs a little more clearly, for tomorrow?"

"Oh, *all* right," Merlo grumped. "Won't be seen anyway, I suppose. Here, let me put 'em in order. Call it out again, Barry, would you?"

"Marnie first," Barry said, "then Horace . . . then Ogden . . ."

As he read, Merlo played a sort of shell game with the chairs. He finished and stepped down, glaring at the actors with his hands on his hips, virtually daring them to find something wrong. They sat down, all of them almost as gingerly as Ogden, but the chairs didn't collapse, so they started looking reassured.

Then they found out that they had to duck down to get their heads through the holes.

"This is ridiculous!" Marnie fumed. "Demeaning! What do you expect me to do next, Barry? Crawl into place?"

"If the script calls for it, yes." Barry sighed. "Though in this instance, it does not. I suppose we could have Merlo and Ramou pick up the table and lower it over you . . ."

"Oh, that won't be necessary, thank you," Ogden said quickly.

I resented that. What did he think we were going to do, drop it on him?

It couldn't have been much worse than bending over and scooting his chair forward, for him. All that belly got in the way, and he did have to try to fold down kind of low. When he straightened up, he clipped his head on the edge of the hole. "Ow! Barry, is this really necessary?"

"I'm afraid so, Ogden. Of course, I'm sure one of the younger men would be willing to take the role, though neither of them could possibly look the part so well as you. But than, makeup does do wonders—"

"That won't be necessary, thank you," Ogden said hastily. "I'll endure it." He looked about, wearing a countertop for a collar. "I say! This *does* resemble a bar, doesn't it?"

"Wanted you to feel right at home, old fellow. Now—"

"I don't suppose a glass of brandy goes with the set?"

"I'm afraid not." Barry sighed. "We will do that vice for our next selection. For now, though, think virtuously."

"This *can't* be right," Suzanne said through clenched teeth, her head tilted back so that her chin could clear the edge of the hole.

"It certainly can't!" Lacey was scrunched down.

"Why are you folded up so, Ms. Lark?" Barry asked.

For answer, Lacey sat up straight, and lifted the whole countertop with her shoulders. Marnie squawked in alarm, and Winston protested, "Easy, there!"

Seemed there was a slight discrepancy in chair heights. Merlo had told me that all human beings are built more or less the same, and scoffed when I reminded him that sometimes that means less, not more.

I was right, though.

Barry stared. Then he turned to Merlo. "Got the measurements off a little, did you?"

"Yeah, we sure did." Merlo turned to me. "Okay, okay! So I *should* have let you measure the girls six ways from Sunday!"

"Just from hips to shoulder, was all I asked," I protested. "I could see Lacey's got a lot longer torso than Suzanne."

"Been studying them, have you?" Merlo gibed, and Larry glared at me, clenching his fists.

"Only visually, boss," I sighed. "Just doing my homework."

"As long as you don't do it at home."

"You could have asked *me* for their measurements, Merlo," Grudy said gently.

"That's confidential!" Lacey snapped.

"And a costumer never tells," Grudy sighed. "They should have us take a vow for silence of the confessional before they give us our union cards."

What were she and Larry doing there? Everybody had come to watch, and Barry hadn't kicked us out yet. I mean, there wasn't anything else to do in the evening—and when you can say that when you're sitting on a planet near its biggest city, that's pretty bad.

I didn't tell Merlo that watching the girls wasn't just my homework—it was also my hobby. I think he had guessed, though—along with everyone else aboard. What can I tell you? I'm healthy.

So are they.

"How *did* you measure them, Merlo?" Horace asked.

"With a tape measure."

"No, no! I mean, what dimensions did you check?"

"Their height. From there, I went by standard proportions."

"In this instance, we seem to need to account for a bit more individual variation," Barry said. "Can you have it corrected by nine tomorrow?"

"Sure. For the meantime, I suppose we can . . ."

Suzanne squawled, startled. "Ramou! Not in public, *please*!"

"I *told* you to lift up," I said, wounded.

"Well, yes, but I didn't realize it was a threat."

I held my hands up in plain sight, shoulder high. "I'm clear. You can sit down again."

Suzanne did, and looked pleasantly surprised. "Oh. You might have told me what you were doing!"

"Sorry." I sighed. "I thought you could see I was bringing a cushion."

Lacey was watching all this with a very jaundiced eye.

"That appears to be high enough," Barry said. "What can we do for Ms. Lark, though?"

"Couldn't the two of us just trade chairs?" Lacey asked.

A look of surprise came over Merlo's face. "Why didn't *you* think of that, Ramou?"

"More fun my way," I said.

Lacey and Suzanne ignored me, ducking down, rolling out, and swapping chairs. When they ducked back up, Suzanne's chin was just barely clear of the countertop, and Lacey's shoulders were just barely clear of the underside.

"It will work for tonight," Barry sighed.

"Are we really going to have to remain in these idiotic positions for an hour?" Marnie demanded.

"An hour and a half, I'm afraid," Barry said, "since you will have to be in place before the house opens."

"And we have to hold our faces immobile all that time?!"

"No, we will cover each of your heads with a black veil. We don't want the audience to see you prematurely—and we want the advantage of surprise when we unveil each of you."

"I shall die of claustrophobia!"

"Really, Barry," Ogden rumbled, "isn't there any way we can sneak into place just before curtain?"

"Merlo?" Barry looked up. "Is there any offstage space?"

"*Off* stage? There isn't even a stage!"

"I'm afraid not, Ogden . . . Ramou, what *is* the matter?"

I'd been looking very excited, but trying not to wave or jump around. Fortunately, just the look in the eyes and the eager nod had gotten through to Barry. "We could cobble up an ornamental screen to put around the table, Mr. Tallendar."

"Hey, good idea!" Merlo's eyes lit. "Something ornate, maybe even baroque! Let the locals have fun studying the decoration and guessing what we're hiding!"

"If you think you can have such a thing ready on time, then do, by all means," Barry said slowly.

"Capital!" Horace said. "Then we can relax at our ease while we wait!"

"We might even imbibe some liquid refreshment," Ogden suggested.

"Nothing but tea, darling!" Marnie fixed him with a glare. "We still haven't learned if there is a prison sentence mandatory for possession of liquor!"

"I don't want to possess it," Ogden said, "I want to *drink* it."

"Then it will possess you," Marty pointed out. Ogden gave him a black look, but he had gotten to liking Marty too well to mean it. Anybody who would listen to him talk about the old days, he wasn't about to alienate—and Marty loved to hear history from someone who had seen it, while he took notes on all the comic acts and bits of business that were so old they would seem new again. He claimed he wasn't much on originality, but that he had a great memory. He billed himself as a humor historian. That, I believed. The first part, I didn't.

"Well, we seem to have taken care of the boredom *before* the performance." Marnie didn't look all that happy about it having been dealt with. "What about during?"

"We suffer in silence, and the appearance of good nature," Ogden told her stiffly, "like any good trouper."

"What's a 'trouper'?" I whispered to Horace—I was still up near the countertop.

"An actor who bears all trial and tribulation cheerfully and with good grace," Horace answered, far more loudly than I had asked. "Troupers never complain, because they know it will wear down the spirits of the other actors, making it more difficult for everyone, and damaging the performance of the company as a whole. Sorry, Ramou—I should have told you much sooner."

The lounge got very quiet, all of a sudden.

Then Marnie turned slowly and gave Horace a look that should have gone right through him and come out the other side. If looks could kill, he would have been starring in a funeral that instant.

Since they couldn't, though, he just sat there blinking up at me earnestly, as if he hadn't the faintest idea anyone else might have heard.

Marnie turned pale. The only thing she could take worse than criticism was being ignored—and we knew she wouldn't be ignored for long.

13

It wasn't just *me* that Horace should have told about being a trouper, apparently—Lacey and Larry had joined Marnie in the dirty looks department, frowning at him, looking both resentful and thoughtful.

Ogden, however, took the implied rebuke well. "Quite so. My apologies, Horace—and Barry, too, of course. One must suffer for one's art, eh? No, quite unprofessional of me."

He didn't look at Marnie while he said it, but she got the point and glared in outrage. "If you think a star of my caliber has to put up with this sort of insolence and endure this kind of privation—"

"Yes, and I am sorry that I must ask it of you," Barry cut in. "But you see, no one here knows that we are stars."

That brought Marnie to a jarring halt. Suddenly, she was aware of where she was, and why, all over again. Slowly she turned, to fix Barry with a poniard glare. But she didn't say anything.

"If you really find it aggravating, Marnie, I suppose I could impose upon Grudy . . ."

"No, I shall manage, Barry!" Marnie made her exasperation very clear. "What we must do, we must do, I suppose. But I shall expect compensation when we perform on a civilized planet."

"If we ever find one," Marty murmured, and Marnie shot him a glare before she settled down to immobile martyrdom.

"*Thank* you, Marnie," Barry sighed and went over to the lectern. He laid his script on it. "Now to begin. 'Attend, good people, and listen to a tale of vice and shame! It happened very long ago, and we all know who to blame—

blame for tempting folk to fall, and bringing them to ruin! We'll show their moral turpitude, and the trouble it was brewin'!" He looked up, nonplussed. " 'Brewin' '?"

"Does it *have* to rhyme, Barry?" Marnie said, exasperated all over again.

"Does it?" Barry stared. "My heavens, it does! Charles . . ."

Charlie shrugged, spreading his hands. "It just came naturally, Barry. I suppose we could find a few synonyms, if it is truly annoying . . ."

"I thought it was kinda making it clear to them who cared, that this was all really tongue in cheek," Marty said.

"Well, it does begin the piece with a tone of levity . . ."

"Thank heaven!" Marnie sighed. "I thought you were trying to be serious!"

"We hope that the good folk of Citadel will think so," Charlie said.

"The bad ones will know better," Marty sniped.

"Now, Marty!" Charlie said. "You know very well that both of us really subscribe to the moral principle being illustrated here—that a person's greed can turn back upon him."

"True," Marty admitted, "when you put it that way—and you do, at the end. It's just the excesses people go through on the way, that I can't help kidding."

"A matter of attitude, not of principle," Charles agreed.

"Gentlemen—if we might rehearse?" Barry hinted.

"Oh, of course! My apologies, Barry!"

"Yeah, sorry," Marty seconded.

" '. . . the trouble it was brewin',' " Barry repeated. "I think that line might need work, Charles, even if you lose the rhyme."

Marty shrugged. "It was a slant rhyme, anyway."

"The villain's one we all know well, and Herod was his name!" Barry orated. "Wicked, cruel, and treacherous—but his wife was more the same!" He pantomimed lifting a cloth off Marnie's head. "Vamp display, Marnie . . . Herodias was the viper's name, a strumpet ill and fell! In his declining years, old Herod fell beneath her spell! She taxed the people, slew her foes, made Israel a churning stew! I tell you, people, there's no end to the harm a bad woman can brew!"

Lacey frowned, not sure she liked the direction the speech was taking—but the next section mollified her.

"Now, a good woman is a blessing rare, for all the world to hold. She heals the sick, comforts grief, and helps us bear our woe. She makes this weary life a joy, lets hidden blessings show—but even as a virtuous woman lifts our souls, a wicked one can do more harm than living flame and coals!"

"The rhymes just came, huh?" I muttered to Marty.

He shrugged. "So some of them needed a bus ticket."

"This shrew of malice had become old Herod's latest toy. . . ."

Marnie glared up at him.

"She gave him pleasures old and new, since he was closed to joy . . . Let me think about that one, Charles . . ."

"Do." Charlie nodded. "And I hope the good folk of Citadel will think about it, too."

"She reawoke his guttered lust, roused up his faltering zeal—and whispered in his ear that he should grant her treasures real. She raised within, his ghost of youth—he felt as one who's callow may—and her brightest tool to fan his flame was her daughter, Salome." Barry pantomimed lifting a veil from Suzanne's head. "Bewitch the audience, Suzanne . . ."

Suzanne gave Marty and me an inviting smile and a slow, intimate wink. I started up, but Marty pulled me back down into my chair. "Down, boy. You were just making eyes at Prudence this morning."

"If those were the new eyes, I'll take the old ones!"

Barry gave us a severe glare and turned back to his script. "This juicy child made Herod drool—to watch her sashay by made him long to touch and taste—but she knew her mother's rule—that he might look, but never touch. For that, he'd turn to Mum. Then she would slake the thirst now raised, and charge a heavy sum. He had to gouge the Israelites for cash to buy her jewels, and judged each case as she saw fit. He was, for her, a fool." He paused, pursing his lips as he scanned the next few lines. "The rhyme and meter stop here, Charles."

"Intentionally." Charlie nodded. "It should enhance the impact."

"The rhymes stopped coming," Marty explained.

"Very well . . . But there was one man, at least, who saw what Herodias was doing, and scolded her for it."

Marnie was all outrage, glaring around.

"Of course, he didn't scold her in private—he wasn't in the palace. No, he scolded her by preaching to the nation, to all the people, telling them that she was trampling on the laws of God even as she trampled on the people. He was John, the Baptist." He whisked an imaginary veil off Horace's head. "We think of the Baptist only as the herald of Christ—we tend to forget that he was a prophet of God, in a time when the prophets spoke the word of the God of Israel to his people, telling them when their sins had become too offensive to bear, when they were straying from the path he had marked out for them, and chiding the rulers when they fell into sin. That means, of course, that he criticized Herod unmercifully—and very courageously, too. But the people of Israel feared God more than Herod, and Herod feared the people, so the king left the Baptist alone.

"But when John began to tell all the people that Herodias was a whore and a vile sinner, she told Herod to slay John . . . See if you can't work out some byplay here, gentlemen . . ."

Horace turned to Marnie, looking sternly righteous as he mouthed criticisms. She turned to storm silently at Ogden, who turned a slow and wicked glare on Horace.

"At first," Barry said, "Herod was afraid—but she begged and pleaded, and threatened to leave his, ah, house. Finally, the king gave in—and the Baptist confronted the king, the tyrant, the mass murderer!"

Horace took his cue and spoke silent ultimatums to Ogden, who mouthed thunderous curses, growing red with rage at Horace. Horace raised his chin, looking noble and righteous; Ogden scowled, mouthing imprecations.

"Ah, that might be a bit much, Ogden," Barry cautioned. "There might be someone in the audience who can read lips."

"Never fear," Ogden assured him. "They're nonsense words."

"Well, if you're sure." Clearly, Barry wasn't. He turned back to his script and began reading again. "Herodias nagged him day and night—she never let him rest, begging him to slay the prophet, so her conscience might find rest. But Herod feared the people's wrath, feared John the Baptist, too . . ."

Horace glared fiercely and reproachfully. I didn't blame him, with lines like that—but Ogden met his gaze, and I realized they were ad libbing pantomime that might go with the speech. So help me, Ogden began to swell with rage. His eyes seemed to bulge, his color deepened.

"Frightened more of John than of his wife," Barry said, "Herod now stood firm against Herodias' pleas . . . Mug appropriately, people . . . till Salome came through. It seemed she'd formed her own dislike, did not the Baptist trust, and told her mother she would help, in any way she must. So Herodias went to the king, a bargain for to make—if he would promise to grant Salome's wish, she'd dance to make him quake with lust, which Herodias would slake. Even then, old Herod stalled—with protest he did wail—so Herodias bartered for his oath, the Dance of the Seven Veils!"

Marnie must have seen that she was about to be upstaged, because she protested, "Mug? Is that all we are to do in this infernal piece—just sit here and *mug*?"

"I fear so," Barry said apologetically. "When one is deprived of one's body as a means of expression, one must do everything with facial contortions."

"Deprived of speech, too," Marnie snapped. "I don't suppose we could take time for a little genuine motivation here, Barry? Some vestige of real acting?"

"If you can, why, by all means do," Barry said slowly. "There is a progression of emotion, after all, and the fundamentals of character . . ."

"Fundamentals! Caricature, you mean!"

"You couldn't expect us to take this seriously," Marty protested. "Not just in an extended monologue."

"I have seen some monologues that were quite serious, and quite excellent," Marnie retorted.

"Quite so," Ogden agreed, "and the fact that the story is a classic should strengthen the piece, not weaken it." He turned to Marnie. "Yes, by all means, let us try to make it as genuine as possible—but not tonight, if you please, Marnie. I should like to have the blocking of emotions, the sequence and the overall sense of wholeness, before I devote any real emotion to it."

Marnie stared at him. "You're talking about this piece of tripe as if it were worth doing!"

Ogden shrugged. "Anything played before an audience is worth doing as well as we may—but more immediately, something resembling effort might relieve the boredom. Let us try to get an overall sense of it, eh?"

Marnie glared up at Barry. "You might try to do a little directing here!"

"Why?" Barry asked, leaning on the lectern. "You two are doing so wonderfully by yourselves."

"Let us continue," Horace said quickly.

"If we must." Barry sighed and turned back to his script, enjoying every minute of it. He frowned at the lines for a few seconds, then looked up at us, the audience, and orated.

"They called it the Dance of the Seven Veils, my friends, because Salome was dressed only in those seven veils when she began to dance. Mind you, they were large veils, very large, certainly enough to conceal her completely—but as she danced, she took off one veil after another, until she was completely nude!"

"Do we dare use that term here, Barry?" Horace asked.

"The deacons have the script, and have not yet informed us of anything they specifically wish to see cut," Barry answered, "though it is quite possible that they are only now reading it closely, and may inform us of cuts tomorrow . . ."

"Probably just before the performance," Winston said darkly.

"We must be prepared for all eventualities," Barry replied, and went on. "Herod's mouth watered. He wanted to see Salome, *all* of Salome, more than he had ever wanted anything—it seemed. He promised, promised blindly: Whatever she asked, he would give, if first, she would dance the Dance of the Seven Veils before him.

"So she did, my friends—good luck dancing with only your head, Suzanne . . ."

Don't ask me how, but Suzanne was doing it. The way

her eyelids drooped, the way her head curved and swung, somehow you *knew* she was doing a slow, drawn-out strip tease as Barry described it. Of course, the table wasn't draped, and those of us watching had the benefit of seeing what the rest of her body was doing, to give her the feel of the part. She didn't take anything off, of course, but her hands pantomimed it, luxurious, caressing, as she sighed—and, seated or not, her body moved, undulated; her feet moved, too, so that her legs followed in sinuous patterns. I felt a sharp pulse of that hunger of Herod's and told myself I was a fool—she wasn't really *doing* anything.

No, but she sure made you *feel* as if she was.

"She turned, slowly at first, her feet stamping out the rhythm, then turned again, her hands beginning to move, playing with the veil, teasing its fringes. The tempo of the drumbeats quickened; she let the first veil slip, then slip some more as she turned, and turned again, undulating, pretty little feet moving in intricate patterns. The veil slipped lower, lower, then fell away entirely, revealing. . .

"Another veil."

"To have a part like this," Suzanne moaned, "and only be able to use my head!"

"You are dong superlatively, my dear," Barry assured her.

"I'll second that," I muttered.

"Sit still, Ramou," Marty muttered back. "Try. Just try."

Ogden was staring at Suzanne's face as if it was the most provocative of erotic pictures, swallowing, eyes bulging. I hoped he was acting—especially at his age. If he was really feeling what he was showing, he might have another heart attack.

"Again the drums quickened!" Barry cried. "Again she turned and turned, this time slinking across the floor to the king himself, beckoning, dainty hand caressing the air only inches from his face—but even as he reached, she was gone, and his hands caught only . . .

"The fringe of a veil."

Ogden groaned, and began to pant—not comically, but as if he were really in distress from internal pressures. I was amazed.

"I didn't know anybody could do that without going for a laugh," Marty whispered.

"I guess he really *can* act," I whispered back. "What was he like forty years ago, Marty?"

"I wish I'd been there to see," Marty whispered back.

But Barry wasn't waiting for us. "Salome spun away, the veil tearing loose, revealing another veil—and a bare, smooth shoulder. She wheeled, she writhed, fingers playing with the corners of her veil, the edges of her veil. The drums throbbed like heartbeats, the lyres sang, and she slipped the veil loose to fall about her shoulders like a cloak, pirouetting, turning and turning like a dervish, closer and closer to Herod. He reached out, plucked the edge of the veil as it spun . . . and it came away! Another shoulder was bared for his inspection, both shoulders and her neck!"

Suzanne groaned again. She was really getting into it now, her "unseen" body shifting and swiveling, so that her head nodded with the rhythm of imaginary drums as her eyelids drooped, then opened, her head rolling around as if taken into transports as she gave herself over to the sound of drum and harp. Lacey was watching her acidly, and I could tell she was adding to her stock of sarcastic remarks every second, just aching to use them.

"She turned away again, stamping with the quickened rhythm of the drums!" Barry cried. "She swayed, she writhed, she churned—and the fourth veil seemed to loosen with each movement. It belled out about her, spinning lower and lower, until it fell to the floor and she stepped over it, clad still in three veils that covered all but her dainty feet, her arms and hands, and shoulders. But she whirled faster and faster, the fifth veil coming loose, spinning aside to fall over the king's face. He clawed it loose, panting, eyes bulging, as he watched the sixth veil weave and waver, as Salome danced entranced, all her being subsumed in the drumbeats and the lyres, thinking only of making the movements of her body one with the music—and the sixth veil fell away!"

"Is it necessary to be so graphic, Charles!" Marnie said indignantly.

Barry jarred to a halt, then turned to frown at her, and his color deepened. Only the older actors would have had the privilege of interrupting a rehearsal that way, and of them, only Marnie would actually have done it—especially for so weak a reason as feeling that she was being upstaged.

But Charles sat calmly, nodding. "If you'll check the text, Marnie, you'll see that I don't actually *name* anything. We give the impression, we give general descriptions of movements—but we don't actually describe her figure, or go into any detail."

"It certainly *sounds* as if you do!"

"That is solely due to the excellence of Barry's reading."

"And the intensity of Suzanne's performance," I breathed. Marty nodded agreement.

Suzanne sat frozen during the interchange, panting, eyes closed, head back, trying to hold to the mood she'd worked up, trying to hang on to her concentration.

Barry saw and turned back to the script before Marnie could come up with a retort. "Herod groaned, for everything he wished to see was still covered by the seventh veil—but Salome danced and danced, whirled and wheeled with wild abandon, closer and closer, and Herod reached out to whip the seventh veil loose! Salome spun away as a top does when you've pulled its string—then sank down kneeling, bowing low, facing the king, hands folded beneath her chin in supplication, eyes downcast, forearms covering her so well that she might still have been clothed—but Herod had seen one glimpse of what he truly wished to see, and he ached for more. Hoarsely, he cried, "Enchanting! Entrancing! The king thanks you, the king's favor lights upon you! Name your gift, and you shall have it!"

And Salome, panting, said, "The head of John the Baptist on a silver salver!"

I turned to frown at Marty. "Silver salver?"

"It's euphonious, it sings!" His eyes were glued to Suzanne's face. "Okay, so it's artistic license. It works!"

At the lectern, Barry went on. "For a heartbeat's space, that throne room held in silence. Then Herod cried out, wailing. 'Not that! Ask for gold or jewels, ask for half my kingdom—but not ask for the head of John the Baptist on a silver salver!' "

"Oh, to be able to take the lines!" Ogden groaned.

"I know, old fellow, but we really mustn't," Barry said sympathetically.

Horace dropped character, too, turning to Ogden and explaining, "If anyone but Barry talks, they'll declare it a play, and no longer a legal lecture."

"I know, I know! But the piece has finally developed some validity! It's painful to see it go by!"

In the center of the controversy, Suzanne waited again, head thrown back, eyes closed, holding fiercely to her concentration. I felt my heart turn over and couldn't help thinking what a waste it was for a woman like that to be single.

Barry noticed, and said, "Let us finish while we've worked it up, then. . . . But Salome had sought to flirt with John the Baptist, as she flirted with every man of her mother's court, promising everything, giving nothing—but that holy man spurned her! He turned her away! Worse, he rebuked her for her loose ways and preached to her the virtues of God! The lust for revenge burned as hot in her as the lust for her burned in Herod, so even though her mother looked uncertain, tempted by the offer of a kingdom, Salome insisted, 'The head of John the Baptist on a silver salver!'

" 'No!' Herod cried. 'Do not ask it, do not demand it! The people shall rise in anger, the God of Israel shall smite us! Ask for anything, but not the head of John the Baptist!'

"But Salome had wished to kiss the lips of that wild desert prophet, had ached to know that he, too, was moved by her beauty, for he was, after all, a man, and human, as much prey to the frailties of the flesh as any of us—but he had twice the moral fiber, he was a giant of faithfulness to the Lord and the law, and he had spurned her. Spite and anger seared her heart, and she demanded, 'I wish for the head of John the Baptist on a silver salver!'

In the audience behind us, Larry snorted. "Silver salver, indeed! Don't you think you overused that a bit, Kemp?"

"No, actually," Charles answered, in a tone that would have frozen freshmen, "I don't think I did."

"The repetition builds nicely," Marty explained obligingly.

Larry sat back, simmering.

Barry went on, blithely unaware. " 'Not that!' Herod

cried. 'Ask me for the world, ask me for Rome itself, but do not ask for the head of John the Baptist on a silver salver!'

" 'I will have the head of John the Baptist on a silver salver,' Salome insisted, 'and nothing else!'

" 'You have given your word, husband,' Herodias reminded. 'You have accepted Salome's gift of dancing the Dance of the Seven Veils; you must stand by your word.'

"Then Herod groaned, and turned his eyes away, and bade his soldiers do the deed. And Salome caught her veils about her, and rushed to hover near the dungeon door, to hear the cries of horror and pain—but no cries came. She chafed, she rubbed her hands—and Herodias watched with a gleam in her eye, to see the fulfillment of her revenge."

"This is sounding somewhat familiar," Larry muttered.

"We steal from none but the best," Marty retorted.

"Then up the soldiers came, and Salome cried out in horror, for they bore to her the head of John the Baptist . . . and here I whisk a veil off the table about your neck, Horace, and we see a silver plate where there should be a collar . . . the head of John the Baptist on a silver salver!

"Salome screamed and fell back against the wall—but the guards knelt before her, holding the bloody thing so close that she could not escape. She screamed and screamed, and Herod turned away his eyes and groaned.

"But Herodias sat smiling, eyes gleaming with vindictive pleasure."

Larry leaned forward and hissed, "At least you didn't keep the bit where she kissed the head!"

Marty nodded. "Charlie wouldn't let me. Said it was too Wilde."

Larry groaned as he fell back in his chair.

"And that is the end of it, good people!" Barry pantomimed putting the veils back over the heads. "That is the degradation that lust can lead a man to; that is the horror and savagery to which vanity can lead a woman. But more than anything else, thus are people corrupted and brought down—for you know the end of the story, of Herod's ignominious death, and Salome's end; you know how Herod's grandson, in his false pride, followed his grandfather's folly. These things are in your Bible, or in the books of history, and the moral is clear: Turn away from the commandments and the Lord, and you will come on evil days, then sink to your undoing. People, we must always be strong, holding ourselves firm against the temptations of those who would breach our integrity; we must be firm and steadfast, for they will be unrelenting. Do not let the tempters lead you into behaving like someone else, someone other than he or she whom you truly are, or you will lose track of yourself, and of the still, small voice within you that keeps you true to yourself, and the path of right."

We couldn't help ourselves; we broke into applause. Barry had done it wonderfully.

The applause took Marnie by surprise. She stared, then recovered and moved in to steal a bit of thunder. "Really, Barry! We must add the Oscar Wilde play to our repertory!"

"Ohhh, yes!" Suzanne moaned, eyes still closed. "We must!"

Lacey glared at her. You could almost hear her thinking, *And I get Calpurnia!*

Barry looked up as the applause died, surprised. "Well, thank you. But it will be better tomorrow night."

"You did my lines full justice," Charles assured him.

"Justice? He did them mercy!" Marty stepped up to shake Barry's hand. "I'll come up with a speech for you any time, Mr. Tallendar."

"Thank you, Martyn—but it *was* a bit overdone."

"Only a *bit*?" Marnie sniffed.

But Charles was shaking his head. "The style suited the script, Barry, and you must talk to these people in a style similar to the one they're used to. I suspect their preachers speak much in the same manner as you have just done."

"Perhaps." Barry riffled the pages. "What was the time on that?"

"Fifty-three minutes," Merlo said.

Barry looked up, surprised. "It seemed far shorter."

"Why, thank you," Charlie purred.

Barry looked up, amused. "Yes, it *is* a good script . . ."

". . . for what it is," Marty said.

"Yes, quite."

Charlie smiled, pleased, and shrugged. "It owes as much to Oscar Wilde as to my own originality."

"Yes, well, let's not mention that to the good folk of Citadel, shall we? Or even the bad ones; they just might know how Oscar Wilde spent his latter years, and I don't think they would approve. Fifty-three minutes, you say? Well, certainly there's no point in doing *Caesar* on the same bill. If we start a little late . . ."

"Which we surely will," Horace interrupted, standing up carefully. "The audience is bound to be tardy coming in."

Barry nodded. "I think that will suffice for the first evening, yes. We'll keep tomorrow's rehearsal schedule as planned, of course—might as well start on *Caesar*, since we will probably need it within the next few days."

He didn't add, *If we're lucky.* We all knew that.

Merlo said, "I could cobble up a sound track."

Barry cocked his head to the side, considering. "Just harps and drums?"

"Can do," Merlo promised.

"Well . . . why not?" Barry grinned. "After all, they can only indict us for the words we say, can they not? And they have already approved those. Yes, by all means, music."

Personally, I didn't see that it could hurt—but I did think the deacons might suddenly develop selective amnesia, forgetting that they'd approved the script. Still, though, it wasn't as if the audience was going to see Suzanne's body dancing with the seven veils—just her head.

Of course, that had been enough to wreak havoc with me on more than one occasion. That reminded me of Prudence, and I glanced at Suzanne with some irritation. Where were her hints and promises when I needed them?

14

We started early the next morning, very early—before dawn. We packed the lighting equipment on a dolly—we weren't using enough scenery to justify a truck, and besides, we didn't have any local cash to hire one—and headed off in the predawn darkness to set up.

Publius had gone over to officially rent the hall from Mr. Langan as soon as the deacons had given their okay. Renting apparently hadn't taken too long, since he arrived back at the *Cotton Blossom* with Barry and Horace. But Barry wanted Merlo and me to escort our publicity teams—and truth to tell, I wasn't at all loath to, myself; kind of looking forward to it—so we had to set up by dawn's early light. Before, really; the excuse was that we had to have darkness to focus and do a dry run. Merlo had called Langan late the afternoon before, to set it up, and had given Langan the choice of staying late, to have us come in and set up by night, or of coming in very early this morning—and Langan chose morning! Something about it would be right after milking, which he minded a lot less than missing sleep. I think I've figured that out now, but I wish I hadn't. The notion that some people routinely get up at four o'clock in the morning is enough to give me shivers. I mean, that's usually maybe two hours after I've gone to bed! Maybe no hours at all, some nights.

There was a bonus—the sleepy customs guard was too weary to give us the full treatment. He just had us walk through the tunnel, verified that the metal detector had indeed detected lots of metal but that all of it was technical material, and sent us on our way. So we hiked out into the predawn darkness of Hadleyburg.

We waited for the monorail, stamping and rubbing our

hands, neither of us talking much. Fortunately, customs hadn't impounded our coffee cups, so we each pressed the heating patch and sipped while we waited.

We didn't have to wait long—Merlo had checked the timetable, and the car was right on schedule. We could hear it first, a low humming that rose in pitch, and Merlo put his cup in the holder on the dolly. "Here we go, Ramou. Remember, we've only got five minutes to load."

"Four, if anybody's getting off the train," I said.

Somebody was. The mono pulled in and stopped, the doors opened—and who should climb out but Elias and Prudence!

She was looking fresh, bright, and incredibly desirable. Early morning or not, my whole body rejoiced to see her, though my brain just had time to register wariness before the hormones hit it. Then I grinned and took a step forward. "Good morning, Miss Prudence—and Elias."

They both looked up, startled. Then Prudence's face lit with delight, and she ran over to catch my hand. "Ramou! How good to see you! But what are you doing up so early?"

I just barely managed to keep from saying that seeing her would be reason enough, and said, "We have to set up lights and sound early, while it's still dark enough to see what the lights are doing."

"Good morning, Mr. Hertz," Elias was saying, and Merlo was off, asking enough questions to keep him out of my way for a minute or two.

I echoed one of them. "What are *you* doing out here at five o'clock in the morning?"

"Oh, we have new jobs!" she cried gaily. "Elias will work the early shift on the field, and I will work in the cafeteria! Only for breakfast, this first morning—they want me to train for a day or two before I start full-time."

"Nice coincidence for me," I said. "Why so early?"

"They begin to serve at five-thirty, for those who must come early, like Elias. The poor man, he only comes this half hour before to escort me."

"A dutiful brother," I agreed. "You're lucky to have him."

"Aye, as brothers go." Her voice softened, lowered. "But

a girl always wants more than a brother, of course. Could not men say something similar?"

What the hey, I was going on the train in a minute—no way for flirting to get out of hand. "You bet." I stepped a little closer, letting my own voice lower. "Every man wants more than a sister." I paused one beat, long enough for it to register, not long enough for her to start replying, then, "Even Elias."

Surprise, then merriment. "Aye, and I hope he will find her! But for myself . . ."

"This car will leave in two minutes," the mono informed us.

"Jump, Ramou!" Merlo called.

How the hey had I missed the last couple of calls? " 'Scuse me, Prudence! Gotta load up!" I ducked away before she had time to try to stall, and started handing pipes up to Merlo. Elias pitched in, saying, "Good morning, Ramou."

"Morning, Elias!" I started handing up spotlights. "Good to see you."

"And you." Elias handed me a Fresnel.

I handed it on up. "How do you manage to be so bright and cheery so early?"

"Why," Elias said, astonished, "is not everyone?"

" 'Scuse me—gotta get the board." I stepped past him, hefted the control board, and lifted it up to Merlo. "Could you give me a hand with the dolly, Elias?"

"Surely." He took the other end—it scarcely weighed anything, with the fans still going—and he hefted it up. I jumped after and turned to wave. "Thanks!"

"Surely." He beamed, waving back.

So did Prudence, behind him—and she actually winked. Not very well, she had obviously just learned it—probably from watching Suzanne—but she managed. Fortunately, the door closed before I could respond.

"Well, that will get your blood pumping," Merlo said, as I settled down in the seat across from him. He handed me my cup.

"Great way to start the day. She can stand in for my alarm clock any time." I pressed the heat button again and sipped.

"I won't tell Suzanne and Lacey," Merlo promised.

I grinned, and I'm afraid it was a little sly. "Why not? Might do them good."

Me, too, of course.

We unloaded at the Hadleyburg plaza, and unloaded fast, before the car could take off again. With everything reloaded, we set off on the mile-long trek to the lecture hall, walking fast—partly because of the chill, partly to have some darkness left by the time we got there. There were only one or two other people on the pavement, both men in dark blue coats and light blue or gray pants, walking opposite from us, toward the mono plaza.

Then we turned a corner, and the man coming toward us jumped in surprise, then swerved past us with a muttered apology and disappeared around the same corner we had just turned.

Look, it was early in the morning. Prudence may have started my blood flowing faster, but she had slowed down my mental processes, mostly by occupying a large chunk of my brain capacity; it was two or three seconds before I stiffened, wide-eyed, and cried, "Hey!"

" 'Hey' what?" Merlo asked, then, "Where are you going?"

I had sprinted back to the corner by that time, and returned swearing. "Out of sight already! Come on, Merlo! He probably just ducked into a doorway!"

"And leave the board unguarded? Are you crazy?" He grabbed my arm and pulled as he set off again. "Come on. We've got an appointment!"

"But it was the Man in Gray!"

"Gray?" Merlo frowned. "What would he be doing here?"

"Following us!" My boss is a great guy, but sometimes he has a little trouble remembering anything exists besides sets and lights. "What else would he be doing? Come on!" I turned away, but Merlo caught my shoulder.

"Ramou! Ramou, stop and think."

"Think? Yeah, while I'm thinking, he's getting gone!"

"So what if you catch him? What can you do?"

"Find out why he put the needle in Charlie's tights!"

"And what if he won't tell you?"

"Oh, he'll tell me, don't worry," I said grimly. "The only question is, 'How long?' "

"That's slightly illegal, Ramou."

"So's murder!"

"Can you prove he did it?"

"What do you *mean*, can I prove it? He was coming up the stairs from the locker room, and later we found . . ." Suddenly, I ran out of gas. "Not exactly a smoking gun in his hand, is it?"

Merlo nodded. "Anybody could have been down there, while we had dinner—and there are always nuts around."

"But why Charlie? He's the most inoffensive guy in the world! Well, in the company, at least."

"Blind chance." Merlo shrugged. "Maybe it was the management, trying to shake us up—maybe it was the union, and they don't like Equity. Maybe it was the revolutionaries, trying to persuade us to side with them."

I looked at him narrowly. "You don't really believe any of that, do you?"

"No, but I do think we can't be sure enough to give the cops a good answer if they ask why you're beating the guy within an inch of his life—assuming you *can* outfight him; whatever he is, he's a pro."

I jammed my hands in my jacket pockets and lowered my head.

"We can't *prove* he's after us," Merlo argued, "and if we can't prove it, we can't *know* it. We can feel sure as hell—but we can still be mistaken."

"All right." I glared up at him. "Why do *you* think he's here?"

"To make trouble for us, of course," Merlo said right back, "but legal trouble—and if we try to do anything illegal to *him*, we could get locked up here for the next twenty years."

I remembered having used that same argument on Larry. It's hell, when your own reasoning comes back at you. I subsided, glowering.

Merlo nodded. "Smart man. Let's go do our job, now—and be ready to counter anything that shadow tries to do to us."

I grunted, but I went over to the dolly and started pushing.

Merlo fell into step beside me.

After a minute, I said, "What do you think he's going to try to do?"

"Get us trapped here, where Elector Rudders doesn't have to worry about us spreading whatever kind of ideas he was afraid of," Merlo said. "And the easiest way to do that is to shut us down."

"Shut us down?" I looked up, alarmed. "You mean get the deacons to take back their permission for us to perform?"

"That would do it," Merlo confirmed.

"We've gotta tell Barry!"

"And we will, as soon as we get back to the ship," Merlo said, "but first, we have to set up. Let's move, Ramou."

We moved. We got to the hall just as Langan was unlocking the door. "Didn't know you show folks got up so early," he said.

"We usually don't," Merlo admitted, "but we have to get up whenever the job requires. Can we start setting up, Mr. Langan?"

"Sure—but I've got to watch you." He didn't look suspicious, though—he looked eager.

Not so eager that he didn't fuss about making sure we had enough padding under "those dern heavy wheels you got there," as he called the boom bases—but he allowed as how four inches of pad with firm top and bottom was enough, even when he saw the base sink all the way down to the floor. As long as it wasn't touching his hardwood, he was satisfied. "Them pads fireproof?"

"*Everything* we use is fireproof," Merlo assured him, "except some of the actors." And he sidetracked Langan with the tale of the Great Chicago Theater Fire, while I bustled around setting up.

The story almost slowed me down, though—I hadn't heard it before, and the way Merlo told it, that tale was a real hair-raiser. I thought he was going to have Langan shutting us down right then and there, but he wound up telling the old man that because of the big blaze, every theater tech is very, very careful about fire, and anything that could cause it. I took the lesson to heart.

That didn't stop Langan from looking slowly up the tree of lighting instruments I'd built and demanding, "You sure that base is heavy enough so it won't fall over, with all this weight atop it?"

"Totally sure," Merlo confirmed. "You saw how it took both of us to manhandle it into place."

Langan sniffed. "I've seen little black boxes you could put on a piece of soft pine, that would make it weigh just as heavy as that base thing—and it'd be a lot easier to manage, if you just turned it off."

Merlo nodded. "Mass multiplier. Yeah, they're beautiful. But they run on electricity, Mr. Langan—and what happens if the battery runs down?"

Langan hemmed and hawed, but finally admitted, "Well, you'd have to yell 'timber!' "

"And maybe see that fire we've been dreading," Merlo said, "not to mention what would happen to the people it fell on. No, Mr. Langan, that's why sometimes I prefer the low-tech solution, even if it is a pain to haul around."

Langan seemed reassured, but he glanced up the pole and the tubes and cone sections I had clamped to the cross-arms. "Those far enough away from the wall not to burn my plaster?"

"Plenty far," Merlo assured him. "They scarcely give off any heat at all."

"Not worried about the power going out on *them*, are you? I see you're using electronic lenses, not glass!"

Merlo shrugged. "If the power goes out, the lamp will go dark, Mr. Langan. It's not going to make much matter if the lenses don't work then."

"Yeah, I'd say that's true," Langan allowed. "Well, let's see this fancy control board of yours."

He affected disdain, but we could tell he was excited. We gave him the demo, and he couldn't stop the gleam in his eye, or the tremble in his hands, even though he tried to look bored. It was the small board, too—just operated lights, and only a dozen of them. So we let him try, and his eyes gleamed as he dimmed the lights up and down, then brought up the specials one by one, highlighting each of the holes in the counter where the heads were going to come through, then brought them all up, then all down, beginning to chuckle with glee. Merlo watched, grinning, and even I forgot my troubles watching the old coot have fun. Takes some doing, let me tell you, with something like Prudence on your mind.

Oh, there was a way to get her off my mind really easily—but Suzanne didn't want to give me any promises. I didn't need anything physical, just a simple pledge that we'd be more than mere friends, but she started getting skittish any time I even hinted, so I stayed clear of the issue. Better to have her for a friend, than not to have her at all—but it did leave me vulnerable to pretty faces and shapely bodies that had brains that might be willing to give me a little more emotional security, if a little less freedom.

A little, mind you. I wasn't asking for anything permanent. I'd seen how permanent things were with my parents—or with my mother, anyway. I couldn't honestly say I'd ever seen anything of my father.

So as I told you, watching old Langan playing with the light board made me forget all that. Sure.

The sun did come up, though, and when its light flooded through the windows so that we couldn't see where our own light pools were, Langan stopped playing and sat back with regret. "I see what you boys mean, about needing to do this after dark."

Merlo nodded. "Either that, or blinds."

"Or window opaquers, young man—we may not use such things much, but we've heard of 'em." Langan glanced up at us shrewdly. "It's all just a scam, isn't it? You get those actors to put on a show, just so you can have a good reason to play with your toys."

Merlo looked startled for a moment, then grinned sheepishly. "You might have a point there after all, old-timer. Well, we have to get back to the ship and help out with the rest of the preparations. Mind our gear for us, will you?"

"Safe as in a bank vault," Langan promised us, and do you know, I was absolutely sure it was true. After all, a techie is a techie, and we all know one another on sight—

don't we? Of course we do, and we know what's *really* important in life.

After girls, of course. Or maybe even.

We hopped the mono and got back to the terminal just a little before nine, to meet the others. No point in going through customs again just to come right back out, so Merlo and I each dropped another pill in our cups, filled them with water at the drinking fountain, and settled down on hardwood seats to press the heat buttons on our cups and wait for the rest of the gang.

"Ramou! Twice in one day!"

I looked up. There she was, a vision in indigo broadcloth, my sweet little Puritan maid who, I suspected, was desperately yearning to be a little less pure, but who would have pulled back in horror if she'd known what that entailed. Well, maybe not—after all, she was probably only talking about a *little*. I grinned up at her as I rose. "Hey, I'm in luck! But where's your waitress uniform, Miss Prudence?" Worthless question if I ever heard one—she wore a virtual uniform all the time, but maybe she added an apron in the restaurant. "Or are they keeping you in the kitchens? Naughty of them if they do, depriving all those poor yearning spacemen of the sight of you."

She laughed, blushing. "Ramou, you say far more than you mean!"

"I wouldn't dare," I assured her.

She frowned prettily, trying to figure that one out, so I asked again, "How come they let you out of durance vile?"

" 'Durance . . .'? Oh, you mean work? No, for today, it was only the breakfast shift, so that I could watch how they work, and learn the rules. Tomorrow I'll work the full ten hours—breakfast and dinner, and cleanup. I go home before the supper shift, though."

"Ten hours is a long day," I remarked.

She shrugged. "Everyone works that much, at least. The idle brain is the devil's playground, you know."

"I've heard it said," I admitted.

"What is a 'playground'?" she asked.

I was tempted to tell her it was a night club, but managed to catch myself in time. "A field, usually with a fence around it, where there are all sorts of toys for children to play with—climbing bars, and a fake castle or two, and swings, and seesaws—"

"They make special places for this? Why, we make do at home!"

Of course, I realized. Why waste money making special places just for kids? Besides, if they had to stay at home and just visit one another, you never had to worry about where they were—assuming they weren't lying. I had a momentary vision of what probably happened to the Citadel child who lied, and shuddered.

Prudence mistook the shiver and stepped a little closer, with half-closed eyes and a self-satisfied smile. "Tomorrow you must come to my cafeteria for breakfast!"

So it was her cafeteria already, was it? "I work tonight," I told her. "How about lunch?"

"Done! I will be glad to serve you with my own hands!"

"I would hope you wouldn't serve me with anybody else's," I said.

She stared at me for a minute, not understanding, then burst into laughter.

Which was just when Suzanne stepped out of the customs tunnel, with Lacey right behind her.

They were looking frazzled, but the sound of Prudence's laughter galvanized them both. They stared for a minute, shocked, then came striding over, looking very purposeful.

I pitched my voice so that it would sound intimate, but so that they could hear. "How about *you* come to *my* place of business, then?"

"Where is that?" She lowered her head, but looked up at me, batting her eyelashes.

"The lecture hall, same one you showed us yesterday—only we're performing tonight."

"Oh, yes, you *must* come!" Suzanne swept down on her like an avenging angel, but one that was all smiles and syrup. "You must see our premiere!"

Prudence looked up, surprised and taken aback, then rallied gamely and smiled back. "Why, how sweet of you to invite me! But what is a 'premiere'?"

"Oh, surely you've heard of that before!" Lacey said sweetly, coming up on Prudence's other side.

I was amazed; next to Prudence, they both looked big and ungainly, she was so slender and delicate. But those huge eyes looked up at Lacey without a shred of guile as she protested, "But I do not. In school, we were told that a premier is a head of state of some kinds of countries—but nothing more. What is it, please?"

"The first time a play is performed, anywhere," Suzanne told her, and those huge eyes looked up to the other side, shining with excitement.

"It is to be a play, then?"

"No, they won't allow that, dear—just a lecture. But we're giving the lecture a little bit of interest, at least, and it's a brand-new scri . . . uh, text, that hasn't been perf . . . *presented* anywhere before. You'll get to see it before the people on Terra do."

"Oh, how wonderful!" Prudence cried.

Neither of them bothered telling her that the script would probably never be produced anywhere, ever again—that it was a sheer desperation measure, cobbled together for Citadel alone, and that if they had ever had anything to compare it to, it probably would have been buried forever. But since they didn't, Prudence's eyes were shining with delight—which was a mistake, on the girls' part. The last thing they should have wanted to do was to make Prudence's eyes shine, when there was a man anywhere around.

And there *was* a man around, coming right up behind them—Marty, wide-eyed at the sight of Prudence's wide eyes, and Larry right behind him, interest kindling and smile spreading broad and false as he came up. "Why, Miss Prudence! What a delight to see you this morning!"

She looked up, startled and pleased—then realized why Suzanne and Lacey had hemmed her in, and smiled slowly. "How pleasant to see you, too, Mr. Rash—and you, Mr. Kemp. Well!" She clapped her hands, looking around at them. "Where are you all off to, so early in the morning?"

She probably intended "early" as sarcasm, but it went right past my crew. "Off to peddle our wares," Larry informed her, hoping for a double meaning which she didn't get.

"We're going to tout the show, Miss Prudence," Marty explained.

" 'Tout'?" She frowned prettily. "What does that mean?"

Marty started to say, "It's a guy at a racetrack who . . ." but he came down with a bad case of elbow-in-the-ribs, and Larry said smoothly, "It means 'promote,' Miss Prudence—to tell people the virtues of a commodity. In this case, the commodity is Mr. Tallendar's lecture tonight."

Prudence stared. "You don't mean you're going to walk up to people on the street and tell them to come to your lecture!"

"Sure," Marty wheezed, almost recovered. "Why not?"

"Why, the deacons would never allow it! The watch would be on you in ten minutes!"

" 'The watch' are your local police?" I asked.

"What are 'police'?"

"The watch."

"The deacons have given us permission to answer people's questions," Larry told her obligingly.

"But what if they do not ask?"

"Then we make them curious." Marty grinned.

"Would you care to join us as a spectator?" Larry invited.

Alarm hit Suzanne and Lacey instantly, though they covered it quickly, and Prudence pealed, "Oh, what fun! I should be delighted to watch you bring people to asking questions, Mr. Rash!"

"Perhaps you could even help us a bit, dear." Lacey had recovered quickly enough to go on the offensive. "You go a block away from us, then come toward us and begin asking!"

"Could I really!" Prudence clapped her hands. "What a delicious prank!"

Well, I hadn't thought of it as a prank—but I was glad to be getting her away from us for even a little while; as an audience, she might inspire me to my best efforts, but she was also a Class A distraction.

"Why, what a wonderful idea!" Suzanne said, though she looked somewhat jaundiced. "But let's hold her in reserve, my pets—let us see what we can do by ourselves, first."

"Surely." Larry smiled his warmest. "No point in corrupting innocence if we don't need to, is there?"

Prudence returned his smile with a merry, roguish look of her own and was about to speak when she noticed something just beyond Larry. "Elias!" She waved a hand, then ran to him and caught his arm. "Oh, Elias, guess what! The actor people are going to let us go along to watch them 'tout' their show—lecture, I mean! And let us help, if they do not have enough success! Oh, Elias, won't it be fun?"

Elias looked up at us, startled, then back at Prudence. "Perhaps," he said slowly, "but will the watch allow it?"

"They say they have permission from the deacons! Oh, Elias, say you will come! It will be so much fun!"

"I am not sure—" Elias began.

"It will, it will be such a lark! We must, we absolutely must!" Her tone was beginning to harden; after all, big eyes don't work on a brother, or shouldn't.

"There is work to be done at home, housekeeping for you, and the Good Book to read, for me—"

"It can wait! It *has* to wait most days, while we are at work! It can wait for this one, too! Elias, if you do not, I will never bake shoofly pie again!"

"Shoofly pie?" Marty wondered.

"Don't ask," I said. Me, I was afraid of the answer.

Elias weakened. "Well, if it will give you so much pleasure as that—"

"Oh, *thank* you Elias!" She looked ready to kiss him soundly, but only clasped his hand tightly—because public display of affection was banned? Or because sisters shouldn't kiss brothers? I wondered how they ever learned all the rules.

Suzanne and Lacey were looking decidedly unhappy about it. I wondered how they would have felt if Elias had been as attractive as his sister. He might be, in five years or so, but he was still pretty young—not much over minimum working age, at a guess, and I pegged him for the younger of the two. The only thing that gave him any authority at all was local law and custom. Even so, Prudence had him pretty tightly wound around her pretty little pinky. I felt a pang of sympathy for the guy, and wished him a quick meeting with the woman of his dreams—and a quicker marriage. I'd have been glad to trade places with him, any day. Just altruism, mind you—and to get the poor guy his freedom . . .

I fell in with the girls as we headed for the door, Prudence between Larry and Marty, chattering and laughing at their jokes. Elias fell in on Suzanne's far side, so I stepped in beside Lacey.

"What are you doing all the way back here?" she said sourly. "The male action seems to be going on at the front!"

"And over on your other side." I nodded at Elias. "How did you get loose from rehearsal?"

"The vets seemed to think they wanted some time to work things out without the kindergarten contingent," Lacey said, with a sardonic smile. "So I'm free to play hooky. What's your excuse?"

I shrugged. "I'm hiding."

"Oh, don't hand me that, Ramou! I've seen the way you look at her!"

"Best cover in the world," I assured her, "especially if you mean it."

Lacey looked at me in surprise, then smiled, though with some contempt. "You don't mean the big brave hero is afraid of a sweet young thing who's all innocence!"

"I suspect the innocence is more because of lack of opportunity, than lack of intention," I said. "Just because she's been raised to be good, doesn't mean she will be."

"Oh, and I suppose you mean that about all women!"

"I was just thinking about Puritans, at the moment—men, too. They give themselves very hard rules, but they'll be the first ones to tell you they've got their quota of sinners."

"Yes, but never themselves!"

I shrugged. "Don't know; this sect might go in for public confession."

Lacey shuddered, turning away. "We've got to get out of here!"

"Advertise hard," I said.

We did. As soon as we hit the plaza in Hadleyburg, we split into three merry, chattering groups—Larry and Merlo with

Lacey, me and Marty with Suzanne. And off we went, down Fifteenth Street, which seemed to be the main drag in this town. There were early-morning shoppers out, and people who weren't hurrying, so must have had the day off—or be running errands on company time. For a wonder, the sun had actually risen, and the day was bright and breezy, crisp and clear—and with just enough tang for spice. It was a perfect autumn day, and everybody was out to enjoy it before winter clamped down. My grandpa would have said it was great hunting weather.

I thought so, too.

15

"How do we do this?" Suzanne asked nervously. "I've pitched a show before, but always over coffee, to friends—never to strangers!"

"Just let us generate the questions," I advised. We halted. "Here comes one now."

The "one" was a youngish man—in his twenties, at a guess—who was walking along without wasting time, but not in any tearing hurry.

"It's really great!" I told Marty. "You learn so much, and it's so much fun watching!"

Marty grinned. "Is it really? I thought they had to be dull to be legal."

The man slowed, noticing Suzanne. She gave him an encouraging smile, and he wavered between duty on the one hand, and curiosity and a pretty smile on the other. "Par' me," he said.

"Of course," she answered, all bright and cheery.

"What are you two talking about?" But his gaze was still on Suzanne.

"Our new lecture!" Marty burbled. "Or our boss's, anyway. About vice and virtue—tonight, at the main lecture hall."

"I'm going to be Salome's head," Suzanne confided.

"Salome?" His eyes widened. "Of the Seven Veils?"

"Well, yes, but you don't see the veils," she said, "because all you see is my head. I don't even get to talk."

"But Mr. Tallendar's words make up for it," I hastened to assure him, while Marty threw Suzanne a "shut up" look. "Come on by, if you're not doing anything! Seven-thirty, and it's free!"

"Free?" Suddenly, he looked suspicious.

"Only to the people who come to listen," Suzanne said quickly. "The deacons are paying for it, as a public service."

"The deacons?" He stared. "The deacons themselves approve of it?"

"Must be more than 'approve,' " I said, "if they're willing to foot the bill."

"Yes, it must," he said, looking happier about the idea. "Seven-thirty, you say? At the hall?"

"That's the place," I assured him.

"Who are *you*—or whose head, I should say?"

"Me?" I shrugged. "I'm just a stagehand. That's how I know Mr. Tallendar's so good—I get to watch while I'm waiting."

"You've heard of Barry Tallendar, I'm sure," Suzanne said. "He played the Angel in *Gideon*."

"Did he really! That is one of my favorite 3DT epics!"

"Who're those guys with the blue coats and the shiny buttons?" Marty asked, looking over his shoulder.

Our customer looked up with a guilty start. "The watch! I really must be about my business! Thank you for the good word, friends!" And he bustled off.

"Well, we got the point across." I glared at the Puritans in the knee-length blue coats. "There a law against stopping to talk on the street?"

" 'No loitering'?" Marty guessed. "Or just during working hours?"

"Either way, we'd better plan on short speeches." I gave the watch a jaundiced eye. "So those are the local police. If it weren't for the long coats and the shiny buttons, you wouldn't be able to tell them from anyone else."

"You forgot about the nightsticks," Marty pointed out.

I shrugged. "They don't matter." I wondered why both of them gave me a funny look. "Wonder what those buttons are made of—brass?"

Suzanne shook her head with the eye of a woman who knows her metals. "Too red—well, brown, really—and not enough yellow. They're copper."

"Probably can mine it locally," Marty opined, "but not the zinc."

"What makes you such an expert?" I asked Suzanne.

She smiled, with a toss of her head. "I like to spend my free time in the art museums, Ramou—lots cheaper than 3DT, and just as much fun . . ." Her voice faltered. "Why are you looking at me that way?"

"Nothing new," I said softly, stepping closer.

"Well, yes." She took a half step back. "But just because I said I like art?"

"There's always something new and fascinating about you," I breathed.

"Even if I'm not a demure Puritan maid?" she asked, with an edge to it.

I tried to ignore the surge of guilt, but it must have shadowed my sheep's eyes, because I saw a gleam of vindication in hers. I was about to work a little harder at ignoring, when Marty muttered, "Cheese it, kids! The coppers!"

I stepped back, looking up in surprise.

"I've been waiting all my life to say that." Marty grinned.

But he hadn't been kidding. The guys in the long blue coats and copper buttons were indeed coming up to us with scowls on their faces. "Here, now! Who are you, and what are you doing?"

"Just peaceable visitors to your lovely planet," Marty said, "going about our business."

"Oh, are you, now? And what business is that?"

"We were just going to the lecture hall, officer," Suzanne said, with maximum charm. "Our director is presenting a lecture there, tonight."

"Director?" Instantly deepened suspicion. "Director of what?"

"The Star Company," I said. "We're a troupe of actors who—"

"Oh, aye! I've heard of you! Be sure you mind your own business!"

"Why, we are," Suzanne said, all innocence.

"Indeed! We'll not have you accosting decent citizens on the streets!"

"Accosting?" Marty said, with a jaundiced eye.

Before they could answer, Suzanne said, "We have permission from the deacons to answer questions about our director's lecture, officer."

"That did not look to me like answering questions." He nodded at the retreating figure of the young man.

"But it was," she protested. "He asked the first question of us, not us of him."

The cop's look said, very clearly, that he didn't believe it. "See that you don't," he growled. "We'll be watching."

"Why, thank you, officer!" Suzanne blushed, flattered.

The copper stared at her, not knowing what she was thanking him for, then muttered something and turned away.

"What *were* you thanking him for?" I asked.

"Because I always like having men watch me," Suzanne explained.

"Our partners aren't doing so well, either." Marty nodded across the street.

I looked up, and saw Larry, Merlo, and Lacey conferring with another pair of long-coated men. Larry's voice kept rising in loud protest, and Merlo kept interrupting smoothly, cutting him off.

"At least Larry's registering protest," Suzanne said.

"Sure," Marty said, "but Merlo would have had them soothed and on their way five minutes ago if he hadn't. Come on, folks—let's move, before they hit us for loitering."

We started walking again. "What are we going to do when we get to the lecture hall?" Suzanne asked.

"Keep on going," I said, "and pretend we got lost. When you get tired of hiking, let me know—I brought a folding cup and some coffee pills."

"Oh, I like the walk—so far. I just hope it isn't for nothing."

"We'll find out soon," Marty said. "Here comes another one."

We started our bright, loud chatter again, and Suzanne gave the passerby the warm smile, but he just looked surprised, a bit wary, and kept on going.

So did the next one.

And the next, and the next.

"I think the watch must have gotten to them," I told my crew.

Marty nodded. "Maybe so." He jerked his head behind him. "Or maybe they just saw Prudence."

We turned and looked back. Prudence was still fifty feet behind us, making a big show of looking in the shop windows and chatting with Elias, who was looking distinctly unhappy about it all.

"That would explain the men," Suzanne said reluctantly, "but a few couples have ignored us, too—and you can be sure the men wouldn't dare stop with their wives in tow."

"For us, or for her?" Marty asked.

"Right," I said. "Let's go compare notes." I stepped off the curb, automatically checking for traffic, though I'd only seen the occasional horse and wagon here, and even more occasional truck. I beckoned to Merlo, and he came over. We met in the middle of the road, the rest of our bands straggling along after us.

"Any luck since the watch started watching?" I nodded at the lone bluecoat who was ostentatiously window-shopping a hundred feet down the street.

"Not a nibble." Merlo looked disgusted.

"I'm doing everything short of hiking my skirt up to show my ankle," Lacey said, "and no one's noticing. Or, well, they're noticing, but they're not stopping."

"Lecherous beasts," Larry muttered.

"Same here," I said, chagrined. "Guess it's time to pull out the heavy guns, eh?"

"Yeah," Merlo admitted. "Flag the locals."

"Right." We went back to our respective sides. As I reached the sidewalk, I started staring at Prudence. It wasn't long before she looked up and caught my eye. I nodded, and she fairly beamed with delight. Elias looked decidely upset; I thought of recommending a stomach remedy.

A minute later, they disappeared around a corner.

"Deserted!" I stared, unable to believe it.

"You couldn't really ask her to get in trouble with the watch," Marty said, but he looked troubled, too.

"Ask him, you mean," Suzanne said darkly. "By local rules, if Elias really puts his foot down, she can't do anything."

Marty shrugged. "Or maybe she thought you meant that we could get along without her."

"Then what did she look so happy about? She thought being a shill was going to be a lark!"

"Whup!" Marty stared straight ahead, wide-eyed.

I followed his gaze, and saw Prudence and Elias just turning a corner ahead of us.

"Of course!" Suzanne said. "They couldn't be bumping into us from behind, could they?"

I nodded approvingly. "This kid's got brains."

Suzanne flashed me a look that said she wasn't all that happy about my attitude, then smoothed her expression and started chattering again about how wonderful Barry's speech was going to be. I matched her enthuse for enthuse, until the Puritan pair came up and Prudence caroled, "A lecture? On vice and virtue? How wonderful! Who will be speaking?"

She did her asking in a voice you could have heard a block away, and I decided the kid might have a touch of talent herself. At least she knew how to project.

"Mr. Barry Tallendar," Suzanne answered with full verve—but I could tell it was forced. "You've probably seen him as the Angel in *Gideon*."

I reflected that it was a good thing Horace and Barry had told us about the sweet old battle-ax at the permits office.

"The Angel! And will he be talking about God, then?"

"No," Marty said, "he's going to be talking about vice, and how it can ruin your life."

"Will he truly!" Her eyes were huge and round—overdoing it, of course, but hey, she was a beginner.

Marty didn't seem to notice, though. He was staring into her eyes as if he were about to fall in.

"Will he not speak of virtue?" Elias demanded.

"No," Marty said, "That's *tomorrow* night."

"Where can we hear him?" Prudence asked.

Another strolling couple stopped to listen.

"At the lecture hall," Suzanne told her, in a nice, clear, loud voice, "at seven-thirty tonight."

"Seven-thirty? Why, that just gives us time to have supper and do up the dishes! How long will it last?"

"Only an hour," I said, wondering why Marty was giving me a jealous glare. "But what an hour! You can't believe how Mr. Tallendar will make that old Bible story come alive for you!"

"Bible story?" Prudence turned those big eyes on me. "I thought you said he was speaking on vice!"

"He is—but he's illustrating it by showing how it brought the downfall of Salome and Herod." I didn't mention John the Baptist—after all, he'd gone to heaven.

"Salome, of the Seven Veils?" Elias gasped, shocked.

"Yes, but he's just lecturing," I said quickly. "If you've ever wondered what was wrong about a simple dance, though, friend, come listen tonight!"

" 'Twas scarcely a *simple* dance!" Elias proclaimed, forgetting he was supposed to be a shill. Two more couples stopped, interested—but Prudence looked embarrassed, and gave Elias a beseeching glance.

He didn't even notice.

"Ah, then you've heard the story!" I said.

"Aye, and 'twas most edifying, in teaching us to abhor the temptations of the flesh!"

"And it will be again," I assured him. "It's something we need to be reminded about over and over." *Every time I look at your sister, for example.* Of course, I didn't say that out loud.

"But the temptations of the flesh are only part of it," Marty said. "There's greed, too, and the thirst for power."

Elias turned to him, frowning. "In the tale of Salome? How?"

"Ah, but I can't tell you that," Marty said, grinning. "Nobody can tell that like Mr. Tallendar! Come listen tonight, friends, at seven-thirty in the lecture hall! It's free!"

"Mayhap . . ."

"Right! Now, if you'll excuse us, we've got to get to work," I said, and bulled my way through the half-dozen citizens who had gathered to eavesdrop. I left them murmuring excitedly among themselves, with Marty and Suzanne right beside me.

"I have to admit, she's very effective," Suzanne said.

I had known that all along.

"Good loud voice," Marty said. "I think this may work out, after all."

A few minutes later, Prudence caught up with us, cheeks glowing, eyes alight. "Did I do well?"

"Honey," Suzanne said, "you did marvelously!"

"Never saw a better shill in my life," Marty confirmed, "even when I was one."

She turned to him, frowning. "What is a 'shill'?"

"You are, swee . . . Miss Prudence—or you were, just now."

"A shill is someone in the audience who starts clapping or laughing, or asks questions on cue. . . . I mean, when they're supposed to," Suzanne explained, and turned to beam at Elias. "Your questions were perfect, Elias!"

"Were they really?" he asked, startled—or maybe it was stupefied, just looking at Suzanne.

"Oh, yes!" she bubbled. "You were asking what all the other passersby were wondering."

I nodded. "Just do that well again, okay?"

"But it is lying!" Elias protested.

"Not a bit, silly!" Prudence said, squeezing his arm in chiding. "We are only asking the questions that everyone should."

"But we are pretending we do not already know! That is deceit—and if it is, it is surely a form of lying!"

"What's the matter?" I asked. "Never played a prank on anybody, by pretending not to know something?"

Elias turned to me, amazed. "Why, aye, in school . . ."

"That wasn't lying, was it?"

"Why . . . yes, I suppose it was . . ."

"No, goose! It was a game!" Prudence protested.

Elias turned to her, frowning. "There is no time for games, when there is work to be done."

"But this *is* our work," Marty pointed out.

Elias turned to him, confounded—and before he could start thinking again, Prudence grabbed his hand and pulled. "Come, brother! We must 'happen by' the folk on the other side of the street." And she hauled him away, protesting.

We strolled on down our side, keeping an eye out for passersby, but keeping the other fixed on Merlo and his crew. They started chatting as soon as they saw Prudence start across the street, and she greeted them with the same bright carol she had given us. We heard it loud and clear, and Suzanne muttered, "That girl doesn't need a microphone, anyway."

"Wouldn't I love to be taping one on her," Marty said, eyes glued to Prudence.

Suzanne turned to him in alarm that faded into a very thoughtful look.

I leaned close. "Might be good for him."

"Yes," she murmured back, "or it might be very bad, when she drops him."

I stared. I'd never thought she'd ever pick him up. Then I thought again, and said, "We won't be here that long."

"We have been already," she answered.

Was it jealousy, that Prudence was poaching on her territory? Or honest concern for Marty?

Little bit of both, probably—and the concern was warranted. I don't think Marty had been all that sure whether he was hetero or gay—but right now, he must have been realizing he was hetero. If she dumped him, though, how deep would the wound cut? How many slashes in his self-image? I suspected there were too many of them, already.

I also didn't like the protective look Suzanne was getting as she watched him.

Prudence and Elias thanked our crew loudly and clearly, and sauntered on down the street—but the crowd they had drawn stayed behind, to ask a few more questions.

"Go slow," I whispered.

We did, and sure enough, Elias and Prudence just happened to catch up with us. There was a puckish gleam in his eye, but he still maintained, "It may be a bit of a game, but it is still lying!"

"Pooh!" Prudence said. " 'Tis not as if you were in court, brother!"

"Just have fun with it," I urged.

"Oh, we shall! Will it be enough if we just hurry on ahead for a few yards, then turn back to encounter you? Or do you think we need to go 'round the block again?"

"I think we'd both better go around several blocks." I nodded at the blue-coated gentleman who was living up to his title and watching us. "He might get suspicious if he sees you asking for the same information a third time."

"He *is* swinging his nightstick in an awfully suspicious manner," Marty noted.

"We had better split up for a few minutes," Suzanne agreed. "Is there another street that would be apt to have this many passersby on it?"

"And isn't too far out of the way of the lecture hall?" I added. "We don't want to be too obviously suspicious."

Prudence giggled, but Elias said, "If the watch is suspicious, we are doing wrong!"

"Oh, sad sack!" Prudence scoffed. "The watch is suspicious if they see a young man and a young woman walking within the same block, on the same side of the street! Nay, surely, friends, we shall meet you on Thirteenth Avenue! There is a little park where it meets Thirteenth Street, and you can always claim that you went that far out of your way to rest."

"Little chilly for sitting around a park," Marty said, "but it sounds like a good idea, if you say it."

Prudence turned, glowing, and for a moment, their gazes locked—but all she said was, "Why, it is not chill at all! It is a warm day, for autumn!"

I decided there might be advantages to wearing yards of wool.

"It's all a matter of what you're used to, I suppose," Marty said, his gaze never leaving her face.

"Aye," she said, her voice gone breathy, "but one sometimes wishes for something new."

Elias tugged at her arm. "Come! The watchman will be on us in a second."

Prudence glanced up and, sure enough, the watchman was scowling worse than ever. She sighed and turned away, with a little good-bye flutter of her hand. Elias pulled her along, talking to her in a low, urgent voice. I don't know what she said in response, but she said it with a toss of her head.

I coughed very loudly; Merlo looked up, and I nodded after Prudence. He nodded, too, and started strolling in our direction with Larry and Lacey.

"Could she really be getting a crush on Marty?" I murmured to Suzanne.

All she said was, "Don't be naive, Ramou."

Good advice, I decided, as far as it went.

We managed to attract two crowds on Thirteenth Street before the watch showed up, one on each side of the street. This time it was Merlo who passed me the word that Prudence would meet us on Tenth Street. "You come in at Tenth Avenue," he said, "and I'll come in at Twelfth. That way, it won't be quite so obvious that she's deliberately bumping into both of us."

"Assuming somebody's watching," I said.

"I think we'd better," Merlo advised.

Sure enough, the watch caught up just as Prudence and Elias finished with Merlo's group, and started walking toward ours—which meant he could be plenty suspicious, but probably wouldn't try to do anything about us.

As Elias came up, I could see that he was having to try very hard not to enjoy himself. Prudence wasn't bothering, of course—she was having a high old time. We went through the routine again, drew another crowd, and sauntered on our way. The watchman was just starting to move in when Prudence and Elias turned a corner, heading east, and the watchman slowed down. But when we headed east, too, he got suspicious, even though we were on another street. He stepped up and accosted us. "Here, now. Where do you think you're going?"

"Officer! What a relief!" Marty said. "We're on our way to the lecture hall, but we've kind of gotten lost."

"I should say you have," he grumbled, but he had to admit that, yes, it was east of here, and we should go down two blocks and over one, and he'd be watching us.

"Yes, sir," I said.

"Thank you," Suzanne said, with her best beam, and off we went. He watched from the street corner, glowering, so I had to give Prudence and Elias the nod. They were waiting when we turned the next corner, and we met in the middle of the block.

"That's it for the morning," Merlo said. "We have to get back to the ship now, so the afternoon crew can take over."

"Oh, must you really?" Prudence said, pouting. "It has been such fun!"

"Any more, and we'll have the watch on us," I said regretfully. "Yeah, it has been fun, but enough is enough."

"Is it really?" she asked, with a long, lingering glance at Marty. He colored and smiled tremulously.

Suzanne frowned, then forced a bright smile as she turned back to Prudence. "Thank you *ever* so much!"

"Yeah," Merlo said. "Don't know how we could have managed without you." He shook hands with Elias. "Don't let your conscience bother you, young man—come see the sh . . . lecture tonight, and watch your fellow citizens. Then judge whether it does them harm or good."

"Why—I had not thought it out to the end," Elias admitted.

"Well, the ends don't justify the means, but they do help you feel better about it."

I nodded. "If we really thought we were doing the public any damage, do you think we'd be in this business?"

I found out later that that was a loaded question. The straight answer was that there are a lot of people in show business who never stop to ask themselves what they're doing to their audience. Some of 'em don't give a damn, as long as they make money. Some of them care a lot, but have very different ideas from mine about what's good for the folks out there in the dark. Most of 'em laugh at the idea that a show can have *any* effect on people. I guess they're the ones who really think the argument over censorship is silly.

Merlo and I discussed that as we wended our way back to the ship. Larry and Lacey were discussing something of their own, and Suzanne put in a word now and then, but mostly she seemed to be concerned about Marty, making sure he didn't trip over his own feet as he wandered along in a happy daze.

"I think he's got it bad," she confided to me as we waited our turn for the customs tunnel.

I glanced at Marty as he started in, humming very softly to himself with an abstracted gaze and a slight smile. I nodded. "Yeah. He's got all the symptoms."

Which put me in a pretty bind. How was I supposed to keep making eyes at Prudence, if my buddy was in love with her?

However, it also made it pretty clear that she wasn't in love with *me*. Again, I asked Suzanne, "You don't think she really cares about him, do you?"

"Only so far as she can use him," Suzanne said shortly.

The rest of 'em went back aboard ship to rehearse, and Merlo and I unwrapped the cheese sandwiches we'd brought along for lunch. We heated another couple of pills of coffee and sat around, chatting, until the afternoon shift came through the tunnel—Horace and Ogden; I could see it was going to be a short afternoon. "No Marnie?" Merlo asked.

"You do not think she would lower herself to pitching a show, do you?" Ogden asked.

Merlo shrugged. "Well, there was a chance. How about you, Ogden? You could have begged off easier than she could—pleaded age and infirmity." He didn't quite say Ogden would have been right on both counts.

"Do you jest? I would not miss this for the world!" Ogden strode toward the doorway, a glint in his eye and a spring in his step. "It has been years since I pitched a show, but I have always found it to be delightful fun! Forward, gentlemen! The fish are waiting to be caught!"

I stared after him. Horace smiled rather apologetically. "He takes a prospective customer as a challenge," he explained. "Between engagements, he supported himself selling encyclopedias. The company was always after him to give up his silly show-business idea and stay with them, where he could have made some *real* money."

"For them, or for him?" I asked.

"That's right."

I tell you, it was a joy watching those old-timers operate. None of our subtleties in walking along talking about the show at the tops of our voices—Ogden was much more direct. He'd brace a sucker—pardon me, a prospective customer—and roar out a greeting, dwindling fast to a mutter, "Pardon me, good sir! Have you heard of the wunnrfo lekzhooasabbenindni?"

At which, the citizen would invariably frown and say, "What?"

"The wonderful lecture which is being presented tonight

at the lecture hall!" Ogden would cry at his jovial loudest. "By none other than Barry Tallendar, renowned for his performance as the Angel in *Gideon*! Oh, you'll never see anything like it, my friend—some thoughts about vice, as exemplified by the tale of Salome and Herod! Seven-thirty—don't miss it!"

"I won't," the dazed sir—or madam—would mutter, and go on his—or their—way. They might not understand, but they would remember.

After the third such encounter, Horace reminded Ogden, "Old fellow . . . we're not supposed to accost the good citizens—only answer their questions."

"But I am answering their questions!" Ogden boomed. "You have heard them yourself, Horace! Each one of them distinctly said, 'What?' "

Not that Horace was any slouch himself, mind you. He would tip his hat at a passing couple, saying, "Good day, sir, madam. Wonderful day to hear an angel, isn't it?"

Some of them just smiled, and said, "Good day," and went on by, though I expect two hours later they finally looked at each other and said, "An *angel*?" But most of them stopped right there and then and said, "An angel? What angel?" I think they had visions of the Second Coming.

Horace dispelled them quickly. "The Angel from *Gideon*—Mr. Barry Tallendar. Surely you have seen it on 3DT? And he is here, right here in Hadleyburg, and will be presenting a lecture tonight, for your edification and enjoyment! Seven-thirty at the main lecture hall—some thoughts on vice and how it drags us down, exemplified by the tale of Salome and Herod! Oh, you must not miss it—especially since it is free!"

"Yes, we really mustn't," one of the couple would invariably mumble, as Horace tipped his hat again with another cheery "Good day!" and strolled off down the street after his next victim.

Yes, it was an education watching them work, those two—all Merlo and I could do was stroll behind them to make sure they were okay—and sometimes call, "Cheese it! The coppers!" or "Time for a change of venue, gentlemen!" Whereupon, we all turned at the next corner.

It was just a pity that they weren't up to going more than an hour and a half—but they hit at least as many people as both teams had, all morning. When we were back in the monorail plaza, I said to Horace, "You two guys are unbelievable!"

Horace shrugged modestly. "As W. C. Fields said, 'There's a sucker born every minute—and two to take him.' "

"Nice to know I've met them both," I said.

16

Merlo and I had to be at the lecture hall half an hour before the rest of the gang, of course—we weren't quite done setting up. I unpacked the screen as soon as we got there, and the two of us arranged it to mask the counter where the "heads" were going to sit. I gave it a quick look and frowned. "How come no pictures, Merlo? That would give the audience something to study while they waited."

"Sure would," Merlo agreed. "Give the deacons something to study, too, and the watch. How many pictures have you seen here, Ramou?"

I looked up, startled, then rewound my mental images of the last few days and replayed them. "Not a single one," I admitted, "unless you count the icons on the bathroom doors."

"I don't," Merlo said, "and I'd stay away from that term 'icon' if I were you—it originally meant a religious image."

"Religious image?" I stared. "You don't think . . ."

"These are Puritans, Ramou. Their Bible has a commandment in it that prohibits graven images."

"Only in church! They wouldn't take that outside the doors of the meeting house, would they?"

"Depends on how fanatical they are," Merlo said, "and from what I've seen here, the people may be nice once you get past their initial suspicions, but the doctrine's as hard-boiled as they come."

"Right pretty," a voice called from the back of the aisle. I turned and looked back; it was old Langan, coming down between the rows of seats with a spring in his step and a gleam in his eye. The sight warmed my heart—the old coot was enjoying this. It almost made me feel welcome.

"Thanks," Merlo said. "I designed it to go with your hall."

Langan stared in surprise. "You just did that between yesterday and today?"

"I've got machines," Merlo explained.

Yeah, he had machines. They had rolled out the fabric and the pieces of the frame; Merlo had painted the panels himself, by hand. He had his primitive side—he could have just set up a pattern unit on a computer, told the machine to multiply it to the dimensions he wanted, then fed it into the giant printer and had it roll the whole canvas out in a matter of minutes. But he liked the feel of the brush in his hands. I thought that was great, until I had to clean it.

"Everything to your liking?" Langan asked.

Merlo nodded. "Everything's fine. Of course, it would be nice if we could move the lectern over a couple of feet, to balance the counter, but it's bolted down, isn't it?"

"Well, not all the way." Langan grinned, going up to the lectern; he took a key out of his pocket and put it into the platform floor, turned it, and lifted out a board. I stepped forward and looked—there was a wide track under it, about four feet long. Langan turned to the lectern and lifted a clamp with a loud *clunk*! He slid the lectern over two feet. "Far enough?"

"Uh—yeah!" Merlo stared. "Just fine!"

Langan nodded and pushed the clamp back in place, then took the board apart in the middle, reset the two halves on either side of the lectern, and turned the key in each one. Then he stood up again, looking very pleased with himself. "We had that put in just in case a lecturer wanted to use a display board. First time we've used it, though."

"I'm glad you thought of it," Merlo said. "Looks much nicer this way."

"Why, how quaint!"

I froze. That withering tone could only have come from Marnie.

Langan stiffened, then turned slowly to look back at the doors.

He was just in time to catch the end of Marnie's pause for pose, before she strode forward, head back and sunglasses atwinkle, parading down the aisle with hauteur and disdain. They weren't her only companions—the rest of the company was following more sedately, with looks ranging from apprehension to contempt and envy—that from Lacey, who was doing her best to sneer at Marnie's behavior, but was also very obviously wishing she had enough status to pull it herself.

Marnie swept right past Langan without a word or a look and up onto the platform, where she posed center, scanning the rows and wrinkling her nose. "*This* is a *theater*?"

"Well, no actually," Langan's face was growing red. "It's a lecture hall. And who might *you* be, Miss Fancy?"

"That's 'Ms.' " Marnie glared down at him. "Ms. Marnie Lulala, star of stage and screen, and the leading lady of the Star Company! And who might *you* be, little man?"

"Little, is it?" Langan's face swelled; so did his voice. "I'm Langan, *Mr.* Langan to you, and I'm the man who runs this lecture hall—all the rest of them in the city, too, for that matter! And it's a darn fine lecture hall, too, not a theater!"

"It is now," Marnie said evenly. "Lecture hall? Ridiculous! Though I suppose that's why you feel you have to have plain, barren, echoing walls with never a vestige of decoration!"

"Decoration's a vanity," Langan snapped, "and any pictures are a sin! As to the echoing, the acoustics in this hall are so good you can hear a pin drop on the platform, all the way to the back row."

"How nice," Marnie said sweetly. "That will be a great comfort if I ever wish to drop a pin."

Barry finally managed to reach her and slide between the two combatants. "Mr. Langan! So good to meet you! Merlo has told me how splendidly you keep your facility!"

"*She* don't think so." Langan nodded toward Marnie.

"Nonsense!" she snapped. "You keep it beautifully—since there's not that much to keep!"

Langan started for her, but Barry caught his shoulder. "You must be patient with her, Mr. Langan. She just realized that she had paid you a compliment, and had to counteract it. Merlo tells me you've been extremely helpful."

"That help's about to end!" Langan told him. "If you can't muzzle that she-wolf!"

"She-wolf?" Marnie looked down at him, eyebrows rising above the dark glasses. "What a pleasant compliment!"

Langan's head snapped around, staring at her, appalled. She smiled sweetly back.

"She does have one point, though," Barry confided. "This lecture hall *is* a theater."

"Don't you dare insult my hall!" Langan bawled. "If it's you playactors that make it a theater, then you can all just get out right now!"

"I have to admire your restraint in expletives," Barry murmured, but before Langan could ask, Horace came up to pour oil on the waters with Charlie right behind him.

"*Any* place can be a theater, Mr. Langan," Horace said in his most soothing tones.

Charlie nodded. "The word originally meant only, 'a place for seeing.' "

"Well, a lecture hall's for listening!"

"If that were all we wished," Horace assured him, "we would only have to play recordings."

Langan snorted, drawn into the argument in spite of his anger. "You can still do that, even if you want to see and hear both! Ain't you never heard of 3DT?"

"Three-dimensional television does have its uses," Horace agreed, "but if it were really an adequate substitute, why would people come to your lecture hall?"

That stopped Langan for a moment. Up on the platform, Marnie was beginning to look stormy—she was being ignored.

Barry nodded to Grudy.

Grudy nodded back and stepped up onto the platform. "Now, dear, there isn't all that much time before the house opens, and we really must see to your headress and makeup."

"They come because they want to ask questions," Langan finally said.

"Do they really?" Horace asked, full of interest. "How many do they usually ask?"

"We have plenty of time before the house opens!" Marnie declared.

Merlo looked at his ring. "Twenty minutes."

"Twenty minutes!" Marnie squalled. "That's barely time for me to put on my base!"

"Then we really mustn't waste any time. Merlo, where do we make up?"

"Behind the screen."

"Maybe three or four," Langan admitted.

Horace nodded. "So it's not just the ability to ask and be answered. It's something of the same sort, though—some unspoken interaction between lecturer and audience. We have all felt it at some time, Mr. Langan—the magic of live theater. That is what keeps us working in a profession that, frankly, rarely pays well, if at all."

"Behind the screen!" Marnie boosted her decibels. "Do you mean to tell me this miserable excuse for a performance space doesn't even have a dressing room?"

Langan looked up with fire in his eye. I stepped up on the platform quickly and pointed to a door at the side of the stage. "In there, Ms. Lulala. It may not be very big, but there is at least a place for the lecturer to wait while the audience is coming in."

"Behind the screen indeed!" Marnie gave Merlo a withering glance and turned to parade off to the ready room.

Langan was beginning to look unsure. Good—he was listening, ready to begin thinking.

"Come up here." Charlie climbed up on the platform and beckoned. "I'd wager . . . ah, I would suspect that you have often watched lectures from the back of your hall, Mr. Langan, but never from the platform."

"Oh, I've been up there more'n you think! To help the speakers with their easels and such!"

"Yes, but never as a speaker yourself. Come up for a minute, and look at the seats. Come up, and imagine what it would be like to *be* a speaker."

Langan glowered up at him, but the temptation was too strong. He climbed up onto the platform.

"I suppose the rest of us get to wait behind the screen," Lacey said sourly.

"Yes," I said, "and if you saw the ready room, you'd be glad."

A screech echoed through the walls of the ready room.

"Just a touch of claustrophobia," I explained.

Langan looked up, affronted, glaring at the door. Charlie touched him gently on the arm. "Look out there, Mr. Langan. Imagine those seats filled with faces, looking up at you, listening to you, as you tell them something that's important to you, very important."

Langan stared, then shrank back.

Lacey stared at the closed door in surprise, then smiled with satisfaction and carried her makeup kit behind the screen.

Suzanne lingered long enough to explain, "Marnie always gets keyed up on opening nights."

"Even when she doesn't have any lines?" I asked.

"Of course." Ogden smiled. "She's much better that way." Then he went on behind the screen, too, carrying an enormous makeup kit. I reminded myself to stop behind the screen in a few minutes and check to make sure his spirit gum bottle was mostly gum and not much spirits.

"Yes, it's frightening at first," Horace agreed. "But you begin to see that they are listening, are paying attention, *really* paying attention—and there's a thrill to that, Mr. Langan, a feeling of satisfaction so great that you begin to forget about the fear, begin to become intent on what you're telling them and the looks on their faces as they hear, until there is nothing in the world, for the moment, except your own thoughts and the rapt attention on that sea of faces . . . Have you ever been in the audience, Mr. Langan, when a really good speaker is connecting with his audience that way?"

"Yes, I have," Langan said reluctantly, "two or three times, in this very hall. And you're right about the feeling."

Horace nodded. "You can't get that feeling from 3DT, Mr. Langan. You can only get it by being here, right here in the hall. It's that magic interaction between audience and speaker that keeps us going in spite of grubby living quarters and marathon travel connections, jet lag and exhaustion, long hours and starvation wages, bare subsistence—but we subsist on that glow of contact with the audience, and it makes it all worthwhile."

"You must really believe in what you're saying," Langan muttered.

Horace nodded. "Or in its worth."

"That is why this hall is a theater, Mr. Langan," Charlie said, "because it is a place where that magic can occur. Lope de Vega once said, 'All I need for a theater is two trestles, four boards, two players, and a passion.' These days, we can even do without the trestles and the boards—but we can't do without the audience."

"Yes," Langan muttered. "I can see that."

"So it doesn't really matter where we perform," Charlie said. "Any space can become a theater, so long as it has players and an audience. Though I must say, Mr. Langan, that very few spaces are so pleasant as this, so well-proportioned and harmonious."

It was the bit of flattery that finally did it. Langan relaxed, smiling. "Well, I try to keep it looking nice."

"And you succeed admirably." Charlie took his arm again and led him down off the platform. "Now, if I might introduce you to another member of our company? He is Publius Promo, our advance man, and during the performance, he will function as house manager—so he will need some information from you, if you would be so good as to supply it."

"What's a 'house manager'?" Langan asked, and Charlie led him back to the entry doors, explaining a portion of his own job to him in some detail.

"Bless the day that man auditioned for us!" Barry sighed. "I didn't know we were hiring a natural diplomat."

"A fortunate acquisition indeed," Horace agreed. "But should we not be seeing to your own preparations, Barry? The house must be about to open."

"Oh, my, yes!" Barry glanced at his watch. "I don't think makeup would be appropriate for me under the circumstances, Horace, but I would like to run my lines again. Could you cue me?"

"My pleasure, Barry."

The doors at the back of the hall opened, and Publius stuck his head in to call, "The house is opening!"

An electric thrill went through us all, even though nobody said a word. Everyone sat up a little straighter, stood a little stiffer, felt the adrenaline rush through them—even those of the company who were in the audience tonight. Marty grinned a little wider, and even Larry looked more lively where he sat glowering at being left out. Winston, of course, crossed his legs, leaned back, and became even more nonchalant—but with a coiled eagerness in him, ready to spring out at the slightest need.

Barry glanced at the ready room and shook his head. "I must be out of sight! But where?"

"Back there." I pointed. "Door to the maintenance hall, Mr. Tallendar. Nobody will come there except maybe a janitor. Shall I bring you a couple of chairs?"

"Yes, thank you, Ramou!" Barry said, relieved, and started for the door.

"A pitcher of water, too, eh?" Horace asked, looking back over his shoulder, then scurrying off after Barry.

I went over to the storage closet, took out a couple more folding chairs, and followed after them.

When I'd seen them settled with a pitcher and two glasses, I bethought me to check up on Ogden, speaking of drinkables. I stepped around behind the screen. "Hi there, ladies!"

They both gave the obligatory scream, though neither of them was baring anything more than her hands and face, and Ogden looked up.

"Can I get you anything, Mr. Wellesley?" I stepped up behind him, close—very close.

"A double whiskey and soda, and hold the soda," Ogden sighed. "But since you can't get me that, Ramou, you might as well check through my kit, with particular attention to the bottle of spirit gum."

"Oh, there's no need for that, Mr. Wellesley!" Especially since, if he was calling my attention to it, it really must be filled with spirit gum, even if it *was* large enough to hold a pint. Besides, I'd already spotted the atomizer with its freight of golden liquid—just about the right shade for high-quality cognac. But I didn't see how a tonsilful of cognac was going to get Ogden drunk, and the whole little bottle wasn't enough to even make him tipsy—especially since I'd seen just how much he could hold without falling down. Of course, it only took a couple of ounces to make him woozy, but he could keep on going after that for an amazingly long time. So I just said, "If you don't need anything, I'd better check in with Merlo. Break a leg!" And I went out up onto the platform, down, and up the aisle, wondering why Horace and Ogden were so insistent that we keep that old phrase, "Break a leg!" even though the professionals stopped using it once the amateurs picked it up. The young professionals, anyway.

I ran back to the control board, at the top of the back row. Merlo was already chatting agreeably with some early-comers, so I could relax—as it were—and look at the platform.

Hey, it looked okay, with the lectern moved over a little toward the audience's left—I was beginning to think of it as "stage right," but it still took an effort—so that it would balance the counter with the four "heads." The screen looked really nice, a wood-grain frame that you couldn't have told from the real thing anyplace else but here, where it was right up against genuine wood. The simple fact that it was mahogany made it look artificial, compared to the golden tones of the trim in the lecture hall. That mahogany frame was filled with panels of rose-colored swirls on a cream-colored background. Mind you, it still looked like an impromptu addition—but it looked okay.

"Are these seats taken, young feller?"

I looked up in surprise. A bearded man in the usual denims hovered at the end of the row of seats, with a poke-bonneted woman behind him. "Uh, no!" I said. "Just checking out sight lines. Here, let me slide out." But I didn't—I stepped over the back of the seats, up next to Merlo. What was it with these Citdelites—did they all like to be far away from the stage? Excuse me, platform.

No, they didn't. The front rows were completely full, the middle rows were filling up fast, and people were streaming up to the back rows. I stared. Had our word-of-mouth advertising been *that* effective?

I stepped over to my boss. "Merlo! They're here! They're really here!"

"Sure are, sport." Merlo grinned. "Nice people, too—every farmer in the county is interested in our control board."

I wondered if interest in gadgets was enough to qualify someone as "nice people" in Merlo's book. "But *how*?"

Merlo shrugged. "They're farmers—for them, machines mean a bigger crop. So they're—"

"No, no! I mean, how come they *came*? We didn't hit *that* many people today."

"Oh." Merlo grinned. "No, we didn't, but you have to realize, Ramou, that every single person we talked to told it to five others, and each of *them* told five others, and it grew exponentially."

"Are we *that* interesting?"

"Interesting? Ramou, you check into it, and you'll probably find that we've been the hottest item of gossip in this town for the last three days—probably the hottest item for the whole planet."

I stared out at all that audience. Come to think of it, I suppose it wasn't so surprising, after all—when there's nothing to do on Saturday night, ever, *anything* is a major event.

Then I spotted another reason why we probably had a big audience. Elias was just sitting down in the inner seat of the last two on the aisle, and Prudence was about to sit down next to him when she looked up and saw me. She waved gaily and hurried up the aisle.

I couldn't help myself—I felt the slow grin growing. I scolded myself for it, and remembered Marty's infatuated face. Friendship, yes—nothing more.

"It's so exciting, Ramou!"

My, that girl had a loud voice, especially when it wasn't called for. Of course, to her, it was—she wanted all her friends to see she was on a first-name basis with the famous show folk.

"Glad you think so," I said. "I'm kind of excited, myself."

"Excited?" She stared, her eyes big by accident for a change. "About *Hadleyburg*?"

"Sure am," I confirmed. "I was afraid we weren't going to pull *any* audience. You did nice work for us, Prudence. Thanks a lot."

She blushed and lowered her gaze—she did it well. "Oh, it was nothing, Ramou. I just told a few good friends about it."

"Been telling them all afternoon, though, haven't you?"

I had a notion a large number of those friends were male—and all coming in hopes of seeing Prudence. If so, it had been a bad idea—she might not look so good to them, after seeing Suzanne in makeup and erotic emotions.

On the other hand, she might. That girl was *really* beautiful.

"Well, yes. It was such delightful gossip, I couldn't *possibly* keep it all to myself."

"Glad you didn't," I said. "Drop by backstage after the show and tell us how you liked it."

She lit up like a laser. "Oh, *could* I, Ramou? I'll be ever so glad! Yes, I'll see you then!"

"First call," Merlo said. He waved at Langan, who was lounging next to the switches for the overheads. Langan nodded and turned off the built-in lights. The audience went "Ooooh!" even though the portable house lights we'd brought were still on. Merlo gave it a five-count, then touched a patch, and the lights dimmed down, then came on again. The audience went silent, startled, then erupted into furious questions about whether or not the power had gone out for a moment, or whether it was a signal of some sort.

"It's a signal," I told Prudence. "Means the show will start in a few minutes."

"Oh, yes! I'll see you afterward, Ramou!" And she hurried back to her seat.

I watched her go, wondering how much a treat it would have been if she didn't have to wear such huge billowing skirts, with what must have been three or four petticoats under them—no chance hoping for a bit of breeze to press the cloth tight and give me a fleeting glimpse of her figure. Then I reminded myself sternly that if she wound up wounding Marty, it wouldn't be because of me. I turned to Merlo. "Ready to go?"

"Not quite." Merlo was frowning, one hand pressed to the button in his ear while the other pressed a black dot onto his lower lip—a microphone that would pick up whispers.

"Something wrong backstage?"

Merlo nodded. "What's the delay, Horace?"

* * *

"A last-minute snag," I whispered to Merlo through my intercom. "One of the deacons has come back to greet us with alarming news. I will let you know when we can proceed."

"Okay," his whisper answered me. I turned away from the unit and back to Barry, who stood tall and straight, not letting his alarm show. "Cannot speak?" he asked. "But why not? Is there a problem with my text?"

"No, your text appears to be fine—especially the description of Salome's dance; you seem to have managed to make it clear how sinful it was, without inflaming the passions of the reader."

I noted that he had not yet seen Suzanne's reaction to it.

"Then what can be the problem?" Barry asked.

The deacon looked uncomfortable, then instantly overcompensated by going ramrod straight with a look of stern self-righteousness. "Mr. Tallendar, we have received off-planet information about your company today."

My stomach sank. I am certain Barry's did, too, but he only frowned with polite puzzlement. "Yes?"

"We have been advised, Mr. Tallendar, that the Star Company is subversive!"

"Subversive?" Barry stared, amazed.

So did I. I will readily agree—nay, boast—that our plays did not conform to Elector Rudders's censorship standards, but freedom of expression has been a cardinal principle of democracies since the American Revolution, perhaps even since the English Restoration, and the exercise of that right cannot truly be deemed subversive unless it preaches the overthrow of the existing governmental system.

Then I realized that, to Rudders, *anything* was subversive if it disagreed with him, or impeded his progress toward his own goals, one of which was the gaining of total power—which was anathema to freedom of speech, of course.

Barry recovered and forced a smile. "My company might occasionally be accused of undermining the foundations of art, deacon, by critics who do not comprehend our standards—but of undermining a duly constituted government? Never!"

"Our source says you've already done it," the deacon

said stubbornly, "that you started a revolution on the first planet where you performed."

Barry stared again, but recovered more quickly this time. "I would say that is quite an overstatement, sir—indeed, I would say that it is false. Tell me, how did you receive this information?"

The deacon dismissed the question with an impatient gesture. "How, does not matter!"

But it did, to us—since radio waves cannot travel faster than light, but our ship could. Obviously some other ship had landed that day, with a message from Elector Rudders—and I could easily guess who the courier had been: our nemesis, the Man in Gray.

"What does matter," the deacon was saying, "is the truth of the statement!"

"There is none," Barry said flatly. "The fact is that we were used by a revolutionary underground that had been steadily working for decades to overthrow the company government on New Venus. Everything was in readiness; they only needed some signal for the people to rise. They made the final curtain of our play their signal."

"A play which aroused the emotions of rebellion, sir! What play was it?"

"One of Shakespeare's masterpieces," Barry answered, "The one about the Scottish usurper."

"Macbeth?" The deacon stared, and I winced, reminding myself that it had not been an actor who said it. Nonetheless, the dread of bad luck suddenly overshadowed me—and surely, the deacon himself was proof enough of that. However, there was hope: The only book his forefathers had definitely brought from Terra would have been the Bible—but if there had been two, the second would have been the complete works of Shakespeare.

"But how could a Shakespeare play work the people into a frenzy?" the deacon asked.

"It could not," Barry answered, "unless the people of New Venus had taken their Shakespeare extremely seriously—and judging from their reactions during the first act, I can assure you that they did not. No, Deacon, the fact of the matter is, very simply, that we were used."

The deacon stared.

Barry nodded grimly. "It is not pleasant, sir, to have to acknowledge that we were duped, but I am afraid we were. The revolutionaries used us for their own purposes, without our knowledge or consent."

There were a few details he was leaving out, of course, but that was the gist of it.

"However, the uprising did follow the final curtain," Barry admitted, "so if you have a secret revolutionary movement working on this planet, Deacon, you should indeed forbid us to appear."

"We certainly do not!" the deacon exclaimed indignantly. "No one would have cause, for we live by the laws of the Lord! And none would dare rebel against the Lord!"

I wondered if he had ever read *Paradise Lost*, but did not mention it—if there were rebels, I certainly did not want him confusing them with Satan. I decided that he had not read Exodus terribly well, either, or Chronicles—and from what I had seen, all his people had cause to complain, even to rebel. But that, of course, was the opinion of a secular humanist, not a believer.

"Then you have nothing to fear," Barry assured him. "After all, how could a mere play start a revolution?"

"True, true." The deacon was mollified, but unconvinced.

Perhaps it was unfortunate that the audience chose just that moment to start protesting at the delay. Cries of "It's quarter to eight!" and "What's keeping you?" rose, then a whole hubbub of discontent.

"However," Barry said, "if you feel it is really necessary to cancel my lecture at this eleventh hour, I will ask that you inform the audience yourself."

The deacon didn't shy away, but you could see that he was quailing at the thought. He, too, must have been looking forward to this performance—for that was what they were expecting, really; no doubt they intended to arrest us *after* they had enjoyed the show—and he knew how badly his fellow citizens were looking forward to it, too. The last thing on Earth he wanted, just then, was to have to stand in front of them and explain why they would not be able to hear Barry speak. "Well enough, then," he said reluctantly, "you may deliver your lecture. But we shall be watching, mind!"

"I had certainly hoped that you would be," Barry said, with massive relief. "May I ask that you take your seat now, Deacon? We really should not keep our audience waiting any longer."

17

"Somebody wants your seat, Ramou," Merlo said.

I looked up and saw a gramma hovering expectantly over the two empty seats at the end of the row, right next to Merlo. She was smiling with suppressed delight, and behind her glasses, her eyes were bright with anticipation. "Okay, okay," I muttered, then aloud, " 'Scuse me, ma'am . . . sir . . ." as I passed her husband.

They crowded in quickly, just as Merlo flashed the lights. The audience set up a louder murmur, and I stepped up against the door and turned to watch.

Then Merlo turned the lights out completely, and the audience noise went up, with notes of anxiety to it. Quickly, he brought the stage lights up, and the audience let out a gratified "Ahhh!" It changed to an "Oooooo" again as Barry stepped out into the lights. He went to the lectern and bowed.

They quieted down.

I stared, surprised—no applause? Then I realized that these were people used to hearing real lectures, and it probably wasn't the custom to applaud the speakers. After all, *they* weren't famous 3DT stars.

Barry apparently realized that, too, because he turned and gestured to the screen. Marty and Larry stepped out, lifted the folding screen, and carried it away—Larry had fussed about having to do it, claiming it wasn't his union, but Barry had insisted that the screen was a prop, and this was Larry's blocking, and besides, Ramou was needed at the back of the house with Merlo—for what, I still hadn't figured out—and besides the besides, Larry wasn't scheduled for a part as a head in *Caesar*, and did he really want to leave Citadel without ever having appeared in front of an audience? So Larry had subsided, muttering, and was now carrying one end of a screen.

The screen passed, and there were four rounded cones of black veiling sitting there on a countertop, the front of which matched the screen that had just disappeared. A murmur of wonder passed through the audience, but Barry was turning back to face them, and opening the folder that lay there waiting for him with his script. He touched his ear briefly, and I could see the slight tension under his dinner jacket that showed he was squeezing the trigger for the electronic prompter. It must have been working, because he seemed satisfied, and looked up at the audience and cried out, in his great, ringing voice.

"Attend, good people, and listen to a tale of vice and shame! It happened very long ago, and we all know who to blame—blame for tempting folk to fall, and bringing them to ruin! We'll show their moral turpitude, and the trouble it was brewin'!"

The audience murmured wonder—apparently, this was not what they were used to in the way of an introduction—but also muttered with impatience. They wanted to see what was under those black veils.

"The villain's one we all know well, and Herod was his name!" Barry whisked the veil off the first head—and there was Ogden, leering at the audience. Apparently, Barry had changed the order of seating during the morning rehearsal.

The audience went wild. They booed, they hissed, they shouted in anger, they shook their fists. I shrank back in shock, afraid I was going to have to try to quell a riot single-handed. It must have been at least as big a shock to Barry and Ogden, but they held their places perfectly. Barry was impassive. Ogden, though, only held still till the initial shock had passed. Then he started mugging shamelessly, sneering at the audience, laughing wickedly at their anger, looking down his nose at them with true hauteur.

They loved it. You could tell by the delight in the booing.

I realized these guys had come primed. They hadn't been sure what to expect, but they were ready for it to be a sensation, and even readier to respond to it in kind.

Finally, the noise began to slacken—and Barry was on

them right away, projecting his voice out to the back row louder than any of them, and they shut up fast, so they wouldn't miss a single word.

"Herod!" he cried, to pick up the flow of the lines again. "Wicked, cruel, and treacherous—but his wife was more the same!" He whisked the veil off the next head in line, and there was Marnie, gazing down at them scornfully.

I was braced for them to go wild again, but they didn't—they were silent for a moment, in shock, I suppose. Then the "Ooooooo" began, female voices first, then male—the husbands didn't want their wives to think they really *liked* all that paint and those classic features—rolling up one side of the audience and down the other, then throughout the whole house.

Marnie just held her pose, regarding them with disdain, which may not have required acting, for her. When the noise began to die, Barry went on:

"Herodias was the viper's name, a strumpet ill and fell!"

He was drowned out by more audience noise, this time sounding shocked, with an undertone of anger—maybe because of the word "strumpet," but maybe also because of the way Marnie was flouncing about and looking at them with a knowing half smile; don't ask me how a bodiless head can flounce, but hers did.

Again, Barry waited, and sure enough, the noise slackened. As soon as it did, he orated over its remains, "In his declining years, old Herod fell beneath her spell! She taxed the people, slew her foes, made Israel a churning stew! I tell you, people, there's no end to the chaos a bad woman can brew!"

A roar of anger now, with shaken fists, and women calling out vile insults to the heartless queen—but not to Marnie herself. Apparently she understood the difference—I'm not sure *I* did—because she just smiled like the cat who got into the dairy and stared them down with a look of contempt.

"Now, a good woman is a blessing rare," Barry declared, when the audience had done registering their votes against vice, "for all the world to hold. She heals the sick, comforts grief, and helps us bare our woe. She makes this weary life a joy, lets hidden blessings show—but even as a virtuous woman lifts our souls, a wicked one can do more harm than living flame and coals!"

The audience shouted agreement, and Marnie turned slowly to glare icicles at them. They loved that, they shouted all the harder, and she turned away in disdain. They quieted a little, and Barry was in gear again.

"This preening shrew a widow was, Herod's latest toy . . ."

Marnie glared up at him.

Barry stepped over and shook a finger in her face.

The audience cheered.

Marnie snapped at the finger, almost bit it off—and somebody had a sense of humor, because one male voice let out a startled shout of laughter, quickly smothered.

The whole audience went quiet in surprise. I don't think it had occurred to them that they could laugh in a lecture hall.

Barry inspected his finger for damage, the old ham, as he went back to the lectern. He gave it a shake and looked up at his audience again. "She gave him pleasures old and new, since he was closed to joy. . . ."

The audience muttered to one another, puzzled. Just as Charlie had hoped—they were going to think about it. I began to realize that this audience actually paid attention to the words, every one, instead of just sort of absorbing the story.

They weren't loud enough to merit a pause, though, so Barry plowed ahead. "She reawoke his guttered lust, roused up his faltering zeal—and whispered in his ear that he should grant her treasures real. She raised within his ghost of youth—he felt as one who's callow may—and her brightest tool to fan his flame was her daughter, Salome." Barry lifted the next veil, to show Suzanne's head. She gave the audience a lazy smile, her head moving just a little in a slow, sensuous rhythm, and I swear you could almost hear the drums pounding and the dirty trumpet sassing.

The audience went into pandemonium. Women shouted invective, men hooted, catcalls echoed off the walls.

For a moment, Suzanne froze. Then her smile grew wider, and she began to pick out single men in the audience for a slow, slumberous glance. I saw a few wives turn to slap at their husbands and scold, and the audience noise turned to one of protestations of innocence.

That was low enough; Barry spoke over it. "This juicy child made Herod drool—to watch her sashay by made Herod long to touch and taste—but she knew Mama's rule: that he might look, but never touch."

A scandalized murmur passed through the house, swelling. Barry went on quickly. "For that, he'd turn to Mum. Then she would slake the thirst now raised, and charge a heavy sum. He had to gouge the Israelites for cash to buy her jewels, and judged each case as she saw fit. He was, for her, a fool."

Rumbles of agreement from the audience, and I glanced aside. The men were looking sober and intent, nodding, but the women had little smiles. I wondered.

"But there was one man, at least," Barry cried, "who saw what Herodias was doing, and scolded her for it. Of course, he didn't scold her in private—he wasn't in the palace. No, he scolded her by preaching to the nation, to all the people, telling them that she was trampling on the laws of God even as she trampled on the people. He was John, the Baptist." He whisked aside the third veil, and there was Horace's head—but what a head! The wig was perfect—you'd have thought it was his real hair, especially since it was iron-gray, streaked here and there with black. His complexion was darker, his nose more prominent—and his expression stern, but thoughtful. He looked wise, very wise—and very, very virtuous.

The audience cheered as if he were the cavalry coming over the ridge as the fort was burning.

"We think of the Baptist only as the herald of Christ," Barry said. "We tend to forget that he was a prophet of God, in a time when the prophets spoke the word of the God of Israel to His people, telling them when their sins had become too offensive to bear, when they were straying from the path he had marked out for them, and chiding the rulers when they fell into sin. That means, of course, that he criticized Herod unmercifully—and very courageously, too. But the people of Israel feared God more than Herod, and Herod feared the people, so the king left the Baptist alone.

"But when he began to tell all the people that Herodias was a whore and a vile sinner, she told Herod to slay John."

The chorus of boos and hisses was so sudden and so huge that it made Barry halt, blinking up at them in surprise. He recovered quickly, of course, waited them out, then went on. "At first, Herod was afraid—but she begged and pleaded, and threatened to leave his, ah, house. Finally, the king gave in—and the Baptist confronted Herod, the tyrant, the mass murderer!"

Hisses and boos again.

Since Barry couldn't be heard, Horace took his cue early and turned toward Ogden. Ogden turned to glare at Horace. Horace raised his chin, looking noble and righteous—and the audience started cheering. Ogden scowled, mouthing imprecations, then turned to rant and rave silently at the audience. If ham is better when it's well aged, Ogden was gourmet fare.

And the audience ate it up. The cheers turned to boos again, shouts of outrage building, then finally beginning to slacken. Barry waited it out, letting Ogden have his field day, and probably jotting notes to tell the old man that he was overdoing his overdoing.

Finally, the audience let Barry talk again. "Herodias nagged her husband day and night—made herself a pest, begging him to slay the prophet, so her conscience might find rest. But Herod feared the people's wrath, feared John the Baptist, too, and stood firm against Herodias' pleas . . ."

Marnie turned to Ogden, mouthing and mugging in what she probably thought was pleading—but from her, it looked like hectoring and scolding, while the audience had a field day with booing and hissing. Ogden scowled at her, shook his head, then mouthed back at her. Marnie reddened and mimed shouting.

Ogden turned his back.

The audience went "Ooooo," in that tone that tells you a storm is coming.

Marnie gave it to them. She went red in the face and mimed shouting and screaming at Ogden until the veins stood out on her neck. Finally, Ogden turned back to her and gave her a slow, haughty, frosty glare. Marnie broke off in midshriek and stared.

Barry backed it up half a sentence. ". . . stood firm against Herodias' pleas—till Salome came through."

All Suzanne did was roll her head around and give the audience a slow, lazy smile—but the young men cut loose with whoops like a Rebel skirmish squad. Suzanne took it as her due, her smile widening, eyelids drooping.

Barry shouted them down. "It seemed she'd formed her own dislike, did not the Baptist trust, and told her mother she would help, in any way she must. So Herodias went up to the king, a bargain for to make—if he'd swear to grant Salome's wish, she'd dance to make him quake with lust, which Herodias would slake."

The house fell silent in anticipation, except for a couple of exclamations like "The hussy!" and "Scarlet woman!" in older female voices.

"Even then, old Herold stalled," Barry cried. "With protest he did wail—so Herodias bartered for his oath, the Dance of the Seven Veils!"

This time, no whooping, only a low moan that didn't seem to come from anywhere in particular. It gave me the shivers, but apparently gave Suzanne a different kind—she shuddered, head back, eyes closed. I wondered if it was real, or just good acting. Whatever it was, it made the moans louder. I knew why—I suddenly realized I was moaning, myself. Not that I would have made a sound if I'd been alone, mind you, but when it's coming from all around you, it's hard not to chime in.

"They called it the Dance of the Seven Veils, good people," Barry said, "because Salome was dressed only in those seven veils when she began to dance. Mind you, they were large veils, very large, certainly enough to conceal her completely—but as she danced, she would take off one veil after another, until she was completely nude!"

The moan hiked up another notch.

"Herod's mouth watered." Barry was relishing every word. "He wanted to see Salome, *all* of Salome, more than he had ever wanted anything—it seemed. He promised, promised blindly—whatever she asked, he would give, if only she would dance the Dance of the Seven Veils before him.

"So she did, good people—she danced the dance!"

Suzanne rolled her head around again, eyes closed, and the moan rose louder.

"She turned," Barry said, "slowly at first, her feet stamping out the rhythm, then turned again, her hands beginning to move, playing with the veil, teasing its fringes."

And again, Suzanne wasn't *really* doing anything—but she sure made you *feel* as if she were. The way her eyelids drooped, the way her head curved and swung, somehow you *knew* she was doing a slow, drawn-out strip tease as Barry described it. I found myself imagining what the rest of her was doing underneath the counter and felt the sweat start, even though I *knew* she really wasn't.

But the farm boys didn't. The moan soared upward and broke in a shout, then turned into a loud, excited hubbub that went on and on, women furiously denouncing the harlot, men hooting, inarticulate male shouts that seemed poised between passion and anger. I would have hated to be one of those guys' wives tonight, if I were a Puritan—or maybe loved it; you never knew how people reacted in private.

But if the wife turned away, there was going to be hell to pay.

Suzanne rode it out, or rode it like a surfboard, her head bobbing and weaving, ducking and rolling, while Marnie watched, alternately hissing and beaming with vindication, and Ogden watched, too, bug-eyed, swallowing convulsively. I *hoped* it was acting—anything else, and his heart couldn't take it.

Finally, Barry could make himself heard over the tumult. "The tempo of the drumbeats quickened; she let the first veil slip, then slip some more as she turned, and turned again, undulating, pretty little feet moving in intricate patterns. The veil slipped lower, lower, then fell away entirely, revealing . . .

"Another veil."

The audience moaned and slavered—I swear you can hear slavering. Must have been the way they panted.

"Again the drums quickened; again she turned and

turned, this time slinking across the floor to the king himself, beckoning, dainty hand caressing the air only inches from his face—but even as he reached, she was gone, and his hands caught only . . .

"The fringe of her veil."

The audience fell silent, poised, waiting, and I didn't doubt that there wasn't a man in the house who didn't see the scene in his mind—or a woman either, with her own face atop that veil-clad, luscious body that nobody saw with their eyes, but everybody imagined.

"She spun away, the veil tearing loose, revealing another veil—and a bare, smooth shoulder."

The moans began again.

"Salome wheeled, she writhed, fingers playing with the corners of her veil, the edges of her veil."

Suzanne was back into her head dance again, eyes not quite closed, turning this way and that—and finally revolving completely around, head bobbing in time to the rhythm of the music track that Merlo was dutifully playing, even though no one was hearing—the audience was too loud.

"The drums throbbed like heartbeats!" Barry cried. "The lyres sang, and she slipped the veil loose to fall about her shoulders like a cloak, pirouetting, turning and turning like a dervish, closer and closer to Herod. He reached out, plucked the edge of the veil as it spun . . . and it came away!"

Incredibly, the audience roared.

"Another shoulder was bared for his inspection, both shoulders and her neck!"

The roar had slackened, but it didn't stop—just went on and on.

"She turned away again, stamping with the quickened rhythm of the drums!" Barry cried, caught up in his own spell—and Suzanne's. "She swayed, she writhed, she churned—and the fourth veil seemed to loosen with each movement. It belled out about her, spinning lower and lower, until it fell to the floor and she stepped over it, clad still in three veils that covered all but her dainty feet, her arms and hands, her shoulders."

The roar turned into a moan of disappointment. Here and there, a bespectacled woman glared about her, but apparently she couldn't be sure the noise was coming any more from her husband than from anyone else's.

"But she whirled faster and faster," Barry chanted, "the fifth veil coming loose, spinning aside to fall over the king's face. He clawed it loose, panting, eyes bulging, and watched the sixth veil weave and waver, as Salome danced entranced, all her being subsumed in the drumbeats and the lyres, thinking only of making the movements of her body one with the music—and the sixth veil fell away. Herod groaned, for everything he wished to see was still covered by the seventh veil—but Salome danced and danced, whirled and wheeled with wild abandon, closer and closer, and Herod reached out to whip the seventh veil loose!"

The male moan broke loose in a chaos of shouting, punctuated by women's cries of outrage, but it all died fast; they poised, hushed and breathless, no doubt waiting for a description of Salome sans veils, even though no description could have equalled what they were seeing in their minds' eyes.

So Barry didn't give it to them. "Salome spun away as a top does when you've pulled its string—then sank down kneeling, bowing low, facing the king, hands folded beneath her chin in supplication, eyes downcast, forearms covering her so well that she might still have been clothed."

A moan of disappointment swept the audience, but it lacked conviction, almost had relief. Everyone wanted to treasure his or her own fantasy, even if they didn't know that was what they were doing—and I realized, with the shock of insight, that it wasn't just because they were Puritans.

People, they were human! In all their lives, they'd never been given an excuse to imagine sights like these, never been given an excuse to do it without guilt, even though every cell of their bodies cried out for it. Hypocrites? Do you call yourself a hypocrite if you diet, no matter how hungry you are? Oh, they had the self-control, all right—but for one frantic evening, they'd been told they didn't need it.

Why? Because this was a lecture, that's why—and a lecture the deacons had approved. Don't blame these poor, starved souls if they didn't know how to handle it. Again, just think of the last time you were on a diet—then sat down for dinner at Thanksgiving.

Barry went into a low, hushed tone. "But Herod had seen one glimpse of what he *really* wanted to see, and he ached for more. Hoarsely, he cried, "Enchanting! Entrancing! The king thanks you, the king's favor lights upon you! Name your gift, and you shall have it!"

The house went totally quiet. You could feel the tension build.

Barry spoke through it. "And Salome, panting, said, 'The head of John the Baptist on a silver salver.' "

The audience roared.

They roared furious denunciations, they roared imprecations, they scolded and threatened and argued. They shook their fists, all that furious tension Suzanne had built up in them cutting loose at Herod.

Suzanne sat immobile, head bowed as Barry had described it, eyes closed, lips parted, breathing hard.

Ogden stared at her, appalled. Marnie smiled with not-so-secret satisfaction.

Barry waited for the audience to get the worst of it out of their systems, then went on. "For a heartbeat's space, that throne room held in silence. Then Herod cried out, wailing. 'Not that! Ask for gold or jewels, ask for half my kingdom—but do not ask for the head of John the Baptist on a silver salver!' "

Ogden pantomimed the wails of grief. Suzanne turned slowly to him, face a set mask, obdurate.

"But Salome had sought to flirt with John the Baptist," Barry explained, "as she flirted with every man of her mother's court, promising everything, giving nothing—but that holy man had spurned her!"

The audience gasped; they had never heard this interpretation.

"John the Baptist had turned her away!" Barry cried. "Worse, he had rebuked her for her loose ways and preached to her the virtues of chastity! The lust for revenge burned as hot in her as the lust for her burned in Herod, so even though her mother wavered, tempted by the offer of a kingdom, Salome insisted, 'The head of John the Baptist on a silver salver!' "

Furious denunciations from the audience—but mixed in with it, here and there, the vindictive cry of satisfaction, in a woman's voice. It made my blood run cold.

" 'No!' Herod cried."

Ogden mimed anguish while the audience clamored. As soon as they had quieted halfway, Barry called out, " 'Do not ask it,' the tyrant howled, 'do not demand it! The people shall rise in anger, the God of Israel shall smite us! Ask for anything, but not the head of John the Baptist on a silver salver!"

Barry's voice sank low, for the audience was hushed, numb and waiting the disaster they knew must come. "But Salome had longed to kiss the lips of that wild desert prophet, had ached to know that he, too, had fallen beneath her spell—and she had seen that John was moved by her beauty, for he was, after all, a man, and human, as much prey to the frailties of the flesh as any of us."

A rumble of confusion and denial broke out.

"But he had twice the moral fiber of any of us!" Barry called out to them. "He was a giant of faithfulness to the Lord and the law, and he had spurned her."

They actually cheered, and they meant it. At least, the men did. It made me wonder.

"Spite and anger seared the heart of Salome," Barry orated, "and she demanded, 'I wish for the head of John the Baptist on a silver salver!' "

The audience fell silent again.

" 'Not that!' Herod cried. 'Ask me for the world, ask me for Rome itself, but do not ask for the head of John the Baptist on a silver salver!'

" 'I will have the head of John the Baptist on a silver salver,' Salome insisted, 'and nothing else!' "

The audience booed, the audience reviled her. Suzanne turned to them slowly with flashing eyes, giving them a dagger look, and they booed louder.

Barry waited for them, then went on. " 'You have given your word, husband,' Herodias reminded. 'You have accepted Salome's gift of dancing the Dance of the Seven Veils; you must stand by your word.'

"Then Herod groaned, and turned his eyes away, and bade his soldiers do the deed."

Ogden squeezed his eyes shut, then turned slowly away, bowing his head, and the audience groaned for him.

"Salome caught her veils about her," Barry said, careful to clothe Suzanne in the audience's minds' eyes, "and rushed to hover near the dungeon door, to hear the cries of horror and pain—but no cries came."

Total silence in the house, filled with apprehension, waiting, waiting . . .

"She chafed," Barry said, "she rubbed her hands—and Herodias watched with a gleam in her eye, to see the fulfillment of her revenge.

"Then up the soldiers came, and Salome cried out in horror, for they bore to her the head of John the Baptist!"

Barry leaned over and whisked away a black scarf that lay on the table about Horace's neck, and the audience could see a silver plate where there should have been a collar—and as the scarf flipped past him, it streaked his face with stage blood, from the pool of the stuff that lay in the doughnut-shaped dish.

"The head of John the Baptist on a silver salver!" Barry cried.

The audience howled in anguish; women screamed; they stared in horror at Horace's blood-streaked, eyes-closed face. I saw at least two women who fainted. Their husbands pulled out the smelling salts, though, and they recovered remarkably quickly.

When the worst of it had passed, Barry called out, "Salome screamed and fell back against the wall—but the guards knelt before her, holding the bloody thing so close that she could not escape. She screamed and screamed, and Herod turned away his eyes, and groaned.

"But Herodias sat smiling, eyes gleaming with vindictive pleasure."

Marnie stared out at the audience with a supercilious smile, eyes gleaming true to the script—but again, that was the kind of thing that came naturally to her.

The audience went wild again, reviling the villain and villainess in no uncertain terms—until Barry went back along the counter, dropping veil after veil back in place. As the last one fell to shroud Suzanne's face, silence suddenly fell with it. Barry strolled back to the lectern, taking his time, knowing he was gathering all eyes as he went.

He turned, looked down at his script for a second, then looked back up and said, "That is the end of it, good people! That is the degradation that lust can lead a man to; that is the horror and savagery to which vanity can lead a woman. But more than anything else, thus are people corrupted and brought down—for you know the end of the story, of Herod's ignominious death, and Salome's end; you know how Herod's grandson, in his false pride, followed his grandfather's folly. These things are in your Bible, or in the books of history, and the moral is clear: Turn away from the commandments and the Lord, and you will come on evil days, then sink to your undoing. People, we must always be strong, holding ourselves firm against the temptations of those who would breach our integrity; we must be steadfast, for they will be unrelenting. Do not let the tempters lead you into behaving like someone other than who you truly are, or you will lose track of yourself, and of the still, small voice within you that keeps you true to yourself, and the path of right."

He stood immobile for a second, and the audience caught their breath, not quite understanding—and not even understanding what they weren't understanding, for they'd never been through this before.

Then Merlo dimmed the lights.

The shocked surprise held for a second or two more of silence in the dark. Then, suddenly, someone started to clap, and in a second, the whole room thundered with applause.

Merlo brought the lights up again. Barry stepped away from the lectern and bowed, and the applause redoubled. When it started to slacken, he straightened, stepped over to the counter, and, one by one, pulled the veils off the actors' heads. As each came off, the applause rose again as the actor's head nodded forward in the closest it could come to a bow. The applause crested, then started to decline, then soared up again as the next veil came off. Finally, Suzanne's veil lifted, and the applause smashed against the walls—applause mingled with cries of outrage and condemnation, but also cries of admiration, and outright wolf whistles.

When it finally started to dwindle, Barry nodded, then bowed, and all four heads bowed with him. The applause washed over them in a tidal wave, held, then receded—and the actors straightened as Merlo dimmed out the lights.

The applause went on awhile in the dark. It even went on after Merlo had brought up the house lights. Then, and only then, did the men and women rise with sighs of satisfaction, and regret that it was over, as they gathered up their coats and shawls and headed for the aisles, and the door.

I writhed my way between them, then slipped into the vacated seats and vaulted over them row by row, up onto the stage. I just had to tell them all what a great job they had done.

I found them all clasping one another arm in arm, grinning from ear to ear, and telling one another how wonderfully they'd done, even Marnie.

Then Suzanne started to slump.

18

I was at her side in a second, kneeling and rubbing her hand. I can't imagine what earthly good it could do, but it was what the romances always said the hero was supposed to do when the heroine swooned, so I did it, while I prattled inanely, "What's the matter, Suze?" Then, realizing how ridiculous that sounded, "It's okay now. It's over. No one's going to hurt you."

"I—I didn't really think they would," Suzanne gasped, "but . . . Oh, Ramou! It was so scary, the way they yelled and hooted at me!"

"Tribute to your acting," I assured her.

"But they didn't mean it for Salome, they meant it for *me*!" She turned and flung her arms around me, burying her face in my shoulder, and she didn't start crying, but her whole body trembled. I hugged tight, but not crushing, stroking her back with one hand, closing my eyes to savor the feel of her body against mine, of her against me, and had the good sense not to speak, just to be there.

I looked at Ramou holding Suzanne, and knew that Prudence had lost, if she had ever had any chance of being more than a mild amusement to Ramou, anyway. Suzanne, of course, had won—but she had won months ago, back on Terra. She just hadn't had the good sense to pick up her winnings. I hoped she would, this time, but I doubted it. I had come to realize, though, that her reluctance wasn't really a matter of career being all-important to her, more important than love and bonding—that was only the excuse for something more deeply seated, far more.

"She will be all right, Horace," Barry assured me. "It was a frightening audience, you must admit. I felt as if I were weathering the storm of five generations of pent-up frustration, all coming out at once."

"You probably were." I gazed at Ramou and Suzanne, with Lacey standing behind, ashen-faced, and Marnie towering over them like an avenging angel, just daring any of those hypocritical Puritans to lay a hand on one of her companions. "But yes, I am sure she will be well."

"Mr. Tallendar!"

Barry turned about, and I with him—to find all seven deacons standing there in the hall, fairly glowing with satisfaction—heightened by apprehension. "An excellent lecture, Mr. Tallendar! I have never seen anything like it!"

"It was a rare experience, gentlemen," Barry assured them. "Your people constitute a most enthusiastic audience."

"Aye. We have never heard the like," Deacon Joram said, the apprehension winning out in his face for the moment. "We are somewhat concerned about the intensity of their excitement, Mr. Tallendar. It cannot be good for folk to become so stirred up."

"I am tempted to agree," Barry said slowly, "but I do not think you would find this degree of emotion worrisome, if it were the result of listening to a sermon."

"Well, there is some truth in that," Joram admitted, "for in a sermon, all their feelings are directed toward the actions that lead to salvation. Here, though, Mr. Tallendar, you have finished by aiming them away from vices, but have not sent them toward virtues."

"However, there is no question that you must perform again tomorrow night!" The chairman handed Barry a slip of paper. "Here is the bank draft for your thousand, minus the cost of the hall, as we agreed—but there were easily as many people who could not get into the hall, Mr. Tallendar, as there were people inside! You agreed to a second presentation, under such circumstances."

As I remembered it, Barry had been the one to raise the possibility—but I wasn't about to object.

Neither was Barry. "We will be delighted," he said, taking the check.

"But . . ." Joram glanced at his fellow deacons, then

turned back to Barry. "But perhaps there could be one slight change, Mr. Tallendar."

Barry tensed, though not overly much—he was used to altering the play to fit the desires of the audience, had even undertaken play doctoring as a secondary profession. "What change would that be, gentlemen?"

"As we said, we are concerned about the intensity of the emotion that arose," Joram said. "We think it may have been due to your description of Salome's dance."

Barry frowned. "I would scarcely call that salacious or obscene, Deacon."

"No, no, as it was written, it was in very good taste!" Joram hastened to assure him. "Decorous, quite decorous! But as it was delivered, Mr. Tallendar, with the emotions in your voice and the . . . aura of dancing your lady created, it was far more inflaming than it appeared in the manuscript."

Out of the corner of my eye, I saw Suzanne lift her tear-streaked face and turn to watch us, frowning. I heard Ramou murmur, "It's a compliment, Suze," but she watched us closely anyway.

"I suppose we could gloss over it a bit," Barry said. "I must tell you, though, gentlemen, that the role was far more demanding on Ms. Souci than she had anticipated. We might substitute a different head tomorrow night."

It was interesting to watch the play of emotions on the two young ladies' faces—covetous delight mingled with apprehension on Lacey's, and on Suzanne's, indignation mingled with relief.

Joram nodded. "Excellent, Mr. Tallendar! Truly excellent! Our compliments to your company!"

The other deacons all nodded, murmuring agreement, and Barry smiled.

The murmur of the audience outside the doors to our hallway had been growing, and now, suddenly, we realized that it had shaped itself into words. "More! More! More! More!"

The Deacons looked suddenly distraught.

Barry suppressed a smile. "What am I to tell them, gentlemen? You have just approved another perf . . . presentation for tomorrow night, but those people who are voicing their demands so stridently are not to be in the audience—only those who were turned away."

"Well, yes. That does bring us to another matter we wished to discuss with you, Mr. Tallendar—of presenting a different lecture, two days from now, on Friday evening."

"Why, of course!" Barry purred. "We would be delighted." He nodded at Winston. "Would you be so good as to tell them that, Mr. Carlton?"

"But of course." Winston departed through the double doors. In a minute, we could hear him proclaiming loudly that there would be a new lecture on Friday night, and in the meantime, if the audience could leave in an orderly manner and *not* come back, it would be appreciated, because Mr. Langan would like to close the hall. He didn't mention our own desire to go back to the ship, of course—we veterans were already dreading our attempt to get out the stage door, especially since there was none.

"I take it, then," Barry said to the deacons, "that you wish us to go ahead with the woeful tale of the vices that led to the death of Caesar and his murderers?" He saw the hesitation on their faces and added quickly, "And the deaths of Caesar's friend Marc Antony and his consort Cleopatra, of course."

All three women looked up at the mention of the fabled queen of the Nile.

"That would be most illuminating, of course," Deacon Joram said slowly, "but we would prefer that this time, you spoke of the virtues instead of the vices, Mr. Tallendar."

"That would restore a bit of balance," Barry said thoughtfully. "Did you have anything more specific in mind?"

"We were impressed by the moral you drew tonight, sir, very impressed," the tall, cadaverous old deacon said. "We would like you to expand upon that theme—we would be very interested to hear your thoughts on the virtue of integrity, sir."

"Very interested indeed," several other deacons agreed.

"A most interesting thought," Barry said, brow furrowing, "and I suppose the story of Caesar does exemplify it, in a way . . ."

But it did not, and he knew it—at least, as Shakespeare

had presented the tale. Of course, I suppose you could have said that Caesar was the man of integrity, and it brought his death; Brutus was the man who allowed his integrity to be breached, and that caused *his* downfall and death—but in both cases, integrity caused death. Scarcely the moral that the deacons wished to hear, I think.

"I suppose it could be used in that fashion."

Barry looked up, to discover Charles at his elbow. With relief, he said, "Gentlemen, the initial author of tonight's piece—Mr. Charles Publican."

"It was *you* who wrote this fascinating lecture?" The chairman reached out to pump his hand.

"Only the initial thoughts and sequence," Charles said. "I fleshed it out with the help of my young collaborator, Mr. Kemp . . ."

Marty looked up, raised a hand, and smiled. The deacons looked immensely reassured by Charles' nondescript looks and Marty's homeliness.

"But Mr. Tallendar must take the final credit himself," Charles said, "for he edited and rewrote the lecture to suit his own style and opinions."

"However, we were fully in accord on the moral issues," Barry hastened to assure the deacons. "What would *you* recommend as a story to illustrate the principle of integrity, Mr. Publican?"

"The story of Everyman, Mr. Tallendar."

"Every man?" Joram frowned. "But how can there be one story for every man?"

" 'Everyman' is the name of a famous hero of a Renaissance morality play, gentlemen," Charles explained, "and his story is one that applies to us all—the story of temptation and the struggle for redemption."

Their faces all cleared—no, cleared and became infused with zeal. "Yes, of course!" one deacon cried, and another said, "That *is* the story of us all, is it not?"

"It is," Charles agreed. "Unfortunately, it has millions of variations, and the ending is not always happy."

"So it is one among the millions of variations on a common story that you would tell us?"

Aren't they all, I thought—but Charles was speaking.

"It is. It has a happy ending, of course—and I would

adapt it, in this case, to focus on the virtue of integrity. There would be many temptations, of course, and we would have to show Everyman allowing his integrity to be breached, so that we may show the consequences—but we would then see him mending his ways and his integrity, and winning through."

"Excellent! Excellent!" Joram nodded, with the chorus of deacons backing him. "How soon may we see the text, Mr. Publican?"

"I think I could have something ready by noon tomorrow," Charles said slowly.

Barry stared at him in alarm.

"Right after dinner, then!" Joram fairly beamed. "We will see you in the deacons' chamber, Mr. Publican—and you, too, Mr. Tallendar?"

"Of course," Barry murmured.

"Excellent!" Joram said again—I think it was his only superlative. "At one o'clock, then. Thank you, gentlemen, and good night."

"Good night," we all chorused, waving, and watched them go back out through the doors. Barry stepped forward to close them tightly, then turned to his company . . .

And the eruption started.

"*Another* overnight wonder?"

"Impossible!"

"Really, Barry, I don't know how . . ."

"Are you out of your *mind*?" Marnie cried.

"In all probability, yes." But Barry raised his hands to cancel further discussion. "However, Mr. Langan needs to close the hall, and I find myself immensely in need of familiar surroundings. Shall we discuss this in the lounge, my friends?" Not waiting for an answer, he turned back to exit through the doors.

I looked apologies at them, then followed. Behind me, I could hear Marnie stamp her foot, but I heard her footfalls following immediately after, too.

We went down the center aisle to the big double doors, and on through.

"Oh, Ramou! It was so *wonderful*!"

There she was, coming toward us with arms raised to

hug, which just incidentally gave a hint of her contours, face alight, eyes glowing—and several other girls her age in the background, simmering because she could call me by name and they couldn't.

I grinned, remembering Marty and trying not to make it too broad. "Glad you liked it, Prudence."

Suzanne and Lacey weren't.

But her Puritan code must have frowned on hugging, because she veered aside at the last moment and brought the arms down to clasp Marty's hand with both of hers. "And *you* wrote it? It was magnificent, an inspired text!"

"Well, I helped." Marty gave her his foolish grin—only I suspected that he wasn't clowning.

"I can hardly wait to see *you* as one of the heads, Mr. Kemp! Or even hear you lecture, yourself?"

"You'd get bored real fast," he assured her, but he was gazing at her like a mooncalf—the one they fattened for slaughter.

Finally, Prudence decided to be a little bit politic. She turned to Suzanne. "Oh, Miss Souci! You were excellent!"

"Why, thank you, dear." Suzanne caught her hand, possibly to keep it from coming any closer. "I'm so glad you liked it." She didn't let go, so Prudence had to look over her shoulder to the veterans. "Ms. Lulala, you were wonderful! Mr. Ogden, I hated every second!"

"You say the sweetest things," Ogden rumbled.

"How kind," Marnie purred. "But you must introduce us to your friends."

That was the last thing Prudence wanted to do, of course. She stepped aside. "Oh, no, I couldn't think of keeping you when it's so late. But is it true? Will you perform . . . ah, speak again tomorrow night, Mr. Tallendar?"

"Yes," he said, "but only for those who have not heard me tonight." She looked just crestfallen enough, so he added, "But for one who has given us so much assistance and hospitality, I am sure we could find a seat."

"Yeah, she can sit up by me," Merlo said.

"Oh, *thank* you, Mr. Hertz!" she cried, and Marnie tossed Merlo a whetted glance.

So did I. Up by Merlo would put her up by me, and though that was enjoyable on the surface, I wasn't so sure of it deeper in—especially after I'd seen how Marty looked at her.

"However, as you've noticed, we really must be on our way," Barry said, all regret. "Good night, my dear—and thank you for your kindness." He tipped the hat he hadn't put on yet, and headed out the door.

Prudence fluttered a tiny hand at him and stepped back. Relieved, Elias reeled her in, and we plowed into the mob of young well-wishers, mostly female, who heaped praise on the menfolk and honeyed catticisms on Suzanne and Marnie. Marnie answered them in kind, with a poisonous smile and honey-coated barbs.

At last we were through, and stepping out into the crisp night air.

"You sure you're okay, Suzanne?" I asked. She was really leaning on my arm as we came out of the lecture hall, not just holding it for show.

"Yes, Ramou," she said firmly. "I can hold myself together until we get home." Her lips quirked in wry amusement. "If the *Cotton Blossom* is home!"

It was, I realized. I wondered when that had happened.

"Hello, sweetie," a voice called, and a chorus of wolf whistles echoed it.

Suzanne looked up, sudden fear writing itself across her features.

A semicircle of farm boys was ringing the door to the lecture hall, lying in wait with leering grins.

"Back inside," Horace snapped, and we turned just as half a dozen burly plowboys slid between us and the doors. Suzanne stared, appalled, and Lacey was looking pretty scared, too, but Marnie was furious. "Why, you ill-bred louts! Just what do you think you're doing?"

"Claiming what's there for the taking," one of them answered.

"Women on the inside!" Barry snapped.

"Ouch! You clumsy clown!" Marnie snapped, as Marty jostled her aside. He stood facing the locals, fists clenched, trembling but resolute. So did Merlo and Winston and I; in a second, the girls were inside a ring of males.

"Neanderthals!" Lacey protested, but it was weak and, frankly, undermined by relief.

"Yeah, clown," a voice between us and the doors said. "Better get out of the way before you get hurt."

"Oh, let *me* make a few jokes." The old familiar loose-lipped grin slid over my face as I stepped just a little bit forward, keeping my fists firmly at my sides—for the moment. "Hey, look, we forgot our scripts. Mind getting out of the way?"

"Come and get 'em," the biggest local sneered, stepping squarly in front of the door.

"Good idea." I started to step forward, but Marnie grabbed my arm and hauled me back.

"Let's talk first—they might see reason," Merlo said.

"Reason?" somebody rural scoffed. "We see a woman behaving like a queen bitch and another throwing herself at us! What reason can there be for *that*?"

"Throwing herself at you?" Barry said. "When she only moved her head, only made facial expressions?"

"But her eyes, the look in her eyes!" another voice said, trembling with lust. "They told us it was there for the taking!"

Horace said, "I thought you good folk of Citadel counted it a sin to accept an offer of that sort."

A grumble of anger surrounded us; they didn't like that, didn't like being reminded that they were planning to commit a sin. But it was John the Baptist who was telling them that, so they didn't make excuses—and didn't advance. "You're no better than the rest of them, old man!" a voice said angrily, but his tone was weakened by his own lack of belief.

"Really?" Horace sounded quite interested. "Why is that?"

"Why, because you're not the Baptist!" the man shouted. "You're just an immoral old man who's *pretending* to be the Baptist!"

"I'm very glad that you see the distinction," Horace said quietly. "Then surely you realize that Ms. Souci is not Salome, but was only pretending to be."

That brought them up short for a moment. There was a lot of hoarse, muttered conversation; then a voice spoke up clearly again. "Maybe, but she can't have any better morals than Salome, or she wouldn't have looked at us like that!"

"As it happens, her morals are quite strict," Barry told them.

"Tell us another one, gaffer!" someone scoffed.

"It's true," I told my bozos.

The big one stared. "You can admit it?"

"It hurts to say it," I told him. "Hurts inside, and down deep."

"Sounds lowdown to me," he muttered, but he was sounding less sure.

"The actor is not the character," Barry explained. "The actor only *portrays* the character, to make the meaning of the words more vivid to you."

Their muttering didn't sound convinced—but it did sound doubtful. "She's Salome," one voice stubbornly insisted, "and we want her."

"Then I am Herodias!" Marnie suddenly bulled her way between Winston and Merlo and stood, hands on hips. "Take a look at me, boys! Do you *really* believe I am the storied consort of Herod?"

"Yes," several voices said immediately, and one explained, "Or her in the modern day, anyway—and coming where you have no business! We'd take you, too, if you didn't look so sour!"

"Try!" Marnie glared at them. "Just try!"

They shouted and came for her.

I found out later that Winston and Merlo managed to yank Marnie back behind them before the boys in front closed in, then laid about them with Merlo's ham-fisted haymakers and Winston's own version of martial arts; he did his Christmas chopping early. At the moment, though, all I knew was that there was a barrage of fists aimed for me and Marty, and I knew I had to get rid of my attackers fast, because Marty couldn't hold out alone.

It was no time for finesse or caution, though I did have it ringing through me that I couldn't kill anyone, or we'd never get off that planet. But it was no time for courtesy, or boys' games. I hit the big one in the solar plexus, chopped another guy in the collarbone while the big one was folding, then leaned to the other side to squeeze a nerve. The shrieks were quite unmanly and horrible, and suddenly, I wasn't enjoying this at all—but I kicked the fallen bodies out of the way and left Suzanne guarding them with tack-hammer shoes while I kidney-punched the two who were beating Marty down, just as he collapsed. They howled and stumbled over Marty, falling, just as a huge fist caught me in the head from behind. I felt myself flip over and fall, but all I could see were stars. Then something caught me under the shoulders, and I lashed out with a blind kick. The stars cleared, and I stumbled back up on my feet to see a farm boy curled around his pain and another one's fist coming right at my face.

I dropped to my knees; the fist went over my head, and I surged up, catching him by the shirtfront and kicking his legs out from under him.

And suddenly, it was clear between us and the doors.

"Inside!" I snapped at the girls, but didn't wait to see if they took my advice—I swung around to help out in front. . . .

Just in time for somebody to kick me in the stomach.

I saw it coming a half second early, just enough to start falling back, and it exploded in my belly like a bomb. For a moment, my abdominal muscles locked, and I couldn't breathe—but that had happened to me before, and as my knees hit ground, I reached out and grabbed the other leg, right on the nerve point.

The man screamed, as high and sharp as a woman, and fell down, still screaming. I felt the first stab of breath come back, and staggered up to my feet while I was waiting for my lungs to get back to working full-time. I knew I was going down, but I was blasted sure I was going to take that plowboy with the thick boot down with me.

This time I saw the kick coming a long way off, in time to catch the boot and pull.

He yelled and flipped up, then down. I didn't hear anything snap, though, and I dropped it before anything could. He wouldn't be using that leg again tonight anyway.

I looked around for my next customer—and saw that somehow, suddenly, the way was clear. The farm boys were all down, several of them moaning and rolling on the ground, holding their heads. I glanced up at Barry and Horace, and saw them holding their canes like sabers, eyes glinting, breathing hard. Winston had blood running down from the corner of his mouth, and Merlo was going to need several big orders of beefsteak. Marty was helping Ogden up from under a tangle of farm-boy boots, and I felt a surge of rage—they even had to pick on an old man! I stepped toward him, anxious to check his pulse, but he waved me away, panting. "I am all right, Ramou. No heart attack this time, by some miracle."

"Let us not rely on another one," Barry said. "Back to the ship, friends."

I beckoned to the ladies, and they came out from the lecture hall—they had managed to get back inside a locked door, somehow. They looked about them hesitantly, and picked their way through the moaning bodies gingerly and quickly, as if afraid someone was going to try to tackle them, which was quite possible. I went to meet them, just in case, and ushered them back into the center of our group. We started off down the avenue, with some curious onlookers watching from the sides—audience members, who had stuck around for the late show.

"Barry," Marnie said, "do you suppose, tomorrow night, we could afford a cab?"

"Surely, Marnie," he said, "if there is one."

"Never can find a taxi when you need one," Marty wheezed.

"Especially not when they haven't been invented where you are." I reminded myself to check his ribs when we got home. "Larry, how are you?"

"Why should you care?" he snarled feebly.

I contained a surge of irritation. "Because if you go out of commission, there's one less wall between me and them, if it happens again. Anything broken?"

"I don't think so," he grated, "no thanks to you."

"Ramou knocked down half of them himself," Suzanne protested.

"How about you, kid?" I looked up at her, feeling a stab of anxiety. I didn't know what lay in her past, but I was hoping this wouldn't trigger any bad memories.

"I'm all right, Ramou," she assured me, but she clung all the more tightly to my arm. "I'm all right, because you were there. Don't ever go away, all right?"

It numbed me, but I managed to pat her arm reassuringly. "Just let me know when you're going to need me, okay?"

Prudence must not have liked the sound of that, because she suddenly showed up on the other side of me, towing a red-faced Elias. "I am so sorry, Ramou! So ashamed of my countrymen!"

" 'S okay," I grunted.

"But it is *not*!" Surprisingly, there were tears in her eyes. "They are such beasts! Such savages! They have no care for refinement or elegance, no care for culture, no regard for women! They think we are just objects to be owned and used, just toys and servants!"

"Prudence!" Elias exclaimed, shocked.

She rounded on him. "Do you think you are really any better than the rest of them, Elias? Do you think you will not truly expect a woman to wait on you hand and foot and, aye, warm your bed at your command, when you are married?"

"Such is the natural order of man and woman!" he protested.

"Scarcely natural at all," Marnie snapped.

"It is set forth in the Bible!"

"Not in quite those words," she said witheringly, "and please remember that the Bible was written by men!"

"Aye, because God is a man!"

"Don't tell me you see God as one of those brutes!" Suzanne protested, tears in her eyes.

Elias glanced at her, but he couldn't quite meet her gaze. "We are all imperfect," he muttered.

"But some more imperfect than others, it seems! Why did they *do* it, Ramou?"

"Testosterone overload," I said. "We boiled up a lot of pressure in them." I was careful not to say who had lit their fires most. "They had to blast it out one way or another. They did."

"The steam-boiler theory of male behavior," Lacey said dryly.

"That steam gets a lot of work done," I said, but it went past her; she thought James Watt invented electric light.

Behind us, we heard whistles shrilling.

I halted. "What's that?"

"The watch." Elias glanced behind him uneasily.

"The watch? Where were they when we needed them?"

"Watching," Marty said.

"Be glad they didn't show up while we were fighting," Merlo said. "Loyalty to the home team usually wins out."

Barry nodded. "They probably would have arrested *us* for disturbing the peace."

"There is some truth to that," Larry said, with a glance at Suzanne. She didn't even notice him enough for a glare.

"You wrong our good watchmen," Prudence began, but Elias disagreed.

"If you'll excuse us, we must needs go home—it is nearly curfew. Your lecture was excellent, and I thank you for it. Come, Prudence!"

"Ow! Elias, not so *hard*!" But she didn't try to stop him, just stumbled after, looking back to wave at us. "My apologies for my fellow citizens!"

"Not your fault," I called after her, trying to avoid the look of hurt on Marty's face, though it was almost buried under brooding calculation.

"The watch will clean up the mess," Horace told us, "but I would rather not be part of what they clean up. Let us hurry, friends."

We did.

We were back at the ship in record time, breezing through customs with the speed of familiarity. It still gave the girls the willies, but they were so preoccupied that they didn't pay them much attention.

Once we were back in the lounge, Suzanne relaxed in the safety of familiar surroundings, and was about to collapse when she noticed people needing nursing. She shrugged off her own fatigue and got busy distributing beefsteaks, ice bags, and analgesics; nothing spruced her up so much as having somebody to take care of. I felt the same way about bartending; the simple repetition of an old, familiar job calmed my jitters immensely.

When we were all more or less settled, Barry said, "Congratulations on a marvelously successful opening night, friends."

There were groans of appreciation. "Oh, it was a riot!" Marty answered.

"Unfortunately, I now find it necessary to discuss my conference with the deacons," Barry sighed. "And I fear it cannot wait for tomorrow. Soothe your aching spirits, my friends, and pay heed."

"You sure that's all we'll have to pay?" Marty asked.

19

"Some of you no doubt overheard my impromptu conference with the deacons," Barry said, "but for those of you who did not, the summary is that we would have had a sell-out audience if we had been selling tickets, with at least as many turned away at the door."

Everyone exclaimed with delight—they were too drained to shout.

"The deacons advanced the rental fee for the hall for this first night," Barry said, "and were ready to lose that money if we did not pull enough audience to justify it. However, they also paid us a thousand in their local currency, to make up for the ticket money they would not let us charge; they wanted this first night to be free to all comers."

"A *thousand*?" Marnie exclaimed.

"A thousand," Barry verified.

"Then we have our tank of fuel!"

"No, maybe half of it," Captain McLeod told her.

Marnie frowned at him. "Rather a high price for water, isn't it?"

"It's a big tank. Besides, the water's free—it's just the distilling and delivery they're charging for."

"Through the nose," Marty clarified.

"A very large nose," McLeod agreed.

Marty fingered his proboscis as if wondering if he'd been insulted; I couldn't help myself, the way he did it—I laughed, and a couple of others joined me. It lightened the mood a little.

"So we have to perform again," Suzanne said, pale-faced.

"You need not, my dear. I am sure that Lacey would be willing to take your place."

Triumph warred with fear in Lacey's eyes.

"As per our arrangement with the deacons," Barry said, "we are therefore obligated to give a second performance of *Salome* . . ."

"You mean, *Herod*," Ogden corrected.

"*Herodias,*" Marnie snapped.

"Indeed," Barry said diplomatically. "This time, however, we will have to pay for rental of the hall—tonight's rental, and tomorrow's."

"*Two* nights?" Marnie cried. "We'll still only have half a tank!"

"No, the hall will only cost us two hundred for each night," Publius told her. "Our net will be sixteen hundred."

"Maybe not a full tank," McLeod said, "but enough to get us to the nearest oasis. We'll have to refuel there, but they'll take IDE money."

"So one more night, and we have our escape!"

"*If* we fill the house," Barry reminded.

"Three times, and we fill the tank," Marty pointed out.

"With a slight profit," Barry agreed.

"Please!" Suzanne hugged herself, shivering.

"Hey, *I'll* play Salome!" Marty offered

"We want to attract audience," Larry objected, "not drive them away."

"A second night of *Salome* will suffice," Barry said. "However, there is a price."

Marnie frowned, not understanding. "Yes—sixteen hundred."

"No, a price to be allowed for being allowed to perform again, though it was not stated as such. The first part of that price is that we make the description of Salome's dance even less vivid . . ."

"But that will leave nothing!" Lacey protested. "How can they censor us like that?"

"They are a church, Ms. Lark—the whole planet is one church, and the deacons govern both the Church and the state; they are one and the same."

" 'To the landlord belong the doorknobs,' " Marty quoted.

" 'And the owner of the grocery store may choose not to sell the avocados,' " Barry finished.

Suzanne laid a soothing hand on Lacey's. "Never mind, dear. You wouldn't, if you had been out there tonight."

Lacey's face went bleak as she remembered that she might be on stage tomorrow; "We'll see," she subsided.

"I believe you implied two parts to this price tag," Winston reminded.

"Yes. The second is that we perform . . . ah, present, a different lecture, two nights from now."

"Two *nights*?"

"We can't possibly do it!"

"That's a whole 'nother *script*!"

"Impossible!"

"We have done it once already, and in less time," Barry reminded them. "Charles assures me he can have the script ready by noon tomorrow, since we have to meet the deacons at one . . ."

"Dibs!" Marty called to Charlie. "On the script, I mean, not the deacons."

Charlie nodded. "You're in. Couldn't do without you, Marty."

Larry glowered. "Why is he elected playwright, and I am not?"

"You didn't volunteer," Charlie said, "and it's too late now. Too many brooks spoil the cloth."

Horace looked up. "I don't believe that's quite how the saying goes, old chap."

"You haven't tried to pull the fabric of a play out of the drink," Charlie retorted, smiling.

"So the rough draft, at least, will be ready on time," Barry said, "and I will ask Winston to repeat past performance, by coaching the cast in a read-through, in my absence."

Winston nodded. "Glad to, old fellow—in self-defense."

"However," Barry said, "I intend to do all I can to see that the author delivers the speech, this time."

Charles shook his head with calm determination. "Not a chance."

"I am sure you could do excellently, old chap."

"Martyn could do better."

Larry looked up, indignant, but Marty said, "No can do. I'm not qualified—only a B.A."

Charlie nodded. "And Barry is the one registered as having the M.A., and therefore the qualifications."

"I doubt that I am the only one aboard," Barry returned. "Be honest, Charles—what degree have you?"

"A B.Ed."

"Bachelor of education?" Marty stared.

"Oh, Marty!" Lacey scoffed. "We knew he was a teacher!"

"No, I thought he was a professor."

But Barry's gaze was still on Charlie's face. "Your *highest* degree, Charles."

"Ph.D.," Charles sighed. "That, however, does not automatically make me a good speaker."

"No, but we know that you are one."

"Nowhere nearly as good as yourself, Barry. Marty has said it—I was a professor, not a teacher. Put me at a lectern, and you'll have a lecture."

"But that's what this is supposed to be," Marnie protested.

"*Supposed* to, Marnie," Barry reminded her, "but we all know that our 'lecture' is a thinly veiled performance."

"Of course," she said impatiently. "That's why we were so successful."

"And how successful would we have been," Charles asked, "if it had been a *real* lecture?"

Everyone was silent, contemplating the prospect with horror.

"The defense rests," Charles said placidly.

"So does the prosecution." Barry sighed. "Very well, Charles. I shall speak your words again."

"Don't worry, Barry—you have the auto-prompter."

"And a great consolation it was, tonight. Well, friends, that is the situation. May I recommend that you do a bit of dignified celebrating? We may not be completely out of trouble yet, but the end *is* in sight."

"Won't you join us, Mr. Tallendar?" Suzanne asked.

"For a few minutes, perhaps." Barry smiled, suddenly looking immensely tired. "But I do long for a few hours' somnolence."

"Well, if you want to go to sleep," Marty said, "we could always ask Charlie for that lecture."

* * *

The party was short, but intense—we had a lot of tension to release. Fortunately, there's a limit to how many drinks you can put away in two hours of social pacing, and they're even less when you have to take a break to put Ogden away, too. Suzanne did that—I just helped. On the way back, we talked very seriously and earnestly about the next show, and I wondered what we were both trying to avoid.

So all in all, I was up and about without too much of a hangover, in time to see Barry, Horace, and Charlie off at noon, making sure they were well fortified with coffee and rolls inside. Charlie made sure I was well fortified with a copy of the script, leaving me with instructions to make a dozen copies and get one to Winston right away, even if I had to wake him. I went armed with coffee and doughnuts, so he didn't mind being waked too much. Of course, the glass of juice with Gran'ma Horrhee's Hangover Remedy in it helped—after he got the taste out of his mouth. He flipped through the script and told me to wake everyone and have them reconstructed and assembled by one.

At one o'clock, we were there—not happy about it, but there. I had the lighting dimmed down, but even so, Larry and the girls were wearing sunglasses. Some of us party more easily than others.

They took one look and stared at Winston in horror. *"Everyman?"* Suzanne gasped. "Isn't this instant death?"

"Not the way Charles and Martyn have written it," Winston said with relish. "It has been substantially updated, and, shall we say, made relevant. Barry has left us casting notes. Charles is to be the head of Everyman, surprisingly enough—Barry doesn't seem to be willing to let him off the hook entirely—and Larry is the head of the Playboy."

"Typecasting," Lacey muttered, but Winston went on with blithe unconcern.

"Martyn is the Fool—in the medieval sense, I'm sure—and I am the Tempter. Suzanne is the Temptress . . ."

He went on and on. We listened with growing amazement. Whatever kind of *Everyman* this was going to be, our Renaissance ancestors would never have recognized it.

We were just finishing up when Barry, Horace, and Charlie came in, wearing very self-satisfied smiles.

Winston looked up. "It went well, then?"

"Quite well," Barry said, and Charles nodded. "They liked the script just as it was, only had a few more points they wanted me to make."

Winston lost his own smile. "What sort of points?"

"Oh, stressing that even though he was not native to Citadel, Everyman still had no more in the way of worldly goods than most people do—and showing his redemption in terms of inner happiness, not in regaining all his belongings."

"How utterly naive!" Marnie said disdainfully.

Charles threw her a keen, probing glance, then smiled and said, "Perhaps . . ."

"Nothing objectionable, then." Winston nodded. "I assume they wish us to stick to the letter of the script."

Horace smiled. "I do not think they will object to the occasional bit of mugging, if that is what you mean."

"It will be very difficult to avoid," Winston said, "with a script like this!"

"I hope you have not obligated us to any further performances," Marnie snapped.

"It was quite tempting," Barry sighed, "since I have sensed the glimmerings of fat profits to be made from an extended run—but no, I did resist."

"His ribs will be sore from my reminders," Horace said, "and I am sure that we would be welcome for at least a second night of *Everyman*, if we wished it—but he did not commit us."

"We do *not* wish it!" Marnie said emphatically. "All I ask of this dustball is to let us free!"

"I do not anticipate any grave problem," Barry assured her. "Indeed, if tonight turns out as well financially as I expect it to, I shall ask Captain McLeod to refuel tomorrow."

It was a good thing he specified "financially," because the second night of *Salome* was a howling success in some ways, but a bomb in others. We didn't do badly, of course—I was thinking about the impact.

Ramou's concerns proved unfounded—almost. Everything proceeded as it had the night before, with shouting and whistling and booing and hissing—but we were braced for it, so it was not quite so frightening. I had an excellent view, from my position as John the Baptist's head—and I watched the audience closely as we came to the rewritten description of Salome's dance, which Suzanne would play again, with Lacey's half-hearted blessing.

But as Suzanne began to make her languid head-circles, and Barry began to read the abbreviated version of the dance, the audience began to mutter. The muttering grew substantially when they realized that Salome had discarded the first veil by the end of the second sentence. When the third sentence dropped the second veil, the shouts began: "Last night! Last night!"

Barry paused uncertainly, glanced at Deacon Joram in the front row, then raised his voice and bellowed out the third sentence, but before he could have her discard the fourth veil, the shouts had turned into a heavy, rhythmic chorus: "Last night! Last night! Same dance as last night!"

"How the devil do they know what we did last night?" Ogden muttered.

"Their friends told them, I'm sure." Suzanne was pale. "And I just *know* they made it sound as if they saw a lot more of me than they really did!"

Barry had paused, because even his mighty voice could not be heard. The chanting was becoming even louder and more angry. Deacon Joram waved at him. Barry looked the question, and Joram nodded.

Barry sighed, put away his script, and pulled out the previous night's version. He held it up for the crowd to see, and the applause and cheering shook the walls. As it abated, he muttered, "Sorry, Suzanne. But I assure you, Ramou has found a taxi."

Suzanne took it like a trouper, and if she paled further, who could know, under that Mediterranean makeup base?

They read the dance as it had been the night before, and the catcalls and hooting were deafening. I suppose that Suzanne was right, and that our plowboys were disappointed that the reality of the performance did not live up to its reputation—but they gave us a huge ovation nonetheless, keeping it up long after we had left the stage, and Winston had to go out to speak to them about our new and even more vivid play that would be offered for their edification on the morrow's night.

In the maintenance corridor that served as backstage, Suzanne was recovering nicely, and assuring Barry that he had no reason to apologize.

But we were all braced as we came down the steps to the front door.

They were there, all right—a semicircle of tall, brawny young men in blue coats and denims. Suzanne shrank back, but Ramou said, "No—wait a minute! You folks stay here." He stepped out through the doors, and we could not hear what he said, but we saw his upraised palm, his grin, and saw the largest of the young men step forward to shake his hand. He shook hands with several of the others, too, then turned to beckon us. We came out hesitantly and with the girls in the middle—but we were scarcely through the door when Suzanne stopped, staring, and said, "Why, Zachariah!"

"I'm surprised you remember my name, Miss Souci," he said, grinning, and stepped forward, holding out his hand. "That was one swell performance you did tonight! You, too, Mr. Tallendar—and all of you."

The relegation to subordinate status was not lost on Marnie, who immediately glared at the young man, but the circumstances were not appropriate for a scathing retort.

For myself, I was amazed at how quickly these young folk formed acquaintances—though not terribly surprised that those acquaintances should want to do Suzanne a good turn.

"We heard you had a little trouble last night," Zachariah said, "so me and the boys figured we'd stay around to see you got into your wagon safe."

To judge by the odd shouts and catcalls from beyond the line of his stalwart blue-clad fellows, there were many other young men who had been awaiting Suzanne's appearance with less altruistic motives in mind—but the presence of Zachariah and his friends, not to mention that of the large number of watchmen who happened to be loitering across the way, assured that we did indeed get into the large car that was waiting at the curb—courtesy of the deacons—

without incident. The driver informed us that it was one of the colony's few official vehicles.

As it rose and drifted away, I asked Ramou, "However did you make their acquaintance?" But all he would tell me was, "It was worth a few bruises."

Apparently the audience's demanding the original script did not worry the deacons greatly. It should have.

The opening night of *Everyman* didn't quite go the way we'd planned, you see. Merlo and I had done a little work on the counter, to make it look more modern, so we were expecting the audience to relate to it well—but not all *that* well.

It seemed to start out well enough—when Barry pressed the fake patch that only made a motor-whine sound, but also made it seem as if Charlie's head was raised into place mechanically, the audience oohed and ahed as if it had been a major magic trick. "Everyman was a man like any of us," Barry orated, "with a wife and two children, a hovercar in the garage . . ."

"Garage?" somebody in the audience asked somebody else, and the word ran through the house in tones of puzzlement.

Well, Barry knew how to respond to his audience. ". . . the garage, a small outbuilding where people keep hovercars," he said, "though for most, it is an outbuilding connected to the house. Everyman's house had seven rooms, as most have—a bedroom for each person . . ."

I smiled; that should make the deacons happy—not admitting in public that husband and wife slept together. For all I knew, maybe they didn't, on Citadel—except when the deacons told them to have another baby.

But the noise in the audience didn't stop—it kept on building. It took me a minute to realize that it had changed from puzzlement to incredulity.

In the front row, all seven deacons were sitting very stiffly.

Barry stood there waiting for his laughs, like any seasoned performer—or, in this case, for his audience reaction. When he finally realized that it wasn't going to crest and start to die, it had begun to turn ugly.

But he didn't try to shout them down. Way at the back, I could see his lips moving, but I couldn't hear a gram of what he was saying—and I suddenly realized that the people in the front row couldn't, either. For that matter, I was willing to bet Charlie couldn't, and he was scarcely four feet from the lectern.

The audience finally realized Barry was talking, and they shut up so that they could hear him.

His voice came to me like a thin thread, but it swelled amazingly; he went back to full projection as the audience quieted. I knew the script, having heard it once through at rehearsal, so I knew where he was—only a sentence further than he had been before the interruption. The old pro had repeated the same paragraph again and again until it could be heard.

"Everyman had a wife," he said, and pressed the button again. The motor whined, and Marnie's head rose into view—even she could do that much mime, at least. "She was a fairly ordinary woman, for the most part—a bit prettier than the majority, more skilled in the use of cosmetics to shadow and highlight her eyes and cheeks, but not greatly. They could not afford to have her dress in the latest fashions, of course—that was only for the very wealthy. No, Everywoman had to wait two or three years, until the fashions from Terra came to the chain stores on their home world of Arcadia, where she could buy them with all the other women in town. But she was not content with this, for their fortunes seemed to rise and fall even as the hemlines did . . ."

The mutter of incredulity had started again, and was growing.

"So Everywoman demanded that Everyman find a better job, which would pay much, much more."

A flash of irritation crossed Marnie's face, but she transmuted it into a look of discontent as she rounded on Charlie, pantomiming a scolding. Charlie's head flinched away.

"Now, that was difficult for Everyman to do, for he worked in a factory where all the heavy labor was done by machines, and all the fine work was done by more machines, and all he had to do was watch the machines to make sure they made no mistakes. . . ."

It was almost a roar of incredulity this time, all in male voices, with some outrage thrown in. Barry paused, but the deacons were turning pale. Joram glanced over his shoulder, then back to Barry, beckoning with both hands in a signal that plainly said, *Go on, go on!*

Barry dropped down to a murmur again, and the audience quieted to hear him—quieted very quickly this time.

"So Everyman knew he could not find a better job, because he had no skills or knowledge. But he did not want to go home to another argument, another scolding . . ."

The murmur was mostly female this time, with an undertone of male agreement, but I couldn't quite read the emotion yet.

". . . so he stopped in at the tavern on the corner, to drown his sorrows in drinks that had large measures of alcohol."

Mixed-sex murmurs this time, all shocked.

"Halfway through the second glass, he met . . . a young and flashy woman named Hetaera!" Barry pressed the button, and Lacey's head rose into view with a whine, makeup so heavy she must have applied it with a trowel, eyelids half-closed, lazy, inviting smile on her lips.

The noise from the audience was mostly male, and in tones of awe, with a seasoning of angry female voices. Barry gave them a ten-count, then started mouthing again. "She batted her long eyelashes at Everyman, coaxed him to buy her a drink, then another and another, as she listened to his sad tale of home life gone wrong, of a wife turned to a scold—while the bartender came by . . ." Barry pressed the patch, and up came Winston, with his famous evil leer. ". . . to tell them it was happy hour, and they could get as drunk as they wanted at a bargain price."

Winston inclined his head toward Charlie and Lacey.

"Everyman paid happily, and paid and paid, as his speech grew slurred and he began to weep."

The male voices turned to tones of contempt.

"Hetaera leaned over and whispered to him that his life did not have to be this way, that he could leave his shrew of a wife and come to her, where there would be more . . . consolation . . . waiting, and more, and more . . ."

The hubbub broke out anew, in tones of outrage with an

undertone of longing. It began to turn ugly, though, and a female voice cried out, clarion clear, "Why does it always have to be the woman's fault?"

"I was wondering about that myself!" a basso voice bawled in answer, and a furious argument broke out.

The deacons turned from one to another, alarmed and on the verge of panic. One of them turned away to the aisle and waved to Langan, who nodded and went out.

Barry held his position like a statue, but glanced over at Marnie. I could almost imagine him saying, "Hold your places, friends. I don't understand what is happening or why, but it will no doubt blow over."

Marnie responded tartly, and I expect it was, "Blow up, you mean."

"You there!" the enraged female voice cried. "You, Everywoman! It's a lie, isn't it? It's the man who leaves the woman, not the woman who drives him away!"

Marnie glanced at Barry; then her eye hardened, and she called out, "It is indeed. This nonsense about the shrewish wife is just a male excuse to justify their doing what they want."

Barry turned to her, remonstrating nervously, but a male voice cried out of the audience, "It's the fault of women who can't be content with their lot! Give them more baubles to lust after, and they'll hound a man to his death!"

"A fine excuse for a lazy layabout who doesn't want to work more than he has to!" a different female voice cried.

"Come now, Marnie!" Charles pitched his voice to carry over the crowd. "You know very well that not all women are perfect, and that some do become covetous nags!"

"Some, yes, Charles Publican—but your script presents them as being the norm!"

"Can you deny that there are many on Terra and the old worlds who live in sin?" a male voice bellowed.

"I can indeed," Winston called out. "They live in houses."

There was a stunned silence; then a shout of laughter erupted. It was a brave try, but even as the laughter was dying, an angry rumble was starting.

"Perhaps where you come from, Winston," Marnie said sweetly. "In my neighborhood, most live in apartments!"

"But they are sinners!" the male voice cried. "Sinners all!"

"Not all by any means," Barry protested. "Not even most. Wherever there are people, though, there will be *some* sinners."

The deacons nodded, relieved, but the angry voice bellowed out, "Nonsense! I've been there, and I've seen it!"

Every deacon went rigid.

"You can't tell the good women from the bad, they wear so much paint, and so little clothing! They're decked out in all manner of cheap finery and fake baubles!"

"The finery is anything but cheap," Marnie snapped, "and the baubles are often real gems."

Feminine incredulity this time, mixed with anger that finally found voice in a woman's cry. "Why can't we have such things?"

"They're vanities and sinful!" a male voice shouted back.

"But you pant hard enough after the women who wear them, don't you? No better than any of your kind!"

"Aye!" another woman shouted. "You only go spacefaring to get away from your duties at home!"

"If you women would try to make yourself prettier and more agreeable," a tenor called, "we wouldn't have to!"

"How can we, without your face paint and finery?" a woman demanded.

"Why can't *we* have machines to keep our houses clean, and schools to mind the children," another woman cried, "while we go out and earn, too?"

I stared—I didn't remember Barry saying anything about day care or household robots. He hadn't even mentioned a vacuum cleaner!

"Be still, you discontented cacklers!" the basso bellowed in full rage. "Be grateful for what you have, and do not seek more!"

"Ever the old song!" a woman shrilled. "Never mind that everybody has such things, back on Terra! Is that why our ancestors fled from there? Because women had life too easy?"

"You!" the basso roared. "You players! Do you see what misery you have wrought, you with your sinful ways and vain luxuries!"

Everything considered, I was very glad that, just then, the houselights came blazing on, and Langan led the Watch in.

The audience paid them no attention.

"Better for us you had never come!"

"Aye!" an older woman's voice shrilled. "What are you doing here, but corrupting our young people with notions of vanities? Get you gone!"

"Aye, get out!" a man roared.

"Perhaps that would be the path of prudence." Deacon Joram came up to Barry, frowning.

"No, let them stay!" several young women cried. "Tell us more of the wonders on Terra!"

" 'Tis the deacons who have done this!" an angry young man bellowed, "the deacons who have denied us these delights, who have barred us even from hearing of them!"

"Aye!" another man yelled. "What do you have to say for yourselves, sirs?"

"Surely suppressing news is tantamount to lying!" an older man called. "Can you really be holy if you suppress the truth?"

"We have never suppressed the truth!" The deacon chairman stepped up on the platform, turning in indignation.

"Suppressed the facts, then!" a younger man cried.

"Why would you not even let us *hear* about these marvelous machines that wash dishes and sweep floors?" a woman cried.

"Why would you not let us know that women, too, can earn money even after their children are born?" a young wife called. "Why would you not let us learn that women can even rise to govern?"

"This is not our way, on Citadel!" the chairman protested, hands upraised. "It never has been!"

"Aye, so that the men can keep all the power to themselves and grind the women down!"

"Aye, so that men should never know that they do not *have* to marry!"

"Not to marry is to invite sin!" Deacon Joram shouted. "If a man must satisfy his concupiscence, better that he satisfy it within the bonds of marriage!"

"A fascinating argument," Barry said, ushering his cast

toward the door to the maintenance corridor, "but I think we had better not stay to hear it. Ah, there you are, Ramou! But what of Merlo?"

"He unplugged the board as soon as the lights came on, and went out the front doors," I panted.

"An excellent thought; let us emulate him. To the front doors, everybody!"

We went through the doors into the maintenance corridor, and an older woman came hurrying toward us, Publius on her heels, carrying a strongbox. "No, Mr. Tallendar! Don't go out that way—there's a mob of people clamoring to get in! They want to talk to the deacons, too!"

"Why . . . Mrs. Hannah!" Barry brought up short. "How kind of you to come! But really, the Permits Office should not be involved . . ."

"After you said such brave things for us women, I couldn't just stand by and watch you walk into danger! Come with me, Mr. Tallendar, all of you—there is a back door!"

She hurried on down the corridor. Barry cast us all a look of surprise, then beckoned as he turned to follow her. We all went after, pell-mell.

"It was so brave of you to say all those things!" the lady was saying. "I *knew* the Angel had come to save us from our bondage! Oh, telling us all those things that everybody's been whispering all these years, but never had the courage to come right out and say, for fear of the deacons and the Watch—but you didn't hesitate, Mr. Tallendar! And you didn't shrink from telling the deacons the facts of it, Mrs. Lulala! Oh, it was so brave, so wonderful to behold!"

And, singing our praises, she hurried us on down the hallway.

Dazed at the thought that she had actually done something brave and noble, Marnie followed.

So did we all.

20

Out the door we came, onto a side street. We could hear the crowd shouting, and I turned the other way more or less automatically.

"No, out here!" Mrs. Hannah called. "The deacons have the car waiting for you!"

Well, it couldn't get down the alley, which was only three feet wide, so this was as close as it could come.

"They probably won't notice us," Barry said. "Their attention is elsewhere. But move very quickly, people."

We moved.

As we came out of the alleyway, we saw the crowd.

They were gathered in a huge, ragged semicircle around the doorway, shouting and occasionally cheering. Every now and then, they would suddenly shut up, and you could hear a guy calling out, relaying what was going on inside. As he finished, the crowd let loose with a vast, ugly shout of rage.

"What did we start?" Horace asked, stock-still, staring.

"A riot." I took him by the arm and pulled him with me. "Into the car, Horace. With a crowd in this mood, I don't think it's safe for us to stick around."

I let Ramou conduct me to a seat in the limousine, if you can call it that—more of a small bus, actually, with seats at the front for a driver and his assistant or relay, or whatever.

The seats were arranged around the sides, the row at the front facing backward, so we were able to view one another.

"Good-bye, Mr. Tallendar!" Mrs. Hannah called, "and thank you—thank you all!" Then she pressed the latch, and the door slid closed.

The hover lifted up on its air cushion and slid smoothly into movement.

"What did she mean?" Suzanne asked. "What was all that about?"

"Apparently there has been a good deal of submerged unrest," Barry said. "We unwittingly brought it out into the open . . . It *was* unwittingly, wasn't it, Charles?"

"Why," Charles said, "however would I have known of their grievances? Did *you* know, Marty?"

"Not a hint," Marty said.

Barry still looked unconvinced. He was giving Charles a long, gauging look, as if beginning to suspect why the ex-professor had been so reluctant to deliver the speech.

"It is a good guess," Ogden said slowly, "but we will never know if it is correct."

"Mr. Tallendar is *very* correct."

Horace turned to look, and so did everybody else, surprised. I was, too, but I kept my head down for a moment; I recognized that voice. When I heard Marty say, with awe and wonder, "Hi, Prudence!" I forced myself to turn slowly and smile.

She was sitting in the copilot's seat, looking positively radiant. Her eyes sparkled with excitement, her bosom heaved, her cheeks were flushed. Something lurched inside me; I hoped it wasn't my heart.

"You were exactly right," she said. "For a hundred of years, the deacons haven't even permitted us to talk about what it must be like on other planets. Ever since the merchants started selling our goods to the old worlds, the deacons have prohibited them from telling what they saw on their travels. But they could talk about it with each other, of course, and people overheard, as they will sooner or later—so we have been gossiping about it for a century, wondering what it was really like and whether their tales were true, or some colossal, cruel hoax."

"And we validated it," Barry said heavily. "We made it clear, tonight, how the rest of the people of the Terran Sphere live."

"Yes, and we will never be content with our lot again! To think that most people have their own cars, that their houses have seven rooms, that the wives have face paint and pretty clothes that are only a year or two behind the Terran fashions! The people are there right now, raising a fuss that the deacons will never be able to contain!"

The crowd had even had a little help, I realized. Now I knew why the younger female voice had seemed so familiar—and why I hadn't recognized it at the time; I hadn't heard Prudence sounding strident and militant before.

"They will *have* to allow some changes now, some few luxuries, some 'vanities,' as they call them, or the Church will never stand!"

"Pray Heaven it does," the driver moaned.

I stared, recognizing the voice. "Elias?"

He glanced back with a rueful smile. "Aye, 'tis Elias. How else would Prudence have been in this car with you?"

I hadn't thought he would admit it.

"I didn't know you could drive," Marty said.

"Oh, aye! That was my last job—driving the farm's hovertruck into Hadleyburg with loads of grain; there were a dozen of us who did. That is why I could find a job at the spaceport—driving their tanker that filled your ship with fuel."

"So how come you're driving this car? Don't get me wrong," I said quickly, "it's great to see a familiar face—but how'd you manage it?"

He shrugged. "I had said I was willing for extra work, and the usual driver took ill."

I glanced at Prudence and saw the gleam in her eye. Somehow I had a notion just how come the driver had gone sick.

The radio spoke up suddenly. "Town car! Come in!"

"Driver here," Elias said toward the pickup on the dashboard.

"Do not stop at the terminal door."

We all tensed.

"The cargo gate will be open," the radio went on. "Go in through the cargo gate and take them directly to their ship. Repeat, do *not* stop at the terminal door."

We all relaxed with a single sigh.

"I will not," Elias promised.

"Sometimes," Marnie said, "it is pleasant to find that people do not want you to linger."

Well, if anybody should have known . . .

We pulled up beside the *Cotton Blossom.* The air lock was open and lighted, silhouetting Captain McLeod where he waited for us.

"I can't get home to my nice, safe lounge quickly enough!" Marnie said, and bolted out the door and toward the ramp. We all followed, but Prudence came, too. "Mr. Tallendar."

Barry stopped halfway to the ramp, then turned slowly, forcing a polite smile. He knew what was coming. Horace turned with him, similarly urbane.

"Please, Mr. Tallendar, take me with you!" Prudence clasped his forearm with both hands. "I shall go insane if I have to pass my whole life on this dingy little world! There is nothing for me here, nothing! All the boys are clowns, all the men are surly boors! I shall die if I have to pass all my life tending children and keeping house with never a moment of beauty or excitement! Oh, please, Mr. Tallendar, please!"

"Young lady, my heart goes out to you," Barry said, "but I am afraid it is impossible."

At the foot of the ramp, Marnie looked up, then turned slowly and started walking back.

"Oh, it is not, it is not at all! Elias has agreed, though it will grieve him to lose me—he knows how unhappy I have been all these years! I was on the verge of despair, until your ship came! Oh, please, Mr. Tallendar, do not cast me back to that!"

Barry looked up at Elias. "Do you give your approval?"

"I cannot say so publicly . . ." Elias began.

"Approval!" It was Marnie, swooping down like a Valkyrie. "Why should she need anyone's approval but her own?"

"Possibly because it is illegal for a woman to leave the planet," Barry said, "or for anyone, if he is not a spacehand or merchant. Would I guess correctly there, Elias?"

Elias nodded mutely.

"That is criminal!" Marnie raged. "In fact, by IDE law,

t is virtual slavery! She is a grown woman, and her life is ers alone!"

Prudence cast a look of sheer adoration at her.

Back at the ramp, both Lacey and Suzanne had paused, heir faces turned to stone.

"A good point," Barry admitted. "How old are you, oung lady?"

"Twenty-two, sir!"

"Then you are an adult by IDE law," Barry said, "and nce you are aboard our ship, you are subject to that law, nd no other, not even that of Citadel. Of course, I cannot ermit you to board." He resolutely turned his back, hands lasped on the head of his cane, and looked up at the stars. It is a beautiful night, is it not, Horace?"

"Splendid," Horace agreed, but he looked aghast.

Joy burned in Prudence's face. She didn't run back to the amp, though—she ran back to the car. "Oh, farewell, rother!" She threw her arms about Elias' neck and hugged ard. "Farewell, and thank you, thank you! Become a paceman—come and visit me!"

"I shall," he promised her, and looked up over her shouler. "I trust her to your hands, Mrs. Lulala—to all of you."

"We shall prove worthy of the trust," Marnie assured im—then, to Prudence, "Get aboard quickly, child, before ne Watch come to live up to their name!"

With a little sob, Prudence choked her brother one last me, then hurried away to the ramp.

I followed them up slowly, wondering whether or not I vas happy about this.

arry and I followed Ramou, walking fast, adding our own ace to the conveyor belt's speed.

At the hatchway, McLeod stepped out to bar Prudence's vay, frowning. "I don't know you, Miss."

"In fact," Barry said, "you don't even *see* her—do you, aptain McLeod?"

McLeod looked up, surprised, then took in the looks on ur faces, and Marnie's. He glanced down at the car below, nat was just now turning away, and you could see his mind dding two plus two and arriving at a total of twenty-two.

"Why, no, Director Tallendar," he said slowly, "I don't see anything at all." And he stepped out of the way.

Prudence gave a glad cry, kissed him soundly on his grainy old cheek, and hurried past him into the ship, following Suzanne and Lacey, who were most emphatically not looking back.

The door closed behind us, and I said to Barry, "You know, you could get us all into a great deal of trouble with this."

"Perhaps," Barry said, and there was cold determination in his voice. "But I could not, in any good conscience leave that poor child, who longs for only a little grace and refinement in her life, to be exploited by such a medieval value system!"

I stared at him, amazed, then said slowly, "Why, you old fraud! You're as much of an evangelist as they are!"

We assumed our usual stations on the bridge, while Ramou ran hither and thither about the decks, making sure everyone was webbed in for takeoff—for Barry had made it clear that he did not intend to linger.

So, as it happened, had Citadel Control.

"Are you prepared for lift-off, *Cotton Blossom*?"

"Almost, Citadel Control," McLeod answered. "Just waiting for confirmation that all supercargo is stowed and safe."

Ramou came panting in and dropped down onto his acceleration couch. He pulled the webbing over his body with a rather wild-eyed look.

"Anything out of the ordinary, Number Two?" McLeod asked, in a tone heavy with hidden meanings.

"No, sir. Everything normal," Ramou answered, though he looked at McLeod as if he were crazy—as if we all were.

"All secure, Citadel Control," McLeod said.

"Then lift off in sixty seconds!" Citadel commanded.

"They *do* want to get rid of us, don't they?" I murmured.

"The feeling," Barry informed me, "is mutual."

"Two . . . one . . . lift-off!" McLeod commanded, and below us, the engines roared. A giant kicked us fundamentally, and for a few seconds, the world was only roaring redness filling my vision, and a weight on my chest that seemed that of the whole planet.

Then it let up, and for a moment, I felt giddy, felt as if I weighed nothing, was floating in a primal sea . . . but it was only reaction. Weight came back, and with it, relief.

"Check supercargo!" McLeod snapped, and Ramou turned to his own console. "Confirm successful lift-off, please. Mr. Wellesley . . . Ms. Drury . . . Ms. Lulala . . ."

"*Cotton Blossom!* Abort!" Citadel Control suddenly barked. "Turn your ship around and come back!"

McLeod frowned. "You know we can't do that without taking an orbit around the planet to get ready. What's the problem, Citadel Control?"

"We have just discovered that you have abducted one of our young women!"

"Abducted?" McLeod turned a face of bland innocence to Barry. "Have we abducted anybody?"

"What's he talking about?" Merlo demanded.

"*You* ask him," McLeod advised.

So the only one on the bridge who didn't know about Prudence leaned forward and said to the authorities, "What are you talking about, Citadel Control? We haven't taken any hitchhikers along!"

"Yes, you have! And don't try to pretend you don't know about it!"

"I don't," Merlo snapped, his voice hard. "Are you making formal charges?"

Citadel Control was silent suddenly, no doubt realizing that the *Cotton Blossom* was now in interplanetary space, and under IDE law. But it tried again. "We demand that you go into orbit and search your ship!"

"We'll search," Merlo replied, "but we can't waste the fuel to go into orbit. We'll let you know if we find anything before it's time to go into H-space."

"She's there! Bring her back!"

Merlo scowled, but McLeod nudged him. Merlo looked up, surprised. McLeod nodded at Ramou, and Merlo turned to him, puzzled and alarmed. Ramou nodded slowly, and Merlo stared, appalled.

"We have found her, Citadel Control," McLeod said. "A stowaway, female, age twenty-two."

"That's against the law!"

"It is," McLeod agreed. "But don't worry, we won't throw her in the brig—just make her work out the cost of her passage to our next port of call. We've got a lot of cleaning needs doing."

"It's against *our* law! No Citadel citizen is allowed to leave the planet without official permission! She has no passport! No permit of any kind!"

"Yeah, I know," McLeod growled. "But don't worry, we'll make sure she gets the right IDE documents at the other end of the run."

"You will *not*! You will bring her back here *right now*!"

" 'Fraid we can't do that, Citadel Control. It would use up most of our fuel, and we don't have enough of your money to buy any more."

"We'll *give* you the fuel! Just bring back our wayward lamb!"

McLeod's voice hardened. "I told you, no! We can't spare the time, we don't want to spare the fuel, and we have absolutely no need to! We are under IDE law now! If you don't like it, have one of your captains complain about it to the nearest IDE judge!"

"You *know* we can't get word to a judge!"

"We don't know anything of the kind. You have plenty of ships, plenty of crews and captains. Just tell one of them to file the correct papers at his next port-of-call and send them to our lawyer. Good-bye now, Citadel. Time to go isomorphic with H-space."

"But who is your lawyyyyy . . ."

The last syllable ran down the scale and faded out as the whole ship seemed to squirm at the same time that it stood still. Then we were in H-space, and Citadel Control was gone.

Merlo relaxed with a gust of breath, then turned to Ramou, glowering. "Don't you have enough women falling over you already?"

"Hey, *I* didn't bring her!" Ramou protested.

"He did not, in spite of his obvious attraction to the young lady, Merlo," Barry sighed. "She brought herself."

Merlo turned to him, staring. "You mean she really *did* stow away?"

"She did," Barry confirmed, "with my knowledge and consent."

Merlo just stared at him while understanding dawned. Then he chuckled. "Why, you old knight-errant! You couldn't find the dragon, so you just unlocked her chain and led her off the rock!"

"Why, thank you, Merlo," Barry said. "How nice."

But Ramou asked, "Why tell them the truth? Why didn't we just keep on lying?"

"*I* wasn't lying!" Merlo snapped.

"Quite so," Barry said. "We couldn't have done it without you, Merlo." And, while the first officer of the moment sat there looking nonplussed, Barry explained to Ramou, "To deny her presence completely might have laid us open to interplanetary criminal charges, Ramou—but to acknowledge her presence, to admit that she is here out of her own free will, extends the protection of IDE law not only to ourselves, but also to her."

Ramou stared at him a second, then whirled to McLeod for confirmation. The captain nodded. "If she stowed away, it's her fault, not ours, Number Two—and not our responsibility, either. Not as long as she's twenty-one or more, and not so long as she's under IDE law."

"Well," Ramou said slowly, "I suppose that makes sense."

"I am glad you find it so," Barry sighed. "I only hope the rest of the company does." He loosened his webbing. "Please ask them all to assemble in the lounge, Ramou."

We were all assembled in the lounge, all well oiled with the lubrication that comes out of the beverage dispenser, and Barry was just finishing explaining Prudence's presence to the rest of the company, while Horace sat beside him nodding confirmation, and Prudence sat blushing, with eyes downcast, before them, Marnie sitting protectively near her and glaring down Suzanne and Lacey—and the covetous gleam in Larry's eye.

None of them seemed to notice the adoring, besotted look on Marty's face.

"Well, then! We have an additional member of the company, at least for the time being," Ogden said jovially. "Welcome to the Star Company, young lady!"

It took a moment, but everybody followed his lead, murmuring welcomes and congratulations on her escape.

"But what can she do?" Lacey demanded.

Prudence kept her eyes downcast.

Marnie leaned over to her. "Can you sew, child?"

"Oh, yes, ma'am!" Prudence looked up, all wide eyes and innocence. "We all can, on Citadel."

"All the women, you mean." Marnie turned to Grudy. "Can you use an apprentice costumer, Grudy dear?"

"Why, I'd be delighted," Grudy said staunchly. "Would you like to learn to make costumes, Prudence dear?"

"Oh, yes, ma'am! With all the pretty spangles and laces?" Prudence's eyes kindled with delight. "I would love it!"

Marnie nodded and patted Prudence's head. "That's settled, then."

But I watched Prudence closely and wondered for how long.

"Well then!" Winston said briskly. "We have come away with a new member—but what other profit have we derived, Barry?"

"No one thought to ask me for the evening's receipts." Publius held up a strongbox. "We took in two thousand tonight—and we can exchange it for five thousand therms."

Winston frowned. "I thought you couldn't exchange Citadel currency."

"Not on the planet, no—but off planet, there's quite a market for it, since so many people have to deal with Citadel, and cannot get their money through the usual channels."

"But aren't we breaking their law?" I asked.

"Perhaps," Barry said, "but they did not exchange the money for us, and I do think that we are entitled to some compensation for our evening's efforts."

"Besides," Charles said, "the deacons may resent us, but not the majority of the people—and the deacons did approve the script, after all."

Barry nodded. "As I recall, the description of Everyman's ordinary possessions was inserted at their request."

"It was," Charles confirmed. "I suppose they meant for me to describe Everyman as having no more than the average Citadel citizen—but they did not tell me *that.*"

"A regrettable oversight," Horace agreed, "and one which I am certain they are regretting very thoroughly, at the moment."

"Somehow, though," Barry mused, "I have a notion they will be glad of it, eventually . . . Well!" He slapped his knees. "A successful run, my friends, in spite of it all!"

"And we couldn't run fast enough," Marty quipped.

"Do you suppose we will be able to perform a *real* play again someday, Barry?" Marnie asked. "One that we have rehearsed ahead of time, and adequately?"

"Of course, Marnie," Barry beamed. "After all, our next stop is an affluent and fully civilized planet. On to Corona!"

"To Corona!" everyone cried, with glasses lifted high.

That was when Prudence learned to drink.

The meeting broke into small groups, and I drifted away from Barry to confer with Winston. "Why do I have the feeling that none of this was quite as accidental as it seemed?"

"Why," Winston said, with his diabolical grin, "because it all turned out exactly as this young lady, Prudence, wished it to."

"Surely you would not claim that she engineered the whole affair!"

"Me? Certainly not! I would only note that she seems to live up to her name!" Winston turned to glance at our Puritan maid, where she stood surrounded by every male on board, emptying her second cup of wine, then gasping, blushing, and giggling at a joke as she accepted a third.

"Or perhaps," Winston said, "not."

About the Author

CHRISTOPHER STASHEFF spent his early childhood in Mount Vernon, New York, but spent the rest of his formative years in Ann Arbor, Michigan. He has always had difficulty distinguishing between fantasy and reality and has tried to compromise by teaching college. When teaching proved too real, he gave it up in favor of writing full-time. He tends to pre-script his life but can't understand why other people never get their lines right. This causes a fair amount of misunderstanding with his wife and four children. He writes novels because it's the only way he can be the director, the designer, and all the actors, too.

The tall roan stallion looked up and nickered. The other horses crowded to the doors of their stalls to watch Accerese the groom as he came into the barn with a bag of feed over his shoulder.

A smile banished his moroseness for a few minutes. "Well! *Someone*'s glad to see me!" He poured a measure of grain into the trough on the stallion's door. "At least *you* eat well, my friends!" He moved on down the line, pouring grain into each manger. "And well-dressed you are, too, not like we who—"

Accerese bit his tongue, remembering that the king or his sorcerers might hear anything, anywhere. "Well, we all have our work to do in this world—though some of us have far less than—" Again, he bit his tongue—but on his way out of the third stall he paused to trace a raw red line on the horse's flank with his finger. "Then again, when you *do* work, your tasks are even more painful than mine, eh? No, my friends, forgive my complaining." He opened the door to the fourth stall. "But you, Fandalpi, you are . . ." He stopped, puzzled.

Fandalpi was crowded against the back wall, nostrils flared, the whites showing all around its eyes. "Nay, my friend, what—"

Then Accerese saw the body lying on the floor.

He stood frozen in shock for a few minutes, his eyes as wide and white as the horse's. Then he whirled to the door, panic moving his heels—but he froze with a new fear. Whether he fled or not, he was a dead man—but he might live longer if he reported the death as he should. Galtese the steward's man would testify that Accerese had taken his load of grain only a few minutes before—so there was always the chance that no one would blame him for the prince's death.

But his stomach felt hollow with fear as he hurried back across the courtyard to the guardroom. There was a chance, yes, but when the corpse was that of the heir apparent, it was a very slim chance indeed.

King Maledicto tore his hair, howling in rage. "What cursed fiend has rent my son!"

But everyone could see that this was not the work of a fiend, or any other of Hell's minions. The body was not burned or defiled; the prince's devotion to God had won him that much protection, at least. The only sign of the Satanic was the obscene carving on the handle of the knife that stuck out of his chest—but every one of the king's sorcerers had such a knife, and many of the guards besides. Anybody could have stolen one, though not easily.

"Foolish boy!" the king bellowed at the corpse. "Did you think your Lord would save you from Hell's blade? See what all your praying has won you! See what your hymn-singing and charities and forgiveness have brought you! Who will inherit my kingdom now? Who will rule if I should die? Nay, now I'll be a thousand times more wicked yet! The Devil will keep me alive, if only to bring misery and despair upon this earth!"

Accerese quaked in his sandals, knowing who was the most likely candidate for despair. He reflected ruefully that no matter how the king had stormed and threatened his son to try to make him forsake his pious ways, the prince had been his assurance that the Devil would keep him alive—for only if the old king lived could the kingdom of Latruria be held against the wave of goodness that would have flowed from Prince Casudo's charity.

"What do I have left now?" the old king ranted. "Only a puling boy, not even a stripling, a child, an infant! Nay, I must rear him well and wisely in the worship of Satan, or this land will fall to the rule of Virtue!"

What he didn't dare say, of course, was that if his demonic master knew he was raising little Prince Boncorro any other way, the Devil would rack the king with tortures that Accerese could only imagine—but imagine he did; he shuddered at the very thought.

"Fool! Coward! Milksop!" the king raged, and went on and on, ranting and raving at the poor dead body as if by sheer wrath, he could force it to obey and come alive again. Finally, though, Accerese caught an undertone to the tirade that he thought impossible, then realized was really there:

The king was afraid!

At that, Accerese's nerve broke. Whatever was bad enough to scare a king who had been a life-long sorcerer, devoted to evil and to wickedness that was only whispered abroad, never spoken openly—whatever was so horrible as to scare such a king could blast the mind of a poor man who strove to be honest and live rightly in the midst of the cruelty and treachery of a royal court devoted to Evil! Slowly, ever so slowly, Accerese began to edge toward the stable door. No one saw, for everyone was watching the king, pressing away from his royal rage as much as they dared. Even Chancellor Rebozo cowered, he who had endured King Maledicto's whims and rages for fifty years. No one noticed the poor humble groom edge his way out of the door, no one noticed him turn away and pace quickly to the postern gate, no one saw him leap into the water and swim the moat, for even the sentries on the wall were watching the stables with fear and apprehension.

But one did notice his swimming—one of the monsters who lived in the moat. A huge slaty bulge broke the surface, oily waters sliding off it; eyes the size of helmets opened, gaze flicking here and there until they saw the churning figure. Then the bulge began to move, faster and faster, a V-shaped wake pointing toward the fleeing man.

Accerese did not even look behind to see if it was coming; he knew it would, knew also that, fearsome as the monster was, he was terrified more of the king and his master.

The bulge swelled as it came up behind the man. Accerese could hear the wash of breaking waters and redoubled his efforts with a last frantic burst of thrashing. The shoreline came closer, closer . . .

But the huge bulge came closer, too, splitting apart to

show huge dripping yellow fangs in a maw as dark as midnight.

Accerese's flailing foot struck mud; he threw himself onto the bank and rolled away just as saw-edged teeth clashed shut behind him. He rolled again and again, heart beating loud in his ears, aching to scream but daring not, because of the sentries on the walls. Finally he pushed himself up to his feet and saw the moat, twenty feet behind him, and the two huge baleful eyes glaring at him over its brim. Accerese breathed a shuddering gasp of relief, and a prayer of thanks surged upward within him—but he caught it in time, held it back from forming into words, lest the Devil hear him and know he was fleeing. He turned away, scrambling over the brow of the hill and down the talus, hoping that God had heard his unvoiced prayer, but that the Hell-spawn had not. Heaven preserved him, or perhaps simply good luck, for he reached the base of the hill with the alarm still unraised and sprinted across the plain toward the cover of the woods.

Just as Accerese came in under the trees, King Maledicto finally ran out of venom and stood trembling over the corpse of his son, tears of frustration in his eyes. Yes, surely they must have been of frustration.

Then, slowly, he turned to his chancellor. "Find the murderer, Rebozo."

"But Majesty!" Rebozo shrank away. "It might be a demon out of Hell . . ."

"Would a demon use a knife, fool?" Maledicto roared. "Would a demon leave the body whole? Aye, whole and undefiled? Nay! It is a mortal man you seek, no spawn of Hell! Find him, seek him! Bring the groom who found him, question him over what he saw!"

"Surely, Majesty!" Rebozo bent in a quick servile bow and turned away. "Let the groom stand forth!"

Everyone was silent, staring about them, wide-eyed. "He was here, against the stall door . . ." a guardsman ventured.

"And you let him flee? Fool! Idiot!" Maledicto roared. He whirled to the other soldiers, pointing at the one who had spoken. "Cut off his head! Not later, *now*!"

The other guardsmen glanced at their mate, taken aback, hesitant.

"Will no one obey?" Maledicto bellowed. "Does my weak-kneed son still slacken your loyalty, even in his death? Here, give me!" He snatched a halberd from the nearest guardsman and swung it high. The other soldiers shouted and dodged even as the blade fell. The luckless man tried to dodge, but too late—the blade cut through his chest. He screamed once, in terror and in blood; then his eyes rolled up, and his soul was gone where went all those souls who served King Maledicto willingly.

"Stupid ass," Maledicto hissed, glaring at the body. "When I command, you *obey*!" He looked up at the remaining, quaking guardsmen. "Now *bring me that groom*!"

They fled to chase after the luckless Accerese.

It was the chancellor who found and followed the fugitive's trail to the postern and down to the water's edge, the company of guardsmen in his wake.

"Thus it ends," sighed the captain of the guard. "None could swim that moat and live."

But Rebozo glanced back fearfully at the keep, as if hearing some command that the others could not. "Take the hound into the boat," he ordered. "Search the other bank."

They went, quaking, and the dog had to be held tightly, its muzzle bound, for it squirmed and writhed, fearing the smell of the monsters. Several of them lifted huge eyes above the water, but Rebozo muttered a charm and pointed at each with his wand. The great eyes closed, the slaty bulges slid beneath the oily, stagnant fluid—and the boat came to shore.

Wild-eyed, the dog sprang free and would have fled, but the soldiers cuffed it quiet and as it whined, cringing, made it smell again the feedbag that held Accerese's scent. It began to quest, here and there about the bank, gaining vigor as it moved further from the water. Its keeper cursed and raised a fist to club it, but Rebozo stayed his hand. "Let it course," he said. "Give it time."

Even as he finished, the dog lifted its head with a howl of triumph. Off it went after the scent, nearly jerking the keeper's arm out of its socket, so eager was it to get away from that fell and foul moat. Rebozo shouted commands, and half a dozen soldiers ran off after the hound and its keeper, while a dozen more came riding across the drawbridge with the rest of the pack, led by a minor sorcerer in charcoal robes.

Down the talus they thundered, away over the plain, catching up with the lead hound, and the whole pack belled as they followed the trace into the woods.

They searched all that day and into the night, Rebozo ordering their efforts, Rebozo calling for the dogs, Rebozo leading the guardsmen. It was a long chase and a dark one, for Accerese had the good sense to keep moving, to resist the urge to sleep—or perhaps it was fear itself that kept him going. He doubled back, he waded a hundred yards through a stream, he took to trees and went from branch to branch—but where the hounds could not find his scent, sorcery could, and in the end they brought Accerese, bruised and bleeding, back to the chancellor, who nodded, eyes glowing, even as he said, "Put him to the Question!"

"No, no!" Accerese screamed, and went on screaming even as they hauled him down to the torture chamber, even as they strapped him to the rack—where the screaming turned quickly into hoarse bellows of agony and fear. Rebozo stood there behind his king, watching and trembling as Maledicto shouted, "Why did you slay my son?"

"I did not! I did never!"

"More," King Maledicto snapped, and Rebozo, trembling and wide-eyed, nodded to the torturer, who grinned and pressed down with glowing iron. Accerese screamed and screamed, and finally could turn the sound into words. "I only found him there, I did not kill . . . *aieeee*!"

"Confess!" the king roared. "We know you did it—why do you deny it?"

"Confess," Rebozo pleaded, "and the agony will end."

"But I did not do it!" Accerese wailed. "I only found him . . . *yaahhhh*!"

So it went, on and on, until finally, exhausted and spent, Accerese told them what they wanted to hear. "Yes, yes! I did it, I stole the dagger and slew him, anything, anything! Only let the pain stop!"

"Let the torture continue," Maledicto commanded, and watched with grim satisfaction as the groom howled and bucked and writhed, listened with glowing eyes as the screams alternated with begging and pleading, shivered with pleasure as the cracked and fading voice still tried to shriek its agony—but when the broken, bleeding body began to gibber and call upon the name of God, Maledicto snarled, "Kill it!"

The blade swung down, and Accerese's agony was over.

King Maledicto stood, glaring down at the remains with fierce elation—then suddenly turned somber. His brows drew down, his face wrinkled into lines of gloom. He turned away, thunderous and brooding. Rebozo stared at him, astounded, then hurried after.

When he had seen his royal master slam the door of his private chamber behind him, when his loud-voiced queries brought forth only snarls of rage and demands to go away, Rebozo turned and went with a sigh. There was still another member of the royal family who had to be told about all this. Not Maledicto's wife, for she had been slain for an adultery she had never committed; not the prince's wife, for she had died in childbirth—but the prince's son, Maledicto's grandson, who was now the heir apparent.

Rebozo went to his chambers in a wing on the far side of the castle. There he composed himself, steadying his breathing and striving for the proper combination of sympathy and sternness, of gentleness and gravity. When he thought he had the tone and expression right, he went in to tell the boy that he was an orphan.

Prince Boncorro wept, of course. He was only ten and could not understand. "But why? Why? Why would God take my father? He was so good, he tried so hard to do what God wanted!"

Rebozo winced, but found words anyway. "There was work for him in Heaven."

"But there is work for him here, too! Big work, lots of work, and surely it is work that is important to God! Didn't God think he could do it? Didn't he try hard enough?"

What could Rebozo say? "Perhaps not, your Highness. Kings must do many things that would be sins, if common folk did them."

"What manner of things!" The tears dried on the instant, and the little prince glared up at Rebozo as if the man himself were guilty.

"Why . . . killing," Rebozo said. "Executing, I mean. Executing men who have done horrible, vicious things, such as murdering other people—and who might do them again, if the king let them live. And killing other men, in battle. A king must command such things, Highness, even if he does not do them himself."

"So." Boncorro fixed the chancellor with a stare that the old man found very disconcerting. "You mean that my father was too good, too kind, too gentle to be a king?"

Rebozo shrugged and waved a hand in a futile gesture. "I cannot say, Highness. No man can understand these matters—they are beyond us."

The look on the little prince's face plainly denied the idea—denied it with scorn, too. Rebozo hurried on. "For now, though, your grandfather is in a horrible temper. He has punished the man who murdered your father . . ."

"Punished?" Prince Boncorro stared. "They caught the man? Why did he do it?"

"Who knows, Highness?" Rebozo said, like a man near the end of his fortitude. "Envy, passion, madness—your grandfather did not wait to hear the reason. The murderer is dead. What else matters?"

"A great deal," Boncorro said, "to a prince who wishes to live."

There was something chilling about the way he said it—he seemed so mature, so far beyond his years. But then, an experience like this *would* mature a boy—instantly.

"If you wish to live, Highness," Rebozo said softly, "it were better if you were not in the castle for some months. Your grandfather has been in a ferocious temper, and now is suddenly sunken in gloom. I cannot guess what he may do next."

"You do not mean that he is mad!"

"I do not *think* so," Rebozo said slowly, "but I do not *know*. I would feel far safer, your Highness, if you were to go into hiding."

"But . . . where?" Boncorro looked about him, suddenly helpless and vulnerable. "Where could I go?"

In spite of it all, Rebozo could not help a smile. "Not in the wardrobe, Highness, nor beneath your bed. I mean to hide you outside the castle—outside this royal town of

Venarra, even. I know a country baron who is kindly and loyal, who would never dream of hurting a prince, and who would see you safely spirited away even if his Majesty were to command your presence. But the king will not ask him for you, for I will see to it that the king does not know where you are."

Boncorro frowned. "How will you do that?"

"I will lie, Your Highness. No, do not look so darkly at me—it will be a lie in a good cause, and is far better than letting you stay here, where your grandfather might lash out at you in his passion."

Boncorro shuddered; he had seen King Maledicto in a rage. "But he is a sorcerer! Can he not find me whenever he wishes?"

"I am a sorcerer, too," Rebozo said evenly, "and shall cloud your trail by my arts, so that even he cannot find it. It is my duty to you—and to him."

"Yes, it is, is it not?" Boncorro nodded judiciously. "How strange that to be loyal, you must lie to him!"

"He will thank me for it one day," Rebozo assured him. "But come, now, your Highness—there is little time for talk. No one can tell when your grandfather will pass into another fit of rage. We must be away, and quickly, before his thoughts turn to you."

Prince Boncorro's eyes widened in fright. "Yes, we must! How, Rebozo?"

"Like this." Rebozo shook out a voluminous dark cloak he had been carrying and draped it around the boy's shoulders. "Pull up the cowl, now."

Boncorro pulled the hood over his head and as far forward as it would go. He could only see straight in front of him, but he realized that it would be very hard for others to see his face.

Rebozo was donning a cloak very much like his. He too pulled the cowl over his head. "There, now! Two fugitives dressed alike, eh? And who is to say you are a prince, not the son of a woodcutter wrapped against the night's chill? Away now, lad! To the postern!"

They crossed out over the moat in a small boat that was moored just outside the little gate. Boncorro huddled in on himself, staring at the huge luminous eyes that seemed to appear out of the very darkness itself—but Rebozo muttered a spell and pointed his wand, making those huge eyes flutter closed in sleep and sink away. The little boat glided across the oil-slick water with no oars or sail, and Boncorro wondered how the chancellor was making it go.

Magic, of course.

Boncorro decided he must learn magic, or he would forever be at others' mercy. But not black magic, no—he would never let Satan have a hold on him, as the Devil did on his grandfather! He would never be so vile, so wicked—for he knew what Rebozo seemed not to: that no matter who had thrust the knife between his father's ribs, it was King Maledicto who had given the order. Boncorro had no proof, but he didn't need any—he had heard their fights, heard the old man ranting and raving at the heir, had heard Prince Casudo's calm, measured answers that sent the king into a veritable paroxysm. He had heard his grandfather's threats, seen him lash out at Casudo in anger. No, Boncorro had no need of proof. He had always feared his grandfather and never liked him—but now he hated him, too, and was bound and determined never to be like him.

On the other hand, he was determined never to be like his father, either—not now. Prince Casudo had been a good man, a very good man, even saintly—but it was as Chancellor Rebozo had said: that very goodness had made him unfit to be king. It had made him unfit to live, for that matter—unsuspecting, he had been struck down from behind. Boncorro wanted to be a good king, when his time came—but more than anything else, he wanted to live.

And second only to that, he wanted revenge—on his grandfather.

The boat grounded on the bank, and Rebozo stepped out, turning back to hold out a hand to steady the prince. There were horses tied to a tree branch in waiting, black horses that faded into the night. Rebozo boosted the boy into the saddle, then mounted too, and took the reins of Boncorro's horse. He slapped his own horse's withers with a small whip, and they moved off quietly into the night, down the slope, and across the darkened plain. Only when they came under the leaves did Prince Boncorro feel safe to talk again.

"Why are you loyal to King Maledicto, Rebozo? Why do

you obey him? Do you think the things he commands you to do are right?"

"No," Rebozo said, with a shudder. "He is an evil man, your Highness, and commands me to do wicked deeds. I shall tell you truly that some of them disgust me, even though I can see they are necessary to keep order in the kingdom. But there are other tasks he sets me that frankly horrify me, and in which I can see no use."

"Then why do you do them? Why do you carry them out?"

"Because I am afraid," Rebozo said frankly, "afraid of his wrath and his anger, afraid of the tortures he might make me suffer if he found that I had disobeyed him—but more than anything else, afraid of the horrors of his evil magic."

"Can you not become good, as Father was? Will not . . . no, of course Goodness will not protect you," Prince Boncorro said bitterly. "It did not protect Father, did it? In the next life, perhaps, but not in this."

"Even if it did," Rebozo said quickly, to divert the boy from such somber thoughts, "it would not protect me—for I have committed many sins, your Highness, in the service of your grandfather—many sins indeed, and most of them vile."

"But you had no choice!"

"Oh, I did," Rebozo said softly, "and worse, I knew it, too. I could have said 'no,' I could have refused."

"If you had, Grandfather would have had you killed! Tortured and killed!"

"He would indeed," Rebozo confirmed, "and I did not have the courage to face that. No, in my cowardice, I trembled and obeyed him—and doomed my soul to Hell thereby."

"But Father did not." Boncorro straightened, eyes wide with sudden understanding. "Father refused to commit an evil act, and Grandfather killed him for it!"

"Highness, what matter?" Rebozo pleaded. "Dead is dead!"

"It matters," Prince Boncorro said, "because Father's courage has saved him from Hell—and yours could, too, Rebozo, even now!"

There was something in the way he said it that made Rebozo shiver—but he was shivering anyway, at the thought of the fate the king could visit upon him. Instead he said, "Your father has gone to a far better place than this, Prince Boncorro."

"That may be true," the Prince agreed, "but I do not wish to go there any sooner than I must. Why did Father not learn magic?"

"Because there is no magic but evil magic, your Highness."

"I do not believe that," Prince Boncorro said flatly. "Father told me of saints who could work miracles."

"Miracles, yes—and I don't doubt that your father can work them now, or will soon. But miracles are not magic, your Highness, and it is not the saints who work them, but the One they worship, who acts through them. Mere goodness is not enough—a man must be a saint, to become such a channel of power."

Prince Boncorro shook his head doggedly. "There must be a way, Chancellor Rebozo. There must be another sort of magic, good magic, or the whole world would have fallen to evil long ago."

What makes you think it has not? Rebozo thought, but he bit back the words. Besides, even Prince Boncorro had heard of the good wizards in Merovence, and Chancellor Rebozo did not want him thinking too much about that. What quicker road to death could there be than to study good magic in a kingdom of evil sorcery?

"Will Grandfather ever die?" Boncorro asked.

Rebozo shook his head. "Only two know that, Highness—and one of them is the Devil, who keeps the king alive."

The other, Prince Boncorro guessed, must be God—but he could understand why Rebozo would not want to say that Name aloud. Not in this kingdom—and not considering the current state of his soul.